SHERLOCK HOLMES VS. CTHULHU

THE ADVENTURE OF THE NEURAL PSYCHOSES

Sherlock Holmes vs. Cthulhu
from Titan Books and Lois H. Gresh

The Adventure of the Deadly Dimensions
The Adventure of the Neural Psychoses
The Adventure of the Innsmouth Mutations (2019)

SHERLOCK HOLMES

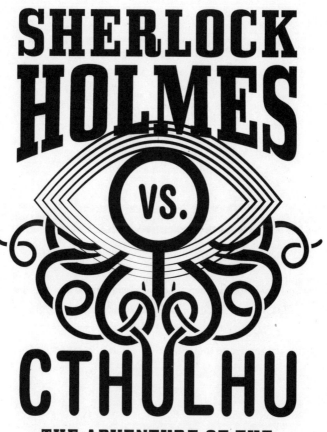

VS.

CTHULHU

THE ADVENTURE OF THE
NEURAL PSYCHOSES

LOIS H. GRESH

TITAN BOOKS

THE ADVENTURE OF THE NEURAL PSYCHOSES
Print edition ISBN: 9781785652103
Electronic edition ISBN: 9781785652110

Published by Titan Books
A division of Titan Publishing Group Ltd
144 Southwark Street, London SE1 0UP

First edition: August 2018
2 4 6 8 10 9 7 5 3 1

A CIP catalogue record for this title is available from the British Library.

Printed and bound in the United States

Did you enjoy this book? We love to hear from our readers.
Please email us at readerfeedback@titanemail.com or write to us at
Reader Feedback at the above address.

To receive advance information, news, competitions, and exclusive offers
online, please sign up for the Titan newsletter on our website:

TITANBOOKS.COM

DEDICATED WITH LOVE TO ARIE, RENA, AND GABBY

WITH GRATITUDE TO ARTHUR CONAN DOYLE
AND H.P. LOVECRAFT

PART ONE

THE ESHOCKERS OF WHITECHAPEL

1

DR. JOHN WATSON

December 1890, London

For two shillings apiece, Sherlock Holmes and I enjoyed a choppy yet pleasant ride down the Thames. My friend is not given to excursions for pleasure's sake alone, so when he suggested a trip to Woolwich upon the new paddle steamer, the *Belle Crown*, I had at first thought to refuse the invitation. I'd recently reunited with my wife and child after the terrifying events of the deadly dimensions, and was still beset by the dizzy spells and strange, kaleidoscopic visions that had first begun to trouble me at that time—I was in no mood for more adventures. But Mary, thinking to lift my spirits, urged me to go. Not wanting to displease my wife or my friend, I relented. So it was that Holmes and I stood contemplating the docks of Wapping from the deck of the *Belle Crown* as it completed its return voyage through the Pool of London.

"You will no doubt remember, Watson," said Holmes, "that the warehouse in which we witnessed the Order of Dagon's meeting is upon that very shore. That is the place where Professor Fitzgerald released the snake-like monsters that attacked him and killed many of his congregation."

I'd been glad to see some color vanquish the death-like pallor that had gripped my friend since our battle with the inexplicable deadly dimensions, but now I wondered if it had been a mistake to venture onto the river so soon after our adventure.

"I remember—of course, Holmes. I'm glad that Fitzgerald is behind bars where he can do no more harm."

Holmes smiled at me. "I understand you, Doctor. You think I am being morbid to dwell on these things. But I have brought us here for a purpose. Those creatures didn't simply slither off to die, I am certain of it. I have not been able to see them from the banks, but here, out in the middle of the river, surely we will see something."

"Holmes," I reminded him gently, "we have twice seen the creatures vanish into thin air. Into another realm, a different dimension."

"That is one theory we must entertain, certainly—that the rational explanation is simply too advanced for us to fully understand. But we must eliminate the probable before we contemplate the improbable, Watson. And I am not altogether convinced they vanished. A trick of the eye, perhaps..."

The Thames surged past as we leaned on the rail of the *Belle Crown*. The craft was sleek as a bullet, pushing against the flow of the river.

Nothing seemed amiss.

Around us, families chattered and laughed, babies cried and gurgled, and everyone's cheeks were as flushed as Holmes's. My eye fell upon a baby not much older than my own Samuel, and I watched with pleasure as he giggled at the sensation of the fast-moving boat.

Despite the 1878 crash of the *Princess Alice*, which had transported Londoners to and from beautiful gardens and parks, we had no reason to think the *Belle Crown* would meet a similar fate. What were the odds that another 900-ton iron-built ship would barrel down the river and kill us? The *Bywell Castle*, the giant craft that had split the *Princess Alice* in half and killed more than 650 passengers, had been an anomaly, representing a once-in-a-generation tragedy.

Holmes interrupted my thoughts.

"The river is gaining momentum. Look at those waves, Watson."

I looked where he was pointing. Black water slammed the side of the *Belle Crown*, then thundered into the downstream current. Froth rode the crests of waves that would have been more at home in the ocean than on the Thames.

"It is choppy," I agreed, "but the weather is unpredictable at this time of year."

"This is more than choppy, and it's more than bad weather," Holmes argued. "The level of the water has risen."

"Well, that means the tide must be rising, surely," I declared.

Holmes shook his head. "The tide should not be coming in yet, Watson. Did you not look at the tide tables when we boarded? And have you ever seen waves like this on the Thames?" He turned his gaze toward the granite clouds, through which weak light trickled down to the water. "It has been overcast all day, but there has not been a drop of rain. I cannot think what could cause the river to swell this forcefully."

I could not continue the argument—he was quite right. The other passengers had noticed the sudden change in the waves, too. The woman holding the baby I had been looking at gasped as the boat jolted us all, water surging in a cold spray onto the deck. She clasped her child to her chest and covered the infant's head with her hand. The man accompanying her took her arm, helping her away from the rail.

Unlike the rest of us, Holmes didn't move from his position. He shielded his eyes from the sky and peered into the water.

"Watson, *look*!" he cried.

"What is it?" I wiped my face on my sleeve. It did no good, for my coat was drenched.

"*Something.* I don't know what, Watson." Holmes also wiped water from his face, but with the back of his hand, then he leaned further over the rail and squinted. "A large shape, moving through the water like a giant squid or an octopus."

Holmes wasn't the type to joke about danger or novel oddities. Alarmed now, I grabbed his arm and tried to pull him from the rail, but he wouldn't budge.

"No. I must see it," he insisted.

A shout from behind attracted my attention. Moving with the flow of water, a small ship sped toward the *Belle Crown*. Men in uniform—*police*—waved frantically, trying to get our attention.

Holmes pointed into the water again.

"Over there," he cried, "look!"

I stared in the direction of his finger. A bulbous shape broke the surface, then disappeared into the black depths.

I'd seen enough. I wrenched Holmes back from the rail as the shape came closer and swirled beneath the water slapping against the ship.

Then—*whatever it was*—it ripped up from the river and curled into a spiral, which then unfurled against the sky. I'd never seen the like of it. It both fascinated and terrified me.

As quickly as it had risen, it slammed back down into the water.

The *Belle Crown* jolted high and teetered. The deck lurched. It cocked at a thirty-degree angle and rode the crest of a wave, but held steady.

I grabbed for the rail, but along with Holmes and everyone else, I lost my footing and fell.

I slid in a pile of humanity toward the other side of the boat, and then my head slammed against wood. Colors whirled. Sharp pain sliced through my skull and radiated through my shoulders.

The boat lurched again—it felt as if something had actually lifted it out of the water—and smashed down. My head cracked against wood, and the whirling colors blackened around the edges as I fought to remain conscious. Hot blood slicked my face. I was on my stomach.

Around me, people screamed.

It happened so quickly and I was so dizzy that it was hard for me to get a clear image. I saw but a tangle of limbs and clothes and a swathe of screaming faces.

Blinking and trying to shake off the dizziness, I strained my neck and looked for Holmes. He sat on the deck, propped against a stout man.

I rolled over and sat up.

Holmes struggled to his feet, and with his back against the side of the ship, he grasped the rail with both hands. Blood streaked down his face, and the wind flicked it off, leaving feathers of red spray on his forehead and cheeks. His hat was gone.

I got on my knees and tried to stand, but the boat lurched, tossing me onto my back. I tried repeatedly, but could not get my footing. People were strewn all over the floor in various states of injury. Some wobbled to their feet, trying to help others, only to be knocked to the floor like me. A few, like Holmes, reached for the rails, anxious to see what had hit the boat.

Someone clawed at me. I turned to see an old man's face inches from mine. His eyes widened. His mouth opened. I'd seen that look many times in the heat of battle. I reached for him.

But the *Belle Crown* tilted in the other direction, and we all went crashing across the deck and against the other side of the boat. The man slammed up next to me, and his eyes glazed into the unwavering stare of the dead.

People tumbled over him, screaming.

Across from me, the boat jutted high at a dangerous angle, and etched against the sky, both hands clutching the rail behind his back, was a tall, lean figure: Holmes. His arms were straight, his legs spread. He leaned precariously toward the rest of us, all heaped upon the deck.

I feared his arms would snap from the strain, but he held fast, his face red, lips pressed tightly together. Should he let go of the rail, his body would crash hard against wood and steel, or possibly, he'd go overboard and be at the mercy of whatever churned beneath the black water.

The boat—still sharply angled—lurched yet higher.

Something had indeed lifted us.

A huge tentacle—wider than Holmes's body, arrayed with suckers, and of a blotched brownish-white color—snapped into the air behind him, and then, much to my horror, it curled and the tip pointed daggerlike over Holmes's head.

"Holmes!" I screamed. "Holmes, let go of the rail!"

The police boat cruised dangerously close to us. A man's voice bellowed, "Duck, sir! Get out of the way! Move, sir, *move!*"

A harpoon sailed behind Holmes and disappeared with the wind. Another harpoon followed.

Harpoons on a London police boat! I thought. *Lestrade must have been busy after the disaster at the warehouse. He must have anticipated more trouble.* And then: *Holmes must get away from that rail. If the harpoons don't kill him, the tentacle will plunge through his head and drill him to bits!*

"Holmes, get out of the way!" I screamed.

The *Belle Crown* jolted yet higher, pushed up from beneath by the giant creature. While we were suspended precariously aloft—*over the surface of the water yet not on any wave I could see*—the deck suddenly leveled. Everyone bounced up, then down onto the hard floor. Wincing, I lifted myself, and on shaking legs, stood. The deck was covered with the dead, the dying, the wounded; women, children, men.

Then I saw the thing behind Holmes.

I'd seen such creatures before: in the Thames warehouse when Professor Henry Fitzgerald had cracked open the ceiling, releasing bizarre creatures from the skies, from... God only knew where. As quickly as they'd appeared in the warehouse, they'd vanished. I had wondered where the creatures had gone.

Now, I knew. Holmes was correct. The creatures had slithered into the Thames.

And now, one was behind Holmes, ready to dash his powerful brain to pieces and kill him.

2

It happened in a flash.

Holmes's side of the boat slammed down, and he whirled to face the creature. It rose, its lumpy head covered in mottled hide. He staggered, either from the shock of seeing such a thing at all or perhaps from the dazzling array of eyes scored into the hide: *dozens* of eyes, each fractured into countless glittering surfaces. A scaly appendage, like a bat's wing, unhooked from a fold over one of those eyes. The giant tentacle quivered over Holmes, still poised for attack.

Holmes reached into his pocket and whipped out a pistol.

He fired, then immediately threw himself down upon the deck. The shot hit an exposed eye beneath the bat's wing. The creature screeched: high and ill-pitched and skittering across bizarre scales. The tentacle crashed into the Thames.

Water soared over the rail and flooded the boat. Holmes toppled and careened across the deck to join the rest of us on the opposite side.

Beside me, a woman huddled with two small children. Her hair was as pale as Mary's, and her eyes were lighter, a blue streaked with lime. Her dress was wet and ripped down one side. The boy, perhaps a year old, cried continually, his face hidden in the folds of her bodice. The other child, a girl, lay unconscious beside them. A gash on her forehead exposed bone. My own head ached, and my mind seemed unfocused and blurred; yet I forced myself to my knees and moved closer to take her pulse. I felt the beat of her tiny heart. I ripped open my coat and pulled my shirt off. Shivering from cold, I tore the cloth into strips as best as I could and wrapped one around the girl's head.

Then I saw another child, and yet another, suffering and in need of my services.

The wind withered. Overhead, the granite clouds thickened, and the light fizzled. The river still shook, but the mighty waves were gone.

The small police boat retrieved several women and children, then sped toward shore.

Holmes wiped blood from a woman's arm. Following my lead, he removed his own shirt and ripped it into strips. He slid the woman's arm into a makeshift sling. Other men were removing their shirts and following suit, trying to help those with broken arms and wrists, gashed heads, and bleeding torsos.

Of perhaps fifty passengers, I had seen at least ten dead.

Three men, five women, one child, and one baby.

Of them all, I think it hurt me the most to see the baby. It wasn't long ago that I'd seen the tram crash in Whitechapel, and had thought my own wife and baby killed. The pain remained real and raw. I'd almost lost my little family to the dangers of living in London—specifically, living with *me* in

London due to my association with Sherlock Holmes.

It *was* a dangerous time to be with my old friend. It meant casting my family into harm's way—from evil men such as Professor Moriarty, nemesis of Holmes, from Professor Henry Fitzgerald of the Order of Dagon; and also from horrors that Holmes and I didn't yet understand, horrors such as the one unleashed upon the *Belle Crown*.

A voice broke into my thoughts.

"We need to get off the boat, Watson."

Holmes had found me. His gray eyes, intelligent and focused, were trained upon me, as if gauging my mental awareness and competence. I didn't want to appear in any way befuddled, for I was *not* befuddled. Sad and worried, *yes*, and a bit off, *yes*... in a way I couldn't quite determine... but, or so I told myself, *not* befuddled.

Holmes stared at me, worried.

"Are you feeling yourself, my dear fellow?" he asked gently.

For a moment, I didn't answer, then I nodded. Before we could say more, we were interrupted by an excited babble of voices. The police had returned, and we lent our efforts to helping the officers load more victims of the river beast onto their boat.

Another boat sped from a dock. More police, coming to get us all to shore.

"I do hope they quicken their progress and send an additional boat or two," Holmes said. "We're going to need more boats, and I mean—"

The deck boards cracked.

I looked down, aware that I was standing in water up to my ankles.

"I mean *now*!" Holmes yelled.

I grabbed his arm.

"Holmes!" I cried.

Water blasted up through the deck boards, and beneath our feet, the boat split in half.

3

A violent cold, as cruel as any knife, sliced through me. The deck stabbed the sky, jutting up at acute angles on either side of me, as the two halves of the *Belle Crown* sank into the Thames. Instinctively, I grabbed a broken board, kicking hard to stay afloat.

In front of me, Holmes also trod water. People flailed and screamed, all trapped inside the double death walls of jutting deck.

Holmes's head slipped under the water, and he disappeared. Had he drowned? Or was he swimming beneath the jumble of kicking legs and feet?

At any moment, the whole ship would smash into the Thames and sink. Whatever I did, it had to be fast. I didn't want to die this way.

Releasing the board to which I'd been clinging, I filled my lungs with air and then thrust my arms down, letting my body spring up as far as possible out of the water. As my body came back down, I thrust both arms out to my sides and up, up over my head, hence shoving my body as far below the surface as possible.

With my eyes shut, I plunged into the icy blackness.

I could feel the agitation of the water from the flailing arms and legs above me, and swam as fast as I could. If I didn't get to the edge of the sinking boat quickly enough, if I didn't get past all these people, then I would surely drown.

A few bubbles of air escaped my mouth.

Despite my best efforts, my body began to rise. My head knocked against a leg, and I grabbed it with both hands and shoved myself past it. I floated yet higher toward the surface.

Expelling the last of my air, I wondered how long I could hold onto life.

With death near, images of my beloved wife, Mary, and our son, Samuel, flashed through my mind. *I love you*, I thought, *both of you, more than anything...* and then my mind shifted to other things, perhaps my last thoughts on this Earth: Sherlock Holmes, Professor Fitzgerald's warehouse on the edge of the Thames, and the eerie keening of the Order of Dagon. In my mind, I saw spherical bones etched with esoteric symbols, a ratcheted bone snake with gold prongs, and the creatures as they fell into the crowd from the warehouse ceiling. I saw the furniture of deadly dimensions. I saw Willie Jacobs shoveling lead into his deadly, gold-producing tram machine. I saw Swallowhead Spring, where Holmes and I had witnessed the deadly production of Bellini's *Norma*. Finally, one image stayed with me, that of Mary and Samuel.

My body begged for release from the freezing water. My lungs ached.

I needed air, needed it badly.

It was then that I realized that nobody's feet and legs brushed against my body, that I was free of the *Belle Crown*.

My head popped above the surface of the water.

I gasped, deeply sucked the cold air into my lungs, and opened my eyes to a wash of prickly color.

Flapping my arms, I trod water with my legs. Still gasping, I rotated, blinking rapidly to clear my vision.

The ship was directly behind me. Dead bodies floated past. A hand clawed at the sky, then sank beneath the water. Blood, clothing, ladies' hats, dolls, and ripped human limbs churned up and down on the black waves. As on the battlefield, I heard the wailing of death, the cries for help, the prayers to God. The wind reeked of blood.

Desperation filled me.

I twisted again into a swimming position, and this time on the surface, I swam away from the *Belle Crown*. It was tough going, as the current was fierce and I was exhausted; but as I finally stroked past the crash site, I let the current pick me up and sweep me downstream: past the ship and past the death scene.

I, too, would die in the River Thames.

Did I pray? I think I did, yes.

Did I ask for forgiveness for the wrongs of my life? I think I did, yes.

Did I have regrets?

Absolutely, I did, *yes*.

Yet I was at peace.

I could no longer struggle against the power of the water.

Nature rules everything. If you doubt for a second that man's place in this world is negligible, put yourself in the middle of a freezing river, and you will immediately understand how weak we are, how dependent on the whims of nature for our very existence.

I stopped trying to swim. The cold clenched me in its death grip.

I peered at the dark water and the distant shore with its lopsided clutch of buildings. *These would be my final visions.*

A fog bell sounded. As I raised my head so that my ears were above water, a man's voice called, "Hold steady! Help is on its way!"

A police boat was bouncing over the waves toward me.

I could barely believe my good fortune. Somehow, I found my last thread of energy. My legs trod water more furiously as I fought to remain aloft with my head above the river. I lifted my right arm and waved.

The small craft pulled alongside me, and two men threw a coiled rope into the water. I slipped it over my head and under my arms. The men dragged me through the waves to the boat. They hauled up the rope, and my hands found iron rings on the side of the boat. I hadn't the strength to hoist myself up. The men did it for me. Strong arms and hands lifted me from that merciless black pit of water and over the side of the police boat. They deposited me on the deck. Stretched on my back, shivering, my eyes closing to the world, I whispered one word:

"*Holmes...*"

"What did you say?" A man's voice was close to my ear. I felt his breath upon me.

"*Holmes,*" I whispered again, this time more strongly.

"Did you say, Holmes?"

Weakly, I nodded.

A second man stooped beside me, and through slit eyes, I saw the uniform of a London policeman.

"Another man swam clear of the *Belle Crown*, as you did, sir. We picked him up, as well, and he rests yonder. We'll take you both to shore and to medical care. You rest now, sir. You rest." He touched my shoulder, then my eyes shut and I saw no more.

The boat careened across the waves. My stomach filled with acid. I swallowed, trying not to be sick. I felt confident that the other man picked up by the police boat was Sherlock Holmes, for I'd followed him beneath the water—or so I assumed. On the other hand, he might have drowned along with the others. I preferred to believe that my thinking had evolved over time to parallel his, and vice-versa. I preferred to believe that, if I'd known that our only safe course was swimming beneath the other passengers, then Holmes would have reached the same conclusion.

Of course, somebody else might have concluded the same.

I managed to open my mouth and croak a few words.

"Holmes. Other man. *Holmes?*"

I opened an eye. The policeman still stooped beside me.

"If your friend is tall and thin with gray eyes and a sharp tongue, then we have your man, yes."

At this, I let myself fall asleep, relief washing over me. Gray eyes and a sharp tongue. Who else but Holmes?

4

Two policemen helped me to my feet. I staggered between them down the wooden planks of the pier. In front of me, between two policemen of his own, stood Holmes, his legs shaking, his tall frame bowed, shoulders stooped. But whatever shape we were in, both Holmes and I were alive, and for this, I was deeply grateful.

He looked over his shoulder at me. His face was bruised, and gashes split his forehead and left cheek. The gray eyes bored into mine. His mouth twitched into a smile.

Then the police prodded him forward, and he turned back to the task at hand, that of stumbling down the pier and onto the London streets, where I assumed, a police cart waited.

My teeth chattered. My body shook from the cold. I smelled terrible. My legs ached, as did my arms. I could barely move the leg that I'd injured in the war. Since my marriage and the rekindling of my friendship with Holmes, I'd grown weary of limping and preferred to suffer pain than show my weakness. This time, however, I had no choice. I limped.

It was hard to move my facial muscles; most likely, I

was as bruised and gashed as Holmes. In particular, my forehead and nose hurt, and I winced, thinking of the stitches a doctor would use to sew me back together.

My ears rang, the noise punctuated by screeching and chanting in a language I didn't know.

"*Q'ulsi pertaggen fh'thagn daghon da'agon f'hthul'rahi roa. Aauhaoaoa demoni aauhaoaoa demoni aauhaoaoa demoni.*"

I clamped my hands over my ears, shook my head, swallowed hard, yet still, the noise persisted. I'd been hearing things and having the most horrid nightmares since working on the tram machine case with Holmes. Any moment, the visions would return: the color filaments floating through the air, the throbbing of items I knew to be stationary, such as buildings and walkways.

"Come on, then, let's get you cleaned up and off you go."

I clasped the man's arm, thankful for his voice, for it broke through the dreadful noise assailing my ears. The chanting withered, the screeching abated. My ears still rang... though faintly.

My rescuers supported me to a standpipe and pumped clean water over me, washing off as much of the river muck as they could. I suffered the force of the water, glad that I had not swallowed any of the foul stuff. They did the same with Holmes, then eased us onto crates, where we waited for the police cart that I'd hoped would be there already. We waited for blankets or warm, dry coats.

"You look as if you've just returned from the war," Holmes said.

"As do you," I said, "and you did not even serve in the war."

He chuckled through blue lips. Blood stained his face. The gash on his cheek puffed along the edges, indicating possible infection; though the swelling might cease, I thought, given appropriate medical care: ointment, bandages, periodic ice.

As if either one of us wanted ice applied to our bodies any time soon...

Holmes stared at the hard dirt of the street.

"That officer told me that most of the passengers died," he said. "Those who were not rescued before the boat broke up. A few men survived the wreckage, though, as well as one or two young women. All the others—infants, mothers, the elderly—everyone else drowned, Watson. The police will be dredging the river for weeks."

"As they did with the *Princess Alice*," I said, "when more than 650 perished in the Thames."

People sauntered past: couples chatting, children laughing as they had aboard the *Belle Crown* right before the crash. Any of these people might have chosen to take a pleasure cruise on the river instead of strolling along its edge. Any of them might now be dead. I wondered, *Has news of the wreck not yet traveled this far downstream?*

Carriages and horses clattered along the cobblestones and dirt. Men with carts called to each other, bargaining over prices and goods. A boy pointed at Holmes and me with our police escorts. His father whispered something in his ear, and the boy looked quickly away.

Holmes chuckled again.

"They probably think we're criminals," he said.

"Or drunken idiots who jumped into the Thames and had to be rescued by police," I said.

"I have my chemical habits, Watson, but drink is not one of them."

"And for that, I'm thankful," I said, thinking of my friend's cocaine habit. My ears had ceased ringing, but I wondered, as I had for this past month, if I were going mad. I wasn't the type to overly indulge with drink, nor did I seek what Holmes referred to as his chemical habits. Something was affecting me, of that I was sure: an infection of the mind, a disease.

A group of men staggered past, clutching at one another to maintain their balance, their faces haggard, their laughter gruff. An old woman stumbled from a crumbling ruin of a building, the siding unpainted and splintering, the windows boarded up with rusty nails.

The Eshocker dens, I thought. *They're everywhere by the docks and even on the side streets where people live.* It was becoming commonplace to see electrotherapy addicts mingling with ordinary citizens.

I glanced at Holmes. He had also noticed the addicts. His eyes sparked with desire. With a start, I realized that Holmes was no stranger to the Eshocker dens. A man who sank into the haze of drugs to fight boredom could just as easily seek out electrotherapy devices.

"There's nothing wrong with electrical stimulation," Holmes had told me many times. "Those of the medical profession, doctors such as yourself, use these devices all the time to cure a vast majority of modern ailments." And it was true, I knew, that doctors were applying mild electrical voltage to treat everything from constipation to blindness and paralysis. Holmes owned an electrical-stimulation hairbrush as well as a belt, and had been enthusiastically testing their efficacy upon his own person, without, I thought, much effect.

But electrotherapy treatment was one thing and Eshocker den addiction was quite another. Pay a price, and you could zap your brain into oblivion.

A boy with a dirt-streaked face darted between two addicts and ran into the crumbling building. He reminded me of Timmy Dorsey, Jr., the boy who lived with his father, a butcher turned murderer, in an Osborn Street building adorned with an unedifying sign that proclaimed *MEAT*. The building was a short walk from where Willie Jacobs had operated the now-simmering tram machine. I shuddered to remember that monstrous beast, with its steel limbs clattering against the walls and ceiling, its coiled tubes and phosphorus pit, its abilities to attack and even kill.

A police carriage clanked around the corner. The officers helped us up and called for the driver to take us to the Royal London Hospital in Whitechapel.

"The Eshocker dens are vile places," I told Holmes as we settled onto the carriage seats. "You should avoid them. They could kill you. All this electricity, we don't know what it really does. Other doctors may have their ideas—the electric aura, the sparks, and vibratory motions, thinking of electricity as some sort of magic fluid that cleanses the body of toxins—but I have my doubts. I see no real proof."

"I will use my belt, and I will use my brush," Holmes said, "as they do me no harm whatsoever, and indeed, they provide mild and enjoyable stimulation."

I didn't answer. I wasn't in the mood for an argument

about anything, much less any of Holmes's less-than-desirable addictions. If I were going to break him of one, it wouldn't be his hairbrush. Rather, it would be the cocaine.

"That creature I shot," Holmes said, abruptly switching topics, "it was not alone, Watson. There are others of its kind in the Thames. The police must keep all boats off the river and must keep all citizens away from the banks. Perhaps the creatures prefer the water—that is why I was looking for them in the river today, though I admit I did not expect them to have grown so large in such a short space of time. Perhaps the Order of Dagon has been careful to release them near water—at Swallowhead Spring and at the warehouse on this very bank not so long ago."

Holmes still sought rational explanations for the creatures' existence, something other than my theory about different realms or dimensions beyond our own. And yet, I feared that his conjectures were only that: conjectures that we would never prove to be fact.

"But why would they prefer water, and on what grounds do you think the Dagonites have released the creatures?" I asked.

"I have no grounds, Watson." He frowned. "I am but trying to draw parallels among the events."

"I agree," I said, "that the families here, enjoying a day by the river, are at risk. Those things in the river… what if they slither up to the shore and enter the heart of London, the streets themselves?"

"Anything is possible," my friend said, and then he shut his eyes. His body trembled with cold, as did mine. We would confront the nightmare of the creatures and their assault upon London in the morning. For now, it would suffice to rest and regain our strength.

But first, I had something more important to consider, and I was not looking forward to considering it, much less taking the necessary action.

I could wait no longer.

I had to send Mary and Samuel out of London and to safety. They'd only returned to me last week, and this time, when Mary left me, she might never come back.

5

DR. REGINALD SINCLAIR

Whitechapel Lunatic Asylum

"Close your right eye. Now tell me, what do you see, Mr. Norris?"

I crouched by the patient, carefully watched his movements, and gauged his reaction to my instructions. He was insane, as were all of my patients, but Mr. Norris's hallucinations—unlike most people's—seemed one-sided. That is, he saw specters with only his left eye and heard demons only with his left ear. I believed him to be an excellent candidate for my Eshocker machine, possibly in extreme treatment mode.

Excitement surged through me, spreading a tingling sensation down my arms and into my fingers. Was this not an electricity of sorts? Excitement galvanized people, did it not? Excitement was the spark of life, whether its cause was natural or induced by electrotherapy.

Ah, the marvels of the modern world. How wonderful to be a medical doctor, a scientist of the brain, in this modern age. How wonderful to control the treatment of patients, to be the director of the Whitechapel Lunatic Asylum.

Mr. Norris squeezed his right eye shut and squinted from his left. Both hands quivered on the arms of the chair. He smelled like decay. His teeth, what was left of them, were chipped and brown. A few strands of gray hair hung over his eyes, and I reached one gloved hand up and swept the strands from his line of vision.

His arm lifted, still quivering, and batted at the air, then dropped again.

"What do you see?" I pressed.

"Th-the heads, they float past me, and such evil lewd grins, sir, such as I see! Th-the hands, they float past, pointing at me, judging me, condemning me. Th-the voices—" At this, the poor man slapped his hand over his left ear. "They threaten me, want to kill me, tell me I'm evil, tell me I am bound for hell, though truth be told, sir, I am already in hell!"

Mr. Norris slammed his fists against both sides of his head. I grabbed his hands and pulled them away from his face. The poor man would beat his head to a pulp if I allowed it.

His right eye popped open as he struggled weakly against me. I guided his hands gently down to the armrests again. He slouched in the chair.

"What do you see, Mr. Norris, *what do you see now*?" I asked.

He blinked. Across the day room, Miss Klune, my nurse, smoothed a vinegar-water lotion across the forehead of Mr. Jacobs, who prattled in a daze from his usual position upon the floor. Several other patients sat, propped so as not to fall from their chairs, and stared into oblivion. Mrs. van der Kolk traced the air with a finger, giggled, and babbled about her undergarments. Mr. Robertson's head lolled to one side, drool coursing down his chin and saturating his night shirt.

I had few women in the asylum and preferred to keep them in the same wing as the men. Had separate wings been a requirement, I would have been forced to toss all of my female patients back onto the streets.

Mr. Norris's body went limp. His head slumped forward.

I lifted his chin and stared into his eyes: pupils dilated, large black circles displaying no intellect, just the emptiness of those whose minds had fizzled. He tilted his head and gazed upward. His lips muttered a short prayer, then:

"My oppressors," he whispered, looking at me again, "they are gone."

"Any floating heads?" I asked.

He shook his head.

"No, sir."

"Any floating hands, pointing incriminating fingers at you?" I asked.

"No, sir."

"And the voices?"

His head bowed, and a few tears trickled down his cheeks.

"They never stop. *Never.*" He began to cry. "The voices are always there. They never leave me alone."

I called to my nurse. I was fortunate to have Clara Klune here at the Whitechapel Lunatic Asylum. Stout, with strong legs and arms, and steady nerves, she was perhaps thirty-five years old to my forty-five; and she believed firmly in my pursuit of electrotherapeutic remedies for neural psychoses. *I'd rather have one Miss Klune than ten male nurses*, I thought with satisfaction.

She tried to comfort Mr. Norris with soothing words and by stroking his arms and hands.

"Dr. Sinclair will help you," she said in a monotone flattened from years of issuing the same promise over and over again, "I'm sure of it. He's the best doctor in the world, Mr. Norris, and you know we only want to help you."

"Yes, yes," my patient blubbered, "but can Dr. Sinclair fight the devil?"

"I can," I replied, straightening myself up and snapping off my gloves, "and I will. Miss Klune, we must give him relief. Is the Eshocker machine ready?"

"I fear we must delay Mr. Norris's treatment for some moments more. We have a new patient. And that pesky man is here again, the one who always upsets you so."

I stared into her ice-blue eyes. Strong and efficient, that was Miss Klune. Ice-blonde hair in a bun, hidden by her white nurse's hat, ice-thin lips emitting soothing words in the same tone they emitted words about my schedule.

"I will see the new patient shortly. In the meantime, restrain Mr. Norris and then send in my visitor, so I can dispose of him as quickly as possible."

She nodded, strapped Mr. Norris into his chair, and hurried away. Truly, she was irreplaceable. She handled various attendants' tasks and never complained, and the money I saved on labor, I plowed into research. Issuing some bland words of comfort to Mr. Norris, I left the patients' day room and returned to my small office.

I rarely used the office, only when shuffling papers and talking business, never for treating patients. Although I was the director of the asylum, I despised administrative duties and much preferred research into the treatment of the insane.

On the wall behind my battered desk were a dozen diplomas, awards, and testimonies. A stack of papers, held in place with a fossil from the Dorset coast, awaited my attention. I had barely settled into my cushioned chair before there was a knock and my office door swung open.

I did not rise as Miss Klune showed the procurement agent into the room. I did not greet him.

He gave me a jagged smile, displaying crooked teeth, and squeezed his massive body into one of the chairs on the other side of the desk.

Miss Klune's lips tightened, and she cast her eyes down and bustled back out of the office. She knew how much I despised this man. He was always squeezing me for more machines and higher profit margins.

My mind was on the new, unknown patient. *Who was he? What was wrong with him? Could I help him? Most important, could my Eshocker cure him?*

My visitor didn't waste time with niceties.

"The Professor requires a massive shipment of den devices. A fortune's to be made, but only if we can equip our dens with more of your machines. How much longer do you intend to make us wait? When will we receive the new shipment?" His voice was soft and low. It always surprised me how calmly this man addressed me. His appearance conveyed an immediate impression of force and violence, of raw brutality. The procurement agent, whose name I didn't know, even after all this time, was well over six feet tall and packed with at least 220 pounds of rock-hard muscle. His hands were thick, the skin tough: a working man's hands. He dressed like a dock worker: cap, jacket, heavy shirt, dirty trousers.

Always, he wanted the same thing: more and yet more electrotherapy devices for Professor Moriarty's Eshocker dens. I was all for the use of electrotherapy. The list of treatments was seemingly endless. However, I wasn't particularly interested in administering jolts of electricity to ordinary fellows seeking thrills.

"You know," my visitor continued, repositioning his bulk in the small chair, "you aren't the only supplier. We can get these devices elsewhere. We can even build them, if we want. There's nothing magical about what you supply, Dr. Sinclair."

"You're threatening me?" I bristled. "I don't like your tone, Mr.—?"

"My name is not important. I've told you that before. What *is* important is giving my employer what he asks of you. Refusals are discouraged. *Strongly* discouraged. We will have these devices, with or without your cooperation."

How dare this man address me in such an insolent manner?

"They're much too dangerous to fool with!" I snapped, jumping up and pounding my fist on the desk. "I own the patent on these devices! You wouldn't *dare*—"

My visitor also stood, flinging his chair aside. It clattered across the floor and hit the wall by the door to my treatment room.

He advanced two steps toward me. Then he paused, cast me a nasty grin, and reached into his pocket.

My heart lurched. What was he going to do? Shoot

me right here in my office? I was a medical doctor, not a criminal. Who would kill a man who had devoted his life to helping others?

He slid brass knuckles over the fingers of his right hand.

I pushed back my chair and stepped back, as if this would do any good. Taking several deep breaths and waiting for my heart to stop racing, I reminded myself that Professor Moriarty and his procurement agent were not ordinary businessmen. They were criminals. They had no respect for decency. When I spoke again, my words were calm and measured—the same way I addressed my patients.

"I'll build the devices for you. Very soon, I promise. Tell your employer that I appreciate his business."

"When will they be ready, and how many?" the other demanded, his right hand balled into a fist, the brass knuckles gleaming dully. They looked worn and scratched as if from overuse.

"Give me a week," I said, "and I'll have my men make five machines. Will that suffice?"

Now it was *his* fist—the one with brass knuckles—that pounded my desk, making me jump. His jagged smile widened, and yet his voice remained soft and low.

"Ten a week, *every week*, until I say, *no more*," he said.

That was a high rate of production for me. I employed the services of two lunatics to build each device. I didn't want any one man to build an entire machine. I didn't want to give away all of my secrets, not even to lunatics. I would have to train more of my patients and set them to work at night. I didn't like the idea. The two who worked for me now were well suited to the task; they'd been machinists and builders before being committed to the asylum.

The money I earned from selling these devices to Professor Moriarty's Eshocker dens enabled me to pay Miss Klune and my other nurse, Miss Switzer. It enabled me to pay for the necessary medicines and foods, whose bills lay upon my desk as we spoke. Without the income, the Whitechapel Lunatic Asylum would be a filthy, cramped, horror house filled with patients I wouldn't be able to help. No bedding. No clothing. No treatment. Just shrieking lunatics in strait-waistcoats.

No. I would not live with that option. My asylum was modern, if small. It was humane. It was a research institution, where I was making major breakthroughs with my Eshockers and on the cusp of filing patents for both hospital mode and extreme treatment mode. The devices I supplied to this man were incapable of giving more than mild shocks. They couldn't hurt anyone; they were used only for pleasure and simple treatments. Certainly, people were addicted, but this was no different from other addictions such as morphine, cocaine, alcohol, and so forth.

Anything good could be used for bad, but the fact remained that my machines existed to do *good*.

"We know how your machines work," Moriarty's man pressed, "and we won't hesitate to build them elsewhere, if you make us. We prefer, of course, that you supply the equipment. It's much easier for us that way. The Professor is not interested in factories or labor problems, only in profit."

The profits must be immense, I thought. I had been told that customers paid a shilling a pop for an electric buzz. But they paid the dens all day every day, selling their bodies, if necessary, to get those shillings. Professor Moriarty's

Eshocker dens were more addictive than opium dens.

"If you build my machines without me..." I wanted to say, *I'll sue you*, but I knew all that would get me was a crack of brass knuckles to my face.

The man laughed at me. He was already halfway to the door. Apparently, he'd guessed what I was about to say, for he answered my unspoken words:

"What will you do, Dr. Sinclair, *sue us*? Just try, and here's what you'll get: the services of another professional. He's called the gravedigger."

I shrank back, afraid to say another word.

What was I thinking, to threaten this man, even in the most weak manner? If I wanted Moriarty to finance the asylum, I had to round up more lunatics to build more machines. It was simple mathematics.

"Make those machines. Ten a week." A fat finger pointed at my face.

I bobbed my head up and down, and Moriarty's emissary left, scowling but without further comment.

I waited a good five or ten minutes, then bellowed:

"Miss Klune! Bring the new patient!"

Let me return to my research, let me study a new malady, let me examine a new patient: anything but worrying about funding, finances, administrative matters, and how on earth I'm going to build ten den mode Eshockers every week.

The nurse, attuned to my behavior after a decade of service, heard my call and rushed into the office. Accompanying her was the surprise of a lifetime. My new patient.

He was someone I knew... *very, very well.*

6

"Y-you're the madman, n-not me!" the new patient shrieked. "Y-you *know* what you are!" Then his words oozed into one long nonsense syllable. He fought to carve the babbling into words, shaking his head, grimacing, stuttering, but to no avail.

Miss Klune waved at someone in the hall, and my other private nurse, Amy Switzer, rushed in behind her. The two of them, as strong as nurses come, pinned Bligh Braithwaite's arms behind his back while avoiding his kicking legs. He struggled valiantly, I had to give him that, but he'd always been a weakling and was no match for even *one* of the asylum's nurses.

My lips curled into a professional fake smile, the one I put on when trying to calm irrational creatures such as Bligh Braithwaite.

"Let's bring him into the treatment room, shall we?" I said.

The two nurses dragged the patient across the office. He continued to struggle, his body twitching, his arms trying to break free. Slobber dripped from his mouth along with a stream of gibberish. His eyes had that foggy look I knew so well: behind them, a dull brain sloshed through dim-witted thoughts. His legs dragged behind him. Miss Klune twisted the knob to the treatment room and kicked open the door.

"Y-y-yooooooo..." Braithwaite slobbered.

"Yes, and what about me, sir?" I said.

"Shall we strap him in, Doctor?" Miss Klune interjected.

Nodding, I followed the nurses and the new patient into my treatment room and gestured at the left Eshocker.

"Use that one," I said.

"Y-y-yooooooo! N-n-n-n-no!" Braithwaite shrieked.

He looked worse than I remembered. His hair was unkempt and wild. His clothes were tattered and hung from his emaciated frame. His beard was perhaps an inch long, like a growth of weeds poking from dirt.

But his behavior certainly hadn't changed. When Miss Klune released him to unlatch the wrist and ankle straps on the Eshocker, Braithwaite doubled over at the waist and twisted his arms and legs in bizarre contortions. His entire body shuddered as if he were experiencing an epileptic seizure, but I knew better. Braithwaite didn't have epilepsy. Braithwaite was insane.

Miss Switzer kept her grip on one of his arms and tried to jerk his body into an upright position. Her face stormed with anger.

"This patient is out of control!" she snapped.

"Aren't they all?" I said.

"Shouldn't you talk to him before rushing into treatment?" she demanded.

When I'd first seen Braithwaite in my office, all I could think was: *he's here, and I don't know why or how he's here, but I must take care of him immediately.* The shock of seeing him in my asylum had made me act before sufficiently considering the situation.

I fingered the watch tucked beneath my vest. I thrust my other hand into a trouser pocket.

Miss Klune trained her ice-blue eyes on Miss Switzer.

"Don't question the Doctor," she said. "He knows what he's doing. This patient requires immediate Eshocker treatment."

"I don't know about that." Miss Switzer shoved Bligh Braithwaite onto the cushion of the Eshocker machine.

Sometimes, I wondered if she was up to the job. She was an excellent nurse, very good with tormented patients, and her calming effect on them was undeniable. Yet there was an underlying anger in her that never seemed to go away. Her eyes were always sharp and glaring. Her forehead bore permanent creases, including a vertical one descending from her hairline to her eyebrows. The sides of her mouth drooped downward. Taller than Miss Klune, Amy Switzer's physique was masculine: broad shoulders, muscular arms, large hands, powerful legs, and as for breasts, I wasn't sure she had anything there.

Miss Klune thrust a ball into Braithwaite's mouth and wrapped gauze around his head to secure the gag. She snapped his wrists and ankles securely into the straps.

Tears streamed down his face. His eyes beseeched me.

I looked away.

"Tell me about this man," I said, but only to appease Miss Switzer.

Miss Klune answered.

"The patient is Bligh Braithwaite. He escaped from the Kandinsky Asylum for the Poor not long ago. Apparently, he was trying to break into our asylum when the police came across him. Imagine! He was gnawing at the chains of the main gate."

I circled the gurney, the cabinet that held my surgical equipment, and the metal examination table. Making my way to the other side of the room, where the second Eshocker stood, I admired the machine. How amazing that a chair with a large wooden box next to it could bring such relief to those afflicted with neural psychoses. The engineering was pure genius. Why use direct current when you could use an alternating current, which could be increased to higher voltages using a transformer? Why use expensive batteries when you could recharge them? Why use steady milliamperes when you could apply varying amounts of electricity based on the patient's needs? Why give a patient toxic medications when you could give him restorative, clean, healthy electrotherapy, all calibrated to his unique requirements?

"Dr. Sinclair?" Miss Klune prompted.

Returning my attention to Bligh Braithwaite, I pictured him gnawing on the chains of the asylum gates.

"How did the police know that this man came from the Kandinsky Asylum?" I asked.

"He told an officer his name—he can speak, though as you have just heard he has a dreadful stammer. It was a simple matter to trace him to the Kandinsky Asylum, which had reported him missing." She considered. "Perhaps he escaped from Kandinsky, went on the run, found he couldn't take care of himself—no food, no place to sleep but the alleys—and he decided to seek asylum, as it were, at another asylum."

Braithwaite had stopped struggling and was limp in the chair. Drool dripped from his open mouth. What a mess he was.

I would help him. In the process, I would also help myself—his fixation with me had obviously reasserted itself. It would probably be best to keep him here rather than ship him back to Kandinsky. It was just as well that I had him in my control.

"Just like a lunatic," I said. "He breaks out of one asylum, only to break into another. Well, he's here now, isn't he? And he knows full well what happens in places like this, doesn't he?"

"I doubt he expected a Dr. Sinclair Eshocker," said Miss Switzer.

"Well, he *is* in for the shock of his life," I said drily. "Nurses, you know the drill. Out with you! *Go!*" I waved them from the room. This was the type of treatment I always handled alone. Just me and the patient. It was critical to the patient's mental well-being. Nobody else would understand what was happening in this room, nor did I want anybody questioning me. The Eshockers were mine, and mine alone.

While I'd patented the den mode Eshocker, I still wasn't ready to apply for patents for the hospital and extreme treatment modes. I needed more clinical trials first, needed to make sure that the two new modes worked as I had planned. Nobody knew how the two new modes worked; *nobody but me*, that was.

The door shut behind the two nurses, and I locked it.

I was alone with Bligh Braithwaite.

"I believe you need extreme treatment," I said, not cruelly but not kindly either.

At this, he squirmed, and his eyes flew open. He stared at me in horror. His arms and legs thrashed against the restraints.

"You shouldn't have come here, Braithwaite. This is a hospital for the insane. I'm the director. What did you think would happen if you showed up? You knew full well what type of treatment you'd receive."

His cheeks puffed in and out. He desperately wanted to scream. The ball and gauze held tight. Sweat poured down his face, which turned red.

"You know I want what's best for you," I continued, twisting off the screws from the top of the Eshocker box. Setting the top on the floor, I stared into the box, admiring my creation. It was beautiful. It was perfect. It was wondrous. A true medical breakthrough.

His eyes beseeched me, but I just shook my head.

"There's no getting out of this, Braithwaite. You came to me for help. I'm going to give you that help. You're a sick man. We both know that. You've always been sick, even as a child. The twitching, the wailing, the gibberish, the spasms. You can't speak clearly to anyone. You can't understand what we try to tell you. You're a lost soul, aren't you, Braithwaite? Lost, and you want me to comfort you. And I will do that, and you know why? Because you're a very special man, that's why."

The dull-wax eyes went wild. They flashed from me

to the door to the gurney to the examination table to the Eshocker across the room. His clenched throat growled, a muted form of howling muffled by the ball and gauze.

I placed a hand on his shoulder, and he shrank back.

"Now, now," I said calmly, "struggling only makes things worse for you. Settle down. Relax. You might even try to enjoy it. People pay for this pleasure in the dens. Addicts would sell their mothers for the dose I'm about to give you."

Moistening his forehead with a wet sponge, I placed two electrodes on him, then stepped back and enjoyed the moment.

"Extreme treatment," I said softly, and when he shuddered, I smiled. "For an extreme case," I added.

I didn't look at him to see his reaction. I'm not cruel.

I turned it on, and the Eshocker rumbled to life. The beautiful sound of electricity filled the air, a steady thrum that made my heart happy just to hear it.

I applied the treatment, and I enjoyed every second of it.

The patient convulsed, wheezed, and fought me like the lunatic he was, and finally, after a lengthy session with the Eshocker, he fell into a deep sleep.

His face relaxed.

Wasn't he better off this way?

Of course, he was.

The man was a maniac. Totally out of control. Who knew what he'd do if let loose in society? He might attack children. He might kill somebody.

But instead, with treatment from the Dr. Sinclair Eshocker, his sick mind floated in the peaceful fold of dreams. In dreams, we hallucinate and hear things, perhaps;

but in dreams, we cannot hurt others, maim or kill them.

Let the lunatics dream.

Later, when Braithwaite awakened, I'd think about giving him further treatment. For now, I had to enlist the aid of my other lunatics, those with machinist skills. I had to build den Eshockers for Professor Moriarty and for the masses, and I had other patients requiring my attention.

My worries centered on Moriarty. He was a dangerous man. He would kill without hesitation. He would kill *me.* Thankfully, he didn't have the *real* Eshockers, the ones that would revolutionize medicine. He had only the den versions. I didn't like negotiating with criminals.

Such prices we pay for medical progress.

Moriarty's demands. Bligh Braithwaite showing up.

I stared long and hard at my new patient.

This was not turning out to be a good day in the lunatic business.

7
DR. JOHN WATSON
London

My wife had stuffed our lives into three large bags that now sat like garbage by the front door. The wall where I'd hung the painting of her father was now a blank slate, waiting for the next occupants of the rooms to put up a picture of their loved one.

Samuel slept in her arms.

She didn't raise her eyes as I entered the room. She'd been crying. Her eyes were puffy, her face was wet.

"Mary," I said simply.

I wouldn't cry. I wouldn't try to convince her to stay. London had become much too dangerous for her and Samuel.

Henry Fitzgerald had sent a man to gas them. Moriarty had tricked and then transported them to a dangerous part of town near Willie Jacobs's tram machine. Strange creatures haunted London and now seethed in the Thames; these must be the creatures that I had heard members of the Order of Dagon refer to as Old Ones, the Others, the Deep Ones—creatures they worshiped, believing they lived along energy lines deep within the earth and beneath the seas. In the same airless room I had heard them speak of another entity, as if they considered it the royal of all royals—they called it Cthulhu.

I sat, resigned, in my favorite chair beside Mary's rocking chair. Outside, the clouds shuddered and dumped rain onto the London pavements. My clothes, bedraggled oddities graciously loaned to me by Detective Harold Bentley, clung to my skin. My near-death in the Thames had left me deflated and weak, fighting a flu or heavy cold; I didn't yet know which, but I feared mentioning my near-death and impending illness to Mary. It was bad enough that I was presenting myself to her with a bandage on my head, where a doctor—less skilled than myself—had applied ragged stitches. I would do nothing that might prevent Mary from leaving me.

"It's gone beyond Sherlock Holmes, and it's gone past me," I said softly, reaching for her hand.

She burst out crying. She clutched my hand, her head bent over our baby.

Samuel stirred, and his tiny eyes opened and blinked at me. He was too young to later remember me at this moment. But I would remember him.

The furniture, comfortable and soft as ever, would feel hard and dead without her. I would not live here alone. I couldn't.

"The newspapers are full of the stories, John," Mary said. "Everyone's talking about it. When you didn't come home yesterday or last night, *I knew...*" She paused. "I knew that you and Sherlock Holmes were involved. These are the same creatures, aren't they, the ones you saw at Swallowhead Spring and in that warehouse by the Thames?"

I nodded.

"There's what I think of as an infestation of these creatures in the river, Mary. Holmes and I saw one of enormous dimensions—a hideous, nightmarish vision, beyond anything we've yet seen—" I hesitated, and then I blurted it out: "We barely escaped with our lives." I made a snap decision to tell her all, because she needed to know, for sure, how dangerous life was in London and how staying with me might mean certain death. I hated scaring Mary in this manner, but her safety came first, so I recounted all that had happened, and tried to end on a more positive note with how the police boat had rescued us, how Detective Bentley had stepped in and made sure we had baths and police beds for the night. Holmes and I had been incapable of anything more.

She attempted a smile. She squeezed my hand a last time, then released it.

"Samuel and I will return, I promise. I'm taking him to a friend of a friend's—I'll give you the address down south." She supplied the information, then added, "When London's safe again, we'll come back to you, John."

"I understand," I said. "I'd hoped that Holmes and I were done with these terrifying creatures. I see now that we are far from done. I must help him, Mary, I must see this through to its conclusion. I want you and Samuel to be safe. I didn't know how to ask you to leave. It pains me, Mary."

My mind felt hazy, perhaps because I had spent a dangerous amount of time in the unclean river yesterday, but most likely, due to whatever had infected me during the past few weeks while Holmes and I resolved the case of the deadly dimensions. The visions, the terrible nightmares: I feared that I had been infected with a disease that caused madness. After I'd seen the effect the case had on Holmes—it had almost broken his belief in a sane world—I'd wished there was a way to travel back in time and run far away from London with my little family to spare *them* from all that had transpired and all that *would* transpire. I had not made that decision in time to spare Mary from suffering and worry.

I didn't pack my family into a cab right away. Instead, Mary and I dawdled, unable to part. I won't relate here what transpired, for I maintain the belief that some matters in this world should remain private, and this was one of those times. I trust you can imagine the difficulties we both had in parting, and especially, how wretched I felt when finally I did tuck Mary and Samuel into a carriage and bid them farewell.

Her final kiss lingered on my cheek. I pressed my hand to it, hoping to imprint it into my flesh.

I had now done what I should have accomplished much earlier: protected my family from whatever threatened them in London. I felt relief, but also, a great sadness. How long would it be before I would see them again? How big would Samuel be? What would I miss?

8

"But surely you have no need to alter your mind or body with electric shocks, Holmes. You cannot possibly be bored. We have a case to solve like no other. Believe me, I am afraid of nothing, but these monsters in the Thames, well, I don't know what to make of them. All London is hysterical. Mrs. Hudson is afraid to go out!"

I swung from the window to face my old friend. We were fellow lodgers again. He'd kindly offered to take me back into 221B Baker Street.

"Only until London is cleared of these creatures," he'd said, "and then, we'll send for Mary and Samuel, and you can return to your home. But for now, it's best that you stay here as in former times."

Yet despite his acknowledgment that his skills might be required to rid England of this plague of creatures, Holmes had insisted on frequenting the Eshocker dens down by the river.

When I'd pressed him about it, he'd cocked his head and slyly suggested that I join him.

"It will help alleviate your melancholy," he'd said, "and forget Mary for a space of time."

"I don't want to forget Mary," I'd spat back. "Even if it means that I'm melancholy, as you put it, I prefer to remember my family. Besides, my mind's been fogged for more than a month. It's as if I'm in a stupor. The last thing I need is to cloud my senses any further."

Now I settled into my old armchair by the fire, while Holmes sat across from me, his eyes narrowed, his mouth sucking in smoke from his pipe then releasing it in curls.

"Perhaps you are suffering from nervous exhaustion, Watson. I agree that these creatures are bizarre entities, and yet, what do we know, as scientists, of the ocean and the multitude of life that swarms within its cradle? Perhaps these creatures come from the sea, have migrated into our Thames, have mutated into their current forms. Perhaps these creatures can indeed exist on land as well as water, and perhaps Professor Henry Fitzgerald and his underlings concealed them upon the warehouse roof that night. Perhaps—" his fingers tapped his pipe stem—"perhaps Fitzgerald's gang unleashed them from that roof to provide the *illusion* of creatures snapping into existence seemingly from nowhere."

He looked quite delighted with himself. He crossed his legs, then rapidly uncrossed them and leaned forward in his chair, elbows on his knees. He stared intently at me. It was the stare I knew so well, the one that often made me pull my eyes away from his due to its sheer intensity.

"Perhaps, but as you always point out, Holmes, guesses do not equate with truth. We have insufficient facts."

"I am aware of that," he said simply, settling back into his chair.

"I need tea," I said, "and some of Mrs. Hudson's biscuits. Where *is* she? Is it *not* tea time?" Yes, I was irritable but knew that Holmes would correctly intuit that my family troubles were upsetting me.

"Speaking of food," he said, continuing his train of thought, "what do these creatures eat? Have you considered how they're surviving in the Thames? If we deny them whatever it is they eat, then *perhaps*—to use that word you apparently despise—they will migrate elsewhere and leave us alone. They'll return to the deep sea, if that is indeed their source."

The image flashed in my mind of the giant tentacle poised over his head. I dared not tell him that I thought *he* was a potential food source for these creatures, and with him, every inhabitant of London.

Abruptly, Holmes leapt from his chair, excited by something, then turned and bellowed over his shoulder, "Mrs. Hudson! *Mrs. Hudson!*"

From beneath our flat, the landlady's heels clicked across the floor and then up the stairs. In the meantime, Holmes wrenched a journal from his desk drawer along with two metal belts. He flipped open the journal and thrust it at me.

"Read it," he commanded. When I looked at him, confused, he said, "The advertisement, Watson. It's from Pulvermacher and Company here in London. 1886."

I glanced at the page. Indeed, it was an 1886 advertisement, but in the *Irish Journal of Medical Science*. Pulvermacher had been forced to stop running similar advertisements in

British medical journals such as *The Lancet*.

"You see," Holmes continued in a state of excitement, "these galvanic belts, of which I possess two types, strengthen both muscles and nerves, re-energize and reduce the very nervous exhaustion from which *you* suffer."

He shoved both belts into my hands. I dropped the journal onto my lap and clumsily grabbed the belts. The heaviest of the two was a Pulvermacher hydro-electric chain, a rudimentary electrotherapy device sold and promoted by doctors of much less standing than myself. I scoffed and set the chain on the floor at my feet.

"My dear fellow," I said, "you don't imagine—?"

He laughed, three quick bursts, and gingerly lifted the belt by its two large handles. He placed the belt—in truth, merely assorted wooden rods with copper and zinc wires wrapped around them and threaded all together—around his waist and gripped the insulated handles.

I shuddered.

"Really, Holmes," I said.

"Not to worry," he chuckled. "I've not dipped the belt in vinegar, and also, I don't intend to use it now."

There was a rap on the door and Mrs. Hudson came in.

"Later, Mrs. Hudson!" he cried.

"But... but..." She was flustered, one hand still on the door, the other clutching a handkerchief. "*You* called for *me*, Mr. Holmes."

"Yes, I did," he replied, "but wait a moment, will you? Or better yet, go fetch our tea. The poor doctor might keel over at any moment if he doesn't have some refreshment."

"Yes, yes," she answered. "Right away. I'm sorry, Doctor.

With all the commotion about those monsters, I'm not myself. I'll prepare the tea straight away then."

She let the door close behind her.

"You really should treat her with more courtesy," I said.

"You know I hold her in high regard," he answered curtly. His gaze was sharp.

Yes, I *did* know that Holmes was quite fond of Mrs. Hudson, and I also knew that she would do anything within her means to take care of *him*. Still, there were times when he treated her more like a slave than a landlady.

I gestured at the belt he'd strapped around his waist.

"Why are you showing me these belts now?" I asked.

"I received a note from Mycroft, asking me to visit him. Here it is."

Scribbled in Mycroft's terse script were a few short lines:

Please dine with me at the Diogenes Club tonight and bring Dr. Watson. It involves your Whitechapel acquaintance— look in on him at the asylum today, if you can. His new abode has a shocking link to his previous one.

—Mycroft

"A shocking link?"

"He means the Eshockers, Watson. Thrawl Street has become notorious in the past few weeks for its Eshocker dens. You must have noticed they were being set up even the last time we were there, when I calmed the tram machine."

"I must confess I did not. I had other things on my mind, and the smoke from that machine was oppressive. But what link is there to the Whitechapel Lunatic Asylum?"

"Simply that Dr. Reginald Sinclair, the proprietor of that asylum, has made it his special study to apply electroshock therapy to his patients; indeed, he manufactures his machines himself."

Something occurred to me.

"The Eshocker dens have devices with stronger currents than these belts?" I asked softly.

"*Much* stronger, Watson. You see, with this old belt, the one you dropped on the floor, patients can control the amount of shock they receive using a clockwork interrupter apparatus." He pointed to a protruding knob. "With the new belt, the one you hold, vinegar is no longer required, and the amount of shock is minimal, more like a tingle, I'd say. People are wearing these belts beneath their garments, Watson. Some wear half a dozen at a time, strapped around their stomachs, their chests; their arms, legs, necks, and yes, even the male anatomy. Yet with all of these devices wrapped around them, until the more extreme of them look like mummies—"

I dropped the second belt to the floor and wrinkled my nose.

"Mummies, you say, and wrapped around the male anatomy?" I dared not think what part of Holmes's body this second belt had serviced.

"Not me, my dear fellow!" he cried.

I didn't yet understand how the den devices presented more danger than Holmes's two belts.

A knock at the door announced Mrs. Hudson, carrying a tray of tea and biscuits. As she put it on the table, her eyes were on the belt I had dropped.

"Mr. Holmes," she said, "I hope you are not using those electrical gewgaws on my premises." As we hastened to assure her that was not the case, she added, "You look a sight, Mr. Holmes, since your swim in the Thames, and, Doctor, you've never looked so weary and ill, not since I've known you. All those cuts and bruises. I worry about the both of you, I do. Those monsters in the river are in all the papers. Creatures from another world, the *Daily News* says."

"The *Daily News* doesn't know what it's talking about," Holmes said, as he poured a cup of tea and handed it to me along with a small dish of sweet biscuits. "We won't be here for supper, Mrs. Hudson. My brother Mycroft has asked us to dine with him at the Diogenes Club. Watson, en route we shall stop at the Thrawl Street Eshocker den."

"I must object!" My cup jittered on its saucer. "There will be no Eshocker dens, Holmes, not for you and certainly not for me!"

Holmes gestured at the electrotherapy belts, one now draped across his desk, the other still on the floor by my feet. "You need to see for yourself what transpires in those Eshocker dens before we go to the Diogenes Club. And I've chosen the Thrawl Street den for a reason."

Mrs. Hudson's face went from mottled red to bright pink.

"Willie Jacobs..." she whispered, barely disguising her disdain for our former client. "That tramp. You're going to visit *him*, aren't you?"

Holmes and I both felt more than obligated to help Willie Jacobs in any way we could. We hadn't been able to save him from total mental collapse caused by the phosphorus

pit and the tram machine. He'd saved the lives of Mary and
Samuel. I'd grown very fond of him, as had Holmes. He was
a good man.

And yet...

Willie Jacobs had indeed gone mad.

He'd been committed to the asylum with a diagnosis of
neural psychosis and was under Dr. Sinclair's direct care.

Mrs. Hudson didn't approve of our involvement with
Willie Jacobs.

"No good will come of this," she said, "no good at all.
That tramp may have saved your family, Dr. Watson, but it
was his fault they almost lost their lives to begin with. In
fact, it's his fault that you and Mr. Holmes almost died, as
well—numerous times, as I recall. And now, the tramp is
insane. Who knows how dangerous he is? Who knows what
he will do?"

Slipping into my coat, I took my cane and hat from the
stand by the door, then placed a reassuring hand on Mrs.
Hudson's arm.

"Don't worry. Mr. Jacobs is ill, yes, but underneath the
illness is a very fine and decent man who wants to do what's
best by others. I'm certain that Willie Jacobs is no threat to
either me or to Mr. Holmes. He may very well be able to
help us fight these creatures and pry loose the citizens of
London from these nefarious dens."

I wasn't sure I believed my own little speech, and I
certainly had no idea what Holmes had in mind regarding
Willie Jacobs.

Mrs. Hudson didn't look entirely convinced that Willie
Jacobs might be able to help us.

"Whatever you say, Doctor," she said, frowning and wringing her hands.

In the meantime, Holmes had slipped past both of us and raced down the stairs to the front door.

Not wanting to get into a prolonged conversation with Mrs. Hudson, I bounded down the stairs after him, just catching the front door before it slammed shut.

Holmes was already hailing a cab.

"Thrawl Street," he instructed the driver, "and make it as fast as you can!"

9

DR. REGINALD SINCLAIR

Whitechapel Lunatic Asylum

My master carpenter, Mr. Norris, the lunatic who saw specters with his left eye and heard demons with his left ear, crouched by the coffin-sized mahogany box. The wood was raw, not yet sanded, stained, and polished. Yet to me, it was a vision of glowing beauty straight from the heavens. This box would save lives. It would restore sanity to the lost—men like Mr. Norris, who had gone insane after witnessing the murder of his wife one balmy evening while sailboats bobbed across the water beneath a soft lemony moon.

Mr. Norris hated yellow. He hated boats. He hated water and refused it when taking his medicine or even bathing. It took both of my nurses, Clara Klune and Amy Switzer, to pin him down—after tranquilizing him into a stupor—in order to lather him with soap. They washed Mr. Norris only once every third week. I didn't raise the issue out of fear that my nurses would leave my employment—and who would I find to replace them?

But here he was, Mr. Norris: eyes focused on the rim of the mahogany box, a slight smile upon his lips. With perfect control, he held the chisel in one hand and the mallet in the other. Wood flakes chipped off the box, dusting his knees and drifting to the floor as he shifted his weight.

Gas lamps set high on the walls cast wavering slips of light through the windowless room. It was a miracle, I thought, that Mr. Norris didn't hallucinate in this environment. But I'd been careful with the set-up of the workshop, aiming to keep my patient calm while he chiseled the boxes. Mr. Norris's own equipment filled this room. I'd sent for it when I signed the papers committing him to the asylum.

I surveyed the equipment: rebate saws, one flat and with a large hole, another with an adjustable fence, and yet another with a pistol-grip handle that I knew to be quite rare. Mr. Norris used these saws to overlap and join wood.

He had planes of all types: sun-planes to level barrel tops, toothing planes to scratch surfaces before applying glues, scooper planes. He also had jointers of all sizes and dimensions, as well as chair-maker's saws, bow saws, felloe saws. He had hooks, clubs, augers, axes, glue pots, nail tools, gimlets, even an ancient grindstone. I could not imagine where Mr. Norris had procured such an item.

Not wanting to frighten him, I walked as quietly as I could, and when I spoke, my voice was soft.

"How is the work, Mr. Norris? I must say, your craftsmanship is the most excellent I have ever seen."

When he turned his head and nodded, I placed a hand on his shoulder and gently squeezed it. His eyes glowed, and his smile widened.

"Thank you, sir. It gives me great pleasure to build these devices for you. I almost feel alive again, as if I matter."

"You *do* matter, Mr. Norris," I reassured him. "You matter more than you know. In fact, I wish that I had another two or three men as capable as you are at fashioning wood for my Eshockers."

A bit of drool slipped from his lips. He wouldn't be able to work much longer before the visions and voices gripped him again.

"I'll let you get back to work," I said. "I need as many boxes as you can carve this week."

"I can only do what I can. A proper job requires a week, given my... illness."

"I know, but demand is high, and to obtain food for you and the others, I need to deliver more of the Eshockers."

He returned to his chisel and mallet. Wood flaked to his knees. His hands shook. His fingers trembled. The mallet hit the chisel off-center, and a small wedge of wood fell off the Eshocker box.

I grimaced. He would ruin the box.

"Perhaps that's enough for today." I lifted his emaciated frame to a standing position.

He dropped his tools. His eyes fogged.

"I-I don't like being in the Eshocker!" he cried. "Th-they are not for pleasure! Th-they are for hell!"

"Now, Mr. Norris, settle down. Come and sit down while I call for the nurse."

He beat his head with both fists. Grabbing his wrists, I lowered his arms to his sides.

"F-floating heads!" he cried. "The voices! Why won't they go away? Why won't they leave me alone?"

I held his wrists with one hand and looped my other

arm around his waist. I dragged him from the workshop, kicked shut the door behind me—it automatically locked—and helped Mr. Norris onto the examination table, where I strapped him across the ankles, wrists, neck, and torso. He struggled, but to no avail. Struggling never worked on the examination table.

"I'm going to get Miss Klune," I said in my most gentle and soothing tone. "She'll take care of you, calm you, and help you rest again."

"No Eshocker!" he shrieked, then burst out weeping.

"I promise, Mr. Norris, no Eshocker. Not today."

But tomorrow, I thought, *you will have a long session in hospital mode, and if you can't calm down sufficiently, I'll have to apply extreme treatment.*

How ironic that the very man who helped me build the Eshockers needed their treatment just to function rationally for any length of time at all.

Mr. Norris screamed and wept as I hurried off to find Miss Klune. I had asked her to look in on Willie Jacobs not long before, and so I sought her in the closet just off the day room where I'd stuffed him. Well, it wasn't *really* a closet, just a tiny room that could accommodate nothing more than a small bed. It was all I had been able to offer at such a busy time—all the beds in the larger rooms were taken.

Miss Klune's muscular body barely fitted between the bed and the stone wall. She straightened as I opened the door, and she lifted a dripping needle from Jacobs's neck, her usually neat hair misaligned after the struggle of holding him still. She set the needle back in its box and pushed her hair back in place. Jacobs emitted a stream of gibberish, his usual nonsense about giant snakes, "the beast," and so forth. Miss Klune shook her head, exchanging a glance with me.

"Hurry off and take care of Mr. Norris, would you, nurse? He needs sedation."

"I assume he's strapped onto the examination table?" She certainly knew my treatment methods.

I nodded.

As she bustled down the hall, I sank against the wall, contemplating my choices for woodworkers and machinists. Among the inmates, who could work a twelve-hour shift without collapsing into the ravings of a lunatic?

My work was *important*.

My work was *critical* to the health of those with brain maladies. My breakthroughs could cure countless patients in future generations.

I needed to sell those den Eshockers to Moriarty, needed funds to run the asylum and to complete my clinical trials of hospital mode and extreme treatment mode. I needed to file the patents.

I broke into a sweat.

"Me crinoline an' bustle, they're too tight! Do you like me bustle, sir?"

She burst into giggles. It was Mrs. van der Kolk, my undergarments-obsessed lunatic.

I jerked myself from my problems. A patient required my help. Quickly wiping the sweat from my forehead with the back of my hand, I rushed over to Mrs. van der Kolk, who huddled on the floor by Mr. Robertson's chair. Slumped as usual, eyes shut, slobber glistening upon his chin and dripping to his night shirt, Mr. Robertson didn't notice me or his constant companion, Mrs. van der Kolk.

After I helped her stand, Mrs. van der Kolk leaned on me and shuffled across the room to a chair by the boarded-up window. Spring poked from the cushion, which was covered in a coarse, decades-old fabric. I eased her down. She giggled and said something regarding her private anatomy. I'd heard it all before... many times. Not only was she obsessed with her undergarments, she was also obsessed with what they covered.

Clasping her hands in mine, I tried to catch her attention with my gaze, but her eyes roamed around the room.

"I want to die," she said. "Nobody wants what I 'ave to offer. Me charms, they're gone."

"Mrs. van der Kolk, look at me, dear," I said, coaxing her by placing a hand on her cheek and swiveling her head toward me. "You have much to live for, dear. Your husband, great man that he was, has gone to the greater heavens, where he awaits you. He is still faithful—"

"Faithful?" Her head swung toward me, and her eyes bored into mine. "'E's faithful? *To me?*"

"Yes, dear." I had come to believe that my patient's obsessions were all bound up in a fear that this was not the case, though my reassurances had not so far brought any relief from her symptoms.

"No, 'e's never been faithful, not to me! An' 'e's not faithful in 'eaven, neither, if 'e be there at all! Me 'usband's in 'ell, 'e is, I tell you, in 'ell!"

"Wherever he is, I can assure you that he is indeed faithful to you. He is with no other woman, not in the ways that matter to you. I promise you this, I promise it."

"No other woman? No more? 'E was with so many. 'E said I weren't young no more, nor pretty to 'im. 'E said I were good now only for cleanin' 'is house and feedin' 'im."

"You're worth much, much more than that, I assure you," I said.

"I were with 'im forty years. 'E was with another woman on me weddin' night... and many more ever since."

The problem was, I had no methods of amusing my patients to divert them from their inner turmoil. They remained lost in their heads, all day, every day, and all night, every night.

Suddenly, she wrenched her hands from mine and clawed at her eyes. I wasn't fast enough to grab her hands and stop her. Blood oozed from both of her eyes, and she shrieked.

"Let me kill meself, let me die, let me go to 'im and show 'im what 'e's done to me!"

Miss Switzer emerged from the hall leading to my office and rushed to my aid. The nurse eased Mrs. van der Kolk from her chair and led her toward the room she shared with Caroline Brown, only seventeen yet already as insane as Mrs. van der Kolk. Just in another way, of course. They all differed in their illnesses. Caroline Brown swore she was Joan of Arc.

"Thank you, nurse." I smoothed my jacket and tweaked my collar.

Amy Switzer cast a brief smile my way, but her focus was on the patient, who was weeping that she wanted "death, nothin' but death."

"Would you like the comfort of the Eshocker, Mrs. van der Kolk?" I asked.

Her eyes widened, and for a moment, the weeping ceased. She turned toward me, clutched at my arms.

"Oh, yes, praise you, sir! Shock me, please! Shock me so I think no more!"

How this warmed my heart, how it brought me the deepest joy.

"Miss Switzer, please bring Mrs. van der Kolk to the treatment room in two hours. I have a few more patients who need my help first, and in the meantime, you may give Mrs. van der Kolk a sedative."

"Yes, Dr. Sinclair, right away."

Did I imagine it, or did Amy Switzer look at me just now with adoring eyes? Did she admire, perhaps lust for me? What did I see in her eyes, she who was always angry and scowling, typically so discontent I wondered if she was the right woman for the job? Had I misjudged her? Was her irritation due to female frustration? Did she want me as a woman wants a man?

I could barely imagine it, and as quickly as the thought occurred to me, I shrugged it off.

I had two patients to process before dealing with Mrs. van der Kolk. Both might also be of use to me in building enough den Eshockers to satisfy Moriarty's procurement agent. Each in his own way, of course.

If sufficiently subdued, Bligh Braithwaite had the brains to handle some of the more elaborate wiring that I always did myself.

As for Willie Jacobs, he'd helped his father build and run the infamous tram machine that no authority or scientist had been able to fully shut down. Nobody knew how that machine worked. Rumor had it that even Mr. Sherlock Holmes, considered a genius, had only been able to put the machine on "simmer," meaning it could erupt again, to my way of thinking. Surely, Willie Jacobs could put together den Eshockers for me. Transformers, wiring, resistors: it was all quite simple, really, though few had my knowledge of alternating current and rechargeable batteries.

I could teach Willie Jacobs.

In return, I wondered if he could teach me something about the esoteric tram machine and its inner workings. I might gain useful knowledge that would help me build even better Eshockers with which to treat my patients.

Excited, I hurried down the hall to my office and to the treatment room, where I knew Bligh Braithwaite would be waiting, strapped into the left Eshocker, the ball-gag in his mouth, the restraints biting into his wrists and ankles.

10

"Ah, my old friend. Bligh Braithwaite."

He gurgled behind the ball lodged between his teeth.

Apparently, Miss Klune had tranquilized Mr. Norris and returned the poor fellow to his room. The examination table was wiped clean of slobber and blood.

I turned my attention to Braithwaite. As I looked at him, he squirmed and a muffled howl escaped his lips.

"I see that my nurses attempted to give you a shave," I said, gesturing at his right cheek, which bore razor cuts, and at the left cheek, which remained dense with spiky growths of black hair.

He strained against the wrist and ankle bindings, his face red and his eyes watering.

"So you escaped from Kandinsky and came to me for help. Or did you come here to help with the clinical trials of the extreme treatment Eshocker?" I asked, moving closer to the box that held the mechanisms of the left Eshocker.

I twisted off the screws from the top of the box and peered inside at the electric mechanisms.

"M-mmmrrrrrr!"

"My dear fellow. Relax, would you? After all, you know how this works. I'm going to help you. It may be that you will soon be able to help me, too."

He answered with another muffled scream.

"You were always so testy," I complained, "never satisfied with anything. Tell me, what would you do in my place? I've thought long and hard about your problem, Braithwaite. Obviously, Kandinsky couldn't help you, and that's why you escaped and came here. So I'm not going to send you back. Instead, I'm going to treat your illness to the best of my ability."

I'd made the decision in a flash. It was brilliant, really. He would help me wire the Eshockers for Moriarty's dens. I would sedate him, keep him calm using extreme treatment. Nobody had ever paid any attention to Bligh Braithwaite but me, and I had no reason to think that anyone would pay attention to him now.

His face was wet with tears. He flailed, trying desperately to get free, and the chair wobbled. It wouldn't fall over. It was much too steady for that. I'd designed it with neural psychotics in mind.

I dabbed his head with a wet sponge and then put the two electrodes on his forehead.

"I don't need to remind you that the skin resistance for alternating current is approximately one kilo-ohm, or one thousand ohms," I said. "The DC-to-AC chopped pulse works beautifully in this set-up. I can control how much electrotherapy you receive. You might be interested in the wiring. You used to dabble with electric mechanisms, as I recall."

I stood back and surveyed him.

The eyes beseeched me again. I could almost hear the poor, babbling idiot beg me: *Please, oh please, Dr. Sinclair, don't give me the electrotherapy; please, oh please, let me scream and bash my forehead against the walls and floor, let me twist like a pretzel, drape myself like a monkey over the nurses; please, oh please, Dr. Sinclair, let me make your life a living hell.*

The poor creature.

His body trembled.

So did mine, but for a different reason. I was excited about my clinical trials.

Perhaps, I thought, it was easier for some men to *remain* insane: irrational, lost in their thoughts, avoiding reality. The world was a hard place. To survive, a man had to be rational, rooted in reality, and determined to make his own way. Sinking into fantasies and visions was the easy way out. Nurses gave you tranquilizers and other medications to blot your brain back into fantasyland. You were fed, washed, given a bed.

Pathetic.

"You're going to have to help me," I said.

He shook his head, *no*, and thrashed more wildly.

"I'm afraid you have no choice." I controlled my anger. With a frozen smile, I sweetened the deal. "If you help me build Eshockers, I'll give you more liberties here in the asylum. Would you like a bigger room?"

A muffled shriek, and still, the head shaking: *No, no, no!*

"There are others who would force you to build these Eshockers, Braithwaite, but they aren't reasonable men, not like me. I won't force you. I won't torture you, won't hurt you. I'm a medical doctor. I want what's best for my patients. I want to help them so they don't suffer as you do. In fact, I don't want you to suffer. So help me. In return, I'll tell you what I'll do for you."

"Ehhhhhh? Glurrrrr?" he whined. His eyes sharpened slightly.

I had his attention.

Good.

"I'll make sure the staff provides you with three excellent meals every day. As good as the food I eat myself. I can't offer you anything better than that."

For a moment, he was quiet, considering his options.

Then his shoulders drooped.

He had realized what I already knew, that he really had no choice. He would do as I wanted, and it would be either with better food or with the greasy slop and watered-down soup that my nurses shoveled into the faces of my patients.

He caught my eye, then looked at his lap.

He nodded.

The answer was *yes.*

"Good man!" My frozen smile warmed into a genuine smile. I was truly delighted.

I touched his shoulder.

He shrank back.

My smile fell.

"All right, Braithwaite, let's get you treated and out of here. Back to your room for rest followed by a good meal. Then later tonight, I'll show you what needs to be done to build those Eshockers I need."

My fingers rested on the wooden handle protruding from the front of the box. My mind flitted through the numbers: sixteen-volt output from the transformer to the resistors in den and hospital modes—along with sliding the variable resistor switch—yielded everything from mild pleasure to euphoria, depending on the person hooked up to the electrodes. Ah, but when I had that little wire in place, the one that shorted the fixed resistor, and when I pushed the variable resistor switch all the way to the right for zero resistance...

Excitement raced through me. My teeth began to chatter. Ah yes, with the switch all the way to the right, maximum current would surge into the fixed resistor with an ultimate yield of 16 milliamperes of alternating current. The impact on the brain would be equivalent to the application of sixty volts of direct current.

"Zap!" I hissed, snapping my fingers.

The door banged open. Miss Klune's key hung on a cord around her neck. Her left shoulder slammed against the door, and she stumbled into the examination room. Her arms were wrapped around Willie Jacobs from behind. Her hands were clasped tightly across his chest. She half-dragged him, while he elbowed her ribs and tried to kick her.

Thankfully, she'd muffled him with a ball and a strip of cloth. But I could hear him, nonetheless, just as I could still hear Bligh Braithwaite's screams beneath his gag.

Now there were two of them at the same time.

Miss Klune shoved Willie Jacobs into the right Eshocker chair, strapped him in tightly and stood back. She was breathing heavily, moisture trickling down her face. She put her hands on her hips and glared at Jacobs.

"Why do they always have to be so difficult?"

"If they accepted treatment and wanted to rid themselves of mental disease, then they would be cured," I answered. "As long as they fight us, as long as they fight *treatment*, then this means they are still mentally diseased."

She tugged at her uniform. Jacobs had ripped the bodice. Blood dribbled from scratches he'd raked down her arms and across her right cheek.

"I gave him a minute dose. I should have given him more," she said, "but sedation costs and we're short on funds." She opened a cabinet behind the examination table, removed a towel, and mopped her face and arms.

Willie Jacobs moaned.

He stared across the room at Bligh Braithwaite.

"Grrrrummmm!" Braithwaite's arms struggled beneath the straps. Even from where I stood by Jacobs, I could see that Braithwaite's arms were both bruised heavily, and yet still, despite the pain he was visibly suffering, he continued to struggle.

Let's get this over with, I thought.

I jerked my head at the door, and Miss Klune scurried out. She knew to leave me alone during Eshocker treatments.

Willie Jacobs, master machinist, squirmed in the right Eshocker. Bligh Braithwaite, master electrician, squirmed in the left Eshocker. I had attached two electrodes to each man's forehead.

"Are you ready, gentlemen?"

Neither could respond. They could only gurgle and scream behind their gag balls.

I stepped to the right unit, the one closest to me. I slid the wooden handle all the way to the right: to zero for minimum resistance and maximum current. I lifted the blue wire from where it hung off the metal plate between the variable resistor and the fixed resistor, then attached the free end of the wire to the metal plate on the right. A simple turn of the twist screw, and I finished. No tools required.

I repeated the procedure on the left unit, the one that would service Braithwaite. He screamed and strained against the straps holding him in place.

Willie Jacobs, on the other hand, neither thrashed nor screamed. His body slackened. His voice left him. Jacobs seemed resigned to his fate.

Carefully, I grasped the wooden handle attached directly to the copper knife switch on the left side of Jacobs's Eshocker box. I did not want to touch the copper part of the knife that extended all the way from the wood to the copper hinge. The design was brilliant, flawless. DC power flowed from the wall socket into a standalone dynamo used to recharge the batteries. While not charging, such as when I was using the Eshocker, the two-volt rechargeable battery inside the box would surge DC power into a motor, and from there, via a set of rotating rods, into the DC-to-AC chopper. As soon as I pulled the copper knife from its upright position, where it was secured into a copper U on an upper metal plate, and attached it securely into the copper U on the lower metal plate, extreme treatment would commence.

Two volts of current would surge from the rechargeable

battery through the upper metal plate, down the copper part of the knife, through the copper U on the lower metal plate, and from there, directly into the DC motor.

"*Get ready*," I said.

Jacobs squeezed his eyes shut, and sweat dripped from his balding head over his eyebrows and lids, and off the tip of his nose. Braithwaite's eyes remained wide open and bloodshot, trained upon me with a look of such horror and dread that I had to turn away.

My own hand was sweating. I wiped it on my trousers and then grasped the handle again. This time, I immediately tugged the handle down and latched the copper knife into the lower U.

Buzzzzzzz!

Zzzzzzzap!

Electricity surged.

Jacobs's back straightened, hard, against the back of his chair. His neck arched. He shrieked behind his gag ball.

I raced across the room and flipped the other copper switch on Braithwaite's Eshocker.

Again:

Buzzzzzzz!

Zzzzzzzap!

The sound filled the treatment room. I stood between the two men, my body quivering, my mind inflamed with the possibilities of my creation. I envisioned a huge room filled with these machines, the treatment of hundreds of patients at once, the calming of mankind, the treatment of all sorts of ailments instantly, the happiness of all men, women, and even children as they hugged me and thanked me profusely for the medical gift I had bestowed upon them.

Happiness for everyone.

Peace and harmony.

Yes!

Current equals volts divided by resistance.

$I = V \div R$.

I = sixteen volts divided by zero (variable resistor slid all the way to the right) plus one kilo-ohm (head resistance) = sixteen milliamperes of alternating current to the head.

A stunning value.

Buzzzzzzz!

Zzzzzzzzap!

The smell of feces. I snapped from my calculations and my daydreaming, and the excitement rushed out of me. Willie Jacobs—*my patient*—spasmed violently and then collapsed in his chair, chin on his chest, body vibrating.

He had passed out.

Rushing to his Eshocker, I yanked the wooden handle up, securing the copper knife to the upper U. This stopped the flow of current through the DC motor and the DC-to-AC chopper, stopping all current through the transformer and the two resistors.

He shuddered violently, but only once, and then remained still. His body had ceased vibrating.

To my right, Bligh Braithwaite continued his struggling and muffled screaming. For the moment, I ignored him, as I checked Willie Jacobs's vital signs: heart beating, still breathing, *good*. Then I hurried to Braithwaite's Eshocker and also flipped it off.

I yanked open the door between the treatment room and

my office, and screamed for Miss Klune.

It took several minutes, longer than usual, for her to heed my summons. When she appeared I saw she'd washed the blood off herself and changed her uniform.

"Yes, Dr. Sinclair? You need my help?"

She looked from Braithwaite to Jacobs, and I thought I noticed concern on her face but it quickly passed. Nothing shocked my nurse. She was the most professional nurse in all of England, I was sure of it.

"Doctor?" she pressed, hurrying across my office and grabbing my elbow.

Gently, I removed my elbow from her grasp. I straightened myself, remained calm.

"Return Willie Jacobs to his bed," I said, "and keep an eye on him." I sniffed. "You might also want to clean him up a little."

"Yes, Doctor."

She began moving toward Willie Jacobs, and this time, it was *I* who grabbed *her* elbow. She swiveled, the ice-blue eyes calmly meeting mine.

"You'll have to drug Bligh Braithwaite," I said. "Even extreme treatment hasn't helped him, not yet, anyway. *Drug him.*"

She nodded.

"I'll drug him. Of course, Dr. Sinclair. Anything else?"

"Yes. One more thing," I said, remembering my promise to Bligh Braithwaite. "When he awakens, give him a hot meal, something good, something that the cook makes for you. In fact, don't ever give this man the usual food prepared for patients. From now on, only give him the best."

Her forehead creased ever so slightly, then smoothed again. Her eyes never wavered.

Perfectly calm and sane: that was Miss Clara Klune.

Everyone else at the Whitechapel Lunatic Asylum?

The total opposite.

11

DR. JOHN WATSON

London

Holmes and I turned the corner and faced Thrawl Street for the first time since he'd figured out how to subdue the murderous tram machine built by Willie Jacobs and his father. The first thing I noticed was the stench of unwashed bodies and cigarette smoke. The second thing I noticed was the shadow, the swathe of gloom, cast over the street by the tram machine building.

The buildings were as bent and tattered as the people hobbling along the street. Several men slumped—sleeping or dead, I knew not which—in the gutter. A child of two or three years old wailed in the arms of a woman who lay unmoving before a dirt-brown building that leaked the telltale smoke of an opium den. Several children scampered from building to building, their laughter much too hysterical by any standards.

I turned my head away, and my gaze fell upon a horseshoe that had fallen from a nearby door—not two months ago, the inhabitants of this street had been hanging them up to ward off the evil of the tram machine. I suspected that nobody was salting their windowsills anymore.

I remembered Holmes's words: "Superstitions, as if salt and horseshoes will help cure what ails this street. There is only one cure, and that is to turn off Willie Jacobs's machine."

But Holmes had not turned off the machine. Instead, with his insights into chemistry and matter, he'd attempted a scientific experiment—one that had thankfully worked—and in doing so, had switched the machine from violent operations to a slow simmer.

Holmes stared at the scene before us, looking very out of place in the shabby street. Like me, he was dressed for dinner at the Diogenes Club, in a top hat, black coat with tails, and white shirt with silk tie held in place at his neck by a gold button. He tapped his cane once, sharply, and turned to me.

"Since our last visit here, things have grown worse. This street is no longer home to anyone," he said. "It is an encampment, Watson, a vile strip of opium dens and Eshocker dens, where wretches seek hallucinations, elevated thoughts, and any escape from reality. They no longer fear the tram machine building, nor devils, nor demons. They are no longer participants in this world, but in a fantasy brought about by opium and electric shocks."

The scene before us was appalling, but how different were the abuses he spoke of, I wondered, from Holmes's own cocaine habit, and his experiments with electricity belts?

"You think me hypocritical, Watson."

"That is no great deduction."

"The occasional use of cocaine by a bored mind is nothing compared to what is happening in the Eshocker dens." He waved a hand that took in the still bodies, the wailing child. "These dens must be shut down, Watson." He spoke softly, and when I looked at him again, his eyes were drinking in the scene. His face sharpened, and he raised his cane to point. "We go *there*," he said.

He marched down the street over the rubble and past the bodies toward the tram machine building. I hurried after him, hoping that the tram machine building was not our destination. If we never opened the door to that building again, if we never saw those drooping cables and the steel limbs, if we never smelled the stink of the phosphorus pit— *never* was an understatement for the length of time in which I hoped to avoid that foul building with its foul machine.

A rusty iron fence encircled the tram machine building, and inside the fence, ten or more policemen stood guard. A lot of good they would do, I thought, if anyone truly wanted to break into the building and re-infuse it with life: phosphorus, chemical energy, *deadly energy*. Ropes hung from the fence, dangling warning signs decorated with skulls and crossbones: DANGER OF DEATH! DO NOT ENTER.

So fixed was I upon the signs that I neglected to track the whereabouts of Sherlock Holmes.

He had apparently ducked into one of the many side buildings, one of the dens. I had no idea how I would find him other than tramping from one to the next, seeking his tall, gaunt frame in the dim haze that no doubt suffused these places of suffering and lunacy.

Feeling rather light-headed myself, I stumbled over a body, and a man muttered at me in his sleep. I leaned against the wall of a building, and from inside, the sad cried and the hysterical screamed. Painful shrieks rang out.

The door beside me banged open, and in a cloud of smoke, a man stumbled from a house—whether opium or Eshocker den, I could not be sure. He lost his footing and fell across the body that I had so recently tripped over.

A young boy raced out, and the door slammed shut. I placed him at approximately eight years old. He wore filthy clothes, though that was not unusual in these parts. His face appeared more blood and dirt than flesh. His eyes, large and round, held no innocence. Indeed, they were also the color of blood and dirt, and as cold as the Thames in the dead of winter.

"You be off, worm!" the boy yelled.

To my horror, he lashed a steel chain across the back of the man who had fallen over the body by my feet. I jumped back. The chain came down three times, and each time the man winced but did not cry out. After the third blow, the man clambered up, and screaming, grabbed the boy's neck with both hands.

"No, you be off! Let me go!" The boy's small hands tried to pry the man's fists from his neck.

The boy was Timmy Dorsey, Jr. Why was *he* in the dens?

I didn't have time to think about it. Light-headed though I was, I shook my head, trying—*unsuccessfully*—to clear my mind, while I dove for the hands around Timmy's neck.

"Dr. Watson," Timmy choked out.

"Get your hands off the boy!" I shouted.

"Who're you?" the man snarled from purple lips. Up close, I saw the nightmare that he was: rotting from the inside out, malnourished; bleary eyes, the whites tinged yellow, and jaundiced skin to match. It took little strength to wrench the man's fists off Timmy's neck.

The boy gasped for air, clenching his neck and staggering back against the door to the den.

"Be off, like the boy said." I spoke sternly as if to one of my worst patients, those who refused their medicine. "Go! You've had enough opium for today, sir."

The man's purple lips split into a nasty smile, revealing black teeth.

"It's not opium I'm after," he said. "It's the Eshocker. Full blast. Full time. No limit. An' yes, with Old Ones Serum in me belly an' me 'ead, there's no limit at all to me Eshocker ride."

"'E's broke," Timmy said, his voice still raw from the choking. "'E wants Professor Moriarty's Eshockin' for free, 'e does." The boy puffed out his chest and lifted his chin high. "I'm the Professor's man an' I do 'is biddin'. 'E's like a dad to me. 'E provides for me, same as for me dad."

I shooed off Timmy's attacker. Inching along and clutching at buildings, he maneuvered his way past the other addicts toward Osborn Street.

"Your father works for Professor *Moriarty*?" I asked Timmy.

"'E's 'is top man, 'e is."

"I see. Timmy, have you seen Mr. Holmes?"

His rusty-brown eyes looked up at mine. I saw the mind calculating behind those eyes, then the brief shrug of the shoulders. Timmy Dorsey, Jr. was following the path of his father just as Willie Jacobs had followed his father's path: it hadn't done either boy any good, not so far as I could tell.

Timmy still wore the same tattered jacket and trousers that he'd worn when he'd scampered from the tram machine building during Holmes's chemistry experiment. Willie Jacobs had made sure the boy left the building before Holmes directed the experiment, which ultimately slowed the machine. Jacobs had grown up with the senior Timmy Dorsey and knew that he was a scoundrel of the lowest type.

"Mr. 'olmes is in the den down the way." Timmy gestured at a clutch of grimy buildings halfway toward Osborn Street.

"Which one?" I asked.

"They're all dens. See where the girl's asleep?"

Yes, I saw her. No more than eleven or twelve years old, she slept in a heap of rags by a door. Someone had lit a fire in a large barrel by the street in front of that particular building. Soot rose into soot. Eshocked den addicts huddled around the fire, rubbing their hands together for warmth.

Timmy pulled on my sleeve.

"I'll take you to 'im. That girl, she's for any man who wants 'er. So long as they pay for 'er Eshockin', she gives 'em whatever they ask. She don't care."

As I followed him to the building where the girl slept, I asked Timmy where he had been living since he'd left the tram machine building, and how he had come to know Moriarty.

"The Professor controls the space on this street, all but for the tram buildin'. Coppers patrol that—keeping out all who might want the gold. The Professor wants the machine. 'E wants to give it the Jacobs chemicals an' make it come alive an' spit out gold again. I think 'e'll send me dad an' me dad's gang in to 'ave it out with the coppers." Timmy tugged on my sleeve again. "Come on, then. Time is money." His eyes lit for a moment as he added, "On account of me dad's service, the Professor hired me to do a man's job, too."

"And what is that job, Timmy?" I asked, as we stepped over the girl and Timmy kicked open the door to the den. As if this were a signal, I saw those huddled by the open fire ungroup and move toward us. Glazed eyes, outstretched arms: they looked already dead to me. Their minds and bodies were gone but for the basics of walking, breathing, and I supposed, eating and drinking.

I stepped inside after Timmy to the roar of machines cranked to full throttle. The noise was enough to hurt my ears, and I clamped my hands over them and groaned.

"Shut the door!" Timmy barked, pointing at the addled creatures stumbling toward us.

As I reached for the door, one of the drugged—or, I presume, Eshocked—men clutched at his stomach, cried out, and doubled over in pain. My medical instincts kicked in.

"What is it, my man? What ails you?"

A crooked grin split the bottom of his face. Two eyes jittered in their sockets. He looked over my shoulder and shuddered as if in a state of rapture.

The man was no more ill than I was—*by Jove, he was faking the stomach pain.*

"What's wrong with you, mister? *Shut the door!*"

Hearing Timmy's command, I quickly slammed the door, and it hit flesh and bone. From the other side, the man cried out in pain again, only this time it was real.

Scrambling to latch the door, I swung the wooden bar

into its metal holder. Fists pounded, and the door shook.

Timmy laughed.

"Don't worry, Dr. Watson. That door is strong. Now, *come*!"

A wash of color swept across my vision and snaked up the door. The metal holder melted into what I can only describe as a squid shape, and as I blinked, desperately trying to clear my vision, the wooden bar curved into a toothy grin.

What had happened to me? What was this hideous infection, this madness, that gripped my mind?

I hit my head with my right hand, again trying to clear my vision while rapidly blinking.

Feeling more befuddled by the moment, I swung around to face the small room. Stretched around all four walls were the machines, Professor Moriarty's Eshockers, and they came in many varieties. The people using the equipment also came in many varieties. A woman with sparse hair tied into a weak bun at the nape of her neck swilled something from a bottle with a medical-style label upon it.

"Old Ones Serum," Timmy told me, seeing my eye upon it. "Specially bottled, close to the tram machine as they can get it; the air's thick with it round 'ere."

Thick with what? I wondered. The woman turned the bottle upside down and shook it, cursing. Then she hurled it at a man wearing what appeared to be a metal corset with a matching helmet: all fixed with wires. In each hand, the man held a control, and his thumbs rapidly pressed large buttons on these controls. With each press, his body stiffened, then his back arched, and he let out a long "ooooo" sound. When his thumbs released the buttons, his body went slack, but only for a moment, because he kept pressing and pressing those buttons. I could barely take my eyes off him.

Luckily, the woman was drugged half out of her mind, and when she hurled the empty bottle at the man, she missed him by a wide margin. The bottle crashed against a large wooden box that rumbled next to another man strapped into a chair with electrodes on his forehead.

What the deuce was going on?

There must have been ten such wooden boxes and electrode chairs in this room, and every chair was occupied by a mumbling, weeping, wailing person. Small, tall, fat, thin, young, old: it didn't matter. All pulled levers on the sides of their boxes, and from the way their bodies shook and their backs arched and their lips drooled, I assumed they were Eshocking themselves. Those not strapped into the chairs writhed on the floor, in a mess of wood shavings coated in vomit and other vile matter. They wore helmets, belts, and mummy-like wraps around their torsos. I saw more Old Ones Serum, bottle after bottle being consumed by these pathetic souls, all deluded by Professor Moriarty's promises of happiness and good health.

There was no happiness in the den.

There was no good health.

In its place were filth and disease, misery and pain.

Glancing back at the door, I saw that the metal holder and wooden bar appeared as they should: no squid, no toothy grin. I returned my attention to the room and its inhabitants, acutely aware that what I was seeing was *real* and not some concoction devised by my weakening mind.

Wedged between the wooden boxes and electrode

chairs—the Eshockers—several other devices shook violently, with people strapped into them, their faces red, heads bobbing, eyes rolling, bodies shaking. I knew about these machines. They'd been around for years, some for decades, but only doctors lacking scruples would contemplate using them on patients.

Timmy lowered his voice.

"The Professor calls those ones quack machines," he said, gesturing at a device I recognized as a violet ray electrotreat. "They do no good. Only Eshockers are safe an' provide the correct buzzin'."

I doubted that the Eshockers were much safer, if at all, than the Professor's quack machines. For example, I thought, as a fat man inserted a long, thin tube into his ear, the violet ray electrotreat was no treat at all, nor did it use violet rays. With an electrotreat, very high voltage pumped into a gas-filled tube—and the tubes came in a wide variety of sizes and dimensions so as to fit into any orifice—sparking a violet-infused tinge to the gas. It looked impressive, and it certainly provided a jolt to its user. But the jolt was dangerous, particularly given that, in the case before me, the tube was in a man's ear.

"Everyone gets the amount an' time of Eshockin' they want," Timmy said. "See that girl over there?" He pointed. "She paid at the door for five minutes. Now watch. There, *there*! See 'ow she slides the 'andle?"

"Yes," I said slowly. "When in pain, she slides the handle to the left, and her face relaxes. And now she wants more, doesn't she? So she shoves the handle to the right, and her face twists again in pain."

"Ain't no pain. Just pleasure," Timmy corrected me. "The man at the door will remove 'er after 'er paid-up time. You see, Doctor, it's the customers what control their Eshockin'. It's safer pleasure than the quack machines." He leaned toward me, and when I stooped, he whispered, "The Professor plans to rid 'is dens of the quacks. 'E's waitin' for more Eshockers."

"What surprises me the most, Timmy—indeed, *shocks* me—is that your customers come from all aspects of society. Young, old, well dressed, and... not."

"Yes, they *all* come," the boy said. "They're all sick in the 'ead. Eshock will be me fortune, Dr. Watson. See that woman there, she's with child, but she don't care none. She's drinkin' down the Old Ones, an' she cares for nothin' else, not even the baby in 'er belly."

Indeed, there was a young girl, heavily pregnant, collapsed against a wall with an Old Ones Serum bottle on her lap. She had passed out. I shook my head, trying unsuccessfully again to clear my vision. I felt weak and dizzy. The leg I had injured at the battle of Maiwand ten years before hurt more than usual, and I begged Timmy to find me a chair.

"No chair 'ere," he laughed, "except for an Eshocker chair, an' I don't think you want *that* chair, Dr. Watson."

The boy helped me to the wall, where I crouched and hung my head, taking long, slow breaths. Nausea rose, and the dizziness washed colors around the room. Everything seemed to pulse with color, in and out, in and out. The ceiling throbbed with geometric shapes, from simple triangles to complex three-dimensional objects.

My face was hot, and sweat saturated the bandage on my forehead, which still ached.

"Have... to... have to..." I gagged from the nausea. "Timmy," I managed to whisper, "get me out of here. Quickly, please."

"But your friend, Mr. 'olmes, 'e's over there in the chair." Timmy jostled my elbow, nudging me to lift my head and peer through the dim room at an Eshocker.

Sure enough, Holmes's gaunt figure hunched in one of the chairs, his head bowed and bobbing slightly in rhythm to the electric pulse of his machine god. His hand clutched a lever on the side of his Eshocker box. He slid the lever all the way to the right, sending his body into violent spasms.

"Get him," I hissed at the boy. "It's time for him to leave this place."

Timmy scampered over to Holmes and slid the Eshocker lever all the way to the left. As the boy lifted the wooden handle attached to a knife-like copper strip on the side of the Eshocker box, Holmes slumped forward, held in place by the restraints. The machine clattered to a halt. Timmy unstrapped Holmes's wrists.

"No," the detective cried, "I paid for more!"

Holmes slapped away the boy's hands, but Timmy avoided him and unstrapped Holmes's ankles and torso from the chair. Then he removed the electrodes from Holmes's forehead.

"Your ride's over, Mr. 'olmes," Timmy said, steering Holmes off the chair and toward me. A girl who had been loitering immediately took Holmes's place on the chair.

I took over from Timmy, steering Holmes from the den and back onto Thrawl Street, but first, I made sure to thank Timmy for helping me rescue Holmes.

"It's a temporary rescue," the boy cautioned.

That I knew. Holmes would return to the dens. He couldn't resist their allure. His insistence that his den visits were *research*—well, I'd never felt so ashamed of Holmes as I did in that moment.

"And you have a bottle of that damnable serum, too, don't you?" I asked Holmes.

His eyes unsteady, he reached up and tapped a bottle tucked into his coat pocket, and the liquid sloshed.

Outside the den, the fire barrel was a whirl of color amidst a fog of smoke.

Unable to see or think very clearly, it occurred to me that I was, perhaps, misjudging Holmes. Yet I could not escape the fact that he was in a stupor induced by the Eshocker and the Old Ones Serum.

How would his great brain be damaged from the Eshocking and the serum? Dare I consider such a terrible thought?

In our current confused states of mind, Holmes and I tottered toward our next destination. We had to make it to the Whitechapel Lunatic Asylum, where I felt sure they would take one look at us and lock us both up.

12

"You obviously don't understand, sir. Mr. Jacobs passed out during treatment. He's not well. You've not come at an opportune time."

The woman glaring at Holmes towered over me and possessed a more imposing frame than most men. Straddling her feet with her arms dangling loosely by her sides, she seemed to be preparing for a fight. She had the palest blue eyes I'd ever seen, the sort of blue I'd always associated with an Arctic ice thaw. Her mouth was a sliver of ice set in an angular face. I didn't remember this woman from our previous visit to the asylum, when we'd had Willie Jacobs admitted. Another attendant had taken care of things for us.

Thankfully, our walk to the Whitechapel Lunatic Asylum had cleared both of our minds—sufficiently, at least, for us to pass as being of reasonably sound mind.

Holmes swept off his hat, bowed slightly, and graced the ice woman with a smile.

"I'm Mr. Sherlock Holmes, and this is my associate, Dr. John Watson. And your name, dear lady?" he asked.

She shifted position. Her muscles tensed.

"Clara Klune, head nurse. Don't try anything with me, sir," she said. "I don't care who you are."

In the distance, a man shrieked. I heard what sounded like pounding, and then a chorus of wailing rose:

"No, not me!"

"Get off, I say, get off!"

Holmes's eyes widened.

"My dear madam," he said to Miss Klune, "we are here to visit our old friend, but also we're on government business."

That's a stretch, I thought.

"You must be aware of the Eshocker dens all along Thrawl Street, only a short distance from here," Holmes quickly continued. "I'm investigating those dens with their Eshockers, and that means a visit to the Whitechapel Lunatic Asylum is in order." He studied her expression—or lack thereof—for a moment, then added, "I believe the inventor of the Eshocker runs this asylum, does he not? Dr. Reginald Sinclair?"

At this, she flinched, but quickly regained her composure. I had the feeling that Miss Klune had ample practice in remaining calm under any circumstances.

She addressed me.

"Dr. Watson, do you specialize in diseases affecting the brain?"

"I'm a general practitioner," I said, "but more to your point, I'm not here in my capacity as a doctor. Although," and following Holmes's lead, I stretched the truth, "I am helping with the Thames infestation and the resulting diseases, injuries, mental aberrations, and of course, deaths."

Her eyes narrowed, but before she could speak, a burly orderly raced into the hall.

"What do you want, Michael?"

"We need you in the day room. The new patient is having a terrible reaction to the sedative you gave him. He's vomiting and attacking anyone who comes near him."

"Oh, God," she said, "there's always something, isn't there?" She returned her attention to Holmes and me. "Now, you two go back to the waiting room. I'll fetch you if Dr. Sinclair becomes available." She pushed the door open and waved us back into the waiting room. "Remember, I have eyes and ears all over this asylum, and if you dare try entering again without following procedure, I will have you banned from this institution. See that Mr. Holmes and Dr. Watson wait for admittance this time." This last she addressed to the waiting room attendant we had slipped past earlier.

She closed the door between the waiting room and the hall. I knew that the door locked people in, but it didn't lock people out—this was how Holmes and I had gained access.

We turned to see the now-hostile waiting room attendant, another burly man in his late twenties, standing over a decrepit fellow writhing on the floor by the fireplace, which had burned out. The fellow on the floor was chewing the skin off the back of his left hand.

"Stop it!" The attendant slapped at the man's hand. "I've told you. There's no bed for you here. We're full. You'll have to leave."

The man spat his flesh to the floor in a spasm of blood.

I raced over to him and felt his forehead, which was blazing hot.

"This man needs medical attention," I told the attendant.

"Then *you* help him," he retorted.

I'd been in asylums before and witnessed the lack of regard for patients. Asylums were nothing more than jails for lunatics. But this situation was appalling. Here was a man clearly in need of help, who had apparently found his way to the asylum on his own, and what were they doing? They were ignoring him.

"This is preposterous," I said, standing and gesturing at the bleeding man. White foam bubbled on his lips. "I insist, sir, that you help this man or find someone who can. I am not authorized to do so, nor do I have my bag with me."

"You deemed yourself authorized enough to slip past me earlier, didn't you?" demanded the other.

At this, Holmes intervened, still standing by the door that led into the asylum.

"This man has been here before, yes?" When the attendant nodded, bewildered, Holmes continued, "And you've asked Dr. Sinclair to help him. Dr. Sinclair refused. You badgered the good doctor to no avail. Indeed, your employer threatened to end your employment here if you persisted in trying to help this poor, suffering individual." Holmes pointed at the sick man on the floor.

"How do you know that?" I asked, as bewildered as the attendant.

"Yes, how?" the man repeated.

"It is obvious, sir. I see the blood droplets upon your collar. I see the encrusted white foam, dried now upon your cheeks. I saw how you overlooked our presence, enabling us to pass undisturbed into the asylum, how fraught with anxiety you were about this man's condition. And yet, upon Dr. Watson's request that you call Dr. Sinclair to help this man now, you steadfastly refuse. Thus, I conclude that you've tried to get help for this man in the past, but failed."

In response, the attendant blurted out his story:

"You're right—about all of it, Mr. Holmes! This man is my sister's husband, Mr. Malcolm Demane. They have five children, Mr. Holmes. Malcolm was just like you and me, but in the past few months, he's been like *this*—drooling, chewing his own skin, foaming at the mouth. He's sick, Mr. Holmes, and I can't get Dr. Sinclair to see him. The family doesn't have the money for hospital. I'm the only one with any job at all. My sister begs me, night and day she begs, 'Help him, help my Malcolm,' but always, I fail. The last man on the door left last week, and I got this position only recently, having spent many a year in the kitchen washing dishes. I prefer not to return to the kitchen. I prefer not to lose my job, and I prefer that my sister stop pestering me."

Holmes did not move from his position by the door. Normally, he would have tried to comfort the man. I inched toward the door myself, thinking Holmes would again dash into the asylum at any moment. And, while I wasn't wrong in my conclusion, how it happened did take me by surprise.

"Will you talk to Dr. Sinclair for me, or at least to Miss Klune?" the man asked. "She's the head nurse and has a lot of power. The Doctor often listens to her advice. Will you help my brother-in-law get into the asylum?"

Holmes straightened himself.

"I'll do all that I can," he said. "I give you my word, sir."

"And I, as well," I added.

The man turned his back to us.

"Do as you will, then," he said. "As before, I'm busy with Malcolm, and let us say that I see nothing else. I dare not lose this job. But please, help him."

Holmes cast me a determined glance, then twisted the door knob and dashed back into the asylum. Together, we darted down the hall and around a corner.

We had entered a day room, of sorts. There were no picture windows, no teapots, and no maids adjusting flowered curtains. Instead, I saw one tiny iron-barred window, set high up in the wall, and where in a hospital I might expect to see at least one dead plant, this miserable cell lacked even that. Several heavily drugged inmates sat propped on chairs. A few more had curled into fetal positions for naps. The room reeked of urine, excrement, and rotting flesh. One man waved at imaginary things in the air and talked to them, another threatened murder when he spied us. A woman eagerly let out a stream of obscenities about her undergarments. Most of these inmates were past their prime, though here and there were a few younger patients, drooling and babbling along with their elders. Certainly, Malcolm Demane would fit in without a problem.

"Willie Jacobs isn't here," Holmes whispered. "Come, let's check farther down the next hall, but beware, Watson, of that nurse or any other staff member."

We passed a door marked *Dr. Reginald Sinclair*. I heard nothing from within: either the doctor was out of his office, or he was reading in utmost quiet. I supposed we would return to his office after visiting Willie Jacobs. We had promised to ask Dr. Sinclair to help Malcolm Demane. As a fellow doctor, I felt confident that I'd be able to persuade Dr. Sinclair to extend some form of minimal treatment to the poor fellow.

"You're the one is mad!" someone screamed.

Holmes curled a finger and gestured at me, and together, we crept toward a door, from which we'd heard the scream emanate. I could tell from Holmes's face that he also recognized the voice: it was Willie Jacobs. A terrible sadness fell upon me, for it was our fault—Holmes and mine—that Jacobs was in this predicament. We had checked him into this place. We'd had no choice.

Holmes paused before the door. His face, typically bleached of color, was tinged pink. His eyes softened.

Then he twisted the door knob, and we both entered Jacobs's room. He looked even worse than on the day we had checked him in. Holmes and I were speechless. Shocked at his condition, we just stared at him.

Shoved into a room the width of two coffins, and squirming on a ratty bed, Willie Jacobs appeared an inch from death. Although only in his mid-twenties, he was bald except for a few wisps of hair. Scabs littered his face and brown-splotched scalp. Yellow skin hung loosely from his face and neck. With his right knuckles, he jabbed rhythmically at his enlarged nostril. Although his clothes were filthy and torn, he smelled faintly of cheap soap. He had already lost a lot of weight, and he'd not had much meat on him when we brought him here. What was most striking was that he had lost his *vigor*. He did not rise when we entered the room. He did not seem to recognize us. Indeed, he did not seem to realize that anyone was in the room at all.

His face and chin bore the red imprints of a strap, which, I assumed from the marks, must have held something that covered his mouth. On his forehead were two red circles, one on each side. Had they gagged him before treating him with an Eshocker? This was my first thought, for I knew that Dr. Reginald Sinclair used his Eshockers in the asylum, only a short distance from Thrawl Street and its insidious pleasure dens.

Willie Jacobs's eyes focused on the ceiling. He spewed constant gibberish about the tram machine—"It wants to kill me!"—about his father—"The beast killed me dad!"—and about Holmes—"You can't stop the beast! You'll fail, an' you'll always fail, Mr. 'olmes. The beast is smarter than you!"

"Mr. Jacobs," Holmes said gently, and the man's mouth snapped shut. His eyes at last focused on us.

"Mr. Jacobs, it is I, Sherlock Holmes, and here is Dr. Watson. We have come to see how you are."

Knuckles jabbed the blood-encrusted nostrils. I'd thought Willie Jacobs had phossy jaw, but now I wondered if something unknown had infected him. I had felt changes in myself that frightened me, and I didn't have phossy jaw. In my case, my nightmares were filled with warbling and screeching, and while awake, I often saw wisps of color in odd places and tendrils of bubbles floating in the air and along cracks in buildings and walkways. My mind felt fuzzy, unclear. Looking at Willie Jacobs now, I wondered.

Would I end up like him? Did I also suffer from neural psychosis?

13

"Mr. 'olmes," Jacobs rasped, "*it's you, in the flesh*."

Holmes wedged himself between the clammy wall and the bed and clasped Jacobs's hand.

"It is I," he said, and then in a kind tone, "We will do all that we can to ensure your safety and well-being. Tell me, please, what treatment have you received today? What has affected you thus?"

At this, Willie Jacobs trembled, and his body convulsed. Holmes grasped his hand more tightly.

"Please, sir—" he said.

I pushed past a jumble of dirty bed linen and medical paraphernalia heaped on a side table, and I pressed a firm hand upon Jacobs's upper arm.

"What have they done to you?" I asked.

"Th-the... it... it's the Eshockers!" Jacobs cried, wrenching his hand from Holmes and clutching at me. "P-please, Dr. Watson, p-please, 'elp me escape from this place! It ain't safe 'ere! More deadly than—" he broke off, and his body convulsed again—"than the... the beast's buildin'!"

The Eshockers, I thought. *They're much more dangerous than Holmes realizes. Look what electrotherapy has done to Willie Jacobs.*

"Of what do you speak?" Holmes asked.

"M-mercy killin's, done in the name of s-science." Jacobs's voice was barely a whisper. His body went slack. He released his grip upon my arms. "I-I saw 'em kill an inmate. Saw it with me own eyes. *I saw it.*"

Holmes glanced at me, his eyebrows raised. I didn't know what to make of Jacobs's latest outburst. Was it the product of a delusional mind? Was he hallucinating?

"Who killed the patient?" Holmes asked.

"D-don't know. Couldn't see that."

"Do you know the name of the patient, then?"

"N-no, Mr. 'olmes."

"Where did you see this crime take place, sir?"

"Out there, in the 'all."

"Not in a treatment room?"

"No, in the 'all!"

"I see," Holmes said, as he straightened himself and headed for the door. "We'll consider your allegation, Mr. Jacobs. In the meantime, please know that we will continue to follow your case and that you are *not* alone."

Willie Jacobs begged us not to leave. Tilting his head up and rapidly jabbing his nostrils with his right thumb, he began to weep.

"You're me only 'ope, as I tol' you before. You were to save me," he wailed, "and now I'm 'ere. This place, it's 'ell, if indeed there is one, and Mr. 'olmes, it was you what put me 'ere."

All that he said was true. We had promised to help him, and we had brought him to the Whitechapel Lunatic Asylum. The guilt of it all marked Holmes's face as clearly as it must have marked my own.

We remained with Willie Jacobs, trying to comfort him, but eventually the sense of his words was lost again in delirium and he seemed not to see us anymore.

"It is a sad thing to see Willie Jacobs so reduced," I said as we left the room.

Holmes already had other matters on his mind. "Watson, we must find Dr. Sinclair, the creator of these Eshockers," he said. "We do not have much time if we are to dine with Mycroft this evening. There is much to discuss in the matter of the creatures that attacked the boat."

Within moments, we stood outside Dr. Sinclair's office again. Holmes knocked several times, then tried the handle. It was unlocked, and we stepped into the office.

Dr. Sinclair was not inside. The desk was tidy: a bundle of medical and supply bills was piled neatly beneath a large fossil to one side, a pen with ink and an unmarked blotter stood ready. The leather chair looked comfortable and well worn. Judging from the indentation on the seat, Dr. Sinclair was of medium build. Judging from the honors and degrees posted on the wall behind his desk, Dr. Sinclair knew what he was doing.

Suddenly, a door on the inner wall swung open, and a medium-sized man with a neat black mustache and a beard burst into the room. He wore a doctor's white coat with pocket embroidery proclaiming him to be *Dr. Reginald Sinclair, Director.* His immaculate hair was clipped to precision, framing a visage of heavy brows, thick lips, large nose, and bulging eyes. When he saw us his face blazed with fury.

"With what authority do you enter my private office?" He drew himself up and smoothed his white coat.

"I am Dr. John Watson," I said, stepping past Holmes and extending my hand. "Mr. Sherlock Holmes and I are investigating incidents in this area, which may be related to the Whitechapel Lunatic Asylum, on behalf—"

"Mr. Sherlock Holmes, eh?" The other man visibly calmed at the mention of Holmes's name. "Do sit down, gentlemen." He gestured at two guest chairs, an uncomfortable wooden set that didn't invite visitors to stay long. "I understand it was you who committed one of my newest patients, Mr. Willie Jacobs."

"That is correct," I said, sitting down. "We have just been visiting, as a matter of fact. You put up your patients in very small rooms, Doctor."

My words hit a nerve. "We have had quite an intake in the past few weeks, gentlemen, quite an intake," said Sinclair, his face reddening again. "We are having trouble finding the space, I must admit. Why, just this morning I had to take in another fellow, Bligh Braithwaite, who was actually trying to break *in* to the asylum. The madhouse he escaped from doesn't seem to want him back."

I saw from Holmes's distant expression that I had wandered from the point of our visit. "You are providing Eshockers for the local dens?" I asked. When the doctor nodded with a puzzled expression, I continued, "I don't mean to be offensive, I assure you, but I wonder if you know the use your electrotherapy machines are being put to. Are you aware that your machines are being used to drug people into addictive behavior?"

Dr. Sinclair's cheeks quivered, and he settled back into his chair, hiding his hands beneath the desk. His fingers steadily rapped the underside of the wood.

"What is your point, sir? Are you suggesting that I am party to a criminal act? If so..." Sinclair shrugged, clearly trying to appear nonchalant, but his hands shook and his face was still red with anxiety. We had rattled him, of this I was certain.

Holmes looped an arm over the back of his chair.

"We are not accusing you of any crime, sir. We seek to understand the phenomenon behind your Eshockers and their effect on the populace. Frankly, there is concern about the growing addiction to your machines."

Dr. Sinclair pondered his options, then replied, "I sell the machines, yes, but only for a meager profit that enables me to buy supplies, medicines, and food for my patients. If not for the sale of these machines, gentlemen, I fear the doors of this hospital would be forced to close. Certainly, I could not afford to treat as many patients. We would have to turn away many who are dangerous, not only to themselves but also to others. These patients are very ill and suffer greatly, gentlemen." His face glistened with sweat, which he mopped off with a trembling hand.

Again, Holmes tried to soothe him.

"Our objective is to help doctors—like yourself, Dr. Sinclair—make patients well again. There is a man in your waiting room—right now, as a matter of fact—who desperately needs your help, yet he says you cannot admit him."

"As I said, we're overcrowded and underfunded."

Holmes darted a look at me, and this time, I addressed the doctor. "And aren't we all underfunded and understaffed, with our asylums most ill-equipped to help patients as best as we'd like due to regulations and lack of resources?" I said. "I thoroughly understand your points, Dr. Sinclair, for I am also struggling to help patients with mental afflictions. I'm sure you have your patients' best interests at heart."

"I do!" the other cried. "I want only to help them, gentlemen! Surely you do understand this, *yes*? We know so little about the human condition, particularly the brain, which is my specialty. I have poor fellows in here who can't remember their own names, who think they're Jesus Christ, who see visions and hear voices. I have women who think they're Joan of Arc or Catherine the Great. I have women who think they have ten children when, in actuality, they have none."

"Rather than sell Eshockers to these dens to fund your institution, might you instead obtain monies from private benefactors?" I asked.

"Clearly," he replied, frowning at me, "I have attempted to do just that, Dr. Watson, but with little success. Charity goes only so far."

"Yes," I said, "I understand your point. As fellow scientists, we hope you can demonstrate for us how your Eshockers work."

"That's impossible. I'm very busy, as you might guess. Please, if there is no *other* matter...?" Dr. Sinclair rose and clasped his hands behind him. He walked toward the office door, gesturing at us to get out of our chairs, and obviously, to get out of his office.

"One moment. There is the matter of Mr. Malcolm Demane," I said, doing as Dr. Sinclair wanted, walking to the door with Holmes. "As a professional courtesy to me, would you kindly admit the poor man and help him, at least with some minimal treatment?"

Dr. Sinclair put a hand on my back and shoved me, gently, through the doorway. He nodded.

"As a professional courtesy, yes, I will do as you ask. In return, sir, as a professional courtesy, I insist that you stay out of my private business affairs. The Whitechapel Asylum has nothing to do with you. The government can shut down the dens, if it so wishes. That is the government's choice."

"But without den equipment—" I started to say.

"If I don't give these men their equipment," the doctor said sharply, "they'll get it somewhere else. At least, gentlemen, you are assured in knowing that the Eshockers supplied by *me* are safe, when used correctly. Other electrotherapy devices, well, who knows what you're getting?"

"We can't stop your sales to the dens," Holmes told him. "We seek only to further our understanding of how the machines work and how they affect the human mind."

"The details are beyond your understanding," came the curt answer. "Now if you don't mind—" With both hands, Dr. Sinclair waved us away.

We left Dr. Sinclair to his affairs. I knew we would see him again. The matter of the Eshockers was far from over. I knew that something used for good could also be used for evil. Dr. Sinclair's motives might be pure regarding his machines, but those who bought and used his Eshockers might not be so pure of heart.

14

Although Holmes had claimed to be in a hurry to get to the Diogenes Club, where we would dine with Mycroft, he enjoined me to walk with him to the Thames first.

"I would like to see the condition of the river. I would like to know if the... creatures are still apparent in this part of the Thames. We are not far from the place where the *Belle Crown* was attacked, as well as the warehouse where we saw them first released by Fitzgerald, after all."

Sure enough, as soon as we reached the waterfront, we saw things were amiss. Vast bubbles broke the surface of the water, indicating the presence of something massive below. Occasionally, the tip of a tendril flipped into the air before slipping underwater again. I thought I saw bulbous objects—heads, I presumed—here and there, but always, when I peered more closely, the objects disappeared. A cloud of translucent, pearly bubbles drifted above the surface, coalescing into shapes and breaking apart from one another. I was reminded of the sensations I'd had in Professor Henry Fitzgerald's London home. After a tram went up in flames—killing numerous victims in front of me—and after a pole struck my head, rendering me unconscious, I'd recuperated in Fitzgerald's home, where the paintings had felt almost lifelike to me, swirling with odd colors I didn't recognize, with bubbles drifting and arranging themselves before my eyes.

"Hurry, Watson." Holmes interrupted my thoughts. "I'm unnerved by the view."

"Do you see the bubbles?" I asked, surprised.

"How could I not? They are everywhere."

"I'm much relieved, my dear fellow. I thought perhaps I was going mad."

"No madder than I," he responded with a grim expression.

I felt *intoxicated.*

But with what?

"This place makes me feel dizzy. Is it affecting you?" I asked.

He blinked at me, then his eyes sharpened.

"No," he said simply. "It's best we make haste, Watson. I want to talk to Mycroft before dinner. Let us get away from this place and find a cab. It is a pity, Watson, that the local populace is not heeding the police warning to stay away from the river."

I had been so caught up in my own problems, I had not noticed until he pointed them out, but there were more people than usual by the river. This particular spot was well known for its opium dens, and some of the onlookers appeared as though they had staggered out of them. A few were sprawled in stupors on the riverside. Others stared in a daze at the wafting bubbles. We were not the only ones inspecting the river, trying to catch a glimpse of the creatures. But these people pointed and gurgled strange words that I seemed to recognize from my dreams, as if they had lost their wits. Others seemed terrified: grown men fell to their knees, their hands clasped, their eyes staring at the heavens, their lips muttering prayers; children clutched at their mothers' skirts.

Holmes steered me along a side street and then to another, where he hailed a cab. He gently nudged me onto the seat, then leapt up beside me. His cane knocked the top of the carriage, the driver lashed the horses, and with a lurch, off we went.

Nauseous, I closed my eyes.

"Be steady, man. We'll be at Pall Mall soon enough," Holmes said.

I sank back in relief at the thought of it. The Diogenes Club was the most anti-social place imaginable. Mycroft was one of its founders. Certainly, I would get plenty of rest there.

"Holmes, what was wrong with those people?" I asked.

"I cannot be sure." Holmes clicked his tongue against the roof of his mouth. The noise was as loud as a hammer, driving home once again that my mind was dislodged and out of sync with reality.

Most frightening. For all I knew, Holmes hadn't made any sound at all.

Sweat broke out on my face and body.

What was wrong with *me*?

"Holmes, I'm not well."

"I realize that. I'm hoping your vigor returns in good

measure. Your condition grew worse when we were by the river."

"But why?" I whispered.

"I do not yet know," he finally answered. "I don't yet have sufficient facts about much of this, Watson: the creatures, the dens, the obvious neural maladies of those we saw by the river, including yourself. Perhaps Mycroft will help. His brain is a vast repository of information, rivaled only by my own."

Even in my state, I had to suppress a chuckle. Holmes often compared his mind to his older brother's, sometimes saying such things as: "Mycroft could be a consulting detective as renowned as myself, but he lacks physical strength and ambition. He is, in a word, lazy."

While our horses clattered along the cobblestones toward Mycroft, I would learn later that Thrawl Street had turned into a battleground. More death, more destruction.

If we valued our lives, then without knowing it, Holmes and I were traveling in the right direction.

15
PROFESSOR MORIARTY
Thrawl Street

The police were imbeciles. It wouldn't take much for me to divert their attention and break into Willie Jacobs's tram machine building, steal the gold, and quickly get away. Like the police, Sherlock Holmes wasn't as smart as he thought he was. It was interesting, wasn't it, how those who considered themselves to be astounding intellects typically lacked true greatness? Most of their supposed competence came only through misplaced perceptions. In Sherlock Holmes's case, he called himself a consulting detective and had built his reputation on the backs of imbeciles who believed his arrogant buffoonery.

Yet those of us who quietly went about our business possessed true power. People never knew when we'd strike, what we were up to, where we were hiding.

I could watch Holmes's movements—because they were so public—but he couldn't watch mine. He did not know who or what he was truly up against. His idiotic companion, Dr. John Watson, was even more in the dark than the man he idolized. Watson knew next to nothing about me.

What I had in mind now would not be an overwhelming objective. Rather, it would be a straightforward matter.

Holmes had left the tram machine running, though not with sufficient power to cause problems.

But the key point was: *Holmes had left the machine running.*

Before Holmes had tampered with the mechanisms, Willie Jacobs had dumped phosphorus and lead into a pit by the machine, resulting in the production of gold.

I wanted that gold.

I could feel it in my pocket. I could envision it glittering in mounds before me.

The thought of the tram machine gold excited me more than anything else.

I wanted to make that machine pump out so much gold that I would never have to think about money again. I would *make* it happen, and then I would live anywhere I wanted, do anything I wanted, be anyone I wanted. There were no limits.

Already, I controlled all of the dens and encampments on Thrawl Street, where the tram machine building was located. Extricating the gold would hardly be a challenge, now would it?

I peered from a filthy window across the street from the building, where a hastily erected iron fence topped with spikes surrounded the perimeter. Approximately a dozen policemen stood guard inside the fence, hands in coat pockets, ready to pull their guns on intruders.

The fence didn't look particularly strong to me. It was nothing that a decent torch or hacksaw couldn't handle.

Of course, I wouldn't be directly involved in the effort. I would send others to do the work for me. Staying in the shadows, I'd station dozens of men where the police now stood, erect a stronger barrier with my men guarding the outside as well as the inside, then sit back and accumulate gold.

The building would be my personal gold mine.

I'd squash the Dagon gang that had stolen my men and used the machine's gold for their own purposes. This, I would do for revenge, and it excited me almost as much as the gold.

Racing down the stairs to the first floor, I slipped out and onto the street. With my collar turned up against the cold and my hat pulled low, I shuffled like any other person toward the pleasure of the dens. From the corners of my eyes, I saw that none of the guards was paying attention to me.

I knew where little Timmy spent time, working for me, thinking himself such a big man. I wanted Timmy's father.

Loping toward Osborn Street, I passed other men— broken creatures who didn't seem to notice me. I ignored them, as well. Eshocked tramps eagerly sucking down Old Ones Serum—provided by me, of course—were in their own worlds. The real world no longer mattered to them. The only thing these men thought about was when and where to get their next Eshock and dose of Old Ones.

I warmed my hands over a fire barrel by the roadside. Soot-black faces encircled the barrel. Their eyes were shut. Smiles quivered on their lips.

They didn't know it, but I owned them. I could make

them do anything, just for an Eshock or a swig of Old Ones. If I wanted, I could kill them.

But I was a good man. I didn't kill men just for the sake of killing them. I needed a reason. If a man opposed me, spoke against me, took any action contrary to my best interests, then he'd better watch his back because I'd be coming for him. I'd hit him when he least expected it. And, of course, it wouldn't actually be me, not in person. It would be a random man on the street, a shopkeeper, or one of his adversary's friends or family members.

I could blend in anywhere. I faded into crowds. Nobody knew my face, not even that clown, Dr. Reginald Sinclair, and—it made me laugh—certainly not that clown of all clowns, Dr. John Watson.

As I laughed, a woman glanced at me, but quickly fell back into her stupor.

Clutching a hip as if injured, I limped from the fire barrel toward the den. A girl slept by the door, her ripped garments serving as a poor barrier against the cold, hard porch. Her skirt was wadded beneath her hips. Dried blood, bruises, and blisters from the cold riddled her legs.

Without knowing her name, I did know that my men sold this girl to any who wanted her, with the price of her body half the price of a minor Eshock. I'd heard from my sources that the girl sold herself on the side for the price of a full Eshock. She procured sufficient Eshocking to keep her in a state of oblivion, the condition she was in now, as I stepped over her small body and swung open the door to my den.

Quickly, I shut the door behind me, lest the soot-faces

at the barrel try to follow me inside. I wanted them only if they had money for Eshocking, and the soot-faces clearly didn't have money. Otherwise, they'd be strapped to my Eshocker chairs, their brains dripping with hallucinations and melodies and oblivious joy. It took muscle to open the door, and besides, once inside the main room...

"What do you want?" the door thug demanded. He was strong, this one, with arm muscles as thick as boa constrictors, a neck the size of a gorilla's, and a face that betrayed very little in the way of intelligence.

"I'm 'ere for Timmy," I said.

"You 'ave money?"

"I do."

"Show me."

Scowling, I made myself appear annoyed. The door thug was doing what my underlings had hired him to do, keep out everyone without the funds for Eshocking.

"I tell you, I 'ave the money," I insisted, pulling my fist from a pocket and showing my hired thug a few coins.

"Enough for ten minutes," the thug decided. He swept his arm in a grand flourish toward the main room.

Along the walls, Dr. Sinclair's Eshockers vibrated and clanked. Customers swelled with ecstasy, strapped into the chairs. Bleeding ankles and wrists stopped nobody. They screamed for "More! MORE!"

Excitement gripped me. I loved watching the Eshockers at work. With every "More!" and "MORE!", I made more and more money.

Speaking of which...

Annoyance replaced my excitement.

Dr. Sinclair and his monkeys weren't producing Eshockers quickly enough for my satisfaction. The den was polluted with other devices: a torpedo sizzling stunner against the back wall, I saw, and a violet ray electrotreat stimulator along the side. My customers wouldn't pay as much for these quack devices as for the Eshockers, which were much more sophisticated, providing steady and reliable do-it-yourself pleasure... especially if a person Eshocked along with a dose of Old Ones.

If Sinclair didn't do my bidding and supply the machines I wanted, I'd be forced to take action against him, action he wouldn't find pleasurable.

Actions that would hurt more than an Eshock at full blast and of long duration.

Yes, I would make Sinclair's head hurt, and badly.

"Don't get too excited yet." The thug interrupted my thoughts, and I eyed him evenly. Had I displayed the slightest quiver? If so, he'd interpreted it incorrectly as excitement about what he thought was my forthcoming Eshock. He shot me a nasty grin and said, "You best wait till you get Eshocked. You'll be wantin' serum, too?"

I shook my head, still keeping my eyes trained directly on his, until finally, he lowered his gaze.

"I'm lookin' for Timmy," I said.

The thug's eyes narrowed and met mine again.

"What do you want with Timmy?"

"'E runs the dens, don't 'e? I pay 'im."

"You can pay me."

"Timmy. Only Timmy," I said firmly.

The thug growled, but rumbled off to a back room, and

shortly thereafter, returned with my man—or rather, my boy, Timmy Dorsey, Jr.

Timmy recognized me and waved the thug back to his position by the door. Few knew me in person, as I allowed only a loyal inner circle direct access to me. I chose Timmy because he was smarter than any lad I'd ever encountered on the streets, and he knew those streets well. And I was a strong believer in building trust while my associates were still young. It gave me more time to turn them into what I wanted.

My inner circle would do anything for me. They knew I offered prolonged service, and hence, income. My men were career men. Someday, Timmy would be a key member of my organization. He avoided drugs and drink, kept his head clear. He already possessed the authority of a much older man. He reminded me of his father.

I walked ahead of Timmy through the main room, past the twitching, gyrating, tongue-lolling Eshocked clientele to a door guarded not by one, but two of my thugs. They didn't recognize me, but they did recognize Timmy, who ran this den for me with his father. One thug unlatched the door, the other swept it open, and I entered my lair, followed by Timmy.

As the door whisked shut, the sounds of the Eshocked— the groans, the ecstatic cries, and the whimpers—faded. This place might be a dump, but it did have thick walls.

Crates of Old Ones Serum wobbled precariously in stacks around the room. I lifted a bottle from a half-empty crate and took a quick swill. One sip wouldn't kill me. My lips and tongue warmed, the roof of my mouth tingled. Warmth spread down my throat and into my belly, through my shoulders and down my arms.

"Good shipment, Timmy."

He nodded eagerly.

"We Dorseys, we get the job done," he said. "We're makin' you a big profit, Mr. M."

"*Professor* M.," I corrected him. "Privately for you, it's Professor Moriarty."

"Professor Moriarty," Timmy repeated.

"But do keep it at Mr. M. for anyone curious enough to ask." I paused. "Of course, curiosity in our business is typically a trait leading to premature demise."

"Whate'er you say."

The boy didn't understand me but hid his feelings well. I liked that. I smiled... but only briefly.

"Premature demise," I explained, "means that any idiot who tries to force you into supplying my name will be killed as soon as he satisfies his curiosity."

The boy didn't flinch. "I've seen plenty of men die."

"Yes, I suppose you have. Come," I said, "and sit with me. Let's talk." I waved him over to a dilapidated two-seat sofa wedged between two stacks of Old Ones crates.

I sat on the firm cushion, and Timmy plopped onto the shredded one beside me. The springs wheezed beneath him. He sank down and laughed, then he bounced on the cushion to hear the springs again.

Still a boy. I had no children, didn't want any, and in general, didn't like them. They were noisy, needy, and demanding. Why people had children, I did not know. The only advantage I could see was continuation of the paternal line, the creation of a dynasty, perhaps.

Who cared about dynasties? I'd already be dead.

It was best not to be responsible for a wife, a mistress, a mother, a child of either gender. Freedom to do what I wanted: this was all that mattered.

Easing my tall frame against the back of the gray-plaid cloth, I casually crossed my legs, withdrew a cigarette, tapped it once on the armrest, and popped it between my lips. He whipped a box of matches from a jacket pocket, the black cloth greasy from wear and faded to the color of sludge, and proffered a light.

I puffed slowly, holding the smoke in my mouth before expelling it in languid circles.

"We need to buy you a new coat," I said, passing the cigarette to Timmy.

He eyed me warily as he sucked smoke into his lungs. Then his mouth formed an O, and the smoke curled out. All the while, he kept his eyes on me.

His smoke circles were larger and more perfectly formed than mine.

"I'll take you up on that, Professor," he said. "I want me a coat better than yours, though." He pointed the cigarette at my tramp's garb, and I laughed.

"If you help me tonight as I know you will, and if we succeed, I promise you a coat that will show the world you're a man to be reckoned with. A gentleman's coat."

The boy's eyes narrowed. He flicked ashes to the floor.

"Tell me what you need," he said.

"Timmy, when do the coppers change shifts at the tram machine building?" I asked.

"Midnight an' noon," came the answer in a cloud of smoke.

"Can you create a disturbance at 11 p.m. tonight?"

"What kind of disturbance?"

I took the cigarette, burned all the way down, from Timmy.

"Whatever you want," I said, "as long as you don't damage the dens or the tram machine building. I don't care who meets with a premature demise, but promise me, no fires, Timmy. Fires could ruin my dens."

The boy nodded, his face bright with excitement.

"Now. Where's your father?" I asked.

"Me dad? 'E's in the den two doors down. Butchers meetin', 'e tol' me."

Dorsey's gang, the Butchers, had been named for their leader's trade, though the rest of them had no occupation other than thieving and extortion. I stood and took a final puff from the cigarette.

"All right. I need your father and his mates," I said. "Can you get them for me, Timmy?"

The boy leapt from the sofa and darted to the door. He was about to yank the door open and race off when he turned back.

"What you gonna 'ave 'em do?" he asked.

"They're the Butchers, aren't they?"

I stared evenly at him while my right shoe ground the cigarette butt into the dirt.

"Well, that's what they're going to do, Timmy," I said.

16

DR. JOHN WATSON

Pall Mall, London

We made our way down Pall Mall to an unmarked door near the Carlton. This was not my first time at the Diogenes Club, but even so Holmes touched a forefinger to his lips. Silence was the creed of the Diogenes Club. Three utterances, and a man would be thrown out.

Holmes and I stepped into a short hall that smelled of cigars and leather. From here, I glimpsed part of the luxurious smoking room, comfortably furnished, with a fire burning merrily. The publications that lined the mahogany bookshelves touched upon all realms of science and medicine, as well as government affairs and history. The men reading that material were dressed in suits custom-made by England's finest tailors, their cigars imported, the wines superb, and the waiters as impeccable as the butlers and footmen of England's grandest estates.

Holmes waved me on towards the Stranger's Room while he went to find his brother.

Thankful that my trousers were constructed of heavy wool, I perched on a splintered stool by the window overlooking Pall Mall. To my right was a chair large enough to accommodate Mycroft, and to my left was a tattered Gothic chair. Heavy with elaborate carving, the chair reminded me of those in Professor Henry Fitzgerald's drawing room, where I'd seen swirling tentacles crawling along the armrests. I shuddered to remember that room: the paintings of multi-limbed creatures in colors I'd never seen before, the silver trays thick with mistletoe, the portent of dread that clung to the air.

I had felt that same dread as we'd walked the streets of London today. It hung in dark folds, blotting out all sunlight and frivolity. It was a blight. We were being attacked by creatures in the river, and we were electroshocking our brains, perhaps out of hopelessness and fear.

Footsteps left a soft carpet and hit hard wood. I realized that I was no longer alone in the Stranger's Room. Sherlock Holmes and his brother, Mycroft, were staring at me.

Holmes nodded a greeting and reclined in the Gothic chair, his body slouched, his legs stretched out and crossed at the ankles. I remembered from previous visits to the Diogenes Club how he hated that chair, and who wouldn't?

Mycroft was very different from his brother in terms of physique. Though they were of near-equal height, Mycroft was double the bulk of his younger brother. Everything about him was enormous: his cheeks, his neck, his stomach, even his fingers. Exercise for Mycroft consisted of walking a few minutes from his rooms on Pall Mall to his office in Whitehall and back each day.

Wheezing, he sank into the oversized chair, which

wheezed along with him. His cheeks flushed as he settled, and the chair groaned.

"Most uncomfortable," he said. "Now, let us discuss the matter at hand as quickly as possible, then retreat into the club for our repast. I'm hungry, gentlemen, and it's already twenty to seven."

Holmes had mentioned to me some time ago that his brother remained in the club from a quarter to five until twenty to eight each day. Due to our visit, his evening meal was overdue, and he had but one hour left in which to eat. I could only imagine the amount he consumed.

Holmes shifted his body, then shifted again. Finally, he hitched himself up so that his back was stiff against the chair, and he re-crossed his legs. When he spoke, it was in a low tone, and I had to hunch forward to hear him.

"Despite the fact that we are allowed to speak in this chamber," he said, "I would say that the Stranger's Room is less hospitable than the other rooms in the club."

"We do not encourage strangers, nor their chatter," Mycroft said, glowering. "And do keep your voice down, Sherlock."

Holmes pursed his lips, then steepled his fingers beneath his chin. He leaned forward and trained his sharp eyes on Mycroft.

"You have my full attention," he whispered—*very softly.* "Pray, begin."

"I suggested in my note that you visit the dens of Whitechapel today, and I see from your faces that you have done so. Dr. Watson, what did you notice about the people of the East End?" Mycroft asked in a seemingly offhand way. His eyes had a misty cast as if clouds suffused his thoughts. Yet no clouds hampered Mycroft's thoughts. Rather, he was in his own world, his mind grinding through problems, sorting information, cranking solutions.

At that moment, *my* mind faltered. Where it had been clear moments before, now it wandered. Mycroft's question was a simple one, yet I stumbled in answering it.

"Watson?" Holmes tilted his head, eyed me with concern.

"People are... I am... The people of Whitechapel are... They are confused... as am I." My voice broke off. I felt my face flush. I raised both palms to my cheeks, hoping to hide them long enough for the flush to disappear.

"The good doctor is temporarily unwell." Holmes addressed his brother. "You noticed the bandage on his forehead, of course?"

"I did," Mycroft said drily, "but it does not relate to Dr. Watson's mental state. I need not point out to you, my dear Sherlock, that a head injury that costs a man his mind is not treated with a small bandage."

"Nothing—no injury—has cost me my mind," I objected.

"Yes, and so, we return to the question, an elementary one. What have you noticed about the people of Whitechapel, in your time among them?" Mycroft repeated, reminding me with a finger to his lips to keep my voice low.

"You refer to the folk who are behaving unusually in that area?" I whispered. "They stagger about the place as if they have been smoking opium or imbibing alcohol, but I do not believe all of the affected wretches have done so. Some of them seem to have lost the power of speech. I believe these people have been reduced to a state of mental numbness. I suspect from their actions that many of them see and hear... things that are not there."

"Suspect?" Mycroft prompted.

"I am fairly certain," I answered, thinking of my own condition. I already suffered from hallucinations. I already heard nonexistent voices screeching and chanting bizarre words.

"They are prone to addiction, for example to the Eshockers of the dens and to the Old Ones Serum," Holmes said.

"Why are you *fairly certain*, Dr. Watson?" Mycroft asked. "Are you seeing and hearing things?"

I hesitated. Dare I expose my malady, my secret, to Holmes's brother?

"Tell him," Holmes said. "You can trust Mycroft as well as you trust me, and he needs to know how pervasive this problem is."

"I have suffered visual hallucinations and have heard very strange sounds. Both come and go..." I began. "My profound hope is that whatever ails me is temporary, a brain infection that has caused some visual and auditory effects that will clear in time."

With the back of my hand, I wiped the thin veil of sweat from my forehead. A chill swept down my body.

"You fear that your brain 'infection,' as you put it, will *not* clear," Mycroft commented drily. "You are a practitioner, and I might add, a scholar of medicine, Dr. Watson. You, of all people, know that we have no cure for many infections. And—" here he cast an apologetic glance at Holmes—"your particular infection is something new and unknown, something vile that has spread across

London rapidly, cutting across all levels of society. A friend of mine, a dear fellow, has fallen prey to the Eshocker dens, and like you, Dr. Watson, he is not himself. He sees things. He hears things."

Holmes cleared his throat. I felt his hand on my shoulder, and I blinked at him as the moisture trickled beneath my shirt. The chills were due to fear, I told myself, and to my embarrassment at revealing what I perceived as my deficiencies.

"Dr. Watson has been nowhere that I have not gone," Holmes said, "and I am, as yet, uninfected, a word I use loosely in this context. I remain confident that Dr. Watson will pull out of his illness in due course. As for your friend, I pray for his rapid recovery, as well." His tone sharpened and he abruptly switched the subject, for which I was immensely grateful. "Mycroft," he said, "tell us what you know and how you suggest we proceed. You requested my help, and I am here."

"You told me the other day of your recent case of the red-headed man who was hired to transcribe the encyclopedia," Mycroft began. "Your handling of that case was admirable, Sherlock."

To Mycroft, Holmes's deductions were merely *admirable*. To the rest of us, they were the work of a genius.

"You saw two disparate facts. First, that only this one red-headed man—one out of a hundred who could easily have handled the job—was hired. Second, that the man who first brought the job advertisement to his attention was later seen wearing worn, dirty trousers. You connected the two facts."

Holmes knitted his brows. His fingers drummed the arms of his chair.

"You're stating the obvious," he said. "*And—?*"

"And you have two disparate facts at play *now*. First, a number of degenerates in a certain area of town are becoming increasingly addicted to the Eshocker dens and Old Ones Serum, causing mental aberrations. Second, at the same time that these symptoms first came to general attention, a number of creatures appeared in the River Thames; the same type of animal you saw at Swallowhead Spring and in the warehouse at St. Bride's Wharf. We know that these are not hallucinations, since you—Sherlock—who is not unwell, has seen them. So could these creatures be contributing to the mental aberrations? In short, you need to find the link between these two factors. Once I know that, I will be able to sever the connection and rid England of this scourge."

He continued, addressing Holmes:

"I've checked with the authorities, who have agreed to give you funds and equip you as you see fit. Machines, artillery, weapons... but they have limited manpower. This might be the greatest crisis England has faced. The matter is urgent."

"I've yet to meet a case that I could not solve," Holmes said. "I will do all that I can to succeed."

"I expect no less," his brother said.

The two locked eyes.

The game was afoot, as Holmes would say.

We rose to make our way to what Holmes told me would be a small meal. He was anxious to work on the case and did not want to waste time with dining.

"A crumb of bread will do," he said.

"Eat quickly, then go," Mycroft said, with the same lack of charm Holmes often displayed when addressing Mrs. Hudson. Mycroft's eyes sharpened, giving me that same uncomfortable feeling I got when Holmes trained his eyes on me.

"Doctor, I want you to remember a few things. They might help you," Mycroft said.

"Anything," I replied, "please."

"In a book called *Theory of Sight*, H.F. Goblet wrote that (I am paraphrasing) the co-existence of disparate factors does not necessarily imply restrictions in time or space. I infer from Goblet's treatise that our minds can connect factors and perceive truths and realities across expanses of both time and space. And now, I will tell you what this means."

Holmes interrupted him with a wave of his hand and an irritated tone.

"Intuition and creativity both rely on connecting factors in ways that most people might not necessarily view as obvious. Decades could pass, and one might remember something seen or heard, something *thought*, and connect it with something *now*. Perhaps the Eshockers, the serum, even the creatures (though I do not yet know how) are stimulating the minds of affected humans into perceiving things—visions, sounds, thoughts—that are not readily obvious to most of us. It has been shown through scientific evidence that applying electricity to the cerebral cortex of a monkey will make the animal's limbs move.

Electricity applied to the brain *changes* the brain."

Anticipating the silence—but for the ruffling of newspapers and the grunts of old men—that would hold us for the rest of our time together, Holmes and Mycroft traded a few more facts, each trying to outdo the other. I remained quiet. It was enough that I barely understood their discussion.

Mycroft rested his hand on the door knob of the Stranger's Room, saying as he did so, "In 1855, Guillaume Duchenne published scientific evidence of successful brain disease treatment using electricity. His treatise on the subject created a stir in the medical community, particularly among the men of asylums."

Holmes replied, "In 1884, Dr. Alexander Robertson, Physician to the City Parochial Asylum in Glasgow, claimed that he cured a patient who had suffered from seven years of paranoid delusions and melancholy as well as hearing voices. His treatment? Galvanic electrotherapy every other day for several months."

"The patient was so delighted with her treatment," Mycroft replied, "that she insisted upon having her head shaved so she could continue with the electrotherapy." He twisted the knob.

The door opened without a sound. Quiet whooshed from the inner sanctum and washed over us like the soundless weight beneath the sea.

"And yet," Holmes whispered, as we passed into the smoking room, "it has also been proven that too much electricity to the brain causes severe trauma such as epileptic seizures."

"*Shhhhh...*" Mycroft's cheeks jiggled and turned bright red.

A dozen or more heads swiveled in our direction, and two dozen (or more) eyes glared at us.

A smile played across Holmes's lips. He visibly relaxed. For men such as the Holmes brothers, silence in its purest form meant they could dwell within their thoughts. No disturbance from the pesky, inferior minds of others.

17
PROFESSOR MORIARTY
Thrawl Street

Crouching beneath the filthy window across the street from Willie Jacobs's tram machine building, I would watch my conquest without risking discovery.

I wanted to watch the killing of the police and the capture of my gold mine close up. I wanted to see each face as it registered the knowledge of imminent death and then withered into that place from which we do not emerge.

I loved watching death. It fascinated me. My first murder was not accidental. I killed François Geraut when I was twelve because I wanted to see the life drain from his eyes. I remained obsessed by the final flicker, the glassiness, the awareness of whatever lay beyond.

Of course, Geraut had deserved his death. He'd attacked, mutilated, and killed countless women, including my mother.

However, being practical, I preferred to survive and remain uncaptured far more than I wanted to see these specific policemen die.

I peeked over the windowsill. A group of street urchins

hollered and jostled one another's shoulders as they ambled past the tram machine building.

Beyond, in front of a building that I'd stolen from the Klanter family and turned into a den, the boys formed a circle. Their voices rose.

My pocket watch indicated that it was 11 p.m.

Dark shrouded the city, and there were no street lamps in this part of London. Here, the residents still used candles after the sun collapsed behind the heavy clouds.

The policemen in front of the tram machine building joked with each other. One held a lantern, which illuminated his face and cast a feeble light across the street. I could not see the positions of the other policemen ringing the building behind the spiked iron fence.

Pressing my nose to the window, I tried to see more clearly, but then quickly withdrew, not wanting to draw attention to myself.

I kept my head below the sill, letting only my forehead and eyes inch up. My heart was loud in my ears, my breathing shallow. I placed my fingertips on the gritty floor, holding my body steady.

One boy jabbed another on the chin. Two other boys broke out in a fist fight. A fourth punched the first boy in the stomach, and both unleashed what appeared to be knives in the dim glow cast by the policeman's lantern.

I could see little, but what I heard told me the story. Timmy Dorsey, Jr. had enlisted his fellows for a punch-out a short distance from the tram machine building.

Several policemen opened the spiked iron gate and raced over to the boys.

"Break it up!"

"That's enough, lads! Go home! I said, *that's enough*!"

Meanwhile, larger shadows loomed in the street, growing as they neared the lantern's glow. The policeman holding the lantern remained by the tram machine building. He held the light high and peered, clearly trying to see what was charging down Thrawl Street from the fire barrel. I knew what these shadows were: Timmy Dorsey, Sr. and his Butchers.

No doubt, the policeman must know by now, too, I thought, *but does he also know that his demise is imminent?*

The Butchers raised cleavers, knives, and saws over their heads. Several dragged other men by their collars and coat sleeves.

My breath fogged the window.

I could contain my excitement no further. I hurried down the stairs to the front door of the building where I hid, and trembling, watched the scene unfold.

To my left, half of the policemen wrenched the fighting boys apart and admonished them to go home. To my right, the other half tried to wrench the Butchers off the men they dragged with them, leaving only the lone man with the lantern guarding the tram machine building.

The unfortunate souls being dragged were the type who slept in gutters when they didn't have the coins for den use. I knew their sort well. They wore rags, and matted beards hid their faces. They staggered, they fell to their knees when a Butcher pushed their shoulders down, they lacked strength and determination. These were my customers, and their tormentors were my Butchers.

It was the natural order of the world. The strong dominated the weak, and without the strong, the world would cease to have meaning, forward momentum, any fluidity. In the wild, beasts devoured one another. Here in civilized society, we restrained our worst inclinations. Usually, that is...

A tall Butcher shoved a policeman, who fell to the street. As the officer scrambled to stand back up again, my man lifted a cleaver and slammed it down—*straight down*—straight down through the officer's skull.

The head split open, cracked in two, and the body twisted to the side and dropped.

My man—it must be Dorsey, for no other Butcher was this brutal and strong—let out a laugh the devil would have been proud of. He pivoted, and his knife slashed at another officer, who gripped his stomach and doubled over before falling. Another maniacal laugh and now a scream of glee, and Dorsey grabbed a metal chain from another of his men. Dorsey wrapped it around another officer's throat and pulled tightly. The victim clawed at Dorsey's hands.

Abruptly, Dorsey released the chain and kicked the man in the groin, then followed with a blow to the face. The policeman fell just like the one before him had fallen. *Dead*, both of them—*dead*. I almost laughed with Dorsey, but controlled my urge.

With police and Butchers scrapping on both sides of the tram machine building, now was the time to crash through the iron gates and take control. It took all of my self-control not to race across the street and kill that lone officer with his lantern.

Come on, Dorsey, do it! I thought wildly, balling my hands into fists.

The attackers had their boots on the backs of policemen squirming on the street. Knives thrust into bone, cracking it, and into meat, eliciting shrieks of pain.

Dorsey's hands wrapped around the neck of an officer. The man clutched at his throat, and dropped to the ground.

Six policemen ran... or rather, limped back to the tram machine building.

I huddled in the shadows, anger swelling in me. *No*, I thought, *you must kill them all. There must not be any police guarding that gold!* I raced back into the building and growled—low and deep in my throat—as I punched a wall over and over again.

Then I stopped.

Did I hear something, perhaps someone—a policeman?— enter the building?

I swung around, fists lifted, ready to pound the intruder into a pulp.

It was Timmy Dorsey, Jr.

"We'll try again, Professor," he said. "Me dad will get into that buildin' for you, I swear it upon me mother's grave, I do." His voice was calm and steady.

I grabbed the boy and shook him.

"You failed me! Your father failed me! I must have that building!"

Timmy's eyes grew hard.

"There ain't nothin' me dad can't do. I'll see to it. 'E'll get what you want."

At that, my anger ebbed away, and I released the boy.

"Timmy, you'll have one more chance," I said sternly, "only one."

Placing my hand on the boy's head, I ruffled his hair. His body went rigid. He expected a blow, I could tell. There would be no blow, but neither was my affection remotely sincere. I felt nothing other than the determination to succeed.

"I don't give second chances very often," I said.

The boy nodded.

"It will be done." He pulled away from me, shook his shoulders, and then dashed into the shadows, and from there, the street.

18

DR. REGINALD SINCLAIR

Whitechapel Lunatic Asylum

Miss Klune burst into my office, her face flushed, eyes flashing.

"Doctor, come quickly!"

I half-rose from my chair, lifted my eyebrows, wanting further explanation.

"I'm in the middle of critical paperwork," I said.

"No time for that!" she cried. "Doctor, this is serious. There's trouble in the day room. *Bligh Braithwaite and Willie Jacobs!*"

Dropping my pen, I shoved back my chair, and rushed after the nurse. She wasn't the type to interrupt me with such insistence unless it was a serious matter. It took a lot to fluster her.

That damn Bligh Braithwaite, I thought, as I hurried toward the sounds of shrieking in my day room, *he's always been trouble. He shows up, unannounced and unwanted, expecting... what? Gratitude, money, favors? That flaming idiot. He should have known... and now, this. Causing me trouble when I have trouble enough!*

"Stop now and sit down! I command you! The doctor's coming, and you're in for a load of trouble, I tell you!" Miss Klune was already in the day room, screaming at the patients.

The image of my mother flashed in my mind. Stout, short, always cooking fatty meals and breads, always berating my father and her easier prey, me.

"Why do you want to treat lunatics?" she'd exclaimed when I told her my career plans. "Isn't it bad enough you want to be a doctor, dealing with death and pain and blood and disease seven days a week? What kind of life is this? Little money, no rest, that's what kind of life it is. But if you have to do it, Reggie, for God's sake, leave the lunatics to someone else, why don't you? Just deliver babies."

My father would grunt in the corner, head buried in a newspaper, eyes not comprehending what he saw. My father had been the first deranged person I'd known. He'd left our squalid flat every night to roam the streets, coming home drunk, stewing in his own sweat and alcohol all day on brown-stained sheets. When he had spoken, it might just as well have been Mr. Norris or any of my other inmates speaking, all nonsense and self-delusions. On his death bed, my father still thought he was the king of England. For all her faults, and there were many, at least my mother was sane.

"Don't let him Eshock you! He'll kill you, Willie! We must resist, not allow Sinclair to Eshock us! We must *revolt*!"

Oh God, it was Bligh Braithwaite, and as I flew into the day room, I saw the fool in all his glory. His emaciated frame was bent at the waist, legs and arms trembling within his tattered shirt and ripped trousers. The dull-wax eyes registered my presence, widened, and went wild.

The day room reeked of feces and urine. Miss Switzer hauled Jeremy MacMyers, one of our longest-standing inmates, down the hall toward the inmates' rooms. Hopefully, we had enough gowns to fit all the soiled patients.

Bligh Braithwaite's arm rose, shaking, and his index finger pointed at me. He backed away.

"Noooooooooo!" he screamed. "Get away! Evil!"

He fell against the chair propping up Mrs. van der Kolk, and losing his balance, fell into her lap.

Mrs. van der Kolk gurgled.

"Oooo, me man, me man meat!" she warbled, her shriveled hands clutching at him. She'd clawed her eyes to bloody smithereens, and I wondered if she'd lost her vision as a result. "Lookit what me 'usband done to me. I be ready for you, sweet thing. You want to see me pantaloons an' firm, roun' buttocks, do you, eh, do you?"

Mr. Robertson curled into a fetal position on the floor behind Mrs. van der Kolk's chair. He wept like an unfed baby with a soiled nappy, interspersing his tears with howls of fury at the voices he heard in his head.

"Avoid the Eshockers!" he cried. "They're of the devil, they're of death, they'll kill us all! Dr. Sinclair must die! We must *revolt*!"

It was sickening, really. Mr. Robertson was parroting Bligh Braithwaite, imagining that what he actually *did* hear amounted to the devil screaming in his brain.

As I reached for Bligh Braithwaite, Willie Jacobs staggered over and grasped my shoulders. He had no strength, but I let him hold onto me, for now. I had nothing against Willie Jacobs. He was a poor soul with little time left on Earth. My heart warmed to him, for what had he done, really, other than tend to his father's business, which had done him in?

I wanted to help Willie Jacobs, give him relief from his anxieties as he slipped into the netherworld of death. I also wanted him to help me build more Eshockers for Professor Moriarty so I could treat those who suffered like Jacobs. Symbiosis? Yes, certainly.

Jacobs released my shoulders and stood, shaking, before me. His right hand rose to his nose, and a finger jabbed rhythmically into the left nostril, which was inflamed now with infection. Scabs encrusted the entire underside of his nose. I noticed that his face and scalp bore additional scabs from the last time I'd seen him in my treatment room. Jacobs had been picking at the scabs, making them deeper and bigger over time. He couldn't stop himself. I didn't think he had even tried to do so. It was a nervous tic, of sorts, a brain illness.

"You're worse than the murderous creatures from beyon'," he rasped. "You're worse than the Old Ones. You 'urt us for no reason."

I bobbed my head toward Bligh Braithwaite.

"Sedate Braithwaite, nurse, this time with a heavier dose," I said, "and then bring him into the treatment room."

Miss Klune's strong arms pried Bligh Braithwaite off Mrs. van der Kolk's lap.

"I'm in no mood for this, Bligh. Be a good boy and behave. I don't want any problems with you this time."

"Noooooo!" He struggled in her grasp, the legs kicking, the head snapping from side to side.

"Ouch!" Miss Klune let one arm drop and rubbed her chin, where he'd kicked her. As he squirmed loose, her steely hands grabbed his shoulders and shook. "You stop this right now." Her words were cold, calm, and measured.

But Willie Jacobs intervened. He encircled her waist with both arms, trying to pull her off Bligh Braithwaite.

"Leave 'im alone. 'E don't want more of your Eshocks."

She shrugged Jacobs off. He stumbled back, tried to regain his footing, his arms clumsily groping for her.

Miss Klune hoisted Braithwaite up from behind, lifting his struggling body with her hands clenched over his chest. His kicks hit mid-air this time, and in this fashion, she carried him from the day room toward the treatment room.

Around me, half a dozen patients moaned and cried. They wailed about my Eshockers and about evil, about the need for revenge and release and revolt. Miss Switzer would return from handling Mr. MacMyers and take care of them, sedating them all and tucking them beneath their sheets.

I needed both Bligh Braithwaite and Willie Jacobs to build my machines. I couldn't afford to sedate them into constant oblivion, nor could I allow them to be together again. Braithwaite was dangerous. He knew too much. He could poison Jacobs against me. Braithwaite was hopeless. I'd never been able to reach him. So I would try to make my peace with Willie Jacobs, and through him, perhaps I could persuade Braithwaite to behave himself and build those machines.

Revolt? Not when I had medicines and machines at my

disposal, not to mention barred windows and locked doors. I had all the power.

"Come, Mr. Jacobs, let us sit quietly and talk." Gently, I helped him from the hysteria of the day room and back to his tiny closet-sized room. I eased him down on the bed and then sat beside him.

"Mr. Jacobs, my only intention, I assure you, *I promise you*, is to ease your suffering."

"Bligh says your Eshockers *kill*. We patients, we want out of 'ere. You're mad, Dr. Sinclair. You're *evil*."

I did nothing but devote my life to these patients and their well-being. How could they think me *evil*?

Again, I remembered my father.

Insanity.

"Mr. Jacobs," I tried again, using my softest and most gentle tone, "there are medical issues beyond our control, things we are not responsible for, such as what is wrong with you and with our friend—*yes, my friend, too*—Bligh Braithwaite."

"I ain't insane. I'm infected by Old Ones, an' says Dr. Watson, also by phossy jaw."

"Dr. Watson is a good medical man, indeed, but he does not specialize in the brain, as I do. The Eshockers use electricity to cleanse your brain of disease and ill thoughts. Doctors use electrotherapy to cleanse illnesses from all parts of the body."

"Machines are bad, evil."

There was that word again: evil.

"Sometimes, we have to suffer to get well," I said. "Amputations hurt, but they save lives. Removing a bad tooth hurts, but you wouldn't want to keep it and be in constant pain, would you? We pop blisters, we use leeches to suck out poisons. How is electrotherapy any different?"

"It changes me brain," Jacobs whined.

"It changes your brain, yes, but for the better," I said in a soothing voice. "It destroys pain, Mr. Jacobs. It helps those who suffer the most. It cleanses hostile thoughts."

"You ain't got hostile thoughts?" he asked sharply.

Frustrated, I leapt up from the bed and fidgeted by the door, ready to leave.

"Mr. Jacobs, you're not a well man. You know that. I'm here to help you. I feed you, and I tend to your every need. I am a doctor, sir."

But he was curled on his side, and snoring. He was ungrateful, like all of them.

Carefully avoiding any hostile thoughts, I left him to his nightmares.

19

DR. JOHN WATSON

London

After a quick but delicious meal in the dining hall of the Diogenes Club, Holmes and I were anxious to be on our way, but Mycroft signaled us to follow him back into the Stranger's Room. He stood by the window and stared into the night for a while before he spoke.

"In the quiet of the club," Mycroft said, "I thought of your safety, Sherlock. Our Dr. Watson admits to mental confusion, which we all know is not his usual mode of functioning. You, dear brother, admit to no such mental confusion, and yet..."

"And yet, you fear that I will suffer the same fate, since I have been where Dr. Watson goes just as he has been wherever I go."

"Correct," Mycroft said. "I suggest that you remain in a safer environment." Before Holmes or I could object, he quickly added, "Not in my rooms, no, for neither of us could bear such a thing, but rather, I've arranged for a room above the Diogenes for you. I arranged for this... yesterday, just in case I felt the need to house you safely upon seeing you today. And now, I've heard from you and the good doctor, and I've had time to consider."

A room above the Diogenes Club, where Sherlock Holmes would be alone, away from me, as if I were diseased, infectious, and about to contaminate him in some deadly manner—

"This is most offensive!" I blurted out.

"Not at all." It was Holmes who replied. "Consider. I need time alone to reflect upon what ails you, what ails London. The Diogenes Club has vast resources, men who might provide insight and help, medical and government documents of all sorts. Novel creatures are bursting upon the city, unleashed by scoundrels, I suspect, though seemingly through rifts in ceilings, a barn roof, a chair, a table, a steam-powered machine, and indeed, from the waters of the Thames. The creatures flicker in and out of our view—" he snapped his fingers—"yet they attack and kill. Perhaps my brother is correct in suggesting I move to the Diogenes Club."

"But—"

"My dear fellow," Holmes interrupted, "it is for the best. I will gather my things in the morning. You will visit me, as needed, and we'll take our excursions from here. In the meantime, you will dwell at Baker Street and make your excuses, on my behalf, to Mrs. Hudson."

"And what excuse shall I make, Holmes?"

"I am on holiday."

"She won't believe me. You never take holidays."

His eyes twinkled.

"I am away on a case."

"She *will* believe that," I snorted. "But where am I to say you have gone?"

"My dear man," Mycroft interjected, "your Mrs. Hudson is not the issue here. The issue is this neural psychosis and how to stop it. Now, I must retire for the evening. I have much to ponder." He turned to Holmes. "I suggest you visit the dissecting rooms at the Royal London Hospital in Whitechapel post haste—first thing tomorrow would be best, and I've already signaled your arrival via one of our ever-faithful and loyal Diogenes servants." He lowered his voice. "I signaled him over the roast beef."

"Do tell, how did you accomplish this over the roast beef, when talking is strictly prohibited in the Diogenes?" I asked.

"By writing on club cards," Holmes murmured. "Did you not see us?"

"I was not attending. You forget I am not feeling myself."

I had grown weary, as if my mind had sucked the strength from my physical being, as if it required all the strength I possessed just to keep my brain working. I wanted to return to Baker Street and to the warmth of my bed. I wanted Holmes to return with me to his own bed. I was not at all comfortable thinking of him *here* while I was *there*.

"My dear fellow," he said, as if reading my thoughts, "it is you who shall fare better than I, for you will have Mrs. Hudson to feed and tend to you."

"Off, then," Mycroft said, swinging his bulk toward the front door of the club. "Sleep awaits, and puzzles to solve. Royal London Hospital dissecting rooms, tomorrow morning, for you, and then, I expect you here tomorrow night and every night until we rid London of this scourge."

"And what are we expected to dissect at the dissecting rooms?" I asked, fearful that my question would be perceived as naïve.

The three of us shifted from the stale cigar smoke of the Diogenes Club into the brisk London night. As he hailed a carriage, Holmes answered me.

"*Brains*, Watson. If we're lucky, we'll study tissues from those who died from the current infection, perhaps brains dragged in from the Thames."

As grand as the idea was, it revealed nothing of value. Holmes and I arrived at the Royal London Hospital, where, rather than sending us to the dissecting rooms, a technician supplied us with a small private laboratory for a few hours.

Holmes was more at home in a well-stocked laboratory, I thought, than anywhere else. As he'd hoped, the police had indeed secured a couple of corpses from the Thames disaster for our study. Most of the bodies, I knew, would have been claimed by the undertaker. The only corpses available for study, as was typical, would be from the dead who had no family or close friends.

The technician pointed to a series of slides in a box by a microscope.

"I prepared the tissues for you." His expression made it clear he had no idea why we were there and wanted to study brain tissues. His superiors had simply told him to prepare the slides. "I don't know what you hope to find, but I'll leave you to it, gentlemen," he said, leaving us and closing the door behind him.

Holmes's total focus was on the slides in the box. His fingers flicked through them, his eyes examining the tiny print that identified each sample. I stood between two lab benches, each arrayed with jars of chemicals, powders, mortars and pestles, beakers, tubes, and slides.

"Perhaps, Holmes, I can be of service," I said.

He shot me a sharp glance, then returned his attention to the slides.

"See what you can make of this one, Watson," he said.

He thrust a slide at me, then put several others on the lab bench by the microscope.

I nudged the first slide into place and secured it with the screw pin. I peered through the microscope. Nothing out of the ordinary. I gestured at Holmes, feeling somewhat useless, and he took my place at the bench. He stared long and hard at the bit of brain tissue clamped between the two slides under the lens.

"I see nothing unusual," he said finally.

We both studied every sample the technician had supplied.

When we'd studied a sample under the microscope from the corpse of Willie Jacobs's father, while trying to determine the cause of his death in the tram machine building, we'd seen blood cells that didn't appear to be either human or animal in nature. The corpse of Amos Beiler—whose death, in a Dagonite chair of his own creation, had brought his son Kristoffer to Baker Street—had given up similar inexplicable clues: peculiarly, inhuman hairs, bits of oddly shaped bone, an exotic insect.

But this time, we saw nerve cells, long tangled fibers. The cells varied in size, but this was normal.

"It was a long shot." Holmes frowned. "These poor devils might not have been infected by whatever has hurt Willie Jacobs and those in the vicinity of Thrawl Street. They were on a boat, on an outing for just one pleasant afternoon that turned out to be not so pleasant."

"Nor do we know that the victims from whom the hospital took these brain tissues were users of the dens or Old Ones Serum."

Holmes was already at the door with one foot in the hallway.

"These brains are no longer functioning, so even if these people were in the early stages of infection on that very day, the dead tissue displays nothing novel. We need living tissue, Watson."

20
PROFESSOR MORIARTY

Moriarty's Whitechapel Eshocker Den

I am a man of my word. A gentleman. If one of my workers fails to execute my instructions, I don't immediately kill him. Of course not. That is not a gentleman's way.

If my workers possessed my capabilities, they would be in my position rather than living in squalor and doing my bidding.

The men forming a semi-circle around the crumbling fireplace were some of my most capable henchmen. Men are motivated by money: to impress a girl, feed a family, satisfy addictions and demons. But the best workers are motivated by the thrill they get from the work itself.

A few such men stood out—Timmy Dorsey, Sr. and James Buckles, in particular, who towered over the others, eyes keen with intellect and determination.

Dorsey and Buckles, one a meat man and the other a welder, had both worked for me for as long as I could remember. They kept the lower men in control, those others who now huddled by a weak fire, wondering why I had called them to the back room of one of my dens.

My eyes swept to Dorsey, who, like his son, met my stare levelly.

"There are times," I began, "when even the most distinguished among us must turn our backs on our core beliefs to achieve critical goals and provide for all of the men."

James Buckles looked at the shapes ground into the dusty floorboards by countless shoes. He shifted his weight from his left foot to his right.

Dorsey didn't move, just continued to meet my gaze with his own.

A welder—Buckles—would be more useful to me than a butcher—Dorsey. To seize control of the tram machine, I needed men adept at *machinery*, not the carving of delicate choice cuts. However, my butcher, Dorsey, was stronger, faster, and smarter than my welder, Buckles.

Yet, did I really need to terminate the employment of either man? Or could I retain them both, for neither had committed the ultimate sin of disloyalty?

Two men, both from Buckles's gang, *had* committed this ultimate sin. Gregory Choir and Theodore Mann. Both had stolen for me, raped for me, killed for me. Both enjoyed their work and excelled in the quick, efficient execution of my commands. Of the few men allowed into my inner circle, unfortunately, these two had betrayed my trust.

Walking to the fireplace, I lifted an iron poker from the mantle, then turned to face my employees.

I felt no joy in what I was doing. This was an unpleasant business, but necessary.

"Order must be restored," I said. "Professor Henry Fitzgerald, a key leader of the Dagon gang, languishes in jail, where I am certain he will either rot or die, and if the latter, let us hope it is a painful and terrible death. The tram machine building is now under police control, and the machine itself idles and does not produce gold. This is an utter waste."

Murmurs ran through the group. Gregory Choir nodded, as if agreeing with me. He clasped his beefy hands and spread his legs farther apart, rocking nervously on his heels. A stocky man with hard muscles and a thick neck, he was a thug I paid to break down doors and keep various people in line.

Theodore Mann blanched. Short and thin, he could slip into places where few men could go. He hid easily in crowds, and after snatching what he wanted—money, handbags, jewelry—he scampered off as quickly as a rodent. Now, he sucked on a cigarette, barely inhaling the smoke before sucking again.

I stooped and pushed the poker into the fire, let the blaze curl around the iron until it glowed. Standing, I pointed the bright end of the poker at each man as I spoke.

"I sent some of you to secure the tram machine building for me. You failed."

Dorsey drew himself up, as did Buckles.

Fear is good, I thought. *It keeps them under control. Control is good. It leads to power.*

"Don't worry," I continued. "I have no designs on disciplining you for the failed maneuver. *However.*"

The sounds of their breathing halted, as the men waited for a pronouncement of judgment.

"You will attempt to secure the building again, and this time, you must succeed. Otherwise you will pay the full price of failure. Do you understand?"

I directed the question at Dorsey and Buckles, and both nodded. Gregory Choir unclasped his hands and darted a look at Theodore Mann, who trembled and stared at the floor as he ground out his cigarette.

"*However*," I repeated the word, emphasizing it, "I believe you need extra motivation to succeed. You must understand, very clearly, how serious I am about owning the tram machine. We do not fail. We always win. There is no other way. Now, Mr. Dorsey, would you please escort Mr. Choir over to me? And Mr. Buckles, bring me Mr. Mann."

Dorsey registered neither surprise nor fear, but James Buckles's body trembled and his face tightened. Dorsey pinned Gregory Choir's arms behind his back and shoved him toward me. Choir's elbows dug into Dorsey's ribs, but despite his muscle, Choir was no match for the butcher.

"What're you doin'?" Choir growled. "Why me? What 'ave I done, eh?"

Meanwhile, James Buckles, still trembling, did the same with Theodore Mann, who whined, "Lemme go. I ain't done nothin' wrong."

I thrust the poker into the flames again and then held the orange tip to Mann's throat. He craned back his neck and gulped air. Chuckling and shaking my head—what a fool he was—I moved the poker slightly. His neck strained farther back, his eyes grew wide, and he held his breath.

Gregory Choir's body jerked as he tried to release himself from Dorsey's clutch. The butcher's grasp tightened, and a faint smile played on his lips.

A high-pitched wail rang out from a front room of the den. It was a female voice. It died rapidly. Probably some pathetic girl had swilled too much Old Ones Serum and passed out. My men did not react. They were accustomed to both the ecstatic and the pained shrieks of customers, and sometimes their death cries too. Old Ones Serum combined with Eshocking was especially dangerous, and we'd seen plenty of clients expire with their mouths still clamped to the bottle neck.

How amusing that my customers actually believed they were drinking a brew concocted of the strange creatures that plagued the river. Given that this was the prevailing notion, it stunned me that anyone would let so much as a drop pass their lips.

Theodore Mann cringed, as if he knew his fate. In the dim light, I might have seen a tear or two glistening on his cheeks. *Pathetic.* Gregory Choir, on the other hand, didn't seem to grasp the situation. His eyebrows arched high over his dark eyes, his lips twisted slightly.

"Surely you ain't gonna use that poker on me, are you?" he had the gall to ask.

"Surely," I answered, moving the poker from Mann's neck to Choir's, "you're not gonna fail me again, are you? Surely, you understand what happens to men who leave my employment for a low-life low-level operation such as this... this *nothing* of Dagon that dares to call itself a gang."

"It's true that I worked for the Order of Dagon, but only for a short while." Gregory Choir's voice cracked. He was losing his composure, but he remained quick-witted, for he added, "It enabled me to gain valuable information for you."

"Yes, yes, *important information*." Theodore Mann cringed again, although the poker threatened Gregory Choir's throat, not his.

"Both of you were part of the Dagon gang, yes?" I asked.

"Never part of the gang, no," Choir said. "I've only ever been loyal to you."

"Both of you have families. A wife and several children apiece. London isn't kind to widows, much less to orphans," I said. "This organization is a family, and we stay together. When one of us strays, it hurts the family. Wives become widows, and if a man's crimes are sufficiently grave, children become orphans." I asked Dorsey and Buckles, "Do either of you know of this 'valuable information' these men claim to have gathered?"

"No," they answered in near-unison.

"Now, Mr. Choir. Tell me what you know about the Dagon gang."

Gregory Choir shook himself free of Dorsey, who stepped back, arms outstretched, as I nodded at him. James Buckles maintained his hold on the limp Theodore Mann.

"Mann tol' me," Choir said, rolling his massive shoulders and balling his fists, "that the most powerful leader of the Dagon gang is at 'alf Moon Bay. This leader 'as magic powers, Mann said, an' all 'is followers are loyal an' devoted... as I am to you, boss. The Dorset den, which you own, is in territory controlled by this Dagon leader an' 'is—for lack of a better word, for wife or mistress don't make sense to 'im—an' 'is mate."

"What's the leader's name? What's his woman's name?" I demanded.

"Amelia Scarcliffe. She 'as powers almost equal to those of the Dagon leader. But as for *'is* name—" Choir nodded at Theodore Mann, whose lips moved rapidly, uttering nonsensical prayers, *the fool.*

"Yes?" I said, keeping my voice calm.

"Well, Mann tol' me that 'e don't know the leader's name. But there's another powerful one there, in an orphanage nearby." Choir's voice rose with excitement as he contemplated the potency of the information he was about to divulge. "An' 'er name is Maria Fitzgerald!"

Theodore Mann ceased his praying and sputtered.

"Um, yes, yes," he nodded, highly agitated, "an' she's the daughter of 'enry Fitzgerald, 'im that's jailed in London."

"Is the orphan with this Dagonite leader and his mate?" I asked Choir, ignoring Theodore Mann.

"I don't know. The men in the gang tell us that she also 'as enormous an' very strange abilities, just like the leader an' 'is mate."

Between the utterings of Choir and Mann, I also gathered that a book existed, a book of dark spells that brought forth creatures such as those in the Thames.

"It is the *Dagonite Auctoritatem*," Choir spat out. "This Dorset leader probably 'as a copy. There's said to be one elsewhere, owned by a man named Beiler, 'ose barn 'ad odd dimensions that cracked open an' spilled deadly creatures into the countryside. The gold of the tram machine 'as somethin' to do with all this."

Nobody steals my den profits. Nobody steals my gang members. Nobody controls the criminal factions of London. Nobody but me.

"You will secure the tram machine?" I barked.

"Yes!" Gregory Choir cried. "I swear to you, *I swear!*"

"Good enough," I said, then gestured at Dorsey.

"Secure Mr. Choir again, would you?"

"Why? I tol' you everythin' you wanted to know!" Choir started to bolt toward the door, but Dorsey grabbed him, pinned his arms behind his back, as before, and held tight. Choir squirmed and kicked, but was no match for Dorsey.

I plunged the iron poker into the fire, and when it glowed with red-hot intent, this time, I did not wait.

I thrust it into Theodore Mann's neck, right through his Adam's apple. As soon as his scream erupted, it died. Blood gurgled from his lips. His eyes glazed. Dorsey sneered. Buckles released the body, which fell to the floor, twitching.

"Pull it out," I told Dorsey, whose face lit with pleasure. He slammed Gregory Choir into a wall, then stooped and wrenched the poker from the dead man's neck.

"Now kill Choir," I instructed him, turning my back on the men. I contemplated the fire. It had done its duty, and now, Dorsey would do his duty.

"No!" Choir shrieked. "Don't do it, *don't*!"

I heard the poker squelch into the meat and crunch into the bones. I heard the screams, the gurgles, the moans, and the last breath of Gregory Choir. For a moment, it saddened me, for he had been a good soldier, but the rest of these men needed a hard lesson about loyalty and about performing one's job, even if it meant death.

"One more," I said. "Now kill James Buckles."

Fear filled the room. I felt it. I basked in it. I had the power, the control, the potency to do as I wished with these men, and indeed, with all of London.

"Boss?" It was Dorsey, questioning my decision to kill Buckles. I knew they were close friends, my butcher and my welder; but in the end, my butcher was more valuable to me, and it was he who would live to see another day.

"Do it," I ordered, "and make him suffer, for I want all of you to know—" I whirled and faced the shaking group of men, who shrank back from me—"what happens if you disobey my decisions, if you think for a moment you can work for another gang! This man allowed his closest associates to be lured into the Dagon gang. Watch him die, watch him carefully, for you will be next if you don't mend your ways! And next time, I won't stop with you! I'll kill your firstborn sons. I'll kill your families."

James Buckles had sunk to his knees, his hands clasped in prayer, his eyes raised to a god that didn't exist.

"Quit your whining," I screamed, "and die like a man!" I swiveled to Dorsey, who had killed enough men not to mind. "Do it!" I screamed. "Do it, and don't make it easy on him!"

Dorsey grunted with satisfaction. He was good with meat, wasn't he?

I barely paid attention as the poker pierced Buckles's stomach, as Dorsey wrenched it out and plunged it into the man's groin; wrenched it out, plunged it into a thigh, then into an ear—*straight through James Buckles's head.*

My mind was already on the future.

I would visit the Dorset coast and obtain what was rightfully mine, and I would kill all who opposed me. This Dagonite leader would be no match for me.

If Amelia Scarcliffe and Maria Fitzgerald could fool a whole cult into believing they had magical powers, then they would be useful. I would kidnap them, and I would set them to work for *me.*

21

AMELIA SCARCLIFFE

Half Moon Bay, Dorset

Killing Mrs. Chatham had been a simple matter. In fact, looking back on how I'd killed the old woman in my flower shop—how the mistletoe had twisted around her neck and killed her *for* me—I figured that killing *anyone* would be a simple matter.

What made humans think it perfectly fine to tramp over flowers, or pull mistletoe off the trees? The plants were sacred symbols of fertility and tools that helped bring forth the Old Ones, who buzzed in these woods.

My neck flaps vibrated in harmony with the buzzing. Now that I was nearing the birth time, my flaps had swollen with blood. I touched a left flap. Velvet beneath my fingertips, and a temperature oscillating between warm and scorching.

I was on the beach with my acolytes and ready to fulfill my destiny. Soon, the brood would be with us. How many would hatch? Twelve? Two dozen? Perhaps *more*?

Bearing even *one* of Koenraad Thwaite's offspring would make me unlike any other female who had ever bred, for Koenraad—and I felt it my right to refer to him only by his first name—was the Supreme Almighty of the Order of Dagon and of the slab of open waters at Half Moon Bay. Captain Obed Marsh, who had started the Order of Dagon in 1838 after learning of the Great Ones in the South Seas, would have devoted his life—*given his life*—to Koenraad, had Koenraad surfaced back then.

I was the first female to fulfill the third oath of the Order, to bear the child of a Deep One...

... for Koenraad was of Dagon as surely as I was of Dagon.

My acolytes stooped on the rocks heaved ashore from the endlessly vomiting sea. Black boulders poked up from dark water frothed orange from a dying sun.

Mau fetia, the stars, reached down and embraced me.

A cluster of perhaps a dozen men and an equal number of women writhed around me, their backs straining, their arms shaking, their mouths hardened into twisted shapes that emitted the Dagonite sounds.

One mouth, with lips as fat as grapefruit slices but the color of beets, formed a shape only a Dagonite would recognize.

From this opening, a shrillness rang over the water and rocks, a sound only a Dagonite would understand: "*Yog'fuhrsothothothoth 'a'a'a'memerutupao'omii!*"

Another mouth looped into a Dagonite shape even more complex than the first, and from these twisted lips came a screech.

"*Aauhaoaoa demoni aauhaoaoa demoni aauhaoaoa demoni!*"

My followers warbled and squealed in a chorus that, within my depths, I knew the Old Ones sang.

In taiotua, *the outer sea, we join you forever, swelling with pride and happiness.* I had no purpose other than to serve those of the Deep and to spawn the next generation.

"Come," I said in the elder language, "and follow me into the sacred cave, where we will give ourselves to the great Dagon and the Deep Ones."

My webbed feet slopped across the rocks, and behind me, grunting and still warbling and screeching, my acolytes followed. Toe suckers popped from rocks, webbed feet splashed across wet sand.

Before me, the cliff cowered, clamped beneath its burden of dense trees and undergrowth. The birds nesting there were deformed monsters, feeding on mice and cats. I spotted one now, a monster bird whose beak could grip an animal with the power of an alligator's jaw. Diving from a sky-high pine, it crashed through branches, which snapped and fell. Its wings were wide and covered in leathery toad-green skin, beneath which the bird's muscles possessed the coiled strength of wiry rope. A falling feather from one of these birds could cripple a man as if a boulder had hit him.

When I passed the slab of open waters, my gills fluttered and heat rushed to my head. It was here that Koenraad had splayed my legs and seeded me.

Briefly, I rested my head upon the slab, and the slime of my flesh slicked across the mold creeping over the black slate. Slime upon slime. Time beyond time. One creature whole with all else in existence. All creatures united as one.

Humanity had it all wrong. People thought they mattered more than the oceans, the cliffs, the birds, the fish, the caves.

But to whom did they matter?

Only to themselves.

Following my lead, each acolyte rested his or her face, slime upon slime, upon the slab. Each offered to slit his or her own throat with sharp rock.

I declined all such offers, for this was not the time for death sacrifices.

That would come later.

The air was heavy with the mustiness of Old Ones, creatures who came from the Great Beyond, who settled beneath the seas and rivers, emerged into the open air; congregated, bred, multiplied, and infused every breath sucked into the gills of all at Half Moon Bay.

You come, and you wait with us, I thought. *Yog-Sothoth has already opened the way, and now you wait for the great Dagon Himself. But your wait is nearing an end, for the womb-incubation of hatchlings is rapid and most unlike the many months needed by human females to live-birth only one baby.*

Koenraad!

My heart surged. The acolytes and I would chant until we fulfilled Koenraad's true desires, until Dagon and Cthulhu emerged from the sea and reclaimed what was long ago theirs—the land, the air, the sky, the waters, and all of us. We were but receptacles and tools.

Koenraad!

You of the seed must bow back and let me bond with Yog-Sothoth. You must let the female feel her power. You must let it grow. You must.

The chant pounded over and over inside my skull: "*Aauhaoaoa* DEMONI *aauhaoaoa* DEMONI *aauhaoaoa* DEMONI."

At the base of the cliff, I swept aside a tangle of vines to expose a clearing, where a coal fire and a water tank pumped steam into a device that rotated a wheel, which in turn, powered a generator. Two cables throbbed along the ground, providing electricity from the generator to a cave, the Dorset coast den.

I stooped and entered the den. Two candles flickered by the rear wall. Several Dagonites lay in humps across one another, their bodies seemingly merging into a single blob of chartreuse flesh that breathed Old Ones in and out of a tubule jutting from the top.

My acolytes slopped into the cave behind me and collapsed against the walls. Lumpy, warped bodies; limbs more like long boneless snakes than human appendages; bloated heads; eyes filled with pus; their twisted mouths foaming and dripping a viscous sludge: some of the pack already possessed the chartreuse cast of an Old Ones addict. A few slumped into a merged heap, and from this heap of flesh, a tubule popped up and drank of the Old Ones air.

My den operator, Koos, nodded eagerly at me, awaiting instructions. Tall and heavily muscled, he lacked in intellect what he possessed in physical strength. He would do my bidding, no matter what I asked of him.

I commanded him now.

"Koos, strap in a few worshipers and Eshock them. Give the others the Old Ones Serum. After a brief Eshocking, unstrap the first group and strap in a second. Give everybody a chance at Eshocking. Give everybody as much serum as they want."

I squatted between the boulders holding the two candles,

as Koos yanked a few dazed Dagonites into Eshockers, secured the wrist and ankle straps over various malformed appendages, and then moistened the head sponges.

Squawking and chattering with excitement, my followers ripped the tops off wooden crates and whipped out bottles of serum. Webbed fingers tore caps off bottles, heads tilted, lips smacked, people hiccupped and swigged serum.

A young acolyte, no more than ten years old, took one sip of serum and fell against the cave wall. Her back slid down it. Her eyes closed.

The air was so ripe with Old Ones in here, and the power of my presence so potent, that even an innocent and naïve child had fallen into the grip of intoxication, the Old Ones infiltration of the mind.

All fell into its grip.

All became addicts merely by entering this cave. No den in London could compete with the ecstasies of the Dorset coast den.

Add a dose of serum—nothing more than alcohol and opium, really—and some Eshocking, and addiction was assured.

Koos pulled down the side lever on an Eshocker.

Zzzzzzzz...

Flesh sizzled, limbs jerked, smiles blossomed, tubules pumped the dense air in, then out, then in again.

I wailed, my chants begging Cthulhu to show Himself, beseeching Dagon to give me a bountiful harvest of hatchlings.

Koos swapped one batch of followers for another in the machines. All drank of the serum. All chanted and wailed, warbled and shrieked.

We were finite.

The Old Ones were infinite.

We were mortal.

The Old Ones were *forever*.

Infinity.

I gripped the rock floor. The spawn inside me pushed downward, anxious for release. My knees spread. My heart pounded.

Playing against the far wall, a multi-winged Thing seeped from the blackness into the shadows. Multiple eyes glowed, chartreuse flecked with green.

Could it be that I'd unleashed Cthulhu, the Greatest of all Old Ones, He Who Ruled the Earth from the Beginning of Time?

Yet He was to rise from the sea, not from the walls of the cave.

My heart picked up pace. I clutched at my chest. Pain spread, like ink from a broken bottle.

"Take me in this way, yes, O Mighty Cthulhu, yes!" I cried. "Take me, but first unleash my hatchlings!"

The pressure upon my body grew fierce. I fell to my side, then rolled to my back.

The looming Thing on the far wall approached. A thrumming filled the air, a deep-throated static. My gills vibrated. Any moment now, and the hatchlings would come.

An acolyte screamed, and my head snapped up. Koenraad Thwaite stood at the cave entrance, drenched in the glow of candles.

My gills stopped vibrating. The static died. There, by the back wall... there, in the blackness, dark upon dark...

Where was the multi-winged Thing?

It was gone.

It had disappeared as quickly as it had shown itself.

Koenraad had broken my spell, had stifled my ability to bring forth those from the Beyond. Koenraad had *intruded*.

I scrabbled to my feet and hurled myself at him, shoved him to the rock floor, where we rolled—gripped in a fierce embrace—until we slammed against the cave wall.

"You are my mate," he hissed. "I chose you! I made you what you are!"

I rolled on top of him, pinned him down, and splayed my neck flaps across his breathing tubules. Choking, he threw me off, and I skidded across rock, as the hatchlings clawed for release. My head hit the cave wall first, then my back, and pain shot down my legs.

Two hands gripped my upper arms.

Zzzzzzzz…

Flesh sizzled.

Eshockers shocked.

Serum slurped, oozed, dribbled.

"Koenraad!" I screamed.

"You are my mate," he hissed again. "You cannot reject me. If you misbehave, think what the others might do. I am their leader."

My spawn froze in the womb. They would wait for release. They would wait because Koenraad Thwaite had forced himself into my most intimate moments with the Old Ones.

"My power exceeds yours," I said. "You are in the way."

"Everything here belongs to me, including you," he said.

He was wrong. I belonged to the vast unknown. In life, in death—it was the same, a seamless web of existence, of non-existence, of being.

Koenraad had fulfilled his purpose. He was no longer necessary. And yet...

If my spawn did not hatch, did not survive, Koenraad's services might again be required.

"If you misbehave, think what *I* might do," I said.

He released me, sank down against the wall next to me.

"You can't get from the others what you get from me," he said.

"Sperm?" I almost laughed, but he looked so sad and defeated, that instead I said, "Koenraad, go to the sea, swim to the reef."

I knew that he would do as I requested, for we both lived, and some day would die, for the same reason. We existed to do the bidding of Dagon and Great Cthulhu.

22
PROFESSOR MORIARTY

Half Moon Bay

After Mann and Choir's betrayal, I decided to travel to Dorset to see for myself the two females they had told me about. My credulous agents had spoken of magical powers, and though I was far from believing in such stories, I wanted to discern the nature of the trick that had so many people fooled.

As it happened, I knew of a local man, Archibald Pewter, a former merchant sailor who had worked one of my smuggling lines in the past, and telegraphed him that very night to make my intentions known to him. I traveled on the first train of the day, with five of my burliest agents, and he met us at the nearest station and brought us away by cart. Archibald furnished me with all the information I could hope for about Half Moon Bay, and our cart detoured so that we could look from the cliffs down upon the very headquarters of the Dagon gang—an unprepossessing slab of rock upon a sandy beach, upon which a few of the cultists were gathered. There were no lookouts.

We lunched at the *O Tei Hau Ia I Te Rahi* Inn, which nestled in the forest by Half Moon Bay.

When I asked the elderly landlord—whose exotic tones I could not quite place—about the unusual name of the inn, he explained, "It has been here for all time. It was named for that which lies beyond us in the sea, beneath the depths, that which readies itself for domination. *O Tei Hau Ia I Te Rahi*. Roughly speaking, sir, it means, that which outstretches all greatness, that which is greater than the greatest of anything imaginable. For all time, we wait, and it will come when all the sand aligns with the stars."

"Thank you. Clearly, you possess exceptional understanding," I told him.

His head dipped slightly, acknowledging my compliment.

"I oftentimes am taken by the great thing yonder," he sputtered, his diction abruptly changing, "and it speaketh through me." Then he murmured what I took to be "mistletoe" and careened out of the rooms, cane clacking across the battered floor.

I'm not sure if the landlord's explanation mattered to my men, for it made little sense to me. As long as I controlled the bizarre gold-making machine on Thrawl Street and got the Dagon gang out of my way, I cared little for this nonsense about great beings from the beyond.

Following our simple meal, we moved to the front room, where plaster walls sagged and cracks splintered them from floor to ceiling, and where mold stained the cracks like weeds. By the outer door, a window sank in its frame, the view obscured by rotting wooden planks secured with rusty nails. The stench reminded me of a midden.

I dared not sit in the lone chair, an overstuffed monstrosity that had seen better days, some hundred years ago or more.

It would either break or release a flood of insects and vermin; it was best not to take the chance.

"The sooner we succeed at our task," I told my men, "the sooner we go home."

They grunted in agreement, as they jostled for room in the cramped space. I barely knew their names—they were *that* interchangeable to me. If one died in combat, I hired another. If all five were to die, I would simply round up five more men with steel fists, easily obtained on the streets of Whitechapel. Muscle was cheap. For a few coins, these fellows would torture, maim, and mutilate anyone. No questions asked, the way I liked to operate.

"Chester. John. Grant."

As I uttered each name, my men snapped to attention. Three responded with guttural noises. Grant was the largest, a brute with blond hair curling down the sides of a face resembling a small boulder. His nostrils flared beneath a broken nasal bone, still scabbed and purple from a recent fight. His jaw hung crookedly beneath splintered teeth and the puffy remains of his mouth. He towered over me by at least six inches, and I am well over six feet tall. His hands were paws, his arms twice the size of mine.

"Grant," I said, "take Chester and John with you—" I gestured at the other two, whose eyes lit with eagerness— "and plant the dynamite down on the beach, where we saw the big black slab of rock."

"You want it by the rock or the cliff? By the water or on the sand?" Grant rubbed his hands together, already anticipating the fun he'd have with his task—blowing up the most sacred meeting place of the Dagon gang.

"All of it," I answered. "I want the three of you to blow up and completely destroy the entire beach surrounding that black slab of rock at Half Moon Bay. There's an extra sovereign in it for each of you if you eradicate the slab itself," I added, and then: "When they're distracted, you grab the leader—Koenraad Thwaite. Once you've got him, hole up in the place we talked about and wait for my instructions."

"And what do you want with the rest of us?" Michael asked, apparently conscious that he, Lloyd, and Archibald had yet to be called upon. He shot me a greedy look.

"Don't worry. You'll have your reward. We'll make those idiots run to their rocks and their beach, and the rest of us will grab Amelia Scarcliffe, and if we find her, Maria Fitzgerald. Archibald, we shall have need of you to guide us to Miss Scarcliffe's place of abode—where she shall hopefully be alone, unguarded."

At this, Michael visibly quivered. He and Lloyd turned from me, already anxious to get to the door and begin their work.

"Not so fast."

These men were even stronger than the trio I was sending to obliterate the black slab of rock. Kidnapping requires muscle. The dynamite was merely a diversion. Of course, it was a thing of no great consequence to me, blowing up the Dagon gang's headquarters, which happened to be on a beach. My main purpose in doing so was to make the competing gang's men race to their headquarters, leaving Amelia Scarcliffe—and possibly, Maria Fitzgerald—alone and vulnerable.

Michael scratched the side of his head by the left ear. It was a nervous habit that annoyed me more than I cared to admit. I shifted my eyes to Archibald and then to Lloyd, both rock-solid and wearing bloodied gashes on their cheeks and foreheads. Tough as whipcord. Nothing got past these two.

"Go quietly," I told them. "Make your way to the cottage Archibald told us about—the flower shop. There, you will find Amelia Scarcliffe. She has enormous powers, so be careful. I've heard she can flatten men with the flick of a finger." I didn't believe this myself, of course, but I didn't want the woman harmed any more than necessary.

"Ha. That cannot be," Lloyd laughed. "No woman can outsmart us, outrun us, out-*anything* us."

"This one *can*," I said, "you'll need to creep up on her cautiously so she doesn't hear you coming. Wait until you hear two explosions, then wait five more minutes. Wait, I tell you, for the dynamite to do its magic and draw the men to the beach. Only then do I want you to grab the woman, subdue her, gag her and tie her limbs, ready to bring her to London."

"And the other lass?" Michael asked, cracking his knuckles.

"The other is but a girl. She is in an orphanage hereabouts. I hope to get further information from the Scarcliffe woman. Also, beware of the leader, this—" I spat his name—"*Koenraad Thwaite*."

"Black-robed?" Michael asked, confirming what I'd already told my men.

I nodded.

"Short, the one with the froggy body?"

I nodded, my patience withering.

"Beard? Funny-looking feet? Flaps on his neck? Hahaha."

The men broke into nervous laughter, muttering amongst

themselves about their own masculine endowments and superiority over the black-robed, froggy-bodied, bearded man with funny-looking feet and neck flaps.

I knew better. The despicable Koenraad Thwaite was possibly the most dangerous adversary I'd met in my career, possibly more dangerous to my health and wealth than Mr. Sherlock Holmes. Thwaite possessed keen intelligence and had nearly brought down my London enterprise. My sources told me that Thwaite also possessed the same strange powers as his mate, Amelia Scarcliffe. Professor Henry Fitzgerald, tucked away in prison, had been a figurehead of the gang, reporting to Koenraad Thwaite. I was troubled by what I'd heard, that Holmes himself had battled Thwaite's gang in London and nearly been defeated, that the creatures polluting the River Thames were under Thwaite's control.

Could it be?

Logic and science told me that my sources were wrong, but I'd read the accounts in the London newspapers about the creatures, how they'd appeared as if from nowhere in a London warehouse and attacked people. I'd stood on the banks of the Thames and seen them myself, how they flickered in and out of view across the surface of the water.

That despicable Holmes had rebuffed my suggestion that we work together. He obviously wanted the glory for himself. But Holmes hadn't beaten me yet. Not in all these years. The man irritated me and distracted me from my true purpose, that of domination over London's criminal enterprises. Someday, I'd put Sherlock Holmes in his place, and if I had my way, he'd be next to Professor Henry Fitzgerald in prison—either that, or dead, buried and long forgotten.

The thought left a bitter taste in my mouth.

"Get on with it," I barked at my men, who backed away slightly in fear. *That's the way I like it,* I thought, and then softening my tone, said, "Assuming you find the child, kidnap her along with Amelia Scarcliffe. And blow up that beach to get the heat off Michael's group. *Now, go!*"

My men burst out of the inn and into the quiet country lane. I followed the dynamite group heading toward the beach. I have always liked a good explosion.

23

DR. REGINALD SINCLAIR

Whitechapel Lunatic Asylum

Professor Moriarty's procurement agent loomed in my mind. He would return soon—in a few days, I suspected—and demand delivery of ten Eshockers for the dens. If I didn't supply ten machines, he'd snap my neck in two.

Mr. Norris, my master carpenter, had succeeded in carving, constructing, staining, sanding, and polishing three coffin-sized Eshocker boxes. I didn't know if I could push him any further. Right now, he was in the day room, prattling at his nonsensical visions.

Bligh Braithwaite, buffered on good hot meals, had been working twelve-hour shifts. He'd wired all three of Mr. Norris's boxes. In the meantime, Willie Jacobs had already studied my wiring diagrams and knew what to do.

I fell into the leather chair behind my desk, and my fingers drummed the wood. I was much too jittery. To solve my problem, I had to calm down, think clearly.

Here in the asylum, what other patients did I have who could help build Eshockers for Professor Moriarty's dens? Who hadn't I thought of?

Malcolm Demane sprang to mind. He'd recently arrived, and I'd admitted him under duress. I'd been forced to admit him for fear that Sherlock Holmes and Dr. John Watson would make trouble for me. This Malcolm Demane... well, he *was* fairly sane compared to the others.

He didn't have visions.

He didn't mumble nonsense.

He didn't fight Miss Klune or Miss Switzer when they strapped him into the Eshockers or tranquilized him.

I wasn't sure what was wrong with Demane. His brother-in-law, who was employed as an attendant at the asylum, was of no help in elucidating the matter.

"He's been this way for a while, sir," he'd told me. "He may fall to the floor at any time, and he groans and twists his body into knots. We don't know what the foam is that bubbles on his lips, and we certainly don't know, sir, why he insists on ripping at his skin—" here, he shuddered—"with his teeth... and then..."

"Yes, eating his flesh," I completed the sentence for him. "Cannibalizing his own body. It *is* a curiosity."

I didn't want foam and blood all over my new Eshockers. We didn't have time to clean up such messes. We'd be lucky to build the Eshockers and deliver them, untested, to Professor Moriarty.

The situation was desperate, *but still...*

Of what use was a foaming-mouthed self-cannibal who writhed in knots on the floor?

No, I had to think of someone else to help build the Eshockers.

In the end, I settled on Jeremy MacMyers, who had

been in the asylum for most of his life. Miss Klune often let MacMyers play with wood, a hammer, and a chisel. He never hurt himself or the other inmates. He carved patterns into the wood and constructed small boxes that could hold a few trinkets.

Could he translate his skills to the construction of a *large* box?

Knowing what I had to do, I pushed back the chair and rose, then gazed briefly at the honors and degrees on my wall. I'd come a long way, hadn't I? And still, here I was, mired in the muck of administrative and bureaucratic detail. It was such a waste of my talents, when I should be doing nothing but curing the mentally diseased.

I called for Miss Switzer, and she entered, scowling at me, as she was too often prone to doing these days. She pursed her lips, and a bloom of wrinkles spread outward from her mouth. When she spoke, her mouth twisted downward, and the wrinkles kinked into strange formations.

Tearing my eyes away, I looked over her shoulder so I could focus on her words.

"What do you need, Dr. Sinclair?" she snapped. "I'm in the midst of restraining Mrs. van der Kolk. The shameless woman's ripped off her clothes again! She's causing quite the ruckus in the day room!"

Stunned by her insolence, I glared at her, and her face flushed. Her masculine body tensed, as if ready to spring upon me.

"What do you need?" she demanded again.

My nerves skittered, my stomach ulcer flared. I moaned and clutched my stomach, gestured at the nurse to sit in a chair in front of my desk. As she complied, I let a wave of nausea pass.

"Miss Switzer," I said sternly, "as an employee of this asylum, you need to remain calm at all times. Your stress and anxiety translate into bad behavior on the part of the patients."

"Don't you dare lay into me!" she cried, half-rising from the chair.

I waved her back down, then sank into my own chair and leaned over my desk with my hands still gripping my stomach. Pain shot through my chest and shoulders, and down my upper back and arms.

"If you don't come to your senses, and soon, I'll do more than chastise you," I said. "Remember, you work for me, Miss Switzer."

"Yes, *yes*..." She breathed heavily for a few moments with her eyes shut, as if trying to force herself into a calmer state. When she spoke again, her voice was less strident. "I apologize, Dr. Sinclair. Now, what can I do for you?"

"Jeremy MacMyers," I said simply. "Bring him to me."

"That's it?" she said.

"And I suppose you should escort Willie Jacobs, Mr. Norris, and Bligh Braithwaite into my office, as well."

She eyed me, puzzled, but nodded, and when I tilted my chin at the door, she rose and hurried from my office toward the day room.

Would Old Ones Serum, which supposedly helped cure nearly all human ailments, help my stomach pain?

I slid open the upper left drawer of my desk and plucked out a bottle of serum. It was unopened. I'd never tried it.

The label read, OLD ONES SERUM, and in smaller letters beneath, HEALTH AND HAPPINESS.

If only it were so simple, I thought, *that a mere drink could bring health and happiness. Even my Eshocker requires medical supervision and continual applications.*

Nonetheless, desperate for relief, I twisted the top off, tilted the bottle, and took a good swig of Old Ones. Instant warmth spread through me. My stomach pain grew sharper. Maybe I hadn't drunk enough.

Sucking down more of the elixir, I was aware that my mind was relaxing but my stomach pain was increasing. The two offset each other somewhat. I let my mind drift, and with it, went my stomach pain.

A sharp rap on my office door wrenched me from my daydreams, and I stuffed the bottle back into the drawer.

Pain shot through my stomach.

Wincing, I managed to compose myself as Miss Switzer swept in with the four men I'd requested.

Jeremy MacMyers sank into a chair; he was so old he hardly stood up anymore—nobody, not even he, knew how old he was. He rarely spoke, and even then, it was only to grunt or emit a shrill and random high note. His dim eyes focused on nothing. He was so emaciated that his torso was concave. A short man, even shorter than I, MacMyers weighed less than a well-nourished child.

But my attention was on Braithwaite. He had a surly look on his face. What was he up to *now*? God help him, should he try to sabotage my Eshocker program, I'd kill him. Well, I'd throw him out on the street, and that would suffice. The poor sot couldn't take care of himself. Why didn't he realize how vulnerable he was without my care?

Willie Jacobs loitered by the office door along with Mr. Norris. Nobody moved near the door leading into the Eshocker treatment room. Despite all I'd done to reassure them, they still mistrusted my wondrous machines.

"Get up, Mr. MacMyers," I said, opening the door on the far side of my office, which led to the treatment room. "We are not stopping in here."

I gestured at Miss Switzer to remain in my office, then led all four men through the treatment room to my special medical cabinet. I moved books and beakers, reached into a deep crevice in the wall behind the cabinet, and pulled an unseen lever. Then I stepped back as the wall and its attached cabinet swung into the treatment room.

"Come," I told them, ignoring their astonished expressions, and they followed me into the back room, where I built the new Eshockers. What did it matter if they knew about the back room? I had the only keys to the treatment room, and I never allowed anybody in here unless I was present. Indeed, nobody but my nurses was ever present during the routine treatment of patients.

I explained what I wanted. Jeremy MacMyers would learn the trade from Mr. Norris. They would work the night shift, from 9 p.m. until 9 a.m., constructing the boxes out of mahogany and pine. Willie Jacobs would work part of the night shift with them, as I didn't dare team up Jacobs with Bligh Braithwaite; the latter would work alone from 9 a.m. until 9 p.m. every day. Jacobs and Braithwaite would wire the machines after MacMyers and Norris built the boxes.

"Mr. Jacobs," I said, and he raised what was left of

his eyebrows, "for now, you must help Mr. MacMyers and Mr. Norris construct more boxes. Work from 9 p.m. until 1 a.m., then get some sleep. As soon as the boxes are ready, please work as hard and fast as you can to wire them up with the actual machine components. Can you do that for me?"

He shrugged. His right hand crept up to his nose, and he jabbed his enlarged nostril with his right thumb. I'd not been able to break him of the habit. Both nostrils were inflamed with infection, both encrusted with scabs, as was his scalp, which was almost entirely bald.

"I'll do as you say," he said. "I'd rather make Eshocks than be Eshocked, sir."

"Indeed," I said. "Well, then, gentlemen, I believe we're all set. We'll begin the new schedule now. Mr. Braithwaite will return to his room, while the rest of you set to work on building boxes. It's early, but I urge you to work more than a full shift, until 9 a.m. tomorrow. Remember, if you want to eat, if you want beds, if you want me to shelter you, then you must work on these Eshockers rapidly and with precision. All depends on what you do, gentlemen. Your fate rests in your own hands."

I directed Miss Switzer to return Bligh Braithwaite to his room, and relief swept over me as he left my office. I would lock the other three inmates in the back room, where I'd monitor them every hour or two. I didn't want anyone going wild back there, hurting someone else or—a pang of guilt accompanied this final thought—damaging my equipment.

I asked Willie Jacobs to keep things under control. Of the three, he seemed the most capable and even-tempered.

Norris was already drooling and shrieking at his visions.

"Yar, *no*! Th-the heads, condemning, screaming at me! I be bound for hell, they say!"

MacMyers gripped his head with both hands, his lips opening and closing but issuing no words. His toothless gums mashed together, opened, mashed together, opened. Squish, squish.

As for me, my stomach hurt like hell, and I needed rest, so I left the three men in the work room and retreated to my office bed.

I curled into a ball, arms wrapped around my torso. I rode the waves of pain, and after an hour of agony, pushed myself off the bed and returned to the work room.

Norris was on the floor, unconscious, his head in a pool of vomit.

MacMyers looked up at me from where he sat cross-legged on the floor, a chisel poised to chip wood from the beginnings of an Eshocker panel.

Willie Jacobs stood behind a box he'd hammered together in a mere hour. A faint smile flickered across his lips, then faded.

"You'll be wantin' 'ow many?" he asked.

24
PROFESSOR MORIARTY

Half Moon Bay

We clawed our way through vines of ivy clad in sticky berries, through thickets and weeds, toward the sea. As if trying to push us to our task, gusts swept through the forest, rustled dead leaves high on branches and ripped them off, rattled tree trunks until they groaned.

In the opposite direction, three of my agents crept nearer to Amelia Scarcliffe's cottage. They would wait for the explosions, would wait for Koenraad Thwaite's Dagon gang to hurry to the black slab of rock in the hope of saving the gang's sacred ground from the blast.

Archibald had told me that, despite their relationship, Thwaite was hardly ever at Amelia Scarcliffe's cottage. He didn't know where Thwaite slept at night. Perhaps Thwaite moved from location to location, keeping his whereabouts secret in case someone like me showed up and wanted him dead. This was my method. I remained rootless, unlike Holmes, whose 221B Baker Street was a well-known address, where a killer might find him snoring in his bed one night.

I keep myself in good physical shape, but even so, my agents ran much more quickly than I could, and by the time I reached the start of the cliff-path leading to Half Moon Bay, they were already scrambling down it to the beach.

Panting, I settled myself beneath a tree that swayed with the wind. From here I had a good view of the beach. The few Dagonites we'd seen earlier had left. Hunching my shoulders and drawing my coat closely about my neck, I allowed myself a grin. I lived for excitement, for moments like these, for what good was life without your heart racing and without the flush of the chase?

In this, Sherlock Holmes and I were alike. We both craved impossible challenges, which we invariably conquered, and we both lived for the excitement of the chase. Either of us could have ended up running a bank or controlling an arm of the government. Either of us could have been a titan of some random corporation, a man who shook up the world and made things happen and earned a fortune for his efforts.

But those occupations would have been too boring, too dull, too predictable for Holmes and for me. We both needed to be in control, but it wasn't just money that drove us. In fact, in Holmes's case, money didn't seem to matter.

Ah, I see that Grant has reached the beach. He looks smaller from up here, not six feet six inches tall and not the bear he was when he stood beside me. And here come the other two behind him, Chester and John, carrying the sacks of dynamite and matches.

I leaned back on my elbows and stretched out my legs. I was going to enjoy this little scene... *a lot.*

Beyond Half Moon Bay, waves crested beneath storm

clouds, then crashed over boulders that sprayed the water in all directions. Rhythmically, the waves soared then crashed, the water opened like a blossom then fell. Closer to shore, the waves smashed against more boulders, perhaps a reef, and the water shot up in a jagged line before sinking down into violent eddies.

A huge black rock with a polished top surface abutted the lip of water. My smile grew wider as Grant and the other two placed dynamite on the surface.

Suddenly, I realized that when the dynamite exploded, the Dagon gang might come scurrying down the path where I sat high on the cliff. So I turned my back on the scene below and scrambled along the path, circling through the brush until I could sit with a good view yet remain hidden from any intruders.

By now, my men had set the dynamite all along the short beach. They fanned out, each with matches. Though they had trouble lighting the matches due to the wind, these men were professionals and managed to shield the matches, strike them on rock, and then put fire to the dynamite.

My heart banged against my ribs, and I jumped up.

Even with the wind, I heard the *sizzle*, the *crrackk*, and the—

KABOOM!

A bolt of fire shot up over the black rock slab, followed by fire bolts all along the beach. The fire spread—but it spread in mid-air, with flames darting horizontally over the beach beneath a thick cloud of soot.

Where were my men? I peered but could see nothing beneath the black cloud.

KABOOM! I ducked and shielded my head with my arm. Below on the beach, rock and sand exploded up and then slammed down. A blast of wind sucked the rock and sand off the beach and crashed it against the cliff, then reversed direction and whipped it all toward open sea. I'd never seen a wind reverse direction. I couldn't explain it, and it terrified me. Fire erupted again, spewing more rock and sand in all directions.

I gripped a tree trunk with both hands, fearing I might fall over the cliff, so fierce was the wind whirling below me. Never before had I seen dynamite explode with such force that it kicked up a whirling storm of rocks.

And what had been the nature of the black soot cloud and the horizontal flames?

This had been unlike any dynamite explosion I'd ever seen.

Male voices yelled behind me from deep in the forest.

They were coming. The Dagon gang was racing to their revered place of worship.

I had to get out of here, get away from the cliff and the beach. My other three agents—Michael, Lloyd, and Archibald—were probably kidnapping Amelia Scarcliffe from her cottage at this moment. Rather than wait for them at the O *Tei Hau Ia I Te Rahi* Inn, I'd catch up with them at the cottage.

The wind was so fierce that I couldn't tell whether my men were dead. I could see neither the men themselves, nor dismembered parts of them. I had no time to look for them. If they were gone, so be it. I'd cut my losses and replace them. Turning, I was about to hurry up the slope when I noticed something that made me stop in my tracks.

The rocks were settling back into place on the beach, as if they'd never exploded into the air. More unsettling, the large black slab still stood there, *undisturbed*, its top surface polished as if no dynamite had exploded on it.

The male voices continued to yell from behind me, and the sounds were growing near. I had to hurry up the path and out of sight. In fact, it would be wise for me to help my men capture Amelia Scarcliffe.

This business of the beach was another oddity to add to the growing list. It was peculiar, I gave it that much, but how much stranger had the explosions been than the existence of creatures in the Thames, bearded frog-like gang leaders, women with powers to kill men simply by wishing it so?

All I wanted was to put an end to the entire Dagon gang. If Sherlock Holmes did it before me and stopped the creatures and the powers and all the rest of it, I'd give Holmes the win, for my victory would be worth far more. He could have the satisfaction. I'd take the dens and the gold and control of the criminal underworld.

I burst through the door to find my three agents pinning an eerily beautiful woman to a counter. The smell of flowers and black tea laced with bergamot filled the shop. On the floor by the counter, a broken teapot sat in a puddle of steaming liquid.

The woman writhed against the arms of my men. They'd already gagged her to muffle her screams. As she fought them, various bits of needlework fell off the counter:

brightly colored embroideries of cats, shrubs, and flowers.

Nearby, green vines dangled from the ceiling over a chair. I batted at the vines, nearly knocking over the chair, and pushed Archibald out of the way. I took his place near the woman's head.

"Turn her over," I ordered, "and bind her!" While Michael and I rolled the woman to her side, Lloyd and Archibald bound her wrists and ankles with rope they'd brought in their sacks.

She wore a nightgown that covered everything from her neck to her ankles, but still it was obvious that she was heavily pregnant, about to burst. I rolled her onto her back again, swept the long black hair from her face, and stared into eyes that seemed to penetrate my own and pierce my very being. Struggling to get free, she squirmed and her gown shifted and exposed her neck. That's when I noticed the skin flaps.

I pushed aside the gown, then immediately recoiled in horror. My three men, to their credit, gasped but continued to hold her tightly to the counter. Where women have breasts, Amelia Scarcliffe had coiled tumors that twined and folded into mounds that looked like intestines.

I reached a hand toward her, then reconsidered and extended only the tip of my forefinger to her neck. I wasn't going near the "breasts." Gingerly, I touched one of the six jiggling neck flaps.

Pain bolted up my finger, and I jerked back my hand. The fingertip where I'd touched the neck flap was a bruised purple. The edges of the bruise were singed, as if burned.

Lloyd lifted her gown, down by her ankles, and stared up

at body parts that I already knew I didn't want to see.

"Look here!" he cried. "This one should be in a traveling carnival!"

Archibald and Michael followed his gaze. All three chortled.

"I wouldn't have that if she were the only lass left," Lloyd laughed.

Being a gentleman, I am nonetheless not immune to some of the crass and perverse ways of my gender. Yet when I peeked, what I saw between Amelia Scarcliffe's thighs sufficed to switch off any physical desire I might have felt.

Instead, I grimaced and looked away, and then stared—but only for a moment—at her feet. They were huge and flat, with webbed toes.

Lloyd reached to touch one of the nail-less toes.

"Don't touch her!" I exclaimed, waving my bruised-and-singed finger.

She spat the gag out of her mouth with a laugh.

"You're enjoying this, are you?" I snarled. "Well, not for long! Where is Maria Fitzgerald?"

"Fitzgerald was a jealous old fool who would believe anything Lucy Nolande told him," she spat. "That child is no more a Fitzgerald than I am! Her sire was the Dagonite leader in Blois—"

"I don't care whose child Maria is. I only care about her powers."

"Fool. She has *his* power. You will be defenseless against her rage if you hurt her."

"Well, well." I forced the gag back into her mouth and secured it as I spoke. "We shall see about that."

I sank into the chair beneath the vines.

My men lifted the pregnant woman and crammed her into a sack long enough to cover her from foot to neck with her head sticking out. They yelled at her to squat down, and when she refused, they shoved until finally, her knees bent. Quickly, they pushed her head down and pulled the strings along the top of the sack, securing her within. The sack bulged. Miss Scarcliffe's bound feet kicked. The sack was too close to me, and her feet struck my shins. As I fell from the chair, toppling it, the overhead vines descended, bunched, then sprouted needlelike protuberances, which grew longer and longer.

Michael and Lloyd shoved Miss Scarcliffe against the wall beneath the vines and pinned her there.

The vines shivered, then billowed outward and formed a circle over Miss Scarcliffe and the men.

Archibald and I ran toward the door. I was anxious to leave Half Moon Bay and never return. Even the noise and squalor of London beat being in a place like this.

Sherlock Holmes could clean up the crime of Half Moon Bay. Let *him* come here and handle Koenraad Thwaite and these ghoulish creatures.

I looked back at the sack, at Amelia Scarcliffe, at Michael and Lloyd. Over them, the strange vines thickened into a mat. The needles were now six inches long and growing longer by the second.

Dashing back to the counter, I grabbed Michael's elbow and yanked him back. We both tumbled to the floor, and in front of us, was Lloyd... still holding the sack and the squirming Miss Scarcliffe.

The needles—*hundreds of needles*—plunged into the top of Lloyd's head. Instantly, his hands dropped, but his body did not. It remained rigidly in place and suspended in the air by hundreds of needles. His arms and legs twitched, and now his entire body twitched with them. Blood oozed from his hair down his face and neck. As he screamed, the vine mat grew and slunk down over his face, muffling his shrieks. His arms thrashed but could not beat off the intertwined vines, which continued to grow in both length and thickness, forming a tight hood over his head.

The hood squeezed and shrank. The muffled shrieks died. His arms were limp at his sides. The hood expanded slightly, as if taking a deep breath, then squeezed his head so tightly that his skull cracked. With a loud squish, the hood collapsed, and in a gush of blood, Lloyd's brains splashed down over his shoulders and chest.

Releasing the corpse, the needles and the vines withdrew. Blood dripped from the ceiling where they hung. The body fell—headless—to the floor.

On our elbows, Michael and I crawled to the door as quickly as we could, when suddenly, Miss Scarcliffe screamed beneath the gag on her mouth, the top of the sack ripped open, and her head popped out.

Those blood-red eyes with pus-colored irises. That oval face with exotic ridges across the cheekbones, ridges that should have made this woman deformed but instead somehow made her beautiful. In fact, she was so beautiful I couldn't take my eyes off her. I found myself—*me*, a man who could have *any* woman, and often *did* have any woman he wanted—*mesmerized*. I knew what lay beneath her gown, and it wasn't something any man would desire. And yet...

The neck flaps gently wobbled, rubbing against one another. I wanted to touch them, to bury my face in them.

"What's the matter with you, boss? We have to get out of here!" From behind me, Michael yanked on my shoulders. Startled, I realized that he was standing, while I was still on the floor on my back, staring at Amelia Scarcliffe.

The neck flaps beckoned.

I was intoxicated.

Michael shoved his arms beneath mine, and he hoisted me up.

"Boss, snap out of it!"

"Yes," I murmured, my head still whirling with confusion. "Snap. Out of it." Carefully, I shifted my focus from Amelia Scarcliffe and shook my head. "Bring the woman," I said, "but knock her out first so she doesn't struggle, and for God's sake, get her head back into the sack, would you? Such ugliness. I don't want to see her again."

Michael brightened, clearly relieved that his employer had not, after all, taken leave of his senses.

He hit Miss Scarcliffe over the head with a gas lamp from the counter. She slumped forward.

"What an annoyance," I muttered. "Disgusting."

Michael scowled and gathered the sack up and around her head.

"Hit her again, just to make sure," I said, "but don't kill her."

"Gladly. A loud-mouthed hag, that's what she is."

Michael lifted the lamp high over his head. As metal hit skull, I stepped outside and into the wind.

PART TWO

MURDER IN THE ASYLUM

25

MISS AMY SWITZER

Whitechapel Lunatic Asylum

How extraordinary that Dr. Sinclair dared to chastise me, after all I'd done for him. I'd given up my life for the Whitechapel Lunatic Asylum. In my mid-forties, I was long past the age where any reasonable man would want to court, much less marry, me. Orphaned at a young age, I'd been lucky to find work as a nurse all these years, and indeed, I'd devoted myself to Dr. Sinclair and his needs. I'd always hoped that Dr. Sinclair would reward my devotion and loyalty with masculine attention. Just thinking about the possibility excited me.

Late at night, all the inmates snoring in their drug-induced slumbers, and here I was, the ever-faithful Miss Amy Switzer, standing guard in the dark corridors lest someone needed my help. It had been a long day, and my feet ached. I could go home, but home was a one-room dump of a boarding house for stray women down on their luck. Old crones and widows lived in those rooms, paying a few coins of rent out of their savings. As for me, I could barely afford the few coins despite my post as a full-time nurse at the asylum. Dr. Sinclair didn't pay me all that well.

There was nothing to go home for, so I sank onto a hard-backed chair at the end of the hall. I'd volunteered for night duty again, so the staff who had families could get time away from this terrible place.

Darkness settled like dirt on the floor and crept up the walls and doors, obscuring them. It was so dark that I couldn't read the hand-painted room numbers, hastily daubed by Miss Klune and myself years ago. The numbers were worn down from age and inmates' nails.

Looking down the long hall was akin to looking down a tube filled with charcoal paste. A patch of light shone from far away, off to the right of the day room, where a lone gas lamp flickered by the nurses' desk.

I mentally reviewed, one by one, the inmates in each room along the hall. How I pitied them. *If only I could help each and every one of you*, I thought. *Your lives are even worse than mine.*

The nurses' clock faintly ticked down by the day room. It chimed twice, as the time slipped to 2 a.m.

I crossed my legs, studied them. Why couldn't they look dainty and more feminine? Why was I cursed to be so muscular and flat-chested? My hands were huge and coarse, and my face…

Surely, if he were normal, Dr. Sinclair would find my face lovely, wouldn't he?

I raised a strong, hairy finger to my lips, and I pretended that the finger belonged to Dr. Sinclair. Shutting my eyes, I tried to fantasize, but as always, failed. It was too far out of the realm of possibility.

I knew the truth: my face was as masculine and ugly as the rest of me. I forced my lips into a smile. My mouth exercises, as I thought of them. If I sat with a forced smile for long enough, perhaps my mouth wouldn't be perpetually downturned and angry-looking.

It was no wonder I was an old maid. Even Dr. Sinclair, who was single and available, didn't view me as female, but rather, as a piece of muscle he could put to use herding up inmates, slamming them into Eshockers and strapping them onto treatment tables.

My uniform smelled of inmates' vomit and sweat. I'd leave later, clean myself up, and get back here for my day shift. But for now, it was enough to enjoy the simple quiet and peace, the luxury of *calm* in this dark hall.

I shut my eyes and let my head drop. The faint ticking of the nurses' clock lulled me to sleep. So relaxing, *so relaxing...*

"Errrr! You cheatin' scoundrel! Those ain't me undergarments!"

My head snapped up. I almost fell off the chair, but grasped the seat just in time and steadied myself.

Cackling came from Room 18, five doors down from my chair. It had to be Mrs. van der Kolk babbling in her sleep, for had she been awake and thinking about her cheating husband, she'd be screaming steadily. Nothing else stirred on the floor: all the other inmates snored and dozed peacefully through Mrs. van der Kolk's cackling. I hoped she hadn't awakened Caroline Brown, who slept in the same room.

Irritated that she'd awakened *me*, I pulled myself to my aching feet, stretched my neck and shoulders, and yawned.

I'd better go shut her up before she awakened the whole hall. That was all I needed, wasn't it, a hall full of lunatics screaming in the middle of the night, with nobody here to help me subdue them?

Ah, now that Caroline, she was a *true* beauty, everything I was not. Seventeen and in her prime—though sadly, insane—Caroline caught the eyes of all the men who worked at Whitechapel. Even Dr. Sinclair lusted for her, and he never thought about much other than his damned Eshockers.

The cackling subsided, and I sagged back down on the chair seat.

At the far end of the hall by the nurses' desk, someone else started chattering: "The Eshockers! The beast! It ain't nothin' but evil!"

Even in the dark, I knew the sounds came from the broom closet known as Room 5.

Acid rose and burned in my stomach. My nerves started skittering. I willed myself to remain calm, but it didn't work. It rarely did.

That damned Willie Jacobs. He'd wake up the whole lot of them. Of all the lunatics—all of whom I pitied something terrible—only one truly got on my nerves. Only one made me want to scream and bash my head against the wall. Only one—with his shrill screaming voice, his pus, his odors—

Willie Jacobs.

Lately, he'd not been spending the night in his bed. He'd been off somewhere, helping Dr. Sinclair with some strange task until after midnight. I'd hoped to get some peace and quiet tonight, but here he was, as loud and annoying as ever. Dr. Sinclair had gone home early, perhaps releasing Jacobs from his mystery task.

"Get your 'ands off me!" Jacobs shrieked from down the hall. "I won't 'elp you no more! No, don't make me, don't!"

He typically screamed in his sleep.

In fact, he was probably jabbing his nose while he screamed in his sleep. The man couldn't seem to take his hands off his nose, and I couldn't bear watching him to the point that, once last week, I'd strapped his wrists to the bed posts. He'd screamed bloody murder all night, and I'd been forced to unleash his wrists—and with them, his fingers, those jabbing, poking fingers that never left his nostrils.

If I held his hands behind his back, he'd rub his nose on the nearest wall, ledge, or piece of furniture.

Once, I'd actually caught him rubbing his nose on the side of an Eshocker—*while being Eshocked*. Dr. Sinclair had yelled at me to leave the room. He didn't want witnesses to his oh so very clever little Eshocking treatments, as if Miss Klune and I and a host of others who worked here didn't already know what the Doctor was doing. *As if...*

On my feet again, angry now, I padded quickly down the hall, my tread soundless in my special nurse's shoes.

I knew how to be quiet at night.

I knew how to let the patients sleep.

I respected the people around me—*didn't I?*

But Willie Jacobs didn't respect anyone around *him*.

Well, I'd shut him up, and for good.

I had just reached Room 18, where Mrs. van der Kolk and the beautiful Caroline Brown slept, when Willie Jacobs's screaming ceased. I paused, tense, and waited for the screaming to begin again, but all was quiet. He'd settled back into the same drug-induced sleep as the other inmates.

Inmates. Patients. Lunatics. What was the difference, really? They were all the same.

Insane, and sad.

Nothing to live for but death itself.

Like me, I thought, allowing myself a moment of self-pity, but quickly I snapped out of. *No, I'm nothing like the lunatics. I serve Dr. Sinclair, and I serve the Whitechapel Lunatic Asylum. My life has meaning. My life has purpose. I'm essential to the well-being of everyone here.*

I pressed my ear to the door of Room 18. Mrs. van der Kolk's snoring rose and fell in an even cadence. I didn't hear a peep from Caroline Brown, but she never snored. The young rarely snore as loudly as the old.

What must it be like for Caroline, to be locked up at such a young age, knowing she'd never be free?

Yes, this poor girl suffered even more than I did.

There... what was that? A whimper? Did I hear her whimper?

My mind flitted again to Dr. Sinclair, so arrogant, so *commanding*. He demanded that I ease the suffering of these patients. And I knew that, in his heart, he probably did indeed lust after Caroline, and he probably pitied her more than he pitied anyone.

He wants me to help you, Caroline, I thought. *The Doctor commands that I help you. Help you, dear, help you...*

In that moment, my decision was clear. I would help Caroline Brown in the only way I knew how. Then, come morning, Dr. Sinclair would no longer have to pity her. He would no longer feel that he'd failed her. I would save her—for the Doctor.

Creeping down to the nurses' station, I obtained what I needed. Then I slipped back into the dark hall and padded quietly back to Room 18.

I twisted the knob. It turned easily, and silently.

Entering the room, I was engulfed in total darkness, for in here, there was no light, but for the faintest of glimmers from the nurses' gas lamp down the hall. I blinked until my eyes adjusted to the black. And there, to the left, I saw the dim outline of a bed: dark gray on black. A figure heaved up and down, snoring and wheezing. Mrs. van der Kolk. I turned to the right-hand bed and saw the outline of another figure, this one slim, tiny like a child, and quiet. Caroline.

Not such a child, are you? I thought. *You, with your seventeen-year-old breasts and legs, your angelic face, your high cheekbones and blue eyes topped with golden hair. You are everything I wanted to be when I was your age.*

Instead, I had lived on the street, filthy, starving, and sinfully ugly. I could only imagine the favors I would have been granted, the food I would have been given, the perfumes, the shoes, the warm coats, the adoration, hugs, kisses, and more...

Had I just looked like you, Caroline.

From the pocket of my uniform, I removed the hypodermic needle and the vial.

Don't worry, dear. It will be quick.

Mercy.

Patience.

Service.

I was a good nurse.

I stroked her hair. It was long and silky. I knelt by her bed and smelled her hair: fragrant, even in this pit they called the Whitechapel Lunatic Asylum. I stroked her cheek, soft, and her neck, also soft.

Then I almost laughed. *How amusing*, I thought, *that Caroline thinks she is Joan of Arc, one of the strongest and most forceful women in history.* Joan had led men into battle, had crushed the enemies of her king. But in the end, poor Joan had been captured, tried for witchcraft and heresy, and she'd been burned at the stake when she was but two years older than Caroline herself.

Sorry, Caroline, dear, but you won't be named a patron saint of anywhere. You are not Joan of Arc. You are a simpleton. A lunatic. A sad and deranged girl with no future.

I felt the inside of her arm by the elbow. We injected these patients on a daily basis. There, I found the nub where we dosed Caroline to calm her down and put her to sleep.

On the bed, she spasmed slightly, rolled to her back. I thought I saw her eyes flutter open, but only for a moment.

I'd better make this quick.

With my long years of practice, it took no time at all to fill the needle and inject the drug into Caroline's arm.

No more suffering, dear. It's all over now. You can rest easy, for there'll be no tomorrow for you to worry over.

She grunted, and briefly, her arm twisted and tensed. Her body stiffened, then relaxed.

I placed my ear on her right breast—*lucky girl, you are indeed perfectly formed*—and listened to her heart beating. I could feel her lungs gently filling, lifting her breast ever so slightly.

Beat, beat, beat…

Breath, breath, breath…

Beat. A long pause. Breath. A long pause.

And now: *nothing.*

I stroked her hair and cheek again, kissed her forehead, and tucked her in as I would a toddler.

I love you, Caroline. You're safe from pain and harm now. Dr. Sinclair will never touch you. And it won't hurt him to see you suffer so. I love you, Doctor. I did this for you, Doctor.

I would have made such a good mother. It was a shame I was past the age of bearing children.

My heart swelled. *I am so kind, good, and dedicated.*

I slid the needle and empty vial into my pocket, and as I rose to leave, saw something out of the corner of my eye: Willie Jacobs. He'd been in the hall outside the door. Had he seen? Had he seen what I'd done?

I darted to the door, snicked it shut behind me, and peered down the long hallway. The door to Room 5 was closed. Nobody was in the hall.

Had I imagined Willie Jacobs? Was the night playing tricks on me?

I padded to the nurses' station and disposed of the used needle and empty vial. The clock gently ticked. Three chimes told me it was 3 a.m.

Willie Jacobs was insane and dying.

Did it really matter what he'd seen or not seen? Did it really matter whether he lived or died?

26
DR. JOHN WATSON

London

During the day, the smoking room of the Diogenes Club was devoid of all but the most elderly men. Even those wealthy or clever enough to avoid work did not lounge in the club until shortly before the supper hour.

In fact, everyone in the room appeared at least twice my age, if not older. I'd never met my grandfathers, and looking around now, I wondered if any of these gentlemen resembled my kin in any way. Grumpy, scowling, sporting a cane and a twirling mustache? Bald, dressed in a dapper fashion, trim and debonair, preferring which newspaper— the *London Daily News* or the *Morning Post*?

I beckoned to the impeccably groomed butler, holding up the note I had composed. His refined dignity reminded me of Pontose, whose master Lord Wiltshram had been murdered during our adventure in Avebury. Stiff and formal, Pontose had served Wiltshram while privately loathing the latter's occupation as a leader of the Order of Dagon. After the murder, traumatized, Pontose had disappeared. But poise was the only similarity between the two men. This fellow before me now was taller than Pontose, and his face was more narrow with a fat nose that looked oddly out of place on it.

I placed a note for Sherlock Holmes on his silver tray, and the butler bowed slightly then swiveled like a Queen's Guard on parade and walked toward the door leading to the back rooms.

Without Holmes, the rooms at Baker Street felt as empty and silent as the Diogenes Club. No, that wasn't true, his lodgings weren't as quiet as it was *here*, for there I had the company of Mrs. Hudson, flitting about, stuffing me with home-cooked meals and biscuits, worrying incessantly about Holmes's well-being.

Still, it didn't feel quite right to occupy the place without Holmes present. I dared not touch his violin, his chemistry equipment, the papers he'd strewn all over the sitting room. Everything awaited his return.

Someone touched my shoulder. I turned, smiling broadly, but my smile faded for a moment when I realized it wasn't Holmes.

"Inspector Lestrade," I said, offering my hand. "I am delighted to see you."

While he shook my hand, his eyes darted around the room.

I fear my face reddened, for in the surprise of the moment, I'd forgotten that we were in the Diogenes, where speaking was considered a criminal act.

Wordlessly, I mouthed "sorry, sorry" to the elderly members who glared at me before returning to their perusal of the morning papers.

Flustered but motioning to Lestrade to sit, I flipped my tails back, sat in my wing chair, and crossed my legs, hoping to recover my dignity. Lestrade was impatient, jittery, quivering in his chair and nervously fingering the armrests. His eyes continued to dart around the room. This case, with creatures in the Thames and all of London seemingly afflicted with mental conditions, had unnerved him.

The fire crackled. Several men in the surrounding leather seats jumped, glared at the fire, and then returned to their papers.

The library door silently swung open, and Sherlock Holmes stepped into the smoking room. The thick rug muffled any noise his shoes might have made. Upon reaching us, his eyes twinkled and he smiled warmly. It was a fine thing to see him, I must say, and I sprang up to return his greeting, thinking perhaps Holmes missed me as much as I missed him. Certainly, his good cheer could not be explained by the presence of Lestrade.

He motioned at us to follow him to the Stranger's Room, where we could talk, and once again, I found myself perched on the splintered stool by the window. Holmes settled into the Gothic chair, slouched down, and crossed his legs at the ankles, leaving Lestrade to sit in the large chair previously occupied by Mycroft.

"And now," Holmes said, "let us get to the matter at hand."

"Which is?" I asked.

"Mr. Holmes called us here," Lestrade piped up, "because he wants the Yard's help in obtaining farm animals."

"What?" I exclaimed. "What is this, Holmes?"

"Relax, Doctor. The Inspector is playing the dramatist."
Lestrade glowered at him.

"No drama about it," he said, "for you told me yourself,
Mr. Holmes, that you wanted to discuss the procurement
of domesticated animals." The Inspector turned to me,
his short body twitching with anxiety. "Dr. Watson, for
the life of me, I don't know what he wants, but I am so
perplexed by what has afflicted London that I will take
help at any corner."

"And so, Holmes," I asked, "what do you have in mind?"

Holmes drew himself up in the uncomfortable chair and
winced.

"I must talk to Mycroft about the furnishings of this
room," he said. "I know the club discourages visitors, but
for those of us who are forced to entertain others here,
certainly the club can provide more comfortable chairs."
His brow creased, then he trained his eyes on me.

"My dear friend, I encourage you to take more rest. You
are evidently exhausted." Seeing my surprise, he quickly
added, "I don't mean to upset you. I am *concerned*. Do you
still feel dazed, or has your head cleared?"

"I am fine, merely suffering at being apart from Mary
and Samuel," I said, though I was not fine at all. As it did—
more and more often now—my vision had blurred. Wisps
of symbols and colors floated in the air. I could not trust
my own eyes, and I would never admit to anyone, not even
Holmes, how worried I was about my mental condition.
"What is this about farm animals?"

"I asked Lestrade to join us here because I need brain
tissues from creatures that are yet alive. Although the tissue

will no longer be functioning normally after removal, we may yet see processes or structures that no longer appear after a creature is long dead.

"For example," he continued, "you may not know that when we first met I was in the process of testing how far bodies could bruise after death. If skin cells continue functioning for a short time, might not brain cells do the same? I contacted Lestrade and requested his help in this matter."

"Yes," Lestrade murmured, "yes, you did. You see, Dr. Watson, Holmes is worried that, should you and he vivisect a farm animal without a license, we might prosecute and jail you both. Is that correct, Mr. Holmes?"

"It is not," Holmes said curtly. "Vivisection is not an easy skill, and I do not know of any surgeon in England who has the requisite skills for performing such a delicate and dangerous task on livestock. I mean to study the cells after death, Inspector, not before—but as close to the point of death as possible. I have seen reports of livestock showing unusual neurological symptoms. Where can I obtain fresh brain tissue from such an animal?"

"You refer to animals afflicted with the same condition we have seen in humans in Whitechapel?" I asked. "But how do you know that there *are* farm animals with such an affliction?"

"Simple, Watson. Lestrade, please, show the good doctor the news clippings, will you?"

"Certainly." Lestrade pulled a small sheaf of folded clippings from his coat pocket and thrust them at me.

"Why, these are from Avebury," I said in surprise. The same place Holmes and I had risked our lives to root out the Order of Dagon. We'd attended a deadly performance of the opera, *Norma*, and infiltrated the mansion of Dagon leader Professor Fitzgerald. It did not thrill me that strange occurrences yet emanated from Avebury.

"Sheep and cows grazing in the Avebury meadows have been slamming into fences, crying out non-stop," Lestrade told me. "When approached by humans, the animals grow violent, and their eyes whirl. Several farmers, risking economic ruin and the possible starvation of their families, have shot their own animals, fearing an outbreak of the infection."

Holmes frowned. "I think these farmers might be inclined to allow us, Doctor, to take tissue samples from these poor animals, but I don't want to be captured in the act and accused of criminal activity. The voices of anti-vivisectionists have grown strong."

"You have authorized us to obtain the brain tissues?" I asked the Inspector.

"I have arranged for others to authorize it for you," he nodded, "as the matter is considered serious. The Yard won't risk doing something as peculiar as what Mr. Holmes proposes ourselves, but, sir," he turned to Holmes, "we know you well enough to trust your judgment."

It was a high compliment, indeed. While Holmes often helped Lestrade solve his cases, he rarely wanted Lestrade's thanks or admiration. These were not motivating forces behind Holmes's pursuit of truth in matters of crime. Rather, he felt compelled to solve mysteries and puzzles that nobody else could.

Lestrade supplied us with signed documents.

"Present these to Mr. Gerald Waltham," he said, "at the location indicated on the attached map. Waltham fears bankruptcy. His flock of sheep now races around his fields like a pack of mad dogs. He is expecting you."

Holmes jumped up.

"Then there's no time to waste. Shall we, Doctor?"

"One moment, Mr. Holmes," said Lestrade. "The note you sent asking me to come here also asked me to look into a Bligh Braithwaite."

"That's correct," said Holmes. "Watson, you remember that was the name of Sinclair's new patient."

Lestrade went on, "We've found no connection between Braithwaite and those names you mentioned. Not Fitzgerald, nor Ashberton, Wiltshram, Pontose, Jacobs, Beiler. Not Reginald Sinclair, nor Clara Klune, nor Amy Switzer—aside from the asylum connection between those last three and Willie Jacobs, that is. But the funny thing is that the Kandinsky Asylum has been asking Sinclair to send Braithwaite back to them ever since he was found."

"Braithwaite has not come up in our investigation, Holmes. Why ever did you ask about him?" I asked.

"Braithwaite showed up under peculiar circumstances and was admitted to the Whitechapel Lunatic Asylum despite their lack of available rooms. They regularly turn away sick people, even those who sleep on the reception room floor and beg for admittance. So why, I wonder, did the asylum admit Bligh Braithwaite so readily?"

27

PROFESSOR MORIARTY

Half Moon Bay

I'd extracted as much information as I was going to get out of Amelia Scarcliffe—at least, for now. Down four agents, I'd been forced to send her to London with Michael. Perhaps some time spent in the squalor of Whitechapel would bring her round to the idea of becoming my informant.

Archibald galloped ahead of me on the path leading through the woods—inland but parallel to the coast. We'd rustled two horses from their sleeping owners and galloped far from Half Moon Bay at as fast a pace as the animals could manage.

The farther we rode, the sparser grew the mistletoe, the less vibrant the colors of the tree bark, the dead leaves, the evergreens.

Archibald's horse crashed through the brush ahead. It was a fine creature, and hardy, which was just as well, since Archibald was tall and built like a heavyweight champion. He had a strong future, this Archibald. He was brash and intelligent, with a cocky swagger, hard glinting eyes, a face scarred by knife fights. Now was his chance to prove himself.

The kidnapping of Maria Fitzgerald would be a reasonable step in that direction. We hadn't found her anywhere at Half Moon Bay, but Archibald had told me there was only one orphanage in the area.

My horse slowed, ears back, flanks heaving. I kicked it into a reluctant canter, but I had lost Archibald. This was not the place to fail on me. The land north-west of Half Moon Bay was sparsely populated; there were few resting places for two kidnappers. If I could steal another horse, I'd get rid of this one. It was too weak for my taste—unless cooked in a nice stew with potatoes.

Eventually, the trail widened and opened into a village made up of a few cottages set among the trees. Archibald had already dismounted; he flagged me to do the same.

"Horses need water," he said, pulling a cigarette from an inner pocket and striking a match on his shoe. His voice was gruff from incessant smoking. He cleared his throat and spat, then sucked hard on the cigarette so the tip glowed brightly and melted back a quarter inch. He held the smoke in his lungs and eyed me, as if appraising me.

"You agree?" he said in a cloud of exhaled smoke.

I didn't want to stop, and I didn't care about the horses and their need for water. But we hadn't seen any other horses for a long time, and I didn't want mine to drop dead under me—not without a replacement handy.

So I nodded and gave him a quick but cold smile.

"As you say, Archibald. Water it is. But I see no cattle trough here—only a well without a bucket. Come on, let's knock on this cottage door and make our request for a bucket or two of water."

"Aye, sir." His lips did not break into a smile, and I liked that—his purely professional attitude.

We tied our horses to trees, and he tossed down his cigarette and ground it out. We crunched over pine needles and twigs toward the nearest cottage.

"How are you gonna calm down this Scarcliffe woman?" Archibald caught me looking at him and quickly pulled his gaze away.

Good. He was afraid of me.

Sometimes, it was best to keep one's strongest men on the tightest leashes. Keep them closest, for they were the ones with the ambition and intellect to attempt a coup.

"I know how to charm a woman," I answered, "*any* woman."

"She was screaming, boss, and more violent than the ugliest street walker."

"No matter," I said, negotiating the creaking wooden steps leading to the cottage door. "It's almost amusing. She claims she won't cooperate with me if I hurt her dear Koenraad Thwaite or her unborn spawn. Yes, she actually used the word, *spawn*. One has to laugh, doesn't one?"

He chuckled and gave me a knowing look.

"Aye, these women can get silly when they're in the... family way. But she also says her lover, this Thwaite, will kill *you* if we don't return her to him."

I rapped twice on the door. There was no sound from within the cottage.

"You believe this is possible, Archibald? That Thwaite possesses the skill to kill *me*?"

"Oh, no, boss, absolutely not."

I knocked again, then tried the handle. The door swung open. In the middle of nowhere, apparently the inhabitants didn't fear robberies.

Good for us, I thought, *bad for them*.

It was a one-room affair. Stale odor, like ale splattered in an unkempt room. The fireplace was cold, but we found some chunks of what appeared to be roasted rabbit on the table. Archibald stuffed the meat into a satchel along with some home-bottled brew he found in a small cupboard. We found several buckets in a low cupboard, which we filled from the well for the horses. We were happy to come out of the oppressive atmosphere of the cottage; we sat outside with the horses, cracked open the brew and downed it. I hadn't realized my thirst until seeing the drinks, and I was quietly thankful for Archibald's good sense in having us stop. We watched the horses graze, the sweat drying on their skin.

"Now let's get out of here," I said, "before the inhabitant of this place returns. He's a hunting man, for sure, and I don't feel like being hunted today."

As the hours passed, we stopped twice more to water the horses, and to let them graze in a field. Eventually, we swerved up a narrow path leading to a ridge, where we stopped. Tying our mounts to a lone tree, we contemplated the small building that lay before us. A hand-painted sign above the building proclaimed, ORFANS.

Archibald pulled out his sack of meat, stuffed some in his mouth, and chewed. The smell was rancid, and when he offered me some, I refused. Instead, I drank another of the dark beers.

"This must be the orphanage," I said drily. "It does not appear particularly high class."

"All the better for us. We can snatch the girl and make a quick escape."

I grabbed his arm and held him back for a moment.

"Remember," I said, "that Maria Fitzgerald is very powerful, perhaps more so than Amelia Scarcliffe. When the girl strikes, you won't see it coming. Scarcliffe commands mistletoe to kill her enemies. Think about *that*, Archibald."

His rough-textured face, hardened by the wind and winter sun, paled. His eyes narrowed, as he looked nervously at the orphanage. Smoke curled from a chimney in the center of the small structure.

"Your men told me about what's in the Thames: creatures flitting over the water, disappearing before their eyes," Archibald said.

"Take care approaching the girl. By all accounts she's very young," I told him. "But she's dangerous. Do not let her age fool you."

Imagine if I could harness the power of Maria and the Scarcliffe woman, harness the power and the terror of this Dagon gang. Imagine if I could get the females to control the power of those creatures for me! If I could command and control the creatures... I could rule the world, not just London, but the world.

We crept to the back of the orphanage. From inside, we heard sounds of life—chairs scraping across a wood floor, an old woman cackling, a man grunting orders, a child whining. I had no desire to kill children. But I would do whatever was required to kidnap Maria.

My objectives were not grounded solely in greed and power. I viewed myself as Sherlock Holmes viewed himself. A superior intellect trapped in a world gripped by stupidity and boredom. Logic fighting for life in a world saturated in religion and superstition. I knew what was best. With more power, I could make things happen. Perhaps Holmes could achieve my goals, as well, but he was too immersed in solving petty crimes and congratulating himself with his do-gooder arrogance.

For a man to truly be powerful and change the world, he had to be willing to break the rules, to speak out as he thought fit, to take actions that others would think too bold, too outrageous, too cunning, too dangerous.

I signaled for Archibald to break down the back door. I would let him lead the way, subdue any adults stupid enough to think they could fight us off, and then I would follow.

Kicking open the door, he darted inside. I smelled cooking meat, and my stomach growled. I was hungry, and the meat smelled fragrant and fresh and very unlike the rancid chunks my companion had just consumed.

"What's the meaning of this?" a man demanded.

I raced in behind Archibald. To my right, he'd grabbed the man—an old fellow, flabby, with a red nose and a fat neck and swollen cheeks—from behind, wrenching him off his feet. Nearby, a woman, heavily wrinkled with brown blotches marking her face, opened a toothless mouth and shrieked. I whirled her around, shook her, and yelled at her to shut up. Her face displaying shock, she complied, mouth sucking her gums, hand dropping a cane, which clattered across the floor.

Several children huddled in a corner by a rocking chair. Two tiny boys and one slightly older girl—she must be about six years old. *Maria?*

The man struggled and cursed in Archibald's grip, and finally, Archibald snarled, "I didn't want to have to do this, mate," and slammed the man's head against the log wall. The man slumped in Archibald's arms, and Archibald dropped him to the floor, turning to the children. They hugged each other, edging away from him with their eyes glazed in fear.

"Pl-please, d-don't hurt the children," the old lady wept. Without her cane to support her, she had fallen to the floor. "They are but orphans."

"And which one of these fine children is named Maria?" My eyes swept over the three, honing in on the sole girl. "Would that be you, sweetheart?" I asked.

She unlatched herself from the others and scrambled to her feet, drawing herself up proudly, as if no longer afraid of me. A capital mistake.

"I am Maria Fitzgerald." She had a faint accent I couldn't place. "What might you want with me, sir?"

"She doesn't look scary to me." Archibald was keeping his eyes on the flabby man, who twitched upon the floor, his forehead gashed and oozing blood.

"How would you like to join my friend here and me for some lovely tea, some biscuits and perhaps a cake or two?" I asked the girl. "How about a hot meal and a soft bed? We'd like to bring you to London, where you are more suited, you must agree, than you are to an orphanage in the forest."

She shook her head, the mop of black hair on her head

swinging by her ears. Her hair was short, as if it had been roughly chopped by a butcher's knife. Her eyes, wide and green, were highly expressive and beautiful.

"I won't go with you," she said, "for we've not been properly introduced. First, you must tell me, sir, who you are and what you want with me. I also object to the manner in which you've treated Mr. Gunshaw, who has been nothing but kind and generous to me."

I marveled at the self-possession of the child. She exuded a maturity beyond her years.

Mr. Gunshaw, the fellow on the floor, rolled to a sitting position, then grabbed hold of the rocking chair to steady himself. He stood, still grasping the chair, then sank into it.

Behind him, the fireplace roared and filled the small room with tremendous heat. It was a giant round fireplace inside a stone-built circle that stood waist high. A cooking pot swung on a hook over the flames. I was sweating beneath my coat and collar. Archibald's face had broken out with sweat, as well, which he wiped off with a sleeve.

I extended both arms with my palms up. I stepped toward the girl. Toward Maria, daughter of a French Dagonite leader and a dead soprano.

"Your father speaks highly of you," I lied.

"My father?" Clearly, she was startled. "How do you know of my father?" She stepped back, arms stretched behind her. Her eyes grew wider and seemed to bore into me.

"He is a most powerful man, is he not?"

"He is in jail," she said.

Ah, so she still thought her father was Professor Henry Fitzgerald. Her mother must not have told her the truth.

"I want to take you to your father."

"Well, I refuse to see him!" she said. "I didn't know of his existence until a short time ago, and then he refused to acknowledge me. I want nothing to do with him."

"Leave the girl be," Gunshaw said. "She's done nothing to you. Her father sent her here, to an orphanage. Surely, you can't be thinking she belongs back with him?"

"Enough of this," I said curtly, my patience wearing thin. "Every moment I waste talking to you, Mr. Gunshaw, is a moment that costs me *money*. This girl is coming with me, and it's best for you to stay out of the matter."

"But I refuse!" he cried, hoisting his bulk from the rocking chair and throwing himself at Archibald. Stupid man, he started beating Archibald's solid chest with his bloated fists—*like a little girl might fight*, I thought—and Archibald just grabbed both wrists in his hands and shoved the man off him.

The old lady clawed at my ankles. I looked down. She had crawled over to me on her stomach. Now, her face looked up at me.

"Pl-please..." she moaned.

I shook her off and turned my attention back to the girl.

"Come quietly and peacefully," I said, "please." I held out a hand to her.

"No!" She turned on her heel and ran to a little door I hadn't noticed till then, wrenching it open. It took nothing for me to grab her by the waist and pull her back. I kicked the door shut. She squirmed, but I held tight. Reaching into my pocket, I whipped out a cloth, balled it, and stuffed it into her mouth.

I bound her wrists behind her back with some nearby rags and tied her ankles together. Nicely trussed and ready for a long ride, she was.

Blood pounded in my head. My nerves were all a-skitter. I loved this feeling, this rush of excitement that always came when I'd conquered an enemy, acquired a weapon.

In the meantime, Gunshaw had launched himself at Archibald, beating his fists against the mounds of chest muscle to no avail. Archibald put up with it, I have to give him his due, until finally, he'd had enough of the old fool. He shoved Gunshaw into the rocking chair, and the fat man flew back into it with such force that the whole chair crashed over, sending Gunshaw to the floor. At that, Archibald pulled back his right leg. I knew what was coming, and I wasn't disappointed. Several violent kicks later, Gunshaw lay moaning and holding his stomach.

I hoisted up Maria, cradling her in my arms like a baby. She couldn't fight me. She was all trussed up like a goose for dinner.

Gunshaw was openly weeping, more a baby than the little girl, who did *not* cry.

"Shut up," Archibald growled, "I said, *shut up.*" But the man continued blubbering.

I prodded aside the woman—I was gentle, for what danger could the old crone possibly pose?—and stepped gingerly toward the door.

I had Maria Fitzgerald.

I had her!

"Archibald, let's—" I stopped mid-sentence.

Archibald had dragged the fat man by his collar across the

floor to the roaring fire. He thrust the man onto the waist-high stone circle. The meat pot swung on its hook. Already, the flames whipped Gunshaw's shirt, and the man shrieked.

"No! Let me go! No! Don't do this!"

"You don't know when to shut your mouth," Archibald growled, "and I'm going to teach you what happens to a man with a big mouth."

With that, he shoved Gunshaw over and into the fire pit. The fat man's head hit the metal pot with a loud *clang* as fire swept over his body, melting and cooking his flesh. He screamed until the very end, and I stood, transfixed, always loving a good show, be it dynamite or death by fire. His last scream fizzled as the flames consumed him, setting his skin crackling.

In my arms, the girl squirmed. I glanced at her eyes, huge and round and filled with terror. The door to the back room stood open. The two boys were probably hiding under their beds.

Archibald scooped up the old lady, who struggled and shrieked as he hoisted her and tossed her into the flames. She went into the fire in a flurry of apron and skirts, scrawny-bone legs with purple veins, and puffs of white hair. She tried to lift herself, but failed. The fire consumed her neck, her arms, her head. The smoke was so thick in the room that I couldn't breathe, and I choked on the reek of her charred flesh.

She wouldn't have lived long anyway, so what did it really matter?

Archibald hitched up his trousers and laughed. It was a hearty laugh that rang on and on.

"Damn, if that isn't great!" He slapped a wall with his hand and strode to the door, where I stood with Maria.

Maria's green eyes shone like glass, focused, *unblinking*, on Archibald. Bound tightly, she couldn't move her legs or her arms, nor could she speak with the cloth balled in her mouth.

But her eyes...

Her thin eyebrows rose higher, almost reaching her hair. The round face grew rounder, almost to a sphere. On her neck, tiny bubbles of flesh protruded and jiggled. Dozens of bubbles now rocked in harmony, bobbing as if to an unheard melody.

Suddenly, like a bullet, the cloth shot from her mouth and hit Archibald's chest. He screamed and doubled over, then rose slightly and clawed at his chest. When he removed his hands, they were bloody. He stared at them in disbelief, then looked at Maria in shock.

I nearly dropped her, but held on, for I feared the result of setting her free. But my hands shook, and for a moment, I knew not what to do.

She muttered syllables that made no sense.

"*Aauhaoaoa demoni aauhaoaoa demoni aauhaoaoa demoni. Ch'thgalhn fhtagn urre'h nyogthluh'eeh ngh syh'kyuhyuh.*"

Blood soaked Archibald's shirt. His eyes closed. His face went white. And then *something invisible* swept him up and threw him into the fire pit onto the bones of Gunshaw and the old crone.

Archibald was gone.

I stared down at Maria, still in my arms, and suddenly

I *believed*. There was no trickery here; there had been no trickery in Amelia Scarcliffe's cottage. This child—this *creature*—had real power, inexplicable power. I had to get her back to London—but how? What if she killed me?

"You have Amelia Scarcliffe?" she murmured.

I nodded, dumbfounded.

"Then take me to her. I know of her, of others. I know more than you will ever know. Together, she and I are more potent than anything you can imagine, even in your nightmares. If you work for me, if you do my bidding, I'll consider letting you live."

At that moment, I would have agreed to just about anything.

Though once we returned to London, I would keep Maria separated from Amelia Scarcliffe until I was ready to use them both for my own purposes.

The girl shivered when we left the hot confines of the orphanage. The air was sweet and cold, but the smell of burning flesh still clogged my nostrils. It wouldn't do for Maria to get sick, not when I needed her. I returned to the cabin, trying not to breathe the stench of burning flesh. I grabbed a blanket from a back room, where the two boys held each other, shaking, and I wrapped it around the shivering girl.

Outside again, I strapped her across Archibald's horse, and then the two of us rode off into the woods.

28
DR. JOHN WATSON

Avebury, Wiltshire

The wind nearly blew my cap off, and I clamped it to my head with one hand while keeping my other hand tucked into my coat pocket. The carriage that had brought us into Avebury clattered off, its driver anxious to find new custom on a night where nobody with any sense would dare venture from home.

Slicing down my calf, the cold knifed my leg, and I winced with every step. Beside me, Holmes pushed against the gale, his body upright, his eyes focused on the inn that was a blur behind the sleet sweeping past us.

"How are we going to find infected sheep and cows in this storm?" I screamed above the wind.

Holmes shouted something back, but I couldn't make out his answer.

I hobbled by his side, and despite the storm, I can't say that I was anxious to get to our destination, the Loggerheads. We had stayed at the inn during our last visit to Avebury, and our room had been smelly and dilapidated. And all night, I'd been kept awake by incantations and the screeching of tuneless singing; I had never determined the source of the disturbance.

Holmes wrenched open the outer door to the place, and we stepped inside. Instantly, the cold and the wet gave way to the warmth of the fireplace, and the odors of stale beer and rotting fish.

Settled on stools by the fireplace, three men huddled and chattered in a language I did not know. Their words, high-pitched and guttural, wobbling from high to low and then back again, reminded me of the gibberish of the Dagon-worshiping cultists that Holmes and I had encountered at Swallowhead Spring, and later, at the Thames warehouse.

I touched Holmes's arm, and we exchanged a glance.

Their garb was similar to that of other Dagonites we had encountered, which we had found was designed to hide the deformities unique to this group. All three men wore shirts that hid their necks from view. All three wore baggy knee-length trousers slung low on their hips. Beneath the tattered trouser legs, greenish flesh bulged with muscles where no man should have muscles. Enormous slippers, crafted from what appeared to be gray animal hide, clad feet twice the size of a large man's foot. Each slipper bowed outward, forming a vaguely triangular shape.

One man lifted a webbed hand, and with a needlelike fingertip, started to rub the left side of his head—a bloated head, inflated like a toy ball, devoid of hair but splotched with a mahogany-colored scab the size of a bread plate. Rhythmically, he rubbed, up and down, up and down, pricking it, wincing, and then smearing a green ooze of what I presumed to be diseased blood across his forehead.

Another of the men—this one having a flattened face with a nose crushed into it, and two protruding eyes that goggled at me—slopped off his stool. Brown slime dripped from the vacated seat and pooled by his feet.

Holmes regained his composure before I regained mine.

"Gentlemen," he said, "please do not be alarmed. We are mere wanderers in need of a room for the night. My companion and I have stayed here before, and not so long ago. Mrs. Hinds, who runs this place, knows us. Would you kindly tell us where she might be, so that we may obtain our room and get a much-needed night's rest? Our journey has been long."

Something crackled in the fireplace, and the light dimmed. The other two men slid from their stools to stand beside the one who confronted us. The one with the bloated head and green-oozing scab cracked open a smile that slit the lower part of his face in two. I slicked the sleet from my face, trying to appear nonchalant while fear swept through me. The man with goggle eyes lifted a much-too-long arm and pointed at the door we had entered by.

"You best be on your way," he said. "There's no place for you here. You're not one of us."

"And what might you *be*, sir?" Holmes asked, hastily adding, "No offense meant, I assure you."

"Offense taken, *sir*," the other snarled. "Your rules don't apply here. We have no need for human pleasantries. No need for humans at all." At this, all three burst out laughing and muttered guttural gibberish at each other. Then abruptly, one reached to the fireplace implements and lifted the iron shovel.

"I suggest you move along," he said. "The Loggerheads is for our kind now, and only our kind. It's the Loggerheads den." He paused, eyes whirling, then added, "Unless, of course, you're here for Eshocking. Then perhaps we can accommodate you."

This was one of Moriarty's Eshocker dens? I could barely stifle my surprise.

"Yes," Holmes said quickly, his eyes on the shovel, "you have divined correctly. That is what we came for."

With a few grunts, the man rapped the shovel on the fireplace grille three times. Everything always seemed to be in increments of three with the Order of Dagon. Our erstwhile client Kristoffer Beiler had three loggerheads on his braces—an ancestral device, he'd told us. His murdered father, Amos Beiler, had constructed three items of furniture described on ancient hide. Lord Wiltshram had shown us in his Avebury home a painting of the Crest of Dagon— three green octopuses within a yellow nonagon—as well as a cherry divan made by Beiler, which balanced improbably upon three ornate posts.

Mrs. Hinds hobbled into the room, leaning on a cane.

"You know these men?" the bloated-head creature asked her.

"I do. They came when the Beiler demons drove out all the normals." She smacked her gums and eyed us. She looked more hunched over than before, if such a thing were possible. She said to us, "These gentlemen are my kin. They've been here for generations in these rooms. This is a den for contemplation and serenity and devotion."

If only there'd been another inn nearby, Holmes and I

would have raced from this place into the storm. But we did not know where to find another room in this locale, and just weeks ago Mrs. Hinds had fed us good breakfasts and kept out of our way. We'd heard the strange noises at night, but we'd encountered nothing dangerous at the Loggerheads.

"Have you a room, madam, just for one night?" I asked.

Gesturing with her cane at the three men to return to their stools, she told us that our former room was free but the cost had doubled.

"Demand," she explained, "what with the den, which is in the kitchen now, and—" she added, "there's no breakfast anymore."

Holmes assured her the arrangement would suffice. We followed her hunched figure to our old room. The door had not been fixed and still appeared broken as if by an axe. The floor remained warped, the two beds ratty and lumpy, the wallpaper shredded and stripped off where Holmes had used it to sketch diagrams.

After depositing our bags and paying Mrs. Hinds, Holmes and I made our way to the kitchen, which was indeed now one of Moriarty's dens. A bar fully stocked with Old Ones Serum stood against the far wall, and to its left stood an Eshocker, its wooden box wedged between the bar and an ancient stove. Strapped into the Eshocker chair was a creature more hideous than the three who had met us upon our arrival. A crevice dented the top of his bald scalp, and it was like a crater, possibly soft like sand from the looks of it. Veins throbbed along the edges of the crater, which pulsed—not like a heartbeat of a man, but rapidly like some strange foreign beast, I knew not what.

"On," he hissed, "turn it on, I say!"

When neither Holmes nor I complied, he kicked a lever near his foot. His wrists and ankles remained unbound to the Eshocker, unlike what we'd seen on Thrawl Street. The lever slammed against wood, metal hit metal, and *zzzzzzzap*, the room vibrated with electricity. The man's head snapped back, his mouth gaped, and he screamed in some combination of agony and glee. The smell of urine saturated the air. His body banged up and down against the chair with his hands gripping the armrests as if letting go might kill him.

"More, I want more! Fire, give me more fire!"

"Holmes, we must do something!" I cried, racing to the Eshocker and flipping the lever off.

The machine grunted and ground to a halt, quivering and then going still.

The man leapt from the chair, staggered from the impact of the electricity, and fell at my feet.

"Y-you," he cried, "y-you turned it off. I wants my money back. I wants my Eshockin'!"

I helped him to his feet, if one could call them feet. Triangular, lumpy, much too long. As I stared, I also noticed that several bizarre appendages protruded from each side of his trousers. All slim, hinged with bones—*like the snake things in the Thames warehouse*, I thought with horror—all writhing around one another, twisting themselves into braids and untwisting only to flop beneath his weight. He steadied himself upon his huge feet, and the wobbling ceased.

In this windowless room, the only light was from fat

candles set in a black iron candelabra far from the Eshocker. It flickered across his face, exposing dozens of skin flaps and fishlike scales, which shimmered under the licks of light.

Holmes grasped one of the man's arms, and I grasped the other. He looked from me to Holmes and then back again. Finally, he addressed me.

"I needs my Eshockin'," he said, "for I be not well. The pain be fierce." His eyes brimmed with tears, as he staggered and almost fell limp in our arms.

"Holmes," I said, "give the man a bottle of serum. It will ease his suffering."

Holmes released the poor fellow, snatched up a bottle of Old Ones, and opened it. Lifting the bottle to the man's lips, he poured half the contents into his open maw.

Licking his lips, the man sagged backward, and I had to throw an arm around him to keep him upright. I settled him back into the Eshocker chair, where he slouched with a dizzy grin and fluttering eyelids.

From the room by the front door, shrill incantations rang out.

"*Ufatu maehha faeatai tuatta iu iu rahi roa cthulhu rahi atu daghon da'agon f'hthul'rahi roa. Ebb'yuh dissoth'nknpflknghreet.*"

Holmes's eyes grew brighter. Like me, he must have remembered these strange sayings from our earlier dealings with the Order of Dagon.

"Do you think they've been meeting here?" I asked Holmes. The Eshocked man answered me instead.

"Ah," he said, "we been meeting here for generations. We call forth the Old Ones to come upon the Earth, reclaim what's theirs. We—" a webbed hand jabbed at his chest— "we of the Order give our lives in service. The Loggerheads is our home."

"Your home, sir?" I said, as Holmes dripped more serum between the man's lips. "Is this not an inn for travelers?"

He smacked his lips and said something sounding vaguely like "*Hahuhoaoao yuhmoni'khu'eenee'eet... Fhtagn.*"

"Yes, sir." I stumbled over my words. "And this is your home, you say?"

He nodded.

"There's a room or two, at times, for those like you. But for generations, we've lived here, met here, mated here. Now we have serums and Eshockin's, we need nothing more."

"Addicts," I murmured to Holmes, who shrugged as if to say, *Of course, what else?*

Holmes asked the man about additional dens in the Avebury area.

"Yes," came the answer, "out at Swallowhead Spring." Taking the serum bottle from Holmes with both of his webbed hands, he added, "That's where many of us died durin' *Norma*. I lost my wife an' ten children that night." He took a long swig from the bottle, draining it, and sank farther into the chair.

"It's now the Swallowhead den," he added, "run by the most powerful—"

"Lord Ashberton?" I asked.

He nodded. Ashberton was one of the Dagonites we had tangled with on our last expedition to Avebury. The last time I'd seen him, he had been running away with Henry Fitzgerald—abandoning Fitzgerald's young daughter Maria—

after the performance of *Norma* had been attacked by the monsters he worshiped. Holmes had theorized that Ashberton and Fitzgerald had brought the animals to the area to release for the performance—just as he thought Fitzgerald had done with the monsters now in the Thames. I was not so sure.

"Swallowhead den is more powerful than Loggerheads. The powers are strong there and have been for thousands of years. I can't go there again, not me, not after my family died there. I must make do with Loggerheads." He tossed the empty bottle at Holmes, who caught it deftly and put it on the bar.

"Do you know Mr. Gerald Waltham, the farmer? We hear that his pastures are by Swallowhead," Holmes said nonchalantly.

"Aye..." the man breathed the word.

"Then we shall go to Swallowhead in the morning, Watson," Holmes said.

I expected the poor fellow before us to scream that we dare not go there, just as Kristoffer Beiler had urged us not to stay at the Loggerheads. When he was silent, I lifted his chin and stared at his face. His eyes had shut, the lids trembled but slightly. His breathing was even. The crater on his head still beat rapidly, the crater-edge veins throbbing.

All night, I lay awake in my bed while Holmes peacefully slumbered. All night, my head buzzed with the words of Kristoffer Beiler: "Should you hear the shrieking in the elder language, whatever you do, don't leave your room to investigate. You could die!"

Pulling the scratchy blanket up around my neck, I squirmed while I stared at the motifs sketched along the moldering wallpaper, or what was left of it. Colors and symbols danced before my eyes—they could not be real. I shook my head, but no amount of shaking cleared my vision. All night, I prayed for the hallucinations to cease. Outside, hail clanked against the wood siding and the roof. Throughout it all, Holmes slumbered.

At the first peek of morning through the holes in the curtain rags, a cacophony of noise brought us rapidly out of our room—screaming and howling and splintering wood.

Holmes reached the Eshocker kitchen first. Mrs. Hinds was wringing her hands in the doorway. The three men who had greeted us the night before were punching the Eshocked, serum-addled crater-skull fellow, kicking him with their large triangular feet.

He curled on the floor in front of the Eshocker, trying to shield himself from the blows.

"Stop, *stop!*" Mrs. Hinds wailed.

The man with the flattened crushed-nose face slammed his arm down hard on the crater head. Holmes yanked him off his victim. Too late. The fellow on the floor was silent.

He lay in an expanding pool of blood and excrement. Green ooze flowed from the crater down all sides of his head, coating his mangled face. I'd never known of any disease to produce pus or blood of such vivid green. But then, I'd never seen a man who looked anything like this one.

The man with the bloated head kicked the victim's stomach, then his groin, his thighs, and his shins. The victim did not move. Still, the green flowed from the crater.

"Watson!" Holmes cried, shoving the crushed-nose attacker against the wall.

"This is a decent establishment," Mrs. Hinds wailed. "None of this here, boys, not here. Oh, Dr. Watson, help him."

A decent establishment, I thought, *indeed, where members of the Order of Dagon turn into mutated creatures from hell, chanting all night and beating each other up.*

I stooped, ignoring the pain shooting down my leg, and put my ear to the man's chest. Nothing. I stared closely in the feeble light of dying candles at the crater head. Were the veins still throbbing? No. I felt for a heartbeat on the green wrist. Nothing. I felt six of the spindle-like appendages— his legs—and they were as pliant as unbaked dough.

"This man is dead," I announced. "You've killed him."

Mrs. Hinds shrieked in dismay, but the three killers registered no reaction to my news. They simply didn't care.

"What's the death of one creature, Doctor?" the one with the bloated head said. "Death is irrelevant. We ain't the true inheritors of this place where we dwell. It be They from Beyond, and only They who matter. And They never die. They're of all time and of all infinity."

"But you killed him," I insisted, "and we are obliged to report your crime."

The others chortled.

"Try it," one of them threatened, "and you'll wish you never left London."

"Don't be foolish, you," said Mrs. Hinds, seeming to wake up at this. "Gentlemen, you'd best be on your way. I'll see this is reported, of course. The poor soul will be in the cemetery before long, where all his kin lie."

We could see there was little hope in staying longer, and did as Mrs. Hinds suggested.

"I suggest we hasten to Mr. Waltham," I told Holmes, "and then leave Avebury before we're forced to spend another night here."

"Agreed," he said. "Luckily, we can be about our business quickly, as the morning is clear."

Indeed, while ice slicked the walkways and fields, it no longer battered us from above, where instead, the sun cast a trembling light.

Mr. Waltham had rounded up several sheep and two cows for us to examine. He begged Holmes to help his other animals, as well, and pointed to the hill behind the field, where cows tumbled down the ice to the bottom and spilled on top of one another in heaps. Sheep raced in circles, bleating and falling.

"I don't know what to do with them. It's like they're all insane. There's nothing to save 'em," the farmer told us. He looked as if he hadn't slept in days.

Neither Holmes nor I wanted to go near the scene of the opera, where we had seen creatures fall from the wooden scenery and kill members of the audience. We were content to stand on the edge of the field by Waltham's farmhouse, content to be near a solid human home, where the humans still had red blood, craterless heads, and unwebbed hands and feet, where they spoke our language rather than that of the Order of Dagon.

As twenty or more sheep raced over a hill and slid down

the ice, rolling and tumbling into the helpless cows below, I could look at the strange scene no longer. Instead, I stared at an icy patch at my feet. I was glad my feet were not webbed. I was glad that I had but two legs with the usual number of bones—and although my leg hurt, I didn't mind.

"Watson," said Holmes, his eyes still on the animals. "It is certainly true that their nervous systems seem to be affected. They are acting, as we suspected, as if they've been in the Eshockers, as if they've drunk the Old Ones Serum, as if they're infected with something, like—" He stared at me, long and hard. "Like others we know."

He meant me.

Yes, I was infected with something that made my mind whirl with colors and symbols and images that did not exist outside the confines of my skull. Yet I had neither drunk serum nor strapped myself into an Eshocker. Nor had Holmes been infected with whatever ailed me.

Clearly, the infection was not jumping from person to person. But the source must be environmental—it was too much of a coincidence that the disease affected those who had been in the vicinity of an Order of Dagon cell. Were we experiencing a new form of plague, one that entered us from... *where? the air itself?* Briefly I wondered if the old discredited theories were right. No, it could *not* be...

"What are we to do, Holmes?" I asked softly. "I'm a medical man. Your brother has enlisted my aid, and yet, I'm failing to understand this—"

I gestured at the animals, bleating and lowing in death throes, at the ones still alive but racing in circles or staggering and falling.

"With this kind man's help," Holmes gestured at Mr. Waltham, who somberly lowered his head, "we'll get a few of the sick animals back to London, Watson. There are no facilities here that would enable me to study fresh brain samples. Mr. Waltham will ship the animals by train to London, and we'll send Timmy to bring them to us.

"He's young," Holmes continued, "and as such, can be salvaged. I believe Timmy is a good lad, for he's already helped us. As for his father, that's another matter. He's a career criminal. But Timmy reminds me of—"

"Yes," I said. "He reminds me of them, too. I assume you mean the Baker Street irregulars. Good lads, all."

Holmes nodded, and our eyes met.

For the first time in days, a glimmer of hope rose in us, a bit of sunshine.

29

AMELIA SCARCLIFFE

Whitechapel Eshocker Den

The Dorset coast and my sacred forest buzzed with life, even in the dead of winter. Brown leaves decorated the snow and skipped across the ice. Animals scavenged for food or curled beneath the frozen earth for warmth. The mistletoe hung still, awaiting my command. We connected in our vast web, their silence palpable as much as my heart pattered out to them. We pitched through winter together.

But I was no longer in my beloved home.

I was *here*...

Here, in the dead of London, where everything truly *was* dead. It would be dead come summer, for the streets lacked the vibrancy that comes with knowledge and awareness. A dead leaf in my woods held more potency and knowledge of the universe than the entire population of London. They, who believed themselves masters of this planet, of all that stretched beyond it—they knew nothing.

Curled on the floor between crates of Old Ones Serum and a sagging sofa, I stroked my swollen neck flaps, and with each stroke, a wave of heat flushed through me. I tensed my toes, stretching the webbing between them to the limit. Of what use were my large webbed feet and toe suckers inside this London den? My soles longed to clench rock, to sucker the sand, to flip through the depths of Half Moon Bay. My gills fluttered, aching for the rush of water. My nose desired the perfume of bergamot.

Moriarty told me that his men had kidnapped Koenraad Thwaite and imprisoned him in a remote cottage north of Half Moon Bay. The humans would control Koenraad briefly, I felt sure, before the Deep One, father to my spawn, broke free and killed them all. Koenraad's second-in-command, the giant Koos, roamed free, and like all Dagonites, his heart beat in unison with the Others from Beyond—with the swarms of the Thames, with the Great Old Ones, with Dagon, with Cthulhu Himself... and with Koenraad.

Yes, Koenraad would escape.

As would I... for nobody controls one such as myself.

Moriarty was an idiot, who thought mistreatment would make me talk.

The spawn inside me squirmed for release. It wouldn't be much longer before I burst open and set them free. These squalid surroundings were irrelevant. My spawn were all that mattered.

A door whisked open, and with it came a blast of dirt and dust that clogged the filtering pores in my gills. As the door clicked shut, muting the ecstatic moans from the den, I wheezed and pushed myself to a sitting position, and then I pushed air through my gills. After a few heaves, my aching gills dislodged the grit, puffing it off me into a cloud of human-created filth.

My belly bulged before me, and beneath the same ankle-length gown I'd been wearing since the kidnapping, my squirming spawn kicked and clawed at me. I allowed myself a smile, for this type of pain pleased me.

Sweeping dirty hair off my face, I peered through the gloom at my jailer, Professor Moriarty. My eyes adjusted to the murk, just as they adjust to the murk of the deep sea.

He was unshaven and wearing rags. His skin had an oily sheen to it. *It must displease him greatly*, I thought, *to ignore his fastidious standards and façade as a gentleman.*

I gave Moriarty a look that—in other circumstances—would tell a mortal that death was imminent. Thinking I was in his clutches with no escape, my jailer did not flinch.

"You're tough," he said, "I'll give you that." He whipped off a nondescript black hat and tossed it on the sofa. He offered me a hand. "Come on, dear, you're in no condition to fight me. Be a good girl and get off the floor, and let us talk like civilized people." He graced me with a false smile, which instantly vanished when I didn't struggle to my feet.

"What is it you want from me?" I hissed. "To chant some spells to create gold out of thin air? Is that what you desire, Professor? Do I strike you as one attuned to the fake promises of alchemy? Do I look like a snake charmer, an elixir salesman, perhaps someone who peddles what you call Old Ones Serum?"

He bristled, and his body tensed.

"As I thought," I continued. "We both know that Old Ones Serum is a simple mixture of alcohol and narcotics. There is nothing of the Old Ones in it."

He reached for me again, this time grabbing my hand

and wrenching me from the floor. I waited, keeping my eyes level with his, until finally, he released my hand, and with a look of disgust, wiped his own hand thoroughly using a pocket cloth.

"*You* are an Old One, aren't you?" he said, surveying me from top to bottom. "*You* are the same as those things in the Thames, just in a different form." The smile returned to his lips, but this time, the smile was real. He enjoyed solving puzzles and mysteries, this man, and to him, I was a mystery that came with a pot of gold.

He leaned against the stack of crates lining the wall.

"You crave nothing I can offer you?" he said. "Food, a bath, a bed, some wine? Nothing?"

"I wish only to return to Half Moon Bay."

"But how can you survive without food?" he asked.

I filter it from the air, fool, I thought. *It's meager here and does not fill my stomach, but it suffices to keep me alive. Now water is another matter. If you deny me water...*

He regarded me quizzically and interrupted my thoughts.

"So you get your food in a manner other than through your mouth." His smile widened, and his eyes glittered. "I see, my dear. But what you don't see is that you must do as I ask, for I control the very things that you cannot live without."

I knew what he had on me. I knew what he meant.

For a moment, panic gripped me, and dizziness washed over me. I groped for the back of the sofa, and clutched it to keep from falling over. Hanging my head, I let the dirty hair sweep over the sides of my face, obscuring Moriarty's view of me.

"But," I said, enunciating each word as a pick punctures ice, "even if you dig the spawn from my belly now, they are so close to birth that they will survive your assault. They will attack viciously and torture and murder anyone remotely responsible for the death of their mother."

Straightening, I balled my hands into fists, and glared at Moriarty.

"So you see," I said, "you have nothing over me, and you cannot make me do anything."

At that, he grabbed my upper arms, whirled me to the sofa, and threw me onto the exposed springs. As the metal prongs pierced my skin, I cried out, and within my belly, the spawn beat upon me for release. I saw now that he was holding a gun.

Standing but a foot away, he pointed the weapon at my face.

"You will do as I say," he threatened, "or I will fill your belly with bullets. Neither you nor your filthy spawn will survive. Do you understand?"

I nodded, my mind whirling with possibilities—none of them good. He was right. He could kill me with that gun, could kill all of the offspring. The fertility rights of the Order of Dagon demanded their birth. To fulfill the final rule of the Order, to bring forth Dagon and his Deep Ones, to unleash them upon the Earth, I had to give birth to the young of Koenraad Thwaite. He had mated unsuccessfully with many females before me. Ours was an unusual chance—together, we could fulfill the final rule. Without either of us...

"You still have Koenraad Thwaite?" I asked.

Moriarty kept the gun leveled at my face, but nodded, that yes, Koenraad remained alive.

"He's under guard twenty-four hours a day," Moriarty said. "My men have orders not to permit him any freedom, nor is he allowed to utter a single word. He's alive, but imprisoned and in a secure place."

"I cannot simply chant some words and magically make gold appear," I said, lifting myself back to a sitting position, as Moriarty lowered the gun but kept it in his hand. "It doesn't work that way."

"Perhaps you are not powerful enough," he said, and then, "So tell me, how *does* it work?"

"If I help you, will you help me, in return? Will you let me go back to Half Moon Bay to raise my children?"

He snorted. "A devoted mother, eh? Next you'll be darning socks and baking a pie. Tell me, for a start, about the creatures in the Thames—great monsters that flicker in and out of view. They are a part of all this, I am sure. What can it harm you to speak of them?"

"I have not seen them for myself. But I know the things you speak of. They come from another place and time. They can go there, then return, in the blink of an eye."

"Can they be sealed off in that other domain when they go there?"

I snorted at the absurdity of his question. "These creatures are in the air, they infiltrate a human as easily as I obtain food. They can drive a man mad."

"They cause... *insanity?*"

"Whatever term you choose to apply will do," I said. "They mutate a man's internal constitution. They cause deformities, physical and mental. They don't affect *all* people. It depends on an individual's fundamental—let me choose a word you might understand—*composition*."

A mask of concentration settled over his features. He clasped a hand to his chin, the gun slipped back into his pocket. He was deep in thought. When he spoke again, his words were calm and smooth, uttered as if from the lips of one who tutors students in philosophy.

"The reason Old Ones Serum first began to sell so well was that people believe it flushes these creatures into their stomachs and minds. But the serum simply adds to the startling effects of the Eshockers. It lifts the dazed to a higher level. It makes the head swim. But it contains none of these creatures. You are telling me that these creatures are in the air we breathe, they're swimming in the Thames. Very well. But there is another theory about these creatures, and it's the truly important one, Miss Scarcliffe: *Do they trigger the tram machine to produce gold?*"

Again, the infernal tram machine, something I knew of only from my fellow Dagonites. He'd spoken of almost nothing else since plucking me from my home at the Bay. Quickly, I answered, "No."

"No?" he said, as if not believing me.

"No. There *are* splinters in time and space, *yes*. But they alone do not yield gold. For that, you need to feed the machine with the fuel it needs, phosphorus and lead. The fuel reacts in the other place and time, where the creatures go when they are not here."

He struggled to understand, and finally, unclasping his chin and dropping his hand, he told me what had to be done.

"With your help, my men will secure the tram machine building. We will go inside the building, and my men will feed phosphorus and lead to the machine. And then you, Amelia Scarcliffe, will utter your incantations to bring the machine to life and crank out the gold."

I didn't care about the gold, about Moriarty or his greed. I wanted only to crawl back to the beach of Half Moon Bay and into the water, to swim out to the reef with my spawn, bring forth Dagon, the Deep Ones, and Cthulhu. I had no doubt that the Old Ones would take care of the human scourge. Of what use were humans to those who existed infinitely before time and after time and everywhere in between?

If he let me out of this building, this den, then perhaps I could escape. It was worth the risk, wasn't it?

30
MISS AMY SWITZER

Whitechapel Lunatic Asylum

I knelt by Mrs. van der Kolk's bed, listening to the old woman snore and mutter in her sleep about her dead husband's mistresses. Soon, Dr. Sinclair would be done with Willie Jacobs. Although Jacobs hadn't mentioned anything to me, I was certain he'd seen me that night when I laid poor Caroline Brown to rest.

Down the hall by Willie Jacobs's room, Dr. Sinclair continued to praise the lunatic.

"Excellent job, Mr. Jacobs. Your father taught you well. Thanks to you, I should be able to supply enough Eshockers to keep the Whitechapel Asylum donors happy."

"I know not what ails me," the lunatic replied in his hideous rasping voice. No doubt, he was picking at his nose or clawing at the scabs on his scalp. He emitted a stream of gibberish, then stuttered as if trying to stop himself. "It came upon me quick. When the tram machine went wild. After it killed me dad." He uttered the words in spurts laced with gasps and choking noises. "When-when-when those creatures come from beyon' is when me brain started hurtin'. Gaahh! The rest of me ills, they be due to the beast."

"You poor fellow. Get some sleep. I'll do all that I can to make your time in the asylum as comfortable as possible. You're a good man. I'm sorry to see you suffer. Life is unfair, Mr. Jacobs, it truly is." Dr. Sinclair's voice sounded gentle and reassuring. He was so good with the patients that my heart swelled just to hear him talk.

Still crouching by Mrs. van der Kolk's bed, I gripped the metal side rail and bent my head. Tears filled my eyes.

Why, oh why, Dr. Sinclair, can't you talk to me so kindly, just once? Can't you see that I worship you, that I would do anything for you, that I love you?

"Thank you, sir," Willie Jacobs rasped, and then after yet more babbling, choked out, "I'm glad not to be Eshocked meself, is all. And when it's time, I'll be glad for a quick death."

At this, my head snapped up. He had no idea how soon death would come, did he? But I knew that he didn't have long to live. Insane, afflicted with an unknown brain condition, he also had an advanced case of phossy jaw. If he died tonight, nobody would be surprised. Dr. Sinclair would find someone else to help him build Eshockers. I knew how the Eshockers worked. Perhaps I could help the doctor in some way. Perhaps we would become a team, an inseparable couple. I imagined him smiling at me, warmth in his eyes, his hand touching my arm, his lips slowly parting. "What would I do without you, Amy?" He would whisper in my ear. "You're so much more than a nurse. You're everything."

My body grew warm, my heart quickened. I felt my cheeks flush.

"Well, let us hope for the best, shall we?" Dr. Sinclair

said from afar, his voice fading as he padded down the hall away from Willie Jacobs's room—and away from me. The doctor was heading home, leaving Willie Jacobs and the rest of the inmates to me. Of course, he didn't know that I was working tonight, but then, I rarely told him when I stayed overnight in the asylum.

After Caroline Brown died, I'd slipped from the building and hurried home. I'd let Miss Klune find the dead girl in her bed the following morning. Sure, there'd been some wailing and weeping—that was standard when any inmate died— but nobody had thought anything untoward had occurred. There had been no hint of foul play. They'd carted her away as they did with all the dead. And now, her bed was empty. It awaited a new patient, and given how many indigent psychotics roamed the streets of Whitechapel, I doubted it would remain empty for long.

Jacobs's bed squeaked. He grunted, as his shoes dropped to the floor.

Mrs. van der Kolk rolled onto her side. I jerked back, released my grip on the side rail of her bed. Her eyes dimmed, then were still. Her lungs rattled with air. This one wouldn't live much longer, either.

Perhaps I need not bother with Willie Jacobs. Even if he tells Dr. Sinclair that I killed Caroline Brown, the doctor won't believe him. Jacobs is always babbling nonsense.

On the other hand, why take any chances?

Willie Jacobs must have seen me that night. If he spoke up, I could end up imprisoned for the rest of my life. I could end up worse off than the asylum's patients.

Slipping from Mrs. van der Kolk's room, I headed

towards Jacobs's room. The hall was dark, as it always was this time of night. A faint glow emanated from the nurses' station at the end of the hall past the day room. Out in the reception area, the night guard would be sleeping. Had Dr. Sinclair decided to sleep in his office tonight rather than in his bed at home—I imagined it must be soft and large with sumptuous fabric—he wouldn't hear anything. He never did. In the back room, should any of the lunatics be slaving away building Eshockers, they wouldn't hear anything, either, for the walls were heavily padded to prevent noise from going out or in. I never heard the lunatic workers hammering, banging, chopping, or shrieking.

Standing outside Jacobs's room, I slid my hand into the pocket of my uniform and withdrew the hypodermic needle and vial of medicine. We regularly tranquilized the lunatics. When not working on Eshockers, Jacobs remained in a stupor in the day room.

What's the harm in a little more tranquilizer? I thought, suppressing a chuckle.

From within the room, he wheezed and then muttered more nonsense about a beast murdering his father and wanting him dead, too.

"It will kill you all," he muttered several times, his voice rising with each iteration.

I pushed open the door and stared at him in the dark. A frail man, nearly skeletal now, barely forming a lump upon his bed. Thin blankets heaped over him, and yet, he shivered. I crept closer and stepped to the side of the bed.

Willie Jacobs stirred, and his lips flapped as he muttered more nonsense. Even in this dark room, I could see the effects of the phossy jaw: the rotting flesh exposing an inch or two of his teeth and jawbone. If he lived another week, he'd be lucky.

Again, I hesitated. Why not let death take its course? Why intrude and push it along? This man was already dead.

And yet...

His eyes opened. He stared at me, but only for a moment. In a flash, he whipped off the blanket tatters and swiveled to a sitting position. I shoved the needle and vial back in my pocket, then dived for him. Smashing him back onto the bed, I pressed hard—*I'm a big, muscular woman, tall and brutish, or so say the men as they push me away*—and I flattened him, pinning his arms to his sides. He shrieked, and I slammed my right hand over his mouth, making him flinch and cringe from the pain of the phossy jaw.

Nothing made *me* flinch. I was a nurse at the Whitechapel Lunatic Asylum. I'd seen and done things that would give most folk nightmares.

His arms flailed, then his fist beat my shoulder. Poor fellow, he was too weak to inflict even a bruise.

"Shhh," I whispered harshly. "Shhh, and I won't hurt you."

The idiot believed me. The flailing ceased, and he stopped struggling.

"What do you want?" he whimpered, as I released his other arm and dipped my hand back into my pocket.

Fingering the needle, I told him that I'd come to release him from his misery, that he would suffer no more.

"K-k-k-k... you come to bring me to 'eaven?" he asked softly.

"Yes, Willie. Heaven," I said.

His right hand rose from his side. His thumb jabbed his left nostril, then his right, and the pace increased until he was poking them rapidly, one after the other. Blood dripped from one nostril into his mouth. He didn't seem to care. He licked the blood off his exposed teeth and jawbone.

"W-w-why?" he asked.

I pushed the needle into the vial, filled the syringe with medicine. I crouched by his side, gently touched his right arm. It calmed him, and he made a cooing noise as a baby does with its mother. Still, his right fingers jabbed his nostrils, flitting over them in some bizarre rhythm.

"Please," I said, "that is no longer necessary, Willie."

In response, he made a fist and started batting his nose with his knuckles. His left hand flew to his head and picked at a large scab, which cracked open and oozed blood.

"Willie," I said, "please," but all he did was moan and mutter at me.

"N-nurse Amy, you're goin' to kill me?" he managed to sputter, yet he did not struggle.

Oh, this poor man, I thought. *He suffers constantly. The agony must be unbearable.*

Enduring all this pain, he built Eshockers for Dr. Sinclair. He hammered them together, he wired them. I wondered what Willie Jacobs could have done with his life had he not been born to the man who forced him to work in the tram machine building. I wondered what he might have achieved, how long he might have lived. No doubt, he would have married and had children. That's what most people did...

Except for me, of course. But it wasn't my fault. Nobody

had asked for my hand in marriage, much less wished me to bear their children. I was barren. Empty. Devoid. Nothing in here, nothing but a sad heart yearning endlessly for what it could never have.

"I understand suffering," I told him gently. "Now, I want you to relax. Stop picking at your head, Willie. Stop picking at your nose. Let your arms relax by your sides. That's a good boy, that's good." As he did as I told him, I stroked his arm and then his bald scalp and forehead. After I finished with him, I'd get a cloth from the nurses' station and wipe the blood from the left side of his face. He would be more comfortable that way.

I shot a few drops of liquid from the needle, then turned his arm slightly and positioned the needle over the inner flesh in the crook of his elbow. Same place I'd injected Caroline Brown. Same place Miss Klune and I injected all the inmates.

His hand flew out and gripped my arm.

"No!" he cried. "I won't let you do it! I ain't ready to die!"

The needle clattered across the floor. My heart grew hard.

"Shut up," I hissed, clamping a hand over his mouth.

He squirmed and kicked me. I sat on his stomach, squashing him to the bed, and when he beat me with his fists, I again pinned both of his arms down, this time up by his bleeding head.

"You will be quiet," I hissed. "You will take your medicine, Mr. Jacobs. Or I will report you."

He started screaming—wildly now, and I could hear patients awakening up and down the hall. Soon, the front guard would come, maybe Dr. Sinclair himself.

Damn you, Willie Jacobs, I thought. *Don't you see that this is best for you?*

The idiots never saw what was best, though, did they? It was always up to us—the nurses, the staff—to attend to their every need.

Well, I'll take care of you, Willie Jacobs, I thought.

Abruptly, I jumped off the bed, scooped up the needle, whirled, pinned his right arm down flat, and jammed the needle into his flesh.

Jacobs shrieked and cursed, kicked his legs up and down, jerked his body from side to side, slapped at me with his left hand. But it did no good. I was Miss Amy Switzer. I was a professional.

The medicine flowed into his bloodstream, and in a flash, his struggling ceased, his body relaxed, and he fell into a deep sleep.

The other inmates on the floor screamed, but before long, they too fell back into the drug-induced slumber of the insane. After all, shrieking was common in the corridors, whether it be day or night. Even the night guard didn't come to investigate the noise...

I waited, listening to the whimpers die.

The hypodermic needle had ejected a lot of liquid when Willie had slapped it from my hand and it had skittered across the floor. He'd not received the full dose I'd intended for him.

When he moaned and quivered, I knew that I'd failed to put him to sleep... forever, to sleep.

It wouldn't take much for me to retrieve more medicine

from the nurses' station and finish the job...

Returning to the hall, I shut the door and looked in both directions. Nothing. I was about to hurry to the nurses' station and get the medicine when I stopped short. I heard a noise, a chair scraping. Then the door to the reception area creaked open.

Someone was coming.

Quickly, I ran to the other end of the hall and around the corner. I would circle around, and while the guard checked the inmates, I would duck out of the building unnoticed.

31
PROFESSOR MORIARTY

Whitechapel Eshocker Den

Amelia Scarcliffe possessed power beyond anything I'd ever witnessed. Fierce and determined, she cared for nothing but achieving her goals, that of giving birth to hell spawn and unleashing Old Ones upon the Earth. An amazing creature, she could breathe beneath the water as well as on the land. I viewed her as a weapon.

She sat cross-legged on the battered sofa in the room behind the Eshocker den. Webbed fingers shoved raw fish into her mouth. She'd bathed and donned what passed for a clean dress. It was actually a sack with holes cut for her neck and arms. Matted and thick like tangled netting, her hair hung over her face as she ate, and occasionally, she swept it back with a fish-filthy hand.

"Water," she hissed, and I handed her a pail. She dropped bloody fish on her lap, lifted the pail, and drank, letting the water splash over her face and drench her upper body. Then she lifted the fish remains again and chewed. She spat out a bone.

Blood-red eyes with pus-colored irises glared at me. The

light from the gas lamp on the wall played across her face, danced in multicolored hues upon the exotic ridges of her cheekbones. The ridges shimmered like fish scales. Then there were the neck flaps—as she swallowed, they swelled and bobbed against each other, somehow so enticing that I had to jerk my eyes away to keep my thoughts steady.

"You controlled the needles that plunged out of that mistletoe and killed my man, Lloyd, eh?" I asked her.

She tossed fish bones into a pile by my feet, making me hop back a step. She laughed.

"You think you're very smart, Professor Moriarty, but you don't know anything," she said.

"So educate me," I countered. "Tell me all that I don't know. Tell me, Miss Scarcliffe, if you can control aspects of nature itself, if you can kill a man using that control, then... can you also call forth these creatures who inhabit the Thames? Can you make them kill as you did with the mistletoe?"

"You ask too many questions."

With much effort, she lifted her bulk from the floor, clenching her swollen belly. Her giant feet slapped across the floor, the toe suckers popping up with each step. Pointing to the door, she ordered me to open it and release her. I refused. She inched closer to me, and as she spoke, each word came from her lips in a stench of fish breath. I stared down at the shimmering cheekbones, and this close, they were so intoxicating that I broke out in a sweat, my head reeling. Again, she laughed at me.

I broke away, moved to the door, and rested my right hand on the knob. Outside, my agents would make sure nobody came in or out of this room unless I authorized it. This woman, or whatever she was, would not get the better of me.

"Afraid of me, Professor?" she taunted, her belly bulging in one direction and now another. She leapt forward like a frog. Her webbed feet landed by the door. Her hand rested on mine.

It was my turn to laugh at her.

"What are you going to do out there, Miss Scarcliffe? Eshock yourself? Mingle with the decrepit? Get drunk and sing pub tunes? *What?*"

Her gills rippled with color. The neck flaps pulsed in an odd three-quarter rhythm, then skipped to rapid trebles.

I caught my breath. Resisting the beat of the neck flaps— the high-pitched trebles skittering over my nerves—I stared directly into her eyes, knowing they might catch me in their embrace and pull me further under her spell. Nobody outmaneuvered me. Nobody—not Sherlock Holmes, and certainly not this female.

"What I'd like to do out there," she said in a flat monotone, "is kill everyone in the den, kill you, and then leave."

As soon as Timmy Dorsey, Sr. and his latest crew conquered and secured the tram machine building, I planned to send Amelia Scarcliffe over there to utter her incantations and bring forth gold. I would see to it that the machine received its phosphorus and lead. I would do whatever it took to create the gold.

That was the ultimate objective. All the rest of this nonsense—the Eshockers, the Old Ones Serum, the dens, that idiot Sinclair and his idiot asylum, Amelia Scarcliffe,

Maria Fitzgerald—I didn't care about any of that. I wanted the gold.

"You'll have your fun in the tram machine building," I said, then my voice turned cold. "You've eaten. You have water. Now go back in your corner where you belong." Pointing to the rear of the room, where the serum teetered in stacks, I added, "Get out of my way. I have things to do."

"What are you going to do if I refuse?" she hissed.

"Trust me, my dear, you won't enjoy finding out."

She nodded, most likely remembering how we had attacked her, overpowered her, and trussed her in a sack. *With all that power,* I thought, *she can't do the simplest thing, like get loose from a sack.* How amusing.

Her powers were limited, but exactly how or why, I did not know.

As she slunk off to settle in the dust again, I left the room and entered the main den, where a dozen or more men and women slumped against the walls or swooned in the Eshockers. Others wore the electrotherapy belts, girdles, and hats, their bodies shaking, their eyes not registering my presence. They were lost in other worlds, in their fantasies, or perhaps just floating in the nothingness of ecstasy, the high of all highs.

The room could accommodate a lot more customers. My procurement agent had assured me that, any day now, Dr. Sinclair—*that idiot Sinclair!*—would deliver a dozen Eshockers to my men. It just wasn't enough.

My sources told me that Sinclair used super-potent Eshockers that he built and wired in the asylum. I wouldn't mind obtaining some of those machines. But *how*—break into the lunatic asylum, find the Eshockers, and then spirit them out of the building?

Imagine the profits. My current customers would spring ten times the going rate for a super-Eshocking.

Assuming I obtained Sinclair's special Eshockers, I could then dispense with the idiot doctor and hire my own team of machinists to build them.

A high-pitched shriek shattered the air. From the back room, Amelia Scarcliffe warbled and screamed words that made no sense.

"Uriaiava. Auro! Aera aere aero."

The Eshockers shook, the bodies strapped into them shook even harder. Addicts on the floor wailed and held their heads. Those in the belts and girdles screamed in ecstasy. Women writhed, ripped off their clothes. Men fell to the floor, beat their heads against the walls.

Miss Scarcliffe's voice went higher, and as her fists pounded on the back door in beats of three, she continued to wail the strange words.

"Shigeonoth shiggaion pharemake perosephora peresibutero paieti raumea toatoaarii eh toatoa."

My agents, all tough men, ran to the Eshockers and started switching them off. Three remained by Miss Scarcliffe's door. I inched toward the front door, ready to race to the street. *Let my men handle the meat work*, I thought. *That's why I pay them.*

Beating the door like a drum, Miss Scarcliffe continued.

"Ebb'yuh dissoth'nknpflknghreet. Urre'h. Nyogthluh'eeh."

The addicts feebly tried to fight off my agents, who were attempting to pull them away from the machines, but what could they do against my men? They screamed to be released, they demanded the return of their money, and some clearly were so far gone they couldn't open their mouths to utter anything, much less scream.

"Quiet!" I held up my hand, and everyone in the room fell silent, bar a few whimpers.

Miss Scarcliffe had reverted to the English language.

"Great Cthulhu, yearning for land, for us, from Beyond in the great sea. I see you, I hear you, I come to you. Those in the Thames, flicker in and out, stay with us, stay in your homeland, where we serve you and gladly give our lives."

My men distracted, the addicts crawled back to the Eshockers and climbed into the seats. They crawled to the electro belts and the girdles. Their hands flapped at the straps, unable to grab hold and attach the ties to their bodies. The flapping intensified, grew more incessant, the addicts screaming with frustration, their faces red, their eyes dim, their bodies convulsing.

"*Uriaiava. Auro! Aera aere aero! Cthulhu! Cthulhu!*" Miss Scarcliffe shrieked.

"Cthulhu! Cthulhu!" The addicts took up the call and started pounding the floor, the walls, and the Eshockers with their fists.

What does this mean, this Cthulhu? I wondered.

Was this another monster, something like those in the Thames? Was it something *worse*? By bringing Amelia Scarcliffe to London, had I unleashed unutterable horror upon the city, something even I had no power to destroy?

32

DR. JOHN WATSON

Whitechapel

"How are you getting on, Holmes?" I asked, as we passed the butcher's shop run by Timmy Dorsey, Sr. The air was particularly rancid here, as if the day's rain had been blood. The humidity made breathing difficult. Several times, Holmes and I had stopped to wipe the perspiration—a brownish grime—from our faces.

"I assume you refer to my accommodation at the Diogenes Club?" Holmes said in a world-weary tone. "Unlike more civilized clubs, the Diogenes discourages overnight guests in the same way that it does inveterate talkers. I have a small room, ten feet by eight feet, rather like an inmate's room at the Whitechapel Lunatic Asylum. The bed is hard and a little too short, which is why I have been limping half the morning."

Despite the comfort of my Baker Street bed, my war-injured leg hurt all night every night, leaving me drowsy during the day. I understood well what Holmes was experiencing, but in his case, he could choose the easy solution, the return to *his* Baker Street bed.

"But you're not injured," I said. "You are torturing

yourself needlessly on that hard bed. You must have finished your research at the Diogenes by now. Why not return to your lodgings at Baker Street? You're subjecting yourself to the infected London environment every day, not to mention that of Avebury, so what good is it doing for you to sleep at Mycroft's club?"

"Contrary to what you may think, Doctor, I have yet to find any evidence in the Diogenes resources of bizarre brain infestations and mutated animals dwelling in the Thames. However, I require utmost quiet and solitude," Holmes said, his voice lowering, "for now."

"But why?" I persisted.

"I want no distractions," came the curt reply.

As he spoke, a man stumbled through the murk toward us and clutched at me. Without thinking, I slapped his hand—*a webbed hand!*—from my arm, then with horror, took in his visage—crater head, bulging eyes, greenish cast to the skin.

"Serum. *Eh'bbguttth.* Eshockin'. Be goin' to the Thames," the man muttered. "You go, see what's real. *You go.*"

"I'm not going anywhere, my man," I said, "and I suggest that you stay away from the river. There are monsters in the water—they nearly killed us."

Holmes gestured at the man's bowed legs and giant triangular feet.

"How long have you been this way?"

"Like what?" His voice took on a defensive tone, and he wobbled and almost fell. I reached out and steadied him, hiding my disgust at the feel of slime coating his shirt. I gave him a reassuring smile, the one I use with patients whose illness is incurable. Comfort is lacking in this world, and whenever we can supply a small amount, we should. A dose of comfort, if combined with a million other doses, might someday counteract evil.

Certainly, evil surrounded us here in Whitechapel. Wasn't it in the grimy air that reeked of stale blood? Wasn't it in whatever infected this man—infected me?

The man's head drooped, displaying the crater top more clearly. Like so many men I'd seen lately, he was bald with scabs on his scalp. This poor fellow's crater was one big scoop of a scab filled with the brownish sludge that seemed suspended in the very air. When he tilted his head, the sludge oozed slightly forward.

Holmes leaned in to peer at the sludge more closely.

"How long?" he asked again, his right hand dipping into his coat pocket and retrieving a vial containing a small medical swab. *My God*, I thought, *he's going to take a sample of the gore on the man's head.*

"You have been at an Eshocking den, I see," Holmes went on. "You observe, Watson, those scabs on his head? Electrical burns, no doubt, thanks to faulty equipment or misapplication."

Our new acquaintance did not follow this conversation at all, but he reacted to the words he knew well enough by blurting out, "I like the dens, and I be Eshockin' for I dunno 'ow long. Nothin' wrong with it, is there?"

Holmes had already removed the swab from the vial. Before the man could react, he dipped it into his head crater, swirled the sludge on the tip of the swab, and sealed it in the vial.

"What say—?" The man's eyes flashed angrily, then

fell back into the glazed look of the Eshocked. "What...
say..." His voice trailed off. He had already forgotten about
the swab and the vial. He stared at Holmes as if trying to
remember something.

How long before I became like this man? Would I end up
bald with a crater head filled with sludge? Would my feet
somehow grow webbed, my hands? What would happen to
me if I didn't cure myself of my own infection?

As Holmes slipped the vial back into his pocket, I pushed
him along the street away from the strange man, who just
stood there, looking baffled, until finally, he fell against the
wall of the *MEAT* building. He grasped his head with webbed
hands, slipping his fingers into the sludge-filled crater.

"My God!" I exclaimed. "Holmes, we *must* examine
the sludge you collected from that poor man. We *must* find
Timmy and get the animals as quickly as possible. We *must*
solve this case. I believe that all life might depend on it."

"Don't be so melodramatic, Doctor." Holmes touched
his top hat and cast me a sardonic look. "We're on our way
to see Timmy now. We'll have the animals in short order.
We will find out what this infection is. We will find a cure.
We will stop the creatures in the Thames. We will do all of
this, I assure you."

"Do you know how?" I asked, astonished.

At this, he grew silent.

"Holmes, you must come back to Baker Street," I insisted.
"What good is it doing you to sleep on a hard bed?"

We stepped over rubbish and slogged through the
stagnant water clogging the gutters of Thrawl Street. Soon,
we stood before the den, where the fire barrel still crackled,

addicts huddled around it, some curled on the ground.

"Nobody but you, Lestrade, and Mrs. Hudson knows that I am staying elsewhere. Moriarty has been more active and less afraid of showing his face in recent days. Should he send a man to murder me, he will not find me at Baker Street. And the Diogenes is well protected—better than you think."

"My dear fellow, say no more," I said. "I didn't realize—"

"Enough," he said crisply, lifting his walking stick and pointing at the crumbling building before us. "To the den and to Timmy."

Just then, the den door flew open, and a pack of about fifteen men thundered out. Holmes wrenched me back, and we dove into a nearby alley. If the men had seen us, either they didn't recognize us or they didn't care. My guess was the former, for we had acted quickly and the men's focus was in the other direction—down the street towards the tram machine building.

"Get her and bring her!" someone cried.

"I am sorry we didn't bring our guns," Holmes whispered.

Holmes and I peered around the alley corner. A tall man with thick muscles was at the head of the group now, and his right hand clutched a huge, bloodied meat cleaver. It was Timmy Dorsey, Sr. His fellows hooted and waved their weapons in the air—saws, knives, bats, and chains.

Even the addicts who usually huddled by the fire barrel across the street had noticed the disturbance. Muttering and trembling, they tried to get away from the men. Some fell in the middle of the road, others stepped on them. A few reached the other side and stumbled toward an open door.

Three of Dorsey's brutes were stumbling after the others

with a sack hoisted between them. Something struggled within it—*a person*. Muffled screams rang out, which only made the men laugh more loudly. Theirs were blood laughs, the type men make who go to war because they like to kill. I'd seen plenty of this sort on the battlefield, and I despised them.

Killing, even in war, is a horrible thing, and a man should never find amusement in another's misery. Only the weak find joy in the suffering of others. The strongest men I'd fought alongside had always been gripped by sadness after killing men in battle.

I was ready to throw myself into the melee and fight, but Holmes stopped me.

"Come, Watson," he said. "We must get closer if we are to help her."

We ran down the street after the men. None of them looked back. Their attention was upon the tram machine building, and the dozen policemen awaiting them. Once we were within hailing distance, we kept our cover in a doorway, from which I could see the men standing ready, some wielding clubs, others drawing pistols.

Twelve policemen versus fifteen or so killers—the odds were looking bad.

"Careful with 'er. Treat 'er good," Dorsey told the men carrying the sack. "No beatin's."

Grumbling at the instruction, the men lowered the sack to the street and opened the top.

"Gentle," Dorsey commanded, waving his cleaver at them.

The policemen raised their clubs and aimed their pistols. They stood in front of the spiked iron fence surrounding the building. The danger signs were still there, but the gate was ajar.

"I don't think the warning signs are working," Holmes said drily.

"An understatement, if ever there was one," I said.

We'd learned from Lestrade that a group of men had attacked the police at this building only days ago, that one man had choked the life from an officer. Cleavers, axes, knives—the weapons had been the same. The survivors had told Lestrade that their attackers called themselves the Butchers. Holmes and I knew that Dorsey had been behind that attack, and now, he was trying again. But for what purpose? Was he working with Moriarty?

A long-haired woman stepped from the sack and kicked it away, snarling. She whirled, fingers splayed as if ready to claw anything near her, and the men backed away. A hushed respect ensued.

"What is this?" Holmes whispered. "Look at that creature's cheekbones, neck, feet. Whatever this is, it is clearly female and pregnant."

"She looks like those deformed worshipers we saw in the warehouse and at Swallowhead Spring," I said. "Why have they brought a cult member here?" And then the chilling thought hit me—because they wanted her to chant those horrifying incantations that opened the deadly dimensions, released the creatures, and spread death and mental disease.

No sooner had the thought occurred to me than the female began to chant the screeching nonsense syllables we'd heard many times from the Dagonites.

The tram machine building jittered, the boards and

plaster rumbling and clanking. From inside, the beast—as Willie Jacobs called it—groaned. Steel clattered. The overhead door bulged outward, then shrank back, concave, popping back into its usual place.

The pregnant creature raised her arms, spread her webbed fingers, and shrieked more of the strange incantations.

The officers swiveled to look at the shuddering building. In that instant, Dorsey's gang attacked.

Dorsey's cleaver cracked into the skull of a stout officer, who tried to duck but couldn't maneuver quickly enough to avoid the blade. His head split wide open. Blood spurted upward. As the officer dropped to his knees, the butcher slammed the cleaver into the man's head again, breaking it clean down to the neck. I have seen such things in battle before, but I could not mask a groan. Holmes tensed and allowed himself a small gasp of horror.

Despite the carnage before us, I dared not enter the fray; it would mean certain death. Holmes and I could not take on so many heavily armed assassins.

Dorsey's cleaver met the midriff of another officer—it cut clean across the man's stomach. After another blow, the man screamed, then moaned, and then whimpered to a halt, as his body broke in two, bent backwards at the waist, the open-mouthed head and torso hanging there, the arms twitching... before the whole corpse collapsed. Dorsey squashed his boots into the bloody pulp of the corpse, slid through the pool of blood surrounding it, and froze as he looked up and saw another policeman aiming his gun at Dorsey's head.

"Yes," Holmes hissed, clenching his fist, "shoot him!"

I saw the rest in a crystallized haze, in which color

sharpened into crisp delineations of Dorsey, the policeman with the gun, the strange pregnant female.

The female screeched words in a staccato rhythm that seemed designed to jangle my nerves and rattle my thoughts—a fury of sound in a whirlpool reel. I clutched the wall to steady myself as the swirling shrieks hammered my mind.

"Ch'thgalhn fhtagn Yog-Sothoth urre'h nyogthluh'eeh ngh syh'kyuhyuh. Ch'thgalhn fhtagn Yog-Sothoth urre'h nyogthluh'eeh ngh syh'kyuhyuh."

"Steady, Watson. Keep your wits about you." Holmes lowered me to a sitting position.

"We must save them, Holmes," I said, my voice shaking.

"We must wait for the right moment," he said, his voice steady and unwavering. It sobered me.

"Why the deuce doesn't the poor man shoot Dorsey?" I muttered. "What's he waiting for?"

Indeed, the officer seemed unable to move or squeeze his trigger. Even his eyes remained open, unblinking.

The woman's chant droned on.

"Ebb'yuh dissoth'nknpflknghreet.

"Hahuhoaoao yuhmoni'khu'eenee'eet."

The words were high and guttural, issued from vocal cords that had a range unlike any I'd ever heard. Not fully human. Not in any known language. Nothing imaginable— except in my nightmares.

I clamped my hands to my ears.

Dorsey grinned. His boots sprung into and over corpses and bloody gore—human organs, exposed muscle and tissue, detached arms and legs—and in several huge strides, he was in front of the frozen officer.

"Ebb'yuh dissoth'nknpflknghreet.

"Hahuhoaoao yuhmoni'khu'eenee'eet."

Dorsey swung his bloody cleaver, and in a clean chop, claimed the head of the frozen officer. It flew back, fell to the street, and rolled to a stop. Another quick swing, and the cleaver hit the meat of the man's midriff. The sound of the cleaver thwacking into the meat nearly made me vomit, and I had to swallow hard several times.

"How much longer must we wait?" I whispered harshly.

"Any moment," Holmes whispered back, "be patient."

Dorsey stood over his latest victim, raised his cleaver high in the air, and howled with victory. Blood drenched his face and hair, his jacket and trousers. Blood drenched his hands and the cleaver.

Five policemen remained alive, and all were wrestling and otherwise grappling with the surviving gang members, who numbered ten strong.

"At this rate," I whispered, "all the police will be dead within minutes. They stand no chance, Holmes."

"It is the female," he said, "her incantations. They stop the police in their tracks, freeze the men so the gang can slaughter them as easily as they slaughter lambs."

But the female was not happy. Her body trembling, she shrieked the insane words while scanning the street for something unknown.

My eyes followed hers, and I thought I saw a man duck from a window across the street. However, with my vision cloudy yet pricked with sharp outlines, I wouldn't swear to anything I saw.

Suddenly, much to my surprise, Dorsey put a bloody

hand over his mouth and spoke to her. She did not fight him. Instead, she nodded, and her forehead furrowed with desperation or frustration, I knew not which.

Had he threatened her?

An axe hacked an officer into bloody shreds, like the strips of meat Mary used to fry for me in a pan. The smell of blood and dead meat clogged the air, and I wondered if I would ever be able to bathe sufficiently to rid myself of the stink.

Gunshots rang out but missed their marks. How much longer would Holmes make us wait before we ran from this doorway, where we hid like cowards?

Three police. Ten attackers.

"Holmes," I hissed. "We must go now. We cannot wait."

He nodded and sprang to his feet, hauling me up with him.

For a moment, I studied the determined profile and glinting eyes of the man who was more a brother to me than an associate in arms. This might be the last time I saw Sherlock Holmes, and should I die, which was highly probable, I wanted to burn his image into my brain.

Dorsey issued orders to two of his men, who raced back to the den, and moments later, returned with another female hoisted above them.

"Another...?" Holmes whispered. "And she's but a child, Watson."

The pregnant female stopped shrieking. My ears rang with her chants, as if hit by echoes.

"Not her!" she cried, pointing at the girl.

"We tol' you it would come to this if you couldn't do it on your own," Dorsey said, as he helped the other two men with the child, who was perhaps six years old. "This one is younger an' more powerful."

"But not her!" the pregnant female insisted, clutching her giant belly.

"It's Maria Fitzgerald," Holmes said, just as the realization hit me, as well. "Henry Fitzgerald's daughter with Lucy Anne Nolande, the soprano who was killed at Swallowhead Spring."

Yes, it was Maria with her mop of black hair, she who had sat on the rock with Lord Ashberton in front of us during the performance of Bellini's *Norma*.

"Now both of you, sing together, crack open that buildin' for us an' kill them coppers!" Dorsey screamed.

Maria's voice opened into a cascade of music that represented the sounds of hundreds rather than one. Her voice was sweet and high, lyrical, bouncing almost joyfully in rich tones that swirled in my head.

I glanced at Holmes, whose face flushed, his eyes half-lidded, as the music swept through him, too.

"*Yog'fuhrsothothothoth 'a'a'a'memerutupao'omii! Aauh-aoaoa demoni aauhaoaoa demoni aauhaoaoa demoni.*"

Her neck grew wider, and from this distance, I couldn't tell what I was seeing, but it looked as if dozens of bubbles wobbled on her neck, rocking in harmony with her words. Her face grew rounder until it was spherical, and the glittering green eyes shone more brightly through the miasmic air.

The pregnant female joined in the harmony, her voice gritty and grating compared to the beauty of Maria's tone.

As the intertwined voices rose—"*aauhaoaoa demoni*

aauhaoaoa demoni aauhaoaoa demoni"—several Butchers dropped their weapons and tumbled to the ground. They lay still, though I knew not whether they had died.

Dorsey screamed at the little girl.

"What're you doin' to me Butchers, you monster?"

Her voice rose yet higher, and the soothing tones turned strident.

"Now!" Holmes screamed, and we both leapt from the doorway and raced to the scene.

Only three gang members stood, among them Timmy Dorsey, Sr. Of them all, he was the one I wanted.

Maria and the other female turned, saw me, and directed a blast of chanting at me. Stunned momentarily, I froze, as did Holmes, his usually sharp eyes growing fogged and distant. My thoughts jangled in my head, skittering in all directions, as a boat without bearings in a storm. I fell to my knees, only too aware of the lolling figure of a dead policeman before me, his gun still in his lifeless fingers.

I'd been infected by the cursed Dagonite illness for so long that the tones of Maria and the other female *moved* me, *inspired* me, filled me with *strength*.

From nowhere, a Butcher came at us and tackled Holmes. The two were on the ground, wrestling. Holmes clutched the other's neck. His opponent was a flurry of movement, pounding Holmes with his fists, kicking him in the groin.

I couldn't move.

I had to force myself out of the trance that imprisoned me as securely as any rope.

I tried...

One of the frozen policemen jerked briefly to life, whipped

his arm up, and squeezed the trigger of his gun.

The bullet missed its mark and instead hit the structure across the street from the tram machine building.

Dorsey threw himself at me, cleaver dripping blood and aimed at my skull.

No! I will not allow it!

From the ground, Holmes screamed, "Watson!"

With that one word from Holmes, my brain unhooked from its trance. I lunged forward and snatched the gun from the dead policeman's fingers.

I blasted the gun at Dorsey's frame. I squeezed, *bang* and *bang*, a tremor of thrilled delight racing through me as the bullets ripped into Dorsey and sent him flying. He landed on his back, clutching his chest, with his knees bent. He rolled onto his side, facing me. Blood streamed from his chest and merged with all the blood of the many he'd just killed.

Timmy Dorsey, Sr. was dead.

The caterwauling of the two females ceased. They were escaping together—Maria ran and the other seemed to bounce up the street toward the den. A cry from the battleground called my attention to Holmes, who was still in the midst of combat, but even as I ran to help, he got the upper hand. Holmes punched his attacker's jaw, pounding it on both sides, until finally, the man stopped moving. Dusting himself off, Holmes stood, and together, we surveyed the scene.

The remaining attackers, those who were alive, limped and ran after the two females. The surviving police officers staggered back against the fence surrounding the tram machine building, too exhausted to give chase.

The light had returned to my friend's eyes. The fog had lifted from my brain. The colors around me returned to the usual grays of London.

"Should we follow the pregnant creature and Maria?" I asked Holmes.

But he shook his head.

"No, I suspect they are well hidden by now. We're better off contacting Lestrade and getting more officers here to relieve these men, who require medical attention. There will be another attack on this building in due course, I fear, and in the meantime," he said, "we have to find Timmy and obtain the livestock shipped from Avebury."

I tended to the men's injuries as best I could. Word must have spread in Whitechapel that there'd been a battle on Thrawl Street, and before long, additional police arrived with stretchers for their wounded colleagues.

Holmes and I hurried to the butcher's shop and pounded on the door until Timmy answered. His face was covered with tears.

"Is it true?" he asked. "Is he dead?"

Timmy had lost his father. He was now an orphan. If it was the last thing I did, I would save him from turning into a lifetime criminal and killer like his father. I would save him from Professor Moriarty.

33

"Me father were all I 'ad," the boy sobbed, hugging his body and rocking back and forth on a stool in the blood-sopped butchering room. "'E weren't much, 'e weren't a good man, but 'e were me father."

While I consoled Timmy and promised to help him, Holmes poked around the room, which apparently, was the only one in the building. His walking stick jabbed a worn pillow and faded gray-blue afghan. He studied the rows of knives by the butcher's table along the rear wall, gazed at the meat hooks and at the dried blood that permeated every inch of the place. The smell was beyond imagining. I had to put a cloth over my nose to keep from gagging. Holmes did the same.

Eventually, he returned to me—and to the boy—and he rapped his stick twice on the floor. The boy's face snapped up, his eyes aglow with tears.

"You will come with us." Holmes's tone indicated that the boy had no choice. "I don't want Moriarty knowing where you are. I will put you in touch with Wiggins."

"Holmes, that's a splendid idea," I said, and then to Timmy, explained, "Wiggins is our main man in the Baker Street irregulars and helps with many of our cases. You will be paid handsomely for your services."

The boy's eyes fell. He blinked. A few tears fell to his lap. The poor lad. Up close, his face looked older than his years. Coarse skin hardened with lines and knife scars, with bruises fading beneath the dirt. And yet, the eyes bore an intelligence that I rarely encountered among street urchins, a possible exception being Wiggins himself, when he was a child.

"The Professor pays me well," Timmy said, "more than if I be 'omeless where you live. And I've got an 'ome 'ere."

"Indeed, you do," Holmes proclaimed, "with a comfortable bed, I see, and shelter. But it is dangerous, *very dangerous*, for you here, Timmy. On a whim, the Professor might kill you. He is not a good man. Your father, much as you loved him, did not succeed in his latest mission on behalf of your employer."

Timmy's eyes grew wide with alarm. His tears ceased. He jerked his hand from mine and leapt from the stool.

"Mr. 'olmes, you're right about that! The Professor said 'e'd kill Dad, and me, too, if we didn't get that tram gold!"

"Well, that settles it, surely," Holmes said. "You'll come with us?"

Downcast, but eventually agreeing with our assessment, Timmy, Jr. followed us from the only home he'd ever known.

"Wiggins will find you accommodation. He sleeps *somewhere*. I'll ask him to keep you hidden from Moriarty. Tomorrow morning, for a fine fee, you will go to the cattle market on the Caledonian Road, and you will bring back my shipment from Mr. Gerald Waltham of Avebury. When you bring them to me, the animals must be alive, Timmy, do you understand?"

"Alive," the boy repeated, nodding.

"Come now, let us all return to Baker Street," Holmes said, "where you will wash and eat at my residence, and then I will supply you with ample funds for your adventure in the morning. Wiggins will help with the animals, and of course, being the man that you are, you will pay Wiggins and any other help he provides."

"I can do this, Mr. 'olmes. I know me way upon the streets, sir."

"Indeed, you do, Timmy," Holmes said, clapping the boy's back.

I had hoped that Holmes would stay at Baker Street, but after ensuring Timmy had everything he needed, he flagged down a cab and returned to his temporary home at the Diogenes Club.

As for me, Mrs. Hudson's heavy meal of shepherd's pie and bread, along with two glasses of red wine, quickly put me to sleep.

In the middle of the night, I was awakened by heavy pounding on the door to my rooms.

"Dr. Watson!" Mrs. Hudson cried from the landing. "Dr. Watson, there is a man here to see you! Police!"

"It's urgent, Doctor!" a man bellowed. "Open up, and quickly!"

I stumbled from bed, and in my nightshirt, opened the

door. A constable burst into the sitting room, Mrs. Hudson wearily trundling in behind him. She fell, exhausted, into Holmes's chair by the fire. She wore her sleeping attire, with her hair tucked beneath a frilly cap.

Timmy staggered out from Holmes's bedroom to join us. He wore one of my nightshirts. It was huge on him, and he had to lift it to walk. He plopped into my chair across from Mrs. Hudson.

"Why, who's this?" she asked in surprise.

"Mrs. Hudson, this is Timmy. A lad Holmes needed to put up for the night."

"You know I have rules about overnight visitors, Dr. Watson," she admonished me, but I could tell she was too tired to argue the point.

"Doctor," the policeman interrupted, "I have been sent to ask you to travel to Wapping right away. The creatures have risen up again and attacked a number of ships, and while our boys are battling hard, we have casualties you cannot imagine, sir. Inspector Lestrade sent for you personally."

The Thames! If only the businesses that lined the river had heeded police advice and sent their ships to offload their wares on the coast.

"Timmy, you had better go back to bed," I said, immediately alert. "Mrs. Hudson, please treat him as you would treat my own son, Samuel, would you?"

Her eyes fluttered open.

"Of course, Doctor," she said.

Quickly, I dressed and grabbed my medical bag, and in short order I found a carriage that would take me to the river.

Along the waterfront, the tragedy was still unfolding. I could see the wreckage of at least three large ships in the river. Near them, two battleships fired their guns at the creatures. Men dragged dying victims ashore, arraying them rapidly on the ground before diving back into the murk to rescue others. The Thames itself roiled downstream, its thick waves rising into a black sky blotched with charcoal and etched with swirls and odd patterns painted in green. A quiver of terror struck me, for I'd seen those patterns on the spherical bones and the bizarre furniture adorning the homes of Lords Ashberton and Wiltshram, and Professor Henry Fitzgerald, leaders of the Order of Dagon.

A man tugged at my coat and screamed something at me, but I couldn't hear the words over the roar of guns and the thunder of cannons from the ships rocking up and down upon the waves.

Fire flashed and illuminated the green further, drenching the sky in a sickly pallor. The heavy night clouds hung like the sagging cheeks of the diseased dead. Creatures shimmered into view, then faded into the green-bleached sky. Some were immense with long tentacles, wings, and eyes the size of elephants, and some were much smaller, mere blips of glistening flesh coated in phosphorescent fur.

A cannon blasted, and my eyes followed the trajectory of the shot. Another jolt of terror hit me, as the cannonball ripped into the hide of a gigantic beast with several snouts and at least a dozen mouths. Sharp teeth reflected the green, which hit my eyes and momentarily blinded me.

Police officers fought alongside naval seamen, battling

the creatures and dragging the wounded ashore.

Thundering waves, more appropriate on the high seas than the Thames, hurled yet more bodies onto the riverbank, and in some cases, as far as the promenade and the buildings beyond. Still, despite the killer waves, the brave men of the British military dived back in, seeking more survivors.

An army battalion lined the bank and shot at the creatures, hitting few. Elusive targets, these creatures, as they flitted into sight, only to disappear again into that other place from which they came.

Tentacles curled around men and squeezed them until they exploded into flesh and blood that rained down into the water. Giant heads dipped and teeth grabbed men from the decks of cruisers and battleships, grinding the bodies to pulp and swallowing them. Bullets and cannonballs blasted into creatures, with seemingly no effect.

Clutching my bag and steeling myself against the hell before me—telling myself that I'd served in wartime and could handle anything—I slogged through the mud to the nearest victims. Bullets whizzed past me—misfired shots, I assumed, from the cruisers closest to shore. I ducked my head and examined a twitching body. It was headless. I moved on.

The next man had a head but was missing both of his legs. Suffering from massive blood loss, he wouldn't last long. For a few moments, I cradled his head in my arms and whispered words of hope in his ear. Over the cannons and guns, the screams and waves, he probably didn't hear a word I said.

"I'm with you, and so is God. You're going to a better place and time," I tried to tell him.

A better place and time...

Didn't this imply the existence of *another* place and time? Despite Holmes's theory about Fitzgerald releasing them by non-supernatural means, I was sure that the creatures had broken into existence from another place and time. With horror, I wondered if the human afterlife had any parallels with the place these creatures inhabited. *If there is a God, then we don't belong with these creatures anywhere at any time, not even after death. Unless*, I thought darkly, *there is indeed a hell.*

The man gasped his final breath. His head lolled. Gently, I lifted him off me and moved to the next patient.

Eventually, carriages arrived to take the injured to the hospital. Eventually, dawn bled into the green sky, and the green blinked out. Eventually, the skin of the sky stopped ripping and the beasts remained on the other side of the seams. Eventually, the waves calmed.

Hundreds of corpses littered the shore and floated on the river. My hands and arms were stained with blood, my clothes soaked with it. I tended to the sick and dying until other doctors pulled me away and took my place.

When I returned to Baker Street, Timmy and Mrs. Hudson were hunched over a game of dominoes by the fire, which infused the room with a warmth that seeped into my aching limbs. I fell into my chair with a sigh.

I could barely keep my eyes open, but through the tears of exhaustion I saw Mrs. Hudson's worried face inches from mine, and beside her, Timmy was crying.

"You must save 'im, Mrs. 'udson!"

"There's nothing to worry about, Timmy," Mrs. Hudson

said, but her voice sounded shaky. "Dr. Watson's come home bloody and beaten many a time. Let's wash him up and get him to bed. Help me, would you? There's a good lad…"

34
KOENRAAD THWAITE

Half Moon Bay

With Amelia Scarcliffe under Moriarty's control in London and my brethren blown to bits on our sacred beach, my captors kept a close watch on me. If I groaned, they barked at me to remain quiet. If I fluttered my gills or stretched my webbing, they recoiled, fumbled with their weapons, and yelled at me to remain still. Clearly, they feared me more than they feared their employer, this human, Moriarty.

Humans lacking harmony and depth, out of tune with the universe—*which accounted for the vast majority of them*—always feared what they did not understand. More than anything, they feared the unknown.

What these captors did not grasp was that, to one such as myself, humans were irrelevant.

Simpletons, all of them, with no comprehension of the dimensions between their world and all the worlds I had at my disposal. I could flit from the Dorset coast to another time and place whenever I chose. Humans lacked knowledge of the other dimensions, of space and time. They thought themselves so advanced, yet they understood nothing.

Six humans, each armed with multiple guns and knives, guarded me. Two remained outside at all times, while two slept and two watched over me. They rotated positions. As for me, I did not need sleep, nor did I need sustenance. Nothing mattered to me other than the birth of the brood I'd sired upon Amelia Scarcliffe.

How absurd that these idiots thought they had *captured* me.

Let them think what they want.

I reclined on the floor of the sacred cave, where I'd spent many a moon with my acolytes. I clenched and unclenched my toe suckers, watching with amusement as the humans paled and trembled and waved their pistols at me.

"Don't move," they said sternly although their voices quivered, "and say nothin', or we'll shoot you as sure as you breathe."

But did I breathe, *did I?*

Would a bullet kill me, *would it?*

As soon as the hatchlings squirmed from the womb, Yog-Sothoth would come and unleash all of us upon this world. We would return to claim what was rightfully ours from the dawn of time, for we'd owned this world and all within it, upon it, and in the air since the primordial sludge crept from the oceans.

These humans thought that, by threatening me, they'd obtain a copy of the *Dagonite Auctoritatem*. I knew all the chants in that book, and long ago, I'd tucked my sacred copy somewhere very safe and far away.

The man closest to me stuck a gun in my face.

"I can't wait to kill you meself," he snarled. "As soon

as the boss gives the order, you'll be dead, an' then we'll dice your flesh into bits an' fling 'em into the sea. You'll be gone forever, an' we'll be drinkin' an' laughin' for years to come."

He chuckled, no doubt thinking me afraid of the death he threatened.

The two candles by the rear wall where I reclined had burned down to nubs. Strands of light shifted across my would-be assassin—cheeks scarred from knife wounds, one eye permanently closed beneath a browless bone, mean mouth twisted and gray like a dead reef, the stubble on his unshaven face coarse like a rat's fur. Even by human standards, he was ugly and unworthy of life.

Amelia's smell clung to his flesh and hung in the mustiness of the cave. This had been our Dorset coast den, where the acolytes drank Old Ones Serum and jacked themselves to the Eshockers. They had loved the thrills, doled out by Koos, who I hoped had disappeared by now into safer zones.

The other man directly guarding me squatted. He was young, this one, with features less warped by age and a more agile body than the ugly one.

"Thwaite, you smell like you ain't washed in a 'undred years," he said.

I laughed inwardly. I'd never bathed—although I'd spent most of my life in Half Moon Bay and the deep ocean, of course.

What the young human did not realize was that the Old Ones drifted thickly through the air of the Dorset coast den, the sacred cave. He couldn't see them, couldn't feel them, but I knew they were all around us, and in fact, seeping into

the pores of these idiot humans, infiltrating their minds...
taking over.

"I've 'ad enough of the smell," the young one said. "Let's switch."

Nodding, the ugly one grabbed him and shoved him from the cave into the outside air and then followed him. I heard them both sucking air into their lungs, glad to be free of the cave and of me, if only for a while.

The two men sleeping near the cave entrance rolled on their sides, snoring, uninterrupted by the others. The Old Ones of the cave had infiltrated them sufficiently to keep them out of my way.

Strutting into the cave, the two men who had guarded the outside stared down at me, and one was brave enough to kick me with his boot. I groaned and pretended to feel pain, but I felt nothing—not even pity for these humans, for I do not feel pity, not ever.

"Your mate thinks you're in an 'idden cottage somewheres near 'ere," the kicker laughed, a smile spreading across his rat-hair face. He wasn't as ugly as the other rat-hair human. This one was eighteen or so, stocky with firm flesh and bright blue eyes.

Interesting how all the humans differed from each other in appearance, intellect, and mannerisms. Each considered himself unique. But in reality, they *were* all the same—puffs of flesh filled with blood and bone, easily extinguished, with lives so short they did not exist in the span of time.

"Your mate is givin' our boss all the gold about now," the other man said, and this one had yellow hair that clung like vines to his yellow face.

"You're boring me," I said.

The two guards pointed guns at me.

I popped into another dimension, then flitted back into view.

I'd had enough of these humans. I began to chant.

"*Ufatu maehha faeatai tuatta iu iu rahi roa cthulhu.*"

The yellow-haired man dropped his gun and lurched to the cave entrance. The one with bright blue eyes gaped at me.

I vibrated my gills, hopped to the wall, popped to the ceiling, and hung there.

"*Rahi atu daghon da'agon f'hthul'rahi roa,*" I hissed.

"What're you doin'? Get down 'ere an' shut up!"

Bullets whistled, and they ruptured the Old Ones' air, creating a narrow rift that no human could see. The microscopic creatures condensed upon the humans' heads, and I laughed—*aloud this time*—and vibrated into the other dimensional place. I didn't want to stay here for long. I needed to find Amelia and return her to Half Moon Bay, where we would greet Dagon and raise our spawn.

In the other dimensional plane, colors swirled, intense and rich, and filaments curled and spiraled, unwound and wired themselves into elaborate structures unknown to the human world. This was another time and place, where science twisted just like these beautiful filaments, where lead and phosphorus combined to produce gold.

In the human world, everything worked in different ways. A famous human, Sherlock Holmes, had cleverly deduced that replacing phosphorus with silicon would slow the tram machine to a near halt. No longer could the machine open the rift into the other space-times. Without the rift, nuclear reactions involving lead and phosphorus could not create gold, and neither could nuclear reactions involving lead and silicon.

I preferred to stay away from the humans, but back I popped into their world, wanting it to be our world already, to populate it with our own. *We will not share it with these pathetic worms, these humans. Why should we?*

My "captors" were screaming, all six of them now—yes, even those whose brains were infected with Old Ones—and firing their guns at me. *Blam, blam!* Bullets hit my flanks and bounced off, some piercing my flesh, some ripping my organs. I oozed green slime from the wounds, which tingled uncomfortably—

BUT.

I popped back to the place of colors and filaments, and there, I healed rapidly, the equations of the place differing from those in human space-time.

Do not think you can outwit us, Professor Moriarty or Mr. Sherlock Holmes. It is not possible to conquer us, diminish us, or eliminate us. We are forever. You, on the other hand, are disposable worms.

35

AMELIA SCARCLIFFE

Whitechapel Eshocker Den

"Koenraad Thwaite has escaped," I whispered to Maria, child of the powerful Blois Dagonite leader and Lucy Anne Nolande. "I sense it. I feel it."

"I also sense and feel it," she said serenely, squatting as I did behind the sofa in the Thrawl Street den.

"He's in the other place and time," I said. "He's no longer here. He's in the texture of the Other."

"Yes." She nodded. "Oh, that we could do as he has done and slip to that other space-time, as well."

But we couldn't, and we both knew it. Koenraad's abilities exceeded mine in some ways. To escape from Moriarty's den and from his clutches, Maria and I had to escape in physical form in the human world—right here on Thrawl Street. I hated to give her any power over me. I was the one carrying Koenraad's spawn, not Maria. And yet, Maria had powers beyond my own. She'd been sired by the Blois Dagonite leader, just as my spawn had been sired by Koenraad Thwaite.

Potent legacies.

Inheritance, a science humans understood in the most rudimentary way.

"Together," I told Maria, "we possess enough power to escape."

"Agreed," the child answered, "and I will work with you, Miss Scarcliffe, if you promise me one thing."

Did she want me to return her to Professor Henry Fitzgerald, the only father she'd known since birth? Did she want me to break him out of prison?

"And what is this one promise?" I asked.

"You must work with me, Miss Scarcliffe—"

"Yes, *yes?*" I prompted her.

Her little fingers stroked my neck flaps. Her eyes were sharp. Then the tiny mouth opened, and flatly, she said, "We will escape, and then we will unleash such horror upon London that they will wish themselves *dead*."

36

DR. REGINALD SINCLAIR

Whitechapel Lunatic Asylum

As I fidgeted with the right Eshocker, contemplating how long and how large a dose to supply, the door was kicked open, making me jump. Miss Klune dragged Bligh Braithwaite into the treatment room. She'd tied his wrists behind his back. As for his legs and ankles, I suppose she'd hoped that he would walk on his own, but his legs were limp, his heels dragging behind him, and he was offering no help whatsoever. Thankfully, she'd gagged him. Even so, he was letting out a steady stream of muffled shrieks.

I clenched my hands to keep them from shaking. How much more stress could I endure without suffering physical collapse? Ordinary folk had no idea how much their doctors endured for their sakes. It took everything in me to help my patients. I dreamed about their problems and treatments. I worried, and I also suffered with them.

Bligh Braithwaite glared at me. Disgusting, how he lacked control over his emotions. Today, they were on full display. His bleary eyes watered and his face creased with anxiety.

"Strap him in," I told Miss Klune. It was always wise to

make sure the patients knew I was in control.

This is the difference, Bligh, I thought, *between you and me. I can control myself, whereas you cannot, and a man who controls nothing, not even himself, has no worth.*

"M-mmmrrrrrr!" came his muffled howl.

Miss Klune untied his wrists and shoved him into the Eshocker chair. His legs and arms thrashed, and one fist landed on her chin. Her face grew even whiter—and colder—than usual.

"Behave, Mr. Braithwaite," she growled. Slamming him back into the Eshocker, she strapped him in. Both of us ignored his howling.

"Wind another strip of cloth tightly around his gag," I told the nurse, "then I'll get started." As she fetched the cloth from the cabinet behind the Eshocker and wrapped it around Braithwaite's head, I addressed him. "You need to accept that you've lost the battle, Braithwaite. Accept it, and your life will be better. Stop fighting me."

Tears flowed down his cheeks and saturated the cloth ties, which dug into his flesh.

"Mmmmmmmph... nnnnnnnnn... nnnnooooo..."

His head slumped forward. The tears dripped to his lap.

"Do you need my help with the treatment?" Miss Klune's blue eyes, oddly soft beneath the white-blonde hair that had slipped from her cap, were on my shaking hands.

"I am perfectly capable of using my own machine," I snapped.

Her face tightened and her eyes grew cold again—quickly.

Bligh Braithwaite's body went limp. His groans grew softer. He'd given up. He'd take whatever treatment I gave to him, and he'd be better off for it—*he'd see.*

"Leave," I ordered Miss Klune. "Go and take care of Willie Jacobs or Mrs. van der Kolk or Mr. Robertson. Keep the patients calm." I pointed at the door and glared at her.

"Doctor," she whispered.

"What is it, nurse?"

"It's just... I've never seen you this agitated. Is there anything I can do for you?"

Aghast, I waved my finger at the door, my arm shaking.

"I will forgive your impertinence this once," I told her. "Now go about your duties."

Miss Klune losing her coolness and asking personal questions? It was shocking, and I wouldn't stand for it, not in my lunatic asylum.

Without further comment, she stalked away, clicked the door shut behind her.

I circled Braithwaite's Eshocker and slid open a drawer near the bottom of my supplies cupboard. I pulled out a bottle. OLD ONES SERUM. HEALTH AND HAPPINESS. The cork twisted off easily enough, and I drank a heady amount of serum, feeling the heat pour through me. The instant sharp pain in my stomach was soothed by the euphoria of the serum. For a moment, I slouched against the cupboard, my hands grasping the back of the Eshocker box.

I lifted the serum bottle from the counter and drank again.

In his chair, Bligh Braithwaite twitched.

Am I really any different from Bligh Braithwaite? A jolt of terror ran through me. *Am I?*

"Mmmrumpphh, nnnnnnoooo..." he seemed to answer.

I drained the serum bottle. It slipped from my fingers and clattered to the floor.

My head swam. There were rims of color around the Eshockers. I shook my head, but my vision remained cloudy, the colors widening, then shrinking, then widening again. I was lost in the pulse of colors. *Lost.*

"Do as I say. I am the King of England, *King of...*" My father's last words before he died.

"Reggie, leave the lunatics to someone else. Go deliver babies." My mother's constant mantra, delivered shrilly whenever I visited her.

Leave the lunatics.

Lunatics. Lost. Babies. Lunatics. Lost. Babies.

"Shut up!" I screamed, clenching my fists, whirling, and pounding the counter.

Behind his gag, Bligh Braithwaite burst out laughing.

Enraged, I raced around the Eshocker and confronted him. But he just laughed in my face, so I ripped the cloth tie from his face and...

Did I enjoy watching him cringe when I ripped away the fabric? Did I?

I yanked out the gag ball.

"You dare," he shrieked, "to take what is mine! Those Eshockers are mine, Reggie! I built them, not you! Me!" His head snapped back and forth, his eyes flared with anger, his limbs struggled wildly against their restraints.

Ramming the gag back into his mouth, I sneered at him. The shaving scars on one side of his face bulged with reds and blues and greens. On the other side of his face, the coarse black hairs wore halos of yellow. His legs spasmed, his face screwed into a mask of pain. Bligh Braithwaite was no threat. He was insane, and nobody would ever believe him, not about anything.

I twisted off the screws holding the lid of the Eshocker box in place. I set the screws aside. Fumbling—for the serum made me groggy and giddy—I attached the blue wire to the metal plates on the front of the box, hence bypassing the flow of current through the fixed resistor. Braithwaite would get the full dose of current today. Extreme treatment. My favorite mode of operation.

I moistened the electrodes and put them on his forehead. Grasping the wooden handle that connected to the sliding contact switch of the variable resistor, I jerked the resistance to zero and the current to maximum strength.

Current equals volts divided by resistance.

The formula danced in my mind.

I = V ÷ R.

I = sixteen volts divided by zero (variable resistor slid all the way to the right) plus one kilo-ohm (head resistance) = sixteen milliamperes of alternating current to the head.

Buzzzzzzz!

Braithwaite's body jerked violently, and the chair banged against the Eshocker frame.

Zzzzzzzzap!

His fingers splayed, his body arched.

"Oh, isn't this fun," I chortled, "and aren't we having the grandest time?"

His color-rimmed eyes focused on me from beneath half-shut lids, then bulged as the electricity hit him in wave after wave.

And I remembered: Bligh Braithwaite in the old days, Braithwaite nimbly wiring the machines while I scribbled the equations, Braithwaite comforting me in the shadows of alleys when my father threw me out, *Braithwaite...*

And *me*, Dr. Reginald Sinclair, helping *him*, the insane, giving him shelter and food, helping him cope with life.

"Let me help you," I said, and this time, I addressed him kindly. "Please, old friend, you've waited so long for a cure. *Succumb.* Let me release these straps."

I stumbled forward, pushed the handle all the way to the left for maximum resistance and minimum current. Then I pulled up the handle to the left of the Eshocker, turning all the power off. The current fizzled to a halt.

Braithwaite whimpered.

"I'm sorry," I said. "You're getting in the way, that's all. You need to leave things alone and stop causing trouble. Let me help you, that's all I ask."

He was so limp, his arms and legs quivering, that I removed the restraints holding him to the chair. He did not even stretch his legs. Nothing. I removed the ties and the gag. Drool slid from his lips in a fluorescent waterfall, or so it seemed, and the sweat on his face glistened like colored beads.

The Old Ones Serum—it had done this to me, made my eyes see things, my lips say things, my brain unhinge, just enough to—

"The Eshockers are mine," Braithwaite whispered. "I built them."

He struggled to lift his body from the chair but lacked the strength. It was best for him to rest, I decided. Extreme treatment could drain the energy out of the most robust of men, and when it came to my patients, they tended toward weakness rather than strength.

I crouched beside him and placed a calming—yet oddly trembling—hand on his forearm.

"Patents," he whispered, "you…"

"Yes," I reassured him, "I'll file the patents soon. I've been busy with my patients and with Moriarty's demands for den Eshockers." My mind drifted to the problems of building all those den units for Moriarty.

Braithwaite almost fell from the chair, but my hand steadied him.

"You sell to the dens, many," he choked out. "Money, lots."

"Yes," I said, "money, lots, and it all goes into the asylum so I can help you and the others. I already own the den patent, and as soon as I own the hospital and extreme treatment patents, I should have enough funds to provide all of you with the best care anywhere in the world. I give you my word, Braithwaite, that this will happen."

Strands of color drifted around the room, picking up light, twisting into shapes, then untwisting. The air was thick and humid, and I struggled to breathe. My heart ached. My shoulders hurt. My stomach felt sliced by knives.

Before I could tell Braithwaite that, like him, I was not well, he lurched to his feet and reached for me.

My knees could no longer hold me up. Oh, how they hurt! I fell, curled on my side next to my beloved Eshocker, and clutched my belly. The room whirled.

Braithwaite loomed over me.

I turned slightly, reached one arm toward him.

"Doctor," he said softly, "for… for all you've done…"

37

DR. JOHN WATSON

Whitechapel Lunatic Asylum

Holmes struck a match on the counter by the day room and lit his cigarette. His eyes roamed the floor, where patients lay in heaps, writhing and moaning, as he smoked—rapidly as if in time with his thoughts. Huddled by Willie Jacobs, a man with foam on his lips sank his teeth into his own arm and then rolled his eyes upward in an ecstatic swoon.

"Malcolm Demane," I said to Holmes, "the receptionist's relative, the fellow we asked Dr. Sinclair to admit to the asylum."

Smoke billowed from Holmes's lips, and his eyes swung toward the wretch who was now chewing the bits of flesh he'd gnawed from his arm.

"Yes," Holmes said thoughtfully, "a man in dire need of medical attention admitted here only because we pried into the nature of Sinclair's Eshockers. It does not appear that he's received much help."

Inspector Lestrade had sent an urgent note to Baker Street, requesting my immediate presence with Holmes at the asylum. I'd collected Holmes from the Diogenes, where

303

he'd been waiting—smoking furiously and pacing the small corridor by the outer door.

Upon seeing us, Willie Jacobs shoved himself up and then trembled by the wall. Malcolm Demane's bloody arm inched toward Jacobs, one mangled hand grabbing Jacobs's ankle.

"Dr. Watson! Mr. 'olmes! You've come to save me again!" Jacobs cried, just as Demane yanked his ankle and sent him tumbling to the floor. Jacobs cursed and shoved Demane off, rising again to his feet, and this time he lurched toward us.

"Damn insane," he muttered, "why I 'ave to be 'ere, I dunno. I'm sick but not like this 'ere man, eatin' 'imself."

Gazing around for an ash tray yet finding none, Holmes tossed down his cigarette and ground it out, making me grimace. I enjoyed the occasional smoke myself, but it had its time and place.

We helped Willie Jacobs from the day room and gently held him against a wall, where he sagged and moaned. He'd lost more weight and hadn't much strength to walk on his own. His hand quivered as it slowly reached for his nose, and one finger uncurled and dabbed at each nostril. Then his hand fell back to his side.

"What's happening here, Mr. Jacobs?" Holmes asked. "Did you witness the murder of Dr. Sinclair? Who's running the asylum now that he is dead?"

Tears dribbled down his sunken cheeks to the rotting skin around his exposed teeth and jawbone, which were set in a permanent ghoulish grin. He winced as each drop hit the jagged flesh, etched like a ragged sea-cliff around his mouth.

"Inspector Lestrade is 'ere," he rasped so softly that I had to lean in close to the rotting face to hear the words. The decay smelled of imminent death. "'E's with the evil doctor in the evil room."

"Mr. Jacobs, did you witness the murder?" Holmes pressed.

"I see nothin' but evil," Jacobs muttered.

"Come along, then," Holmes said, hoisting the man up and gesturing at me to do the same from the other side of Jacobs's body. "Let's go to Dr. Sinclair's office, shall we?"

"N-n-n-no," Jacobs cried, "I ain't goin' there!" His struggles amounted to the fluttering of a moth beneath one's shoe.

"Holmes," I said, "is this necessary?"

"I need Mr. Jacobs's help," Holmes said curtly, eyeing me as if I were an idiot.

"Yes," I said, knowing when not to pressure my friend, "of course." Silently, I helped Holmes drag Willie Jacobs to the door marked *Dr. Reginald Sinclair.*

Holmes pushed the door with his shoulder, and it swung open. The stench of burned meat roiled out, reminding me of the corpses by the Thames and of the bloody murders on Thrawl Street.

"*What...?*" Holmes whispered.

"It's the machine," Jacobs blubbered.

Dr. Sinclair's desk was as I remembered it: tidy with papers piled on one side, a fresh blotter, leather chair pushed neatly beneath the desk.

The door leading to the examination room was ajar.

"At last, Holmes!" Inspector Lestrade called from the inner room. "I've been waiting for you. Bligh Braithwaite is here. I think he's our man."

As Holmes released Willie Jacobs and strode into Dr.

Sinclair's examination room, I stood by the inner door, aghast at the clouded image I saw through the black smoke that reeked of burned flesh. Jacobs mumbled incoherently, and his body shook.

"M-more death!" he spat out. "M-more killin's by more machines from 'ell! Where's the eyes, the bones, the gold?"

While I wanted to comfort Jacobs, I remained transfixed by the scene before me, unable to take my eyes off the horror, unable to speak... and choking for air.

Finally, I looked at Holmes, who was pacing, his eyes darting to the horror then to the cabinets and the examination table, and then back to the horror. One hand was upon his hip, the other cupped his chin. His eyebrows were furrowed, his eyes sharp with concentration. He was in the place where he goes when deep in thought.

My eyes swept to Lestrade, who stood with Bligh Braithwaite and two nurses—one I recognized as Miss Clara Klune, and the other whose badge identified her as Miss Amy Switzer—near the right Eshocker, all as far away as possible from the pools of blood and lumps of fried tissue and organs littering the floor. The Inspector's mouth twisted with nervous energy, his body stiffly upright as if looking taller would help him control the situation. Miss Klune also stood stiffly, her powerful physique and icy stare making Lestrade appear small and weak.

As for Miss Switzer, she was a fidgety woman lacking any hint of feminine appeal: middle-aged, short, raggedly cut graying hair. Muscular and plump with no waistline yet no roundness where her breasts should swell, she wore heavy black shoes that might have fit *my* feet, and for a man, my feet are not on the small side. Whereas the faces of Lestrade, Miss Klune, and even Bligh Braithwaite were all wrinkled with concern, Miss Amy Switzer's face looked *heartbroken*. Her lips twisted down at the corners.

Noticing my attention, her eyes met mine, and quickly, I looked away. Had she assumed my attention was that of a man *enticed* by a woman? The thought turned my stomach.

"Watson!" Holmes snapped, and his voice brought me back to the horror in the room.

"Yes?"

"Would you care to examine the victim?" Holmes erupted into a coughing fit, whipped out a handkerchief from his coat pocket, and slapped it across his mouth and nose.

I steeled myself, put *my* mind into that place where *it* goes whenever I have to examine the worst nightmares of life, or in this case, death.

Bligh Braithwaite, whose arms and legs kept seizing up and twisting into odd shapes, and Inspector Lestrade, joined Holmes with the two nurses on the other side of the room, where a second Eshocker sat, cold and clean, awaiting its next victim, or rather, patient.

The Eshocker in question was another matter. It was anything but cold and clean. It was where the corpse—*unrecognizable*—had been seated and the source of the burned-meat haze filling the room.

"Who is the victim?" I asked.

"Dr. Reginald Sinclair," Holmes said. "That is obvious, Watson." When I didn't answer, he elaborated. "It's the simplest of deductions. If he were not dead, he would be alive in the room with us now. This *was* his hospital."

"Idiot," Miss Switzer hissed.

Lestrade chuckled.

"Get on with it, would you?" he said, not in an unkind tone.

"Dr. Sinclair might have been out at the time of this… incident," I said.

"But he wasn't. He was right here with Bligh Braithwaite," Miss Klune said coldly. "I know because I left the room shortly before what you refer to as an *incident*, and the two of them were alone, *right here*."

"Where exactly were they?" Holmes asked.

"The patient was in the Eshocker, ready for treatment— much needed treatment, I might add," she said, glaring at Bligh Braithwaite.

The patient's arms suddenly kinked out of joint, and he screamed. Both nurses grabbed him, but he wrenched from their grasp.

His arms twisted unnaturally outward at the elbows, then snapped back into place with a loud clicking noise.

"I-I don't… don't… need…" He could not finish.

"But you do," Miss Klune cooed at him with what I took to be her professional voice, "you do need extreme treatment, Bligh."

"You see, sir, why Mr. Braithwaite is our man," Lestrade said.

"Yes," Holmes replied, "I can see why you *think* this is the case. Tell me, nurse, was this room locked from the inside when you left them alone here? I notice that the door can be locked from either side."

"Dr. Sinclair always locks the examination room from

the inside when he's treating a patient, and he insists upon treating them without help."

"Do you have a key?" Holmes prompted.

"No, there is only one. Dr. Sinclair keeps it on him at all times."

"I see..." Holmes said thoughtfully. "Watson, would you examine the body, if you don't mind?"

I *did* mind—the smell had grown no less appalling with familiarity—but all the same, I held my handkerchief over my nose and mouth and approached the Eshocker. Where Dr. Sinclair had burst upon us in his office only days earlier, now he himself had burst, literally and permanently. Charred remnants of his white doctor's coat curled atop the scorched rags of his trousers and shirt, revealing a body ravaged by fire. Burned to the bone in places. His chest was ripped down the center as if by a scalpel. The blood had coagulated but still glistened; dark, viscous swells had oozed from the volcano of a dead heart.

I moved slowly, not wanting to slip and fall in the blood slicking the floor. I stepped around the bone and lumps of burned meat, but still, some of the bits were so tiny I could not avoid them and my shoes crunched and squished as I worked.

Oddly, at this moment, my mind flashed to my wife, Mary, and our baby, Samuel. If I could finish this job with Holmes, if I were smart enough to help Holmes uncover and catch this murderer, to help him shut down the dens and kill the hideous creatures swarming in the Thames—

I longed for the warmth of home, for the smile of my wife, for the gurgles of my son. After this nightmare finally ended, my family would return to London and to me, and I would be happy enough to be with them and to eat meat pies and take evening strolls and issue tonics to cranky old ladies.

It would be enough.

Get through this, I thought. *Finish the job and get out of this room. Finish the whole job and get out of this way of life. It's not worth it.*

I pulled a notepad from the inner pocket of my coat. While I scribbled with the stub of a pencil, Holmes continued questioning the nurses and Bligh Braithwaite. Coughs punctuated their conversations, and like them, I choked for lack of air while examining the corpse. My eyes watered and burned from the smoke. The room had no windows to open, so it was nearly unbearable and I was anxious to complete my work and leave.

"Inspector Lestrade tells us that another victim was found in the Whitechapel asylum. A young girl? You found her, Miss Klune?"

"Yes, I found her," came the clipped tones, "dead, killed at night in her bed."

"There were no signs of foul play," Lestrade interjected.

"But," the nurse said sharply, "there was foul play, detective."

"Inspector," Lestrade murmured.

"The needle marks on her arm were too fresh," Miss Klune said, "and also too ragged. We don't do things that way here. We know how to give patients injections."

"You were on duty that night, Miss Switzer?" Holmes inquired.

"What of it?" she demanded. "She was alive when I left, and besides, why would I kill her? She was dead enough, being in the asylum so young and for the rest of her life. Why would anyone kill her?"

I listened to all of this while inspecting the remains of the Whitechapel Lunatic Asylum director and jotting down notes.

Legs: both broken at the kneecaps, shattered from knees to ankles, femur stumps on the seat of the Eshocker chair. Exposed thigh muscle on the right stump. Blackened tibia and fibula fragments like ashes around the feet, also burned to the bone.

"You tried to kill me, too," Willie Jacobs rasped. "You evil nurse, tell Mr. 'olmes the truth, tell 'im 'ow you crept into me room at night with the needle. An' you killed others, you called 'em kind killin's."

"I did no such thing," Miss Switzer snapped.

"She has been particularly agitated lately," Miss Klune said thoughtfully, then barked a quick laugh. She didn't strike me as the type of woman who laughed very often. "Why, Amy dear, I do believe you desired our Dr. Sinclair, didn't you? Oh, don't deny it, dear. It's my job to know people and understand what they're thinking. I work in a lunatic asylum. He spurned your love, didn't he, dear?"

I didn't look up from the corpse or from my notes, but my mind was whirling with possibilities. My heart quickened. *By God, what I wouldn't give to know what Holmes will make of all this*, I thought. I wrote:

Two hands still grasp the armrests. A blackened shaft of humerus hangs from the remains of the left shoulder. On the right side of the corpse, the shoulder looks as if someone pounded it with a jackhammer before setting it aflame.

The exposed trachea has cracked midway up the neck, and the head hangs upon the shredded chest, held in place by filaments of muscle.

"I love nobody!" Miss Switzer screamed. "Nor did I try to kill anybody! Not that ridiculous imbecile, Caroline Brown. Not you, Willie Jacobs! And most certainly not Dr. Sinclair, a man I respected more than anyone in this world. What will we do without him? I, too, am a professional, Miss Klune!"

"Calm down, ladies," Lestrade said.

I swiveled to look at them. The nurses both clenched their fists, and had Lestrade not stood between them, I was certain they would hurl themselves at each other in a death match. Vaguely, I wondered how women fought in battle to the death. I was only familiar with the methods of men.

"Doctor," Holmes asked me, "are you finished?"

"One more item," I answered.

I wrote in my notebook:

Top half of head blown off, remains on ceiling and splattered on nearby cabinets. Eyes gone. Nose gone. Black smoke still curling from bottom half of head. Lips exploded. Teeth broken, missing.

Looking up, I announced the cause of death. Nobody looked at all surprised.

"Electrocution by Eshocker," I said.

Holmes turned to Bligh Braithwaite.

"But who strapped him in and flipped the switch?" He spoke as if he already knew the answer.

38

"Can we leave this infernal room?" Miss Switzer demanded. "The smell is going to kill us all. The patients need attention. Someone has to get a cart in here, get the body out. Inspector Lestrade, take control of the situation. There are things to do."

Lestrade nodded and started moving to the door leading to Dr. Sinclair's office, but Holmes grabbed his arm.

"A moment, Lestrade," Holmes said. "I may need you." His eyes twinkled. "If only as a witness."

Wrenching his arm from Holmes, the Inspector muttered something under his breath and gestured at Miss Switzer to leave the examination room. Quickly, before Holmes could object, she raced out, and the outer door to the hall banged shut.

"Why did you let *her* go?" Miss Klune asked. "If anyone's guilty of murder, it's Amy Switzer. I wasn't here the night of Caroline Brown's murder, nor was I in this room when our poor doctor met his fate."

"Yes, yes." Holmes waved a hand at her. "I grow weary of this situation," he said, "and of the plodding nature of the inquiries." At this, he glared at Lestrade, who put his hands on his hips and glared back at him.

"That's enough, Holmes," the Inspector said sharply. "Let's hear what you have to say, so we can all leave. I can't breathe in here, and as the nurse says, I must call someone about the corpse."

Holmes surveyed Lestrade's diminutive physique and agitated manner. Then his attention snapped back to Dr. Sinclair and the Eshocker that had electrocuted him.

"His arms and legs broke from struggling against the restraints during electrocution. The electricity was high enough to penetrate the flesh and burn him, inside out, one might say—yes, I believe the poor fellow was cooked to the point where the meat fell off his bones. The electrodes on the head applied sufficient voltage to cook his brains until the skull exploded." Holmes reflected a moment. "A terrible way to go, and one of the worst cases I've encountered."

"But can the Eshockers actually kill a man in this way?" I asked. "I have seen addicts shocking themselves over and over again in the Whitechapel den, and none of them are seriously hurt—merely addled. Why here and right now, in this particular instance, did the man who created the Eshocker die from own creation?"

"Indeed, a mystery. Miss Klune," he said abruptly, turning to face her, "has anyone quarreled with Dr. Sinclair recently? Have you witnessed any arguments, fights, anyone or anything out of the ordinary in the past few weeks?"

She didn't hesitate with her answer.

"Dr. Sinclair did have a visitor, yes, and he was afraid of this man and avoided him."

Holmes's eyebrows lifted.

"Pray tell," he murmured.

"Dr. Sinclair told me the visitor was a procurement agent, though he never told me what the fellow wanted to buy from a lunatic asylum. A burly man with big fists and big muscles, a threatening manner about him. He stopped by several times, and after each visit, Dr. Sinclair was shaking, unable to speak without a tremor in his voice, and while I hate to say this about our dear, departed director, he took to the bottle a bit, too." She pointed to the door leading to Dr. Sinclair's office. "He keeps alcohol in one of the drawers of his desk. I know. I've seen him eye the drawer when he gets particularly nervous."

Lestrade dashed into the office, and sounds of drawers sliding open and banging shut soon followed. Shortly, he returned with his hand held high, clasping a half-drained bottle of Old Ones Serum.

"Of all the drinks he could have chosen!" Miss Klune exclaimed. "The man had sufficient wealth to take anything he wanted—brandies, fine liquors, wines! But Old Ones Serum? That's what they drink in the seediest of dens."

"The serum is opium and alcohol and nothing more," said Holmes.

"But Holmes, how do you know this?" I asked, astonished.

"Because I've drunk my fill of it, Watson. The taste is not hard to recognize."

My chest tightened. All the time Holmes was investigating the dens for his brother, Mycroft, had his motive extended or been largely driven by his desire to swill Old Ones Serum? The thought sent chills through me.

"Dr. Sinclair's office is tidy, as always, with everything in its place as far as I can see," Holmes declared. "Nobody fought with him in that office today, then dragged him in here and electrocuted him. There was no intruder from the outside office. The murder was not done by this so-called procurement agent." Again, he turned to the nurse. "You told us the doctor locked himself into this examination room with Bligh Braithwaite?"

"Yes," she said.

"And that nobody, not even his most trusted employee—that being you, Miss Klune—"

Not even a glimmer of self-satisfaction crossed her face.

"Correct," she said, "I had no key to get into this room. Nobody did."

Stuffing his handkerchief back in his pocket, Holmes stooped in the blood and muck by the dead man's charred feet and examined the straps around the ankles. Then he peered closely, his face inches from the floor, at the black ashes littering the area. He pulled a small magnifying lens from his pocket and peered yet more closely, then jumped up, his face lit with the thrill of discovery.

"The slightest of footprints, Watson, but I see them! The blood and the ashes obliterated most of the outline, but still, I see them!" he cried. "Lestrade, this is evidence, surely, that there was a struggle in this room, right by this Eshocker, that someone forced Dr. Sinclair into the chair and strapped him down. And that someone, that person, electrocuted him! Briefly, he stood close to the chair as Sinclair was cooked alive—he stood close enough to imprint the outline of his shoes in the dust and the blood on the floor. He moved back and away from the cooking man to avoid the explosion of blood, guts, and brains, didn't he?" Holmes whirled and pointed at Bligh Braithwaite. "It had to be you, sir, for nobody else was in the room!"

Braithwaite's limbs were locked into odd positions, and his head jerked back and forth. It was Miss Klune who spoke up for him.

"No," she said, "it could not have been Mr. Braithwaite. Look at him, Mr. Holmes. He's a very sick man. He's not capable."

"B-b-b-but…"

Everyone swiveled, and all eyes flew to Willie Jacobs, who clawed his way up from his position on the floor by the door and now stood, clutching the door to remain upright.

"Yes, Mr. Jacobs?" I said.

"B-but Bligh an' me… Norris did woodwork on the boxes…"

"Yes?" Holmes pressed.

"A-an' I… I did the fine woodwork, I did the electrical work…" His right hand crept up, shaking, reached for his nose and jabbed the air instead. His other hand gripped his right wrist to keep it steady and then moved the right hand, still shaking, to his head, where he jabbed both nostrils wildly. Pleasure spread across his face. He moaned once, happily. His thumb poked rhythmically at the left nostril then the right, and then his knuckles flew across both nostrils, jamming them with such ferocity that I feared that, in his dilapidated condition and with much of the flesh rotted off the lower half of his face, he would dislodge his nose and it would fall to the floor.

"Please," I cried, running over to him, "please, Mr. Jacobs, do stop!"

I grabbed both hands and tore them away from his face. He staggered against the door and started sliding down, his body angled such that he would fall and probably injure himself further. I looped my arms under his shoulders and propped him up, then stood beside him, holding him around the waist.

"D-don't touch me nose," he whimpered.

Oh, God.

"I promise," I mumbled. The poor wretch.

"I'm too weak to kill." He struggled with his next words. "But B-Bligh! He's the master electrician on the Eshockers. The *master*," he stressed.

"Can I please leave now?" Miss Klune interjected, breaking our concentration on the matter at hand. "I have work to do, patients to tend, and I see no point in you keeping me here, Mr. Holmes."

"Just go, yes, go!" Holmes cried with a flourish of his hands. "Leave us, Miss Klune, if that is what pleases you!"

"*Well, I never*—" she started to say something but then raised her chin, straightened her back, and stalked from the examination room. Again, the outer door to Dr. Sinclair's office banged.

"Tell us, Mr. Braithwaite," Holmes asked, as if he hadn't been interrupted by anything, "where are the new Eshockers built? Where is the room?"

Braithwaite's lips issued a cascade of stutters and babbling, his body refusing to cooperate as he tried to remain standing. Instead, he collapsed to the floor again, writhing and twisting.

Both men, Willie Jacobs and Bligh Braithwaite, were dreadfully ill, and how much longer either would live was anyone's guess. My heart filled with sadness and compassion. I would have done anything within my power to help these men recover, or at minimum, feel more comfortable in their own bodies as they sank into the unknown realm beyond death.

"H-help me," Willie Jacobs whispered, pointing a finger at the medicine cabinets.

I did as requested and helped him stagger past the Eshocker and the corpse, past the blood pooled and coagulating all around the machine.

Our shoes in blood and gore, we stood in front of Dr. Sinclair's medicine cabinet. Jacobs's wavering finger pointed at a shelf containing books and beakers. As I held onto Willie Jacobs, Holmes circled the Eshocker and reached to the shelf, shoved aside the items, finally exclaimed, "At last!" and reached his arm *into the back of the cabinet.*

"What is this?" I cried.

"The lever, pull the lever," Jacobs said with as much strength as he could muster, his eyes dim and unfocused.

Holmes reached far into the wall behind the cabinet, and something groaned—machinery set in motion by the lever—and then we all jumped back as the wall, with its attached cabinet, swung open to reveal a hidden room. Still clutching Willie Jacobs and sliding on the blood, I nearly fell, but I regained my footing and followed Holmes into the interior room. Inspector Lestrade followed, hauling a limp and gibbering Bligh Braithwaite.

"This is where we build Eshockers," Jacobs said. "This is where evil is done."

Wooden boxes and Eshocker chairs in various states of construction were scattered about the room. A couple of tables were strewn with saws and chisels, cables and wires.

Holmes sniffed the air, prompting me to do the same.

"The black smoke," I commented.

"Yes," Holmes said, "it's in this room, but not in a concentrated manner, and even less so than in Dr. Sinclair's outer office. Somebody opened the wall and slipped in here, then closed the wall again before much smoke could get inside. Who did that? Who hid in here and then made his escape—and when did he run away?"

"When the door's closed, there ain't no way out," Jacobs said. "Dr. Sinclair, 'e locked us in to build the Eshockers."

"The murderer must have left the wall slightly ajar," Holmes said. "Tell us the truth, Mr. Braithwaite. When Miss Klune found Dr. Sinclair's body, were you hiding in this room?"

The man refused to answer. He didn't deny the murder, nor did he confess to it.

With a frustrated huff, Holmes searched the walls and floors, even the ceiling. He poked everywhere, and he peered long and hard at everything through the powerful convex lens he habitually carried.

"Nothing," he concluded, "no more hidden doors, no hidden levers opening any of the walls, no trap doors. The only way in and out of this room is via the examination room."

We returned to the room where the dead man with his head blown off and his limbs shattered to gore, with his chest sliced and mangled, with his organs burned, waited for his final resting place.

"Surely, Holmes," I said, nodding at Willie Jacobs, still draped in my arms, and at Bligh Braithwaite, held upright by Inspector Lestrade, "these two are patients, and exhausted ones, at that. How much more do you expect them to endure?"

Holmes pointed to the clean Eshocker across the room.

"Put them over there and stay with them, doctor, and let me ponder in peace such that I may concentrate and conclude this matter, once and for all."

Lestrade eased Braithwaite to the floor behind the other Eshocker and then refused to leave Holmes's side. As for me, I was as exhausted as poor Willie Jacobs, and I sat next to him on the floor near Braithwaite. Jacobs's head fell forward, and he started snoring, lightly at first, but the volume increased as it hissed through his exposed phossy jaw and mangled nostrils. Braithwaite remained awake but highly agitated, jerking and twisting constantly, eyes fixed on Holmes.

My friend spoke as if lecturing Inspector Lestrade on a case study he'd already solved and was teaching to a class. The Inspector appeared annoyed but kept quiet, having long experience with Holmes and his solving of cases for which Scotland Yard received the credit.

"Miss Amy Switzer most likely murdered Caroline Brown while she slept," Holmes said. "She administered a dose of medicine, enough to kill her, but we'll never know for sure. I believe Willie Jacobs, who has never lied to me and has proven himself both loyal and faithful. Remember, Watson," he added, "how Mr. Jacobs stood guard and almost lost his life protecting Mary and Samuel? Mr. Jacobs tells the truth, that Miss Switzer attempted to inject him with lethal drugs. He fought her off, and the administered dose didn't suffice to kill him. Switzer, however, did not kill Dr. Sinclair. She was not in the locked room, nor did she have access to it."

"Holmes," I finally interrupted, "why must we discuss all of this *here*, in this particular room, where Dr. Sinclair is—?"

"Where he's *dead*?" Holmes whirled, and with a grand flourish, waved at the corpse in the right Eshocker.

"Because," he said, "Willie Jacobs and Bligh Braithwaite are going to demonstrate exactly how this Eshocker killed him!"

39

"I suggest we employ the *vacant* Eshocker," I said drily.

"Ha! I wouldn't have it any other way," Holmes said, pinching his nose as he walked past Dr. Sinclair, whose head had ceased emitting smoke.

By now, I was accustomed to the stench in the room, and if anything, felt that I might never get the odor of the dead Dr. Sinclair off me.

"I've always wondered how these den machines work," Lestrade said. "How they make a person so intoxicated, simply with the use of a bit of electricity. Evil stuff," he added, "work of the devil. Feh. Electricity, indeed. Gas is good enough, if you ask me, as are candles."

"Wake up, Mr. Jacobs." Gently, I shook the man until he snorted one final bit of sleep out of him. His bleary eyes popped open, and he squinted.

"We're still 'ere," he said, as if not believing his sore luck.

Lestrade propped up Bligh Braithwaite.

"And you, sir, come along. It's time to show us how you killed the doctor."

Braithwaite resisted, blubbering that the Eshockers were "brilliant devices" and "could not possibly murder" and that, even with "extreme treatment," neither he nor Willie Jacobs had come close to dying.

Jacobs agreed.

"It ain't like the beast, which killed me father. I was electrified by Sinclair enough to know. Extreme treatment, 'e called it. Cannot kill, Mr. 'olmes."

"The sooner you show Mr. Holmes how these machines work, the sooner we can all leave the treatment room," I told both patients.

With Lestrade holding onto Braithwaite and me holding onto Jacobs, we stood with Holmes before the vacant Eshocker.

"You sit in the chair, an' I'll show 'em 'ow it works," Jacobs suggested to Braithwaite.

"N-nooo, you sit in the chair, and I'll... I'll show them how it works," Braithwaite stuttered. "Th-this is my machine, not yours."

"N-no! No Eshockin'!"

"Gentlemen, we do not mean to actually switch the machine on. This is purely a theoretical demonstration. Mr. Jacobs, you need to rest. Please, sit in the chair." I eased Willie Jacobs into the Eshocker.

He looked doubtful, but sat down without further complaint. For what they claimed was such a harmless machine, neither man had much desire to mount that chair and subject himself to the "pleasures" of den electrotherapy.

Braithwaite fumbled with the top of the coffin-sized box and finally gave up, stuttering at Holmes to unscrew it. Holmes did as requested and removed the four twist-off screws, lifting the lid and setting it aside.

I huddled beside Holmes, Braithwaite, and Lestrade, all of us staring at the array of components, wires, and cables in the box. Behind me, Jacobs cried out, and I turned to see him on the floor. He'd fallen from the Eshocker chair.

"S-strap him in," Braithwaite said, and with Jacobs struggling and begging me not to do it, I tied his wrists to the armrests and his ankles to the chair legs.

"A-a cloth... put a-a cloth in his mouth," Braithwaite choked out.

"No!" Jacobs shrieked, thrashing against his restraints.

I assured him that we would not gag him, nor would we turn the machine on. He struggled until his strength gave out, and then he settled down with his head slumped forward.

"Dr. Watson, do take notes," Holmes commanded without looking at me, intent on studying the internal workings of the Eshocker.

Braithwaite, with an air of pride I thought misplaced, mumbled his way through an explanation of the Eshockers. Lestrade held him upright the whole time, with Holmes pointing to components, nodding, and asking follow-up questions. And I scribbled:

Four metal plates are attached to the outside left of the box, and four screws attach each plate to the box itself. On the outside of the box and attached to the top two plates in the upper left, is a dynamo that, in turn, is attached to a DC power wall socket mechanism.

"Th-this dynamo charges th-the Eshocker battery," Braithwaite explained. "Usually, it... it is unplugged from... from the wall."

I continued scribbling, though my knowledge of electric mechanisms was limited and what Braithwaite described was well beyond my understanding.

I hoped that Holmes either understood everything Braithwaite spoke of or that my notes would elucidate details that escaped him.

Beneath the plates attached to the dynamo, a knife switch with a wooden handle and a copper contact turns the Eshocker ON or OFF. A U-shaped holder secures the knife switch when the machine is not in use. With the knife flipped to the ON position, the two-volt rechargeable battery sitting inside the box sends two volts of electricity.

"Holmes?" I said. "Do you understand what he's talking about?"

Braithwaite glowed with pride, while my friend explained in common terms.

"Dr. Sinclair invented a way to keep his machines running on stored electricity in the form of these rechargeable batteries. The mechanisms for all of these things we see in the box are available, but nobody has yet put them together in this manner. This might be one of the first rechargeable batteries, and if I'm not mistaken, over here to the right, this is a DC-to-AC chopper used with a transformer and a series of resistors..."

He'd already lost me, so I let Braithwaite continue while

I scribbled notes as verbatim as I could manage to catch the stuttered words.

A rotating rod connects the DC motor to a DC-to-AC chopper. The motor sends DC current into the chopper. Two volts of AC current flow from the chopper into a transformer unit.

"AC, AC, a miracle," Willie Jacobs rasped from the Eshocker chair. "Me father would 'ave loved to see it."

"Newfangled nonsense," Lestrade said bitterly. "These newfangled devices will kill us all, Mr. Holmes."

"Pray continue," Holmes told Braithwaite, ignoring the Inspector. "I need to know exactly how this works."

"R-right," Braithwaite stuttered, and then he continued explaining the machinery with the pride a father has of a newborn son. I wondered, *did I sound like this after Samuel was born?*

Again, without much comprehension, I documented what Braithwaite told Holmes.

The transformer unit is an iron core with five winding copper coils on the left and forty winding copper coils on the right. Approximately nine inches by nine inches in size, the transformer unit takes the two-volt AC and multiplies it by eight, yielding sixteen volts of AC power.

Holmes interrupted.

"Clarification, sir," he said, pointing into the box. "These two wires coming out of the right side of the transformer unit carry sixteen volts of AC power?"

Braithwaite nodded.

"Yes, AC power, flippin' positive an' negative, positive an' negative!" Willie Jacobs said giddily. "I ain't never seen such machines, not even in the beast!"

I'd always considered Holmes and myself to be hungry for science. I'd always considered this hunger to be the source of my great affection for Holmes and my need to be with him, even when Mary objected. The excitement of using science to solve crimes was a thrill beyond most anything in life. Holmes felt the same, of this I was certain.

Now here we both were, learning about electric mechanisms that we'd never dreamed possible, yet these wires and devices existed in a London lunatic asylum. And stranger still, who was explaining all of this to us? Two patients of the lunatic asylum! It was humbling, to say the least.

"I see that there's a lot of room back here," Holmes said, pointing again, "between this wire behind the two rightmost units and the back of the wooden box."

"N-n-n-n-not much," Braithwaite stuttered.

"But enough," Holmes said. "Now, tell me about these final two units on the right."

Lestrade complained that his arms were growing tired from holding up Braithwaite, that we knew enough about the infernal machine and it was time to get on with it.

"This one goes to jail," he said, nodding at Braithwaite, "and that one—" he nodded at Jacobs—"goes to a proper hospital, I'd say."

"A few more moments, I promise, Inspector. The details

are important," Holmes said, gesturing at Braithwaite to continue.

"I-I will s-say nothing more if you s-send me to jail," Braithwaite insisted.

With Lestrade spluttering and objecting, Holmes reassured Braithwaite that he could remain in the Whitechapel Asylum—at least, for now—and delay any concerns about jail.

"V-very well," Braithwaite said after long consideration, "I'll tell you, and b-being an intelligent man, Mr. Holmes—" he shot a disparaging look at Lestrade—"y-you will see that I-I could not have killed anyone with this... this Eshocker.

"That... that wire," he began to explain, and Holmes pointed to the wire coming out of the transformer and spanning the backs of both of the final two units on the right of the Eshocker box, "y-yes, yes, that wire... it is for den, hospital, and ex—"

"Extreme treatment," Jacobs rasped.

"Y-yes, extreme treatment," the other agreed.

With questions flying back and forth, I simply kept my mouth shut and wrote everything down that seemed pertinent.

The second AC wire comes out of the transformer and attaches to the variable resistor unit, which provides from four to zero kilo-ohms of resistance, or in other terms, resulting in between 1.7 and 3.3 milliamperes of current. The resistor unit is very narrow and sits close to the front of the Eshocker box, and protruding from the front of the box is a wooden handle that slides along a contact switch.

"When in the far left position, the 'andle 'elps the doctor use maximum resistance of four kilo-ohms an' minimum current," Jacobs explained. "When in the far right position, it gives zero kilo-ohms of resistance an' maximum current."

I stared at Jacobs. His technical skill shocked me. While he continued his explanation, I scribbled further notes.

The final unit, a fixed resistor, supplies one kilo-ohm of resistance. It is used for hospital and extreme treatment modes.

"What's this?" Holmes asked, pointing inside the box near the front.

Braithwaite said it was a metal plate, to which both the variable and fixed resistors were wired. In addition, another metal plate on the front of the box had one wire attached to the fixed resistor and another wire—a long one—dangling from the front of the box.

"And this?" Holmes said, gesturing toward one that had caught his eye.

"The blue wire—" this time, it was Jacobs who answered—"is attached to each metal plate in front of the fixed resistor, but only when Dr. Sinclair wants to short out the four kilo-ohms of fixed resistance down to zero. It's for ex-ex—"

"Extreme treatment?" Lestrade asked.

"Only for ex-ex—" Jacobs answered.

"Understood," Holmes said.

He turned to me and told me to write down what Jacobs had said.

"The first wire off the transformer, Watson, goes out

through a hole in the side of the box. At its end is the first electrode that Dr. Sinclair attached to his patient's head. A person's head has—what, Doctor?—approximately one kilo-ohm of resistance?"

I shrugged, not having the answer, and he shot me an annoyed look and then continued.

"The second electrode is hanging here in front of the box. This long wire, Watson. It supplies either zero or four kilo-ohms of resistance, depending on how Dr. Sinclair slid this wooden handle along the variable resistor and whether he attached the blue wire shorting the fixed resistor."

"Damn it all," Lestrade exclaimed, dragging Bligh Braithwaite away from the Eshocker and dumping him by the wall again. "What the deuce does any of this mean, Holmes, and why should we care? Braithwaite killed Dr. Sinclair. That's all that matters. He was in the room. He knows how to use the damn box."

"It matters," Willie Jacobs said.

"*But why?*" the Inspector demanded.

"Because," Jacobs rasped weakly, "the Eshocker don't kill. Dr. Sinclair used ex-ex... used it on me an' Bligh many times for long times. We survived the worst Eshockin'."

"In its largest doses, can extreme treatment kill a man?" I pressed.

"No," Jacobs said.

"No," Braithwaite said.

Finally, to the great relief of all present, Holmes dismissed us from Dr. Sinclair's treatment room. Inspector Lestrade hurried off to get help with Sinclair's corpse, and as for both Bligh Braithwaite and Willie Jacobs, we had no choice—

at least, for the moment—but to return them to the care of Miss Klune. Holmes instructed her to pay particular attention to Willie Jacobs and to ensure that Miss Switzer was never alone with him.

Later, after Holmes and I returned to the Diogenes Club, he tugged me into the Stranger's Room, where we could talk. I was anxious to get home to 221B, dine with Mrs. Hudson, and get some sleep. But Holmes insisted that I write a series of equations in my notepad before allowing me to leave.

"That Eshocker killed Dr. Sinclair," he said, "and Lestrade is right that Bligh Braithwaite did it. And I know *how* he did it, Watson."

40

Per Holmes's instructions, I sketched a drawing of the Eshocker wiring in my notepad and supplemented it with equations. As always, his grasp of complex details amazed me. Had he wanted to sell Eshockers to Moriarty's dens as well as to hospitals across England, he could have built the machines himself.

DEN MODE

$$I \text{ (current)} = \frac{V \text{ (voltage)}}{R \text{ (Resistance)}}$$

$$I = \frac{16 \text{ volts}}{(0+4+1)} = 3.3 \text{ milliamperes max. of alternating current}$$

where:
- 0 is the minimum resistance from the variable resistor
- 4 is the resistance from the fixed resistor
- 1 is the resistance of the forehead

$$I = \frac{16 \text{ volts}}{(4+4+1)} = 1.7 \text{ milliamperes minimum AC}$$

where:
- 4 is the maximum resistance from the variable resistor
- 4 is the resistance from the fixed resistor
- 1 is the resistance of the forehead

HOSPITAL MODE

Make sure the blue wire is detached.
Note that in hospital and extreme treatment modes, the second
4 kilo-ohm resistor is replaced by a 1 kilo-ohm fixed resistor.

$$I = \frac{16 \text{ volts}}{(0+1+1)} = 8 \text{ milliamperes maximum AC}$$

where: • 0 is the minimum resistance from the variable resistor
• 1 is the resistance from the fixed resistor
• 1 is the resistance of the forehead

$$I = \frac{16 \text{ volts}}{(4+1+1)} = 2.66 \text{ milliamperes minimum AC}$$

where: • 4 is the maximum resistance from the variable resistor
• 1 is the resistance from the fixed resistor
• 1 is the resistance of the forehead

EXTREME TREATMENT MODE

Attach the blue wire.

$$I = \frac{16 \text{ volts}}{(0+1)} = 16 \text{ milliamperes maximum AC}$$

where: • 0 is the minimum resistance from the variable resistor
• 1 is the resistance of the forehead

$$I = \frac{16 \text{ volts}}{(4+1)} = 3.2 \text{ milliamperes minimum AC}$$

where: • 4 is the maximum resistance from the variable resistor
• 1 is the resistance of the forehead

"Numbers never lie," Holmes said. "Willie Jacobs was correct that the Eshockers—even in extreme treatment mode—are not lethal. But the equations also prove that Bligh Braithwaite electrocuted Dr. Sinclair."

"But that's a contradiction!" I cried.

"No contradiction," he said. "You're making an incorrect assumption."

"Which is?" I asked.

"I'm surprised you don't see it. *Think*, Watson."

I fumbled for an answer.

"Might there be another way to wire the resistors?"

He stared at me.

"Wrong," he said curtly, and then, "That is a naïve suggestion."

"Then *what* is my incorrect assumption?" I asked, frustrated.

"Your wiring diagram," he pointed at my notes, "clearly shows that there are three modes of Eshocker operation. But what if Bligh Braithwaite used the Eshocker in another way, something outside the normal modes of operation?"

"The Eshocker has a fourth mode," I stated.

"*No*," Holmes said. "Your wiring diagram eliminates that possibility."

Then what? I wanted to scream. *Just tell me!*

But whatever he'd worked out, he wanted me to deduce on my own, so at this point, I gave up and closed my notepad. If I waited long enough, I'd learn the answers along with everyone else.

41

A strapping fellow of eighteen with ragged hair and chipped teeth, Wiggins ruled over the Baker Street irregulars. To request his presence at 221B, I need only put the word on the street that I wanted to talk to him. Wiggins knew what "talking" meant—coins for information brought by the orphans he rounded up.

Just like Timmy.

My Samuel would not end up like Wiggins and Timmy. Even if, God forbid, something were to happen to both Mary and me, we had money in trust for him and friends who would see him safely through to adulthood. But all the same, I hoped that I would soon be reunited with my family and able to protect them once again.

Mrs. Hudson knocked on the outer door and called to me.

"He's here, Dr. Watson. Shall I bring him in?"

Hurrying across the room and sweeping the door open, I ushered Mrs. Hudson and Wiggins into Holmes's sitting room.

"Where's Mr. Holmes?" Wiggins asked, peering around and fidgeting with the worn cap in his hands.

"He's not at home." I motioned at the boy to sit in my chair by the fire. I dared not let him sit in Holmes's chair, not wearing those filthy rags. The boy looked and smelled as if he hadn't washed in a month.

Mrs. Hudson wrung her hands by the door.

"Please bring Mr. Holmes back," she said, "and let us all pray that life returns to normal. Those beasts in the river and the peculiar folk staggering around London have me scared, Doctor, and all my friends, as well. We're afraid to go outside. We're afraid to sleep at night."

Wiggins looked at the holes in his shoes.

"You should 'ear what they say on the street, Mrs. 'udson," he said. "They say we all be possessed by devils."

"They might be right, at that," the landlady answered, with her eyes watering, "but I tell you, if anyone can help us, it is Mr. Holmes. Doctor, please tell me that no harm has befallen our Mr. Holmes!"

"He is as you remember him," I assured her. She continued to stand at the door, wringing her hands and not budging, so I added, "He has asked me to question Wiggins. Would you close the door as you go?"

She snapped out of her reverie, murmuring, "Yes, yes, yes, of course," as she left.

I turned my attention to Wiggins.

"You have Timmy Dorsey safely tucked away?" I asked.

As he nodded, white flakes dropped thick as snow from his hair and fell on my favorite chair. It was the least of my worries. I told Wiggins that both Mr. Holmes and I appreciated what he was doing for Timmy.

"Timmy's a good boy, does what 'e's told," Wiggins said. "Timmy's no trouble."

"Good, good. It's best that I not know where he's hiding, so here—" I pulled a generous amount of coins from my pocket and gave them to Wiggins. "Get Timmy and bring him to the Whitechapel Lunatic Asylum."

Licking his lips, Wiggins slipped the coins into a trouser pocket. Then his eyes darkened, and he frowned. Wiggins was like that: he could be eager to please, yet just as quickly turn as hard as any man I've ever known. Street life did not amount to much of a life. It hardened a man.

"You ain't gonna throw Timmy into the asylum?" Wiggins asked with an edge to his voice.

"Don't worry about *that*!" I exclaimed. "Never, I can assure you! Timmy knows what we need, and he knows what to expect when he arrives at the asylum. Now be off, for there's no time to waste!"

In a flurry of dirt and white dandruff, Wiggins jumped from the chair and hurried to the door. I heard him bound down the stairs, and soon after, the outer door to 221B shut with a click.

Quickly, I hailed a carriage and asked the driver to drop me near Osborn Street. From there, I headed on foot to the asylum, where Holmes waited for me in Dr. Sinclair's treatment room.

The light from the gas lamps illuminated the lines and dark circles beneath Holmes's eyes. He'd neither slept nor eaten well for days.

I pictured Dr. Sinclair's remains on the chair of the right

Eshocker. I pictured his brains dripping from the ceiling. Despite vigorous scrubbing, blood stains splotched the chair and the box holding the electric mechanisms. Stains flowered like fungal growths on the ceiling, the supplies cabinet, and the floor.

"Both nurses, as well as the cleaners, did what they could," Holmes said, "but what happened in this room is not easy to erase." He gestured at one Eshocker, then the other.

"While we wait for Timmy and the animals," he continued, "I'm curious, Doctor, if you've analyzed the equations I gave to you and if you have yet deduced the nature of this crime. I believe that I gave you sufficient information."

His eyes twinkled. He enjoyed giving me puzzles and watching my face as I tried to solve them. I found it unnerving, as if I always had to prove myself to him.

Why couldn't he just tell me what he had deduced? Why must we play these games?

On the other hand, when I did logically arrive at the correct conclusion—or minimally, offer a guess that satisfied him—it gave me a jolt of pride and a sense of accomplishment that I rarely felt elsewhere.

And so, as I always did, I played along.

"Dr. Sinclair's Eshockers, even in extreme treatment mode, could not murder anyone," I said. "To tamper with the Eshocker such that it electrocuted Dr. Sinclair would have required knowledge of the equipment's inner workings. But aside from Dr. Sinclair, only a handful of insane patients who helped him construct the Eshockers knew about their inner workings. Willie Jacobs and Bligh Braithwaite both seem to possess sufficient knowledge about the Eshockers to rewire them. And yet, the Eshocker used to kill Dr. Sinclair had not been rewired. According to both Jacobs and Braithwaite, the wiring conformed to its standard configuration." I paused, considering the puzzle and staring at the bloodstained Eshocker, where Holmes stood.

Abruptly, he lifted a shoe, struck a match, and lit a cigarette. He puffed steadily, his eyes focused on me, with the expression of a professor quizzing his prize student. I didn't feel equal to the task.

"There is another possibility," he finally said. "Simple logic, Watson."

I'd been so focused on his equations and the alternating current and the milliamperes and the three modes of operation that I'd not seen the obvious. *Remove the clutter. See the simplicity.*

"Could the killer," I said, "have rewired the Eshocker, murdered Sinclair, then returned the wiring to its original configuration? Is this the answer?"

He flicked ashes to the floor, where a day ago, Sinclair's ashes and blood had coagulated into a blackened pulp.

"Is it?" he shot back at me. "Think, Dr. Watson. How could Braithwaite have done that?"

"W-why, I don't know!" I exclaimed. "I'm not an electrician, Holmes, and I know very little about electrotherapies."

"But to figure this out," he countered, "you don't need knowledge of electricity or electrotherapies." He burst out laughing, then apologized. "I am sorry. I don't mean to upset you. It's just so simple. *Logic*, my dear fellow."

"Tell me, then, and be done with it," I retorted.

"I will give you one final clue," he said. "There was no way to rewire the Eshocker itself to kill Dr. Sinclair. And now, you can deduce the rest."

If the Eshocker hadn't been rewired at all... then what?

I snapped my fingers.

"I have it!" I exclaimed. "The killer *added* something to the Eshocker. But then, what did he do with it after killing Dr. Sinclair? Where did this added component or whatever you have in mind, Holmes—where did it go?"

"Ah, and that *is* the answer *and* the question all in one," my friend said, glowing.

At that moment, Timmy stepped into Dr. Sinclair's outer office, hauling via rope two small lambs and a calf. The animals barely squeezed through the doorway. Resisting the tugging of the ropes around their necks, they bleated and lowed as if being tortured.

"Get in 'ere, you stupid bleaters!" Timmy barked, and then followed with a stream of cursing. He wrenched the beasts through the open treatment room door, as well.

Appalled by the spectacle, I stood, speechless, but Holmes rushed over to Timmy.

"So Mr. Waltham delivered, as promised. I had faith he would do so," Holmes said. "You had no difficulties at the market?"

"No, sir," Timmy said. "Mr. Waltham's infected animals was waitin' as you said. They gave me trouble, though, in comin' 'ere. I be glad to 'ave Wiggins with me."

"Watson, help him," Holmes demanded.

I broke from my trance and grabbed a rope from Timmy. Holmes took another, and the boy held onto the third rope.

"What kind of trouble did you run into?" Holmes asked the boy.

"We got a cart an' loaded the animals on, but they was crazed, these beasts, an' kept fallin' and makin' messes and tryin' to run in circles. They ain't well, these bleaters."

"I see," Holmes said, but his mind had already raced onward. He handed me his rope, shut and locked the door, and withdrew a vial containing a swab coated in brown sludge from his coat pocket.

"This is the brain matter I collected from an infected man nearby. You recall the fellow, Watson."

Remembering the man from whom we'd obtained the brain matter, I shuddered. He'd been bald with an indentation like a crater on the top of his head. The sludge had filled the crater, slopping over as the man tilted his head.

"We're taking this with us to the dissecting rooms at the Royal London Hospital," Holmes told me, sticking the vial back into his pocket, "along with these animals after Eshocking."

Timmy's eyes widened.

"You're goin' to Eshock 'em?" he said.

"Yes," I said, "apparently so. We have to study the brain tissues, Timmy, of infected animals, of Eshocked animals, of this man we encountered who was infected so badly I fear he is dead by now."

Knowing little about the study of brain tissues, it occurred to me that the bit of gore in Holmes's vial might not contain living cells at all. Of what use would it be?

We tied the ropes of one lamb and the calf to the left Eshocker.

Timmy and I lifted the remaining lamb onto the chair of the right Eshocker. We had to prop the animal horizontally across the seat. Holmes secured the right wrist strap around the tops of the lamb's front legs. He secured the other wrist strap around both of the hind legs. All three animals bleated and lowed something horrible.

Of the three of us, only Timmy seemed comfortable mistreating the animals in this way. I felt cruel, and by the sick look on Holmes's face, he felt the same way.

"Let's get this over with," I muttered. "This is a bit much, Holmes."

"I grant you it's difficult," he answered, "but if we don't examine these brain tissues, we may never find out what causes the neural psychosis. We may never find out how to make you better."

"We're grasping at nothing," I retorted.

"We are not!" he exclaimed. "I never grasp at anything, Watson, without a reason."

You protest too much, I thought. *This time, Holmes, you're not sure what you're up against or how to fix it.* Never had my faith in Holmes been this low.

But I did as he asked, as did Timmy, because if anyone could save London and its people, it was Sherlock Holmes.

The lamb in the Eshocker chair struggled to break free, but Dr. Sinclair had built his machines well. He'd built them so no neural psychotic, no matter how violent, could break free—and neither could a lamb.

Holmes and Timmy unscrewed the top of the Eshocker box, and the detective examined the wiring, then announced that it was in "Hospital mode at 2.66 milliamperes, the minimum dose of current, and ready to go."

With a flourish, he turned the machine on.

Zzzapp.

Muted bleating, wild struggling on the chair—

Holmes turned off the machine, counted softly to himself, then switched it on again, and—

Zzzapp.

This time, the lamb shrieked, and the chair rocked as the poor animal desperately tried to break free of its restraints.

"Holmes," I cried, "really, must we do this?"

"The duration of the treatment," Holmes said, "is equal to the dose."

"*What?*" I said.

"It's not just the milliamperes, Watson, not just the amount of alternating current, the resistors, and all the rest. The duration of the treatment also matters. We don't want to apply a current high enough to kill an animal, or say, a person. Yet we've seen the creatures, in larger form, flit in and out of view right before our eyes—"

"At the warehouse when Fitzgerald broke the gate, the rift, that held the creatures from entering our world—"

"Yes," Holmes said, "and during the performance of Bellini's *Norma* at Swallowhead Spring, when we saw the same thing happen. Therefore, it is logical to assume that the creatures are—dare I say it?—flitting in and out of view—"

"In and out of our world," I exclaimed, "though how

such a thing is possible, I cannot fathom!"

Again, Holmes turned off the machine, and after a short while, switched it on.

Zzzapp.

The lamb shrieked until it lost its breath, and its eyes rolled. Its neck snapped back and forth, and its body convulsed.

Timmy burst out crying, and apologizing quickly to Holmes for leaving, I gathered the boy and ushered him from the treatment room.

"Sit in Dr. Sinclair's office for now," I suggested.

Miss Klune appeared at the door. I shooed her away, telling her that this was "official government business."

I ran back into the treatment room and begged Holmes to stop, but he stared me down.

"Control yourself, Doctor," he said. "I am not torturing this animal. The treatment is no different from what Willie Jacobs received, what Bligh Braithwaite received, what countless paying customers receive in those dens. Why, I myself have received this treatment—and much more—in the den on Thrawl Street."

"We can make the choice for ourselves," I told him, "while these poor beasts in our care cannot."

"They are all infected, Doctor, and will die whatever happens in this treatment room. Keep that in mind. The minute doses of current I'm applying do not hurt human patients, and hence, I assume they will not hurt these beasts. You're a medical man. Act like one."

He glared at me so intensely that I blanched, feeling like a schoolboy who has been chastised by his master. I fell silent and let him continue with his "treatment" of the infected lamb, who still bleated and struggled upon the chair.

"Take note," Holmes said, "that I'm increasing the alternating current to four milliamperes."

With that, he turned the machine back on, and...

Zzzapp.

Again, Holmes turned off the machine, counted softly, and switched it on again.

Zzzapp.

The lamb continued to bleat and struggle within the restraints.

"Increasing to six milliamperes," Holmes proclaimed, and then he went through the whole wretched procedure again.

"Nothing," he concluded. "The beast remains sick. No change in its behavior. See how it hangs its head, rolling its eyes. Look at the cast of the eyes. Red and gray. No, this beast is still infected." He paused and looked at me. "I suggest you join Timmy in the outer room, Watson, if you are not prepared to watch what I am about to do."

"Which is?" I asked as coldness ran down my spine.

"Twenty-five milliamperes could kill the beast," my friend said thoughtfully, "yet twelve milliamperes might do the trick. If necessary, we'll push extreme treatment to the high end, to the full sixteen milliamperes. But for the sake of the lamb, we'll do extreme treatment at twelve milliamperes of alternating current first. Pulse it. Kill the microscopic creatures that are here now. Let more flit into the brain from the otherworld. Pulse the alternating current. Kill them. *Repeat.*"

Not waiting for me to agree or disagree, he turned to the open Eshocker box, attached the blue wire that turned hospital mode into extreme treatment, and adjusted the handle on the variable resistor.

"Not this dosage level!" I cried, stepping forward and wrenching him away from the Eshocker and from the lamb.

Across the room, still tied to the other machine, the second lamb and the calf pulled against their ropes and shrieked.

"This is unbearable!" I cried.

He shook free of me and pushed me away.

"I repeat," he said sternly, "I am not torturing these animals. They are already infected with something that will kill them. They have no hope of survival. They are suffering as it is. In the wild, they were running—*indeed, tumbling*—down hills, slamming into fences, piling into heaps. They were headed for slaughter. Watson, these animals are *sick*. Do you understand?"

"I understand that you're hurting them," I said.

"I am hurting them no more than Dr. Sinclair hurt his patients when he tried to cure them of neural psychoses. I am hurting them no more than you hurt your own patients, Doctor, when you apply treatments."

"But you intend to kill them."

"Twelve milliamperes of alternating current," he said, then pulled the lever on the side of the box, and the Eshocker switched on again.

One minute passed.

The lamb struggled, as before, eyes whirling, head sagging, all four legs pushing against the restraints.

Two minutes.

Still, the lamb bleated and struggled.

Three minutes, now four, and now five.

Holmes turned the machine off and on, applying the current in pulses of five minutes each, repeating the process four times, peering at the lamb, eyes narrowed, seeking a response to the treatment.

Finally, Holmes switched off the machine.

"Holmes?" I whispered.

"The lamb felt a mild sensation," he told me in a clipped tone, "and only mild pain. The current did not destroy its brain, and it certainly did not kill the lamb."

From Dr. Sinclair's office, Timmy was weeping in loud, heaving breaths. I stepped away from Holmes and joined Timmy, holding his hand and kneeling beside him.

Holmes appeared in the doorway, his shoulders hunched, his face drawn.

"It's time for the hospital," he said. "There's a cart waiting outside. The lamb we Eshocked may have been cured of the infection. We won't know until we get to the Royal London Hospital."

"You killed it!" I cried.

"Of course not, Doctor," Holmes said. "I do believe I cured it."

42

"We examined tissue from an infected lamb and calf, as well as from the Eshocked lamb. We also examined the brain sludge from that poor gentleman we encountered on the street."

"Yes, Sherlock, and what were the results?" Mycroft wriggled to cross his legs in the one reasonably comfortable chair in the Stranger's Room. Unable to cross his legs due to their enormous size, he sagged back against the cushions and made do.

Once again—and I hoped, for the last time—I squirmed on the stool, and I answered Mycroft before Holmes had time to pluck the pipe from his lips.

"The brain cells of the Eshocked lamb," I answered, "looked like healthy cells, whereas the brain cells of the infected but not-Eshocked lamb and calf both appeared bizarre."

"Bizarre in what way?" Mycroft asked, and then added, "Please do tell me the results of your efforts, Doctor, without requiring that I constantly prod you along. My time is valuable and I bore very easily."

Holmes blew a smoke ring at his brother, and this time, it was Holmes who spoke before I could gather my wits and respond.

"Boredom does run in the family," Holmes said. "In short, Eshocker extreme treatment killed the infection in the lamb. Mycroft, extreme treatment *cured* the animal."

"Extraordinary," Mycroft muttered.

"That animal's infection would have killed it," Holmes added, "as it was killing the other poor animals in Avebury."

"But what is the nature of this infection?" Mycroft pressed.

"It appears that the infection is caused by or is simply due to the—" he chose his words carefully—"permeation of the brain tissue by microscopic creatures hitherto unknown to medical science. They enter our world from... what I think of as an *otherworld*. By the by, it is the same infection as we have seen in humans. I took a sample from a fellow in Whitechapel the other day that showed exactly the same organisms."

When Mycroft looked at me quizzically, I nodded in agreement. Indeed, this is what Holmes and I had seen beneath the microscope lens: dead creatures with filaments around their edges. Yet the Eshocked lamb's brain cells showed no signs of playing host to such organisms. Holmes had been correct. The voltage had sealed the rift between our world and the otherworld. Perhaps the creatures had brought the Eshocker voltage from our world into theirs. We had no way of knowing, not for sure. The experiment was far from precise.

Holmes dumped the contents of his pipe into a tray set on

the floor by his feet. He refilled the pipe, and then folded his tobacco pouch and tucked it in his coat.

"Test the Eshocker and make sure it kills these microscopic creatures." Mycroft turned his large head and trained his eyes on Holmes and then on me. He grasped the armrest, ready to push himself from his chair and leave us again. "Once you are certain, Sherlock," he said, "you will apply this treatment to those suffering from this neural psychosis malady." As Holmes began to protest, Mycroft waved his finger and said, "No, you don't have to Eshock everyone yourself, Sherlock. Prepare detailed instructions on how to rig these den Eshockers up for extreme treatment. It doesn't sound particularly complex. There's no need to replace the fixed resistor in the dens with the type used by Dr. Sinclair."

"Correct," Holmes agreed, "one need only attach the blue wire that shorts out the fixed resistor entirely. Voilà, extreme treatment."

"*When you are certain*, Sherlock," his brother stressed, "let me know, and I'll contact the appropriate authorities, who will send agents to the rest of England to cure anyone else who has the infection."

Rising from my stool, I stretched my aching legs and back and made a final decision.

"Eshock me first," I said over Holmes's objections. "Cure me, and then I will be sufficiently convinced to help you Eshock the others."

Mycroft lumbered to the door leading to the Diogenes Club, where quiet awaited him.

"One final task," he said, as his hand turned the knob.

"You don't have to tell me," Holmes said. "After I Eshock Dr. Watson, you want me to find a way to use the Eshockers to kill those damnable creatures in the Thames."

"As always, you are correct," Mycroft murmured. "Test the deadly device before you use it on the river creatures. Get some *ordinary* cows from the slaughter house for your experiments."

Holmes cast me a glance.

"These cows are *meant* for slaughter, Doctor," he said. "Yet have no fear. We'll make sure they don't suffer."

"But you said the Eshockers don't kill," I stammered, "yet you intend to use the Eshockers on me. How will the Eshockers kill those creatures? I don't understand—" I broke off.

"One problem at a time," Holmes said. "First we'll Eshock you and then we'll attend to the rest."

43

"I insist, Mr. Jacobs, that I be the first test subject."

"No, Dr. Watson. Step aside. Me death is near anyways. You 'ave a baby an' a wife, an' they need you."

I could easily have shoved the frail man aside and forced him to let me go first. But I thought about what he said, about Samuel and Mary and how they needed me alive and well. With my mind reeling with visions and colors, it had taken all of my strength to help Sherlock Holmes to this point. Weakened, I dreamed only of my family, of seeing them again and perhaps living far away from the horrors, the crime, and the demands of life in London.

Had we not been happy together before I'd visited Holmes and been lured back into his investigations? Yes, I remembered it well: days with my patients, nights with Mary, both of us astonished by the miracle of our tiny Samuel. He'd been born prematurely and barely survived. I wanted him back. But in the end...

"Mr. Jacobs is too weak and might die during treatment," I told Holmes. "Other than the mild infection of these creatures, my health is intact. If one of us has a better chance of surviving the treatment, it is I, so strap me in and give me the treatment first."

Did I see a flash of concern on Holmes's face? Did he fear that I might die from the treatment? If so, he erased the thought from his mind, and without looking at me further, gestured at me to sit in the Eshocker chair.

Willie Jacobs protested, but Holmes refused to listen to him.

"You're a decent man, Mr. Jacobs, one of the finest I've met, but Dr. Watson's point is a good one."

The seat cushion was comfortable enough, though ripped by the lamb that had occupied the Eshocker yesterday. Letting my arms and legs go limp, I watched colors form complex patterns around the room. Whirls within whirls, ten-sided objects within those with fifteen sides, breaking apart and re-forming in seemingly endless arrays.

"The duration of the treatment," Holmes repeated his words from yesterday, "is equal to the dose. Remember, I gave the lamb twelve milliamperes in five-minute pulses, and that is what killed the brain infection or, as I'm coming to think of it, the infestation of the brain by microscopic creatures."

"W-why didn't extreme treatment kill me, then?" Willie Jacobs asked from his slumped position in the left Eshocker. His voice was so weak that I could barely hear him.

Holmes answered: "Because Dr. Sinclair didn't pulse the dose. He applied the treatment for only a short while, never as long as five minutes at a time, and never for a full twenty minutes in total, applied in blasts or pulses."

Holmes restrained my ankles and wrists with the straps,

put the two moist electrodes on my head. My hands grew clammy, and sweat dripped down my face and neck. It curled down my back. I began to shiver.

Perhaps this was a bad idea.

"Sorry, old friend, but the gag…" He popped a clean ball into my mouth and wound cloth around my head. "It's for your own good," he added. "The gag will keep you from biting your tongue."

I'd changed my mind and didn't want to be Eshocked. I didn't like the feeling of entrapment, of not being able to move or speak. I struggled with the restraints, and my voice came out in muffled gurgles.

Holmes's eyes watered but quickly cleared. He removed the top from the Eshocker box, checked that the blue wire was attached to both fixed and variable resistors, adjusted the variable one, and glancing at me, switched on the machine.

A mild tremble swept through me, then a sizzle as if my blood ran a bit faster than usual, my heart raced a bit more. My flesh tingled: my fingertips, my legs, my torso, even my tongue and eyelids. Then there was my mind—it *more* than tingled. It soared, and as it peaked with ecstasy, pleasure streamed through me. I *ached* with pleasure.

Was this the feeling Sherlock Holmes had when he injected himself with cocaine? If so, I could understand the addiction. The Eshocker made me feel as if I never wanted to get out of the chair and face reality again. If I could float forever, happy, *why not?*

But the dose was low, and Holmes did to me what he had done to the lamb. He started with a low current, then turned off the Eshocker, applied greater current for more minutes and then more; and as the current pulsed through me in stronger doses and in longer durations, my mind and body reacted—*violently.*

My body was no longer under my control, nor was my mind. My leg and arm muscles struggled against the restraints, which bit into my skin. Searing pain fanned out from my wrists and ankles. Still, my muscles strained, so hard, in fact, that cramps seized both of my calves, which popped out of joint at the knees. I screamed, but the gag muffled me.

Gripped by terror, shrieking and crying, pain slicing through me—the room was a whirl of colors, and my stomach knotted with nausea—I tried to scream, "Holmes!" but all of my screams came out as "Hhhhhhh." In the background, Willie Jacobs wept and came into view, clawed at Holmes and begged him to release me from the Eshocker.

"Let 'im go, 'olmes! Stop, you're 'urtin' 'im," he whimpered. "This beast is evil, just like the one I built with me father."

"Nonsense, Mr. Jacobs. A pulsed Eshocking will cure Dr. Watson's illness. It will kill the infestation." Using one arm, Holmes easily kept Jacobs away from the Eshocker, and finally, Jacobs disappeared from view, staggering back toward the other side of the room.

Zap. Sizzle.

When I thought my head was going to explode, Holmes finally turned off the machine—this time, for good. The pain subsided, the tingling resumed. Unable to open my eyes, I felt Holmes's fingers unstrapping my ankles and wrists, felt his hands knead the strength back into my calves.

I fell forward, and Holmes caught me. With his arms around my waist, he gently eased me to the floor, where

I lay on my side, sobbing. My left eye cracked open, and through its window, I saw the stain of Dr. Sinclair's blood. Filaments encircled the dark blotch, making it look like one of the bizarre creatures under Holmes's microscope.

44

Several days passed. Worried more about my recovery from the neural infestation than about Moriarty's men finding and killing him, Holmes returned to 221B Baker Street.

Mrs. Hudson catered for both of us as if we were her long-lost sons. She seemed especially worried about me, which warmed my heart. Rather than languishing in my bed while Holmes played his violin for hours on end, I had Mrs. Hudson to keep me company. She kept cool cloths on my forehead, read the newspapers to me, and when I insisted that I was well enough to get back to battle, she urged me to rest. Mycroft sent notes by messenger to Holmes, asking for updates about my condition.

Holmes broke the seal on the latest note and read it to me.

"While I hope that Dr. Watson soon feels better and his brain resumes normal functioning—" at this, Holmes chuckled—"I hope, too, that you are not neglecting your work on the Eshocker that might rid us of the Thames infestation. Watson's recovery from the illness suggests that our plan to eliminate the accursed creatures en masse will also meet with success."

A tall order from Mycroft, I thought, but Holmes didn't appear fazed at all. He just laughed.

"We will do what we can," he said, and he set aside his brother's note and picked up his violin again.

While I listened to Holmes's endless renditions of his repertoire, Mycroft sent agents across England to modify the den Eshockers. Holmes instructed Timmy how to modify the Eshockers in the Thrawl Street den to pulse twelve milliamperes in the manner Holmes had done with me. The newspapers began printing stories that relief had come to London's Eshocked addicts.

Holmes visited the asylum once without me and returned with a report about Willie Jacobs.

"He's not well, Watson, and Miss Klune doesn't expect him to live much longer. He says that, when he dies, he will be thinking of his father but also of you and me, whom he considers his closest friends."

I rose from my clammy sheets, but Holmes eased me back down.

"I've failed Mr. Jacobs," I moaned. "I could not cure him."

"There is no cure," Holmes said gently, "not for phossy jaw at this late stage."

"I know, but—"

Holmes held up his palm.

"Enough, my dear fellow. Gather your strength. We must confront Bligh Braithwaite and persuade him, along with poor Mr. Jacobs, to create this special Eshocker for us. We must do this quickly, for Jacobs is essential and might not last long enough to help. Braithwaite is unpredictable. He's a murderer."

As the snow fell like giant tears on the gray streets, the season crept toward Christmas and the New Year. A fog penetrated the nights and drifted through the days. It was almost 1891, and still, I'd heard nothing from Mary. With my mind clear of the bizarre infection, it filled instead with images of Mary and Samuel.

One morning, I shoved aside Mrs. Hudson's breakfast tray, hauled myself from bed, and confronted Holmes.

"It's time," I said, even as my legs wobbled, barely able to hold my weight. "We can delay no longer, Holmes. We must act, and we must do it now."

Surprised, he set his violin on his chair, peered intently at me, and then straightened himself, having reached a decision.

"To the Whitechapel Asylum, Dr. Watson," he said, "and not a moment to lose."

At this, I struggled into my clothes and grabbed my cane, and together, we hailed a carriage and set off for Thrawl Street. The cold air and snow stimulated my senses, cleared my head further. Drops of ice brushed my face. Numerous folk passed us on the street, lost in their own worlds and oblivious to one another. Boys snatched bread from bakeries and dashed off, women toted food baskets and babies—this was my London, and I would protect it.

I could never really leave, not *permanently*. As soon as Mary returned, I would limit myself to being a good husband and as decent a doctor as I could manage. I would stop fooling myself into thinking I needed the thrill of these adventures with Holmes. I would settle down and be content with the simple things in life.

Lost in my thoughts, no different from all the other men and women passing on the street, I was suddenly jerked back to reality by Sherlock Holmes.

"Bligh Braithwaite will show you how he murdered Dr. Reginald Sinclair," Holmes said. "You will see it for yourself. Then, under threat of *painful* execution unless he cooperates, he and Willie Jacobs will give us an Eshocker to kill those Thames creatures. Brace yourself, Watson, for the true battle is just beginning."

45

Miss Klune sat in Dr. Sinclair's chair as if perched on a throne. She clasped her hands and set them on the desk, then motioned for us to sit in the visitor chairs.

"No need," I said, though I had to place my palm on the edge of the desk to remain steady.

She glanced at the cane in my other hand.

"But surely, you need to sit," she said. "You don't look well, Doctor."

Rather than sit in Dr. Sinclair's office, Holmes strode to the door leading to the treatment room.

"Dr. Watson is fine. He's cured," Holmes said, as my knees buckled and I nearly fell. I pushed myself off the edge of the desk and tottered across Sinclair's office to join Holmes by the treatment room door. He looped an arm through mine, for which I was grateful, and addressed Miss Klune. "Please obtain both Bligh Braithwaite and Willie Jacobs for me, would you? I trust you have no issues with what we are about to do, which in brief, equates to killing those monsters in the river."

With her ice-blonde hair knotted in a tight bun and her ice-blue eyes trained on Holmes, she responded in a clipped voice carefully modulated to betray no trace of emotion. I had the sense that everything about Miss Klune was based on her long years of service at the Whitechapel Lunatic Asylum.

"I understand the urgency of your mission," she said.

"Mr. Jacobs and Mr. Braithwaite, then, and *quickly*?" Holmes pressed.

"Yes, I'll get them." As she left the office, she turned and added, "Then I'll be in the day room, if you need me."

Waiting until she must be far down the hall, Holmes hurried from the room, and I sank into the chair of the left Eshocker. In moments, the bloodstained chair of the right Eshocker would be occupied by a new patient, who might die during extreme treatment.

In short measure, Holmes returned with Timmy and a companion. Although I expected the arrival of the boy and our new patient, my heart sank anyway, and a sadness fell over me. Medical discoveries were often made by those who experimented on animals, and even on human beings. Indeed, we learned about our own bodies by carving up corpses.

As Timmy pushed a calf through the door into the treatment room, Miss Klune followed with an equally reluctant Bligh Braithwaite along with Willie Jacobs.

"Dr. Sinclair would never have permitted this," she said. "His office was a sanctuary. This treatment room was private and carefully controlled. His Eshockers were his life."

"I admire your loyalty," Holmes said, as he and Timmy roped the calf to the Eshocker chair legs and armrests. There was no way the calf could fit on the seat. Its tail swished by the open Eshocker box. Its eyes blinked at the left Eshocker. Chewing and blinking steadily, unaware of what was about to happen—*this is not a patient*, I thought, *but rather, an animal about to be inhumanely used in a medical experiment.*

"Holmes…" I whispered, and then I said firmly, "You know how I feel about this type of experiment. I know that medical science has moved into modern times, that our doctors examine corpses and live animals in hopes of determining how to treat human ailments and save lives. But still, I strongly object to torture, Holmes."

"As do I, Doctor," Holmes said. "It is not my intention to torture this animal. Medicine is your profession, and what we're doing today may save countless lives."

"Yes," I muttered. "Yes, I know, Holmes, but—"

"Timmy procured this poor beast from the slaughter house," Holmes told me, "so its destiny was already sealed. In fact, if Timmy hadn't brought this calf here, you might have dined on it tomorrow."

Timmy, who had learned from his father how to butcher slaughtered animals, nodded in agreement.

"We best be gettin' on with it," the boy said. "Mr. 'olmes figured 'ow to 'elp you with your infection an' also those in the dens. 'E now will figure 'ow to kill the beasts in the Thames. We best let 'im get to work, Dr. Watson."

I limped to the Eshocker across the room, where I fell onto the chair. Timmy was lecturing me about medical experimentation. Of course, the boy was right, but he was accustomed to the brutality of animal slaughter, whereas I healed the sick. We saw things from different perspectives.

"Go ahead," I told Holmes, "do what you must."

Miss Klune glared at Holmes and shook her head.

"Evil," she said, "*evil*. Now, if you're done with me, sir…"

Holmes waved her from the room, told Jacobs to shut the door, and then filled his pipe. For several moments, he puffed steadily and stared at Bligh Braithwaite, who twitched and drooled by the Eshocker we'd previously used on the lamb. Braithwaite seemed more excited than usual. His right hand rose to his mouth, and shaking, wiped off the drool. I knew of no cure for Braithwaite's seizures, his inability to control his limbs, his need to fall on the floor and twist his body into shapes, his gibberish. I wanted to reach out, take hold of the man, comfort him, and return him to his room and bed. But Holmes was certain that Bligh Braithwaite had killed Dr. Reginald Sinclair.

Holmes set his pipe on the counter of the medical cabinet, then eased Braithwaite away from the Eshocker and propped him against the wall, where Willie Jacobs stood on weak and trembling legs. Braithwaite slipped to a sitting position, and Jacobs followed.

Opening the lid of the Eshocker box, Holmes stroked the calf, which lowed softly. Gently, he ran his fingers along the animal's head and its flanks.

"I will gain no pleasure," he said, "from what is about to transpire in this room, but it must be done." Still soothing the animal, he addressed Bligh Braithwaite. "You, sir, knowingly murdered Dr. Sinclair. You were alone in this room with the murdered man. The room was locked, and nobody could have entered it. You acted with forethought and malice. You wanted him dead. The question is, *why?*"

As for me, I remained interested in learning *how*, but upon hearing Holmes, Braithwaite wailed and tears flooded his eyes. Willie Jacobs flinched and covered his ears.

"Let me briefly go over the facts."

"N-n-no..." Braithwaite begged. "I cannot hear it... *no!*"

"You *will* hear it, sir. Further, you will admit to what you've done, and, to avoid a horrible death at the hands of the hangman, you will tell me how to ramp up the voltage of this Eshocker such that it will kill those creatures in the Thames."

"You're correct," Willie Jacobs managed to say from his rotted-flesh mouth with its open sores. With each word, he grimaced, but loyal to the end, he apparently wanted to help us, and so he spoke, enunciating each word slowly and spacing his words so he could cope with the pain. "Bligh's an expert with the Eshockers. He knew 'em as soon as 'e arrived 'ere. 'E 'ated Sinclair more than me. Bligh knows what 'e's done!"

Suddenly, Braithwaite's body spasmed, and he fell across Jacobs's lap, his face turned toward Jacobs. Braithwaite balled his hand into a fist. Jacobs weakly swat at it, unable to grab hold of the other man's wrist. Braithwaite's fist crashed into Jacobs's phossy jaw—the exposed bone cracked, blood trickled down Jacobs's chin, and his head snapped back. He screamed and squirmed sideways and out of the other's reach.

"Y-you shut up! Y-you say n-nothing! Y-you kn-know-

know nothing!" Braithwaite shrieked. His torso spasmed again, his arms twisted outward at the elbows, his tongue lolled from his lips.

I pushed myself from the Eshocker chair and limped to the two men, where I crouched and threw an arm around Willie Jacobs's shoulders.

"Please, sir," I cried to Braithwaite, "you must control yourself! This man is innocent of any wrongdoing!"

"H-he doesn't *know*!" Braithwaite screamed.

"Gentlemen," Holmes said as he soothed the calf, which was now struggling against the Eshocker restraints, "all of you, calm down and be quiet. Remain still. *Please.* Watson, stay with Mr. Jacobs. As for you, Mr. Braithwaite, I am done with your histrionics.

"We will now expose the truth. This man—" Holmes pointed at Braithwaite— "knew how the Eshockers worked when he arrived at the Whitechapel Lunatic Asylum. Although Dr. Sinclair wouldn't treat local men in need of his help, he did treat Bligh Braithwaite. He did not send you back to the Kandinsky Asylum, sir, from which you escaped. You came *here*, sir, and *why*?"

"For God's sake, Holmes, tell us!" I cried, not for the first time in recent days.

"It's elementary, dear fellow," Holmes said calmly, his eyes trained on Bligh Braithwaite, who inched like a worm, straining to reach the closed and locked door. I clamped one hand on his ankle to keep him in place. My other arm remained around Willie Jacobs's shoulders.

"Mr. Braithwaite came to the asylum *specifically* to see Dr. Sinclair. He already knew how the Eshockers worked and how to build them. There's only one way someone locked in a lunatic asylum far away would possess this knowledge. You, sir," he said to Braithwaite, "helped Dr. Sinclair create the Eshockers, didn't you? And you wanted some of the money from the sales of those Eshockers, didn't you? You wanted the credit, you wanted people to know you were the brains behind the Eshockers, that you aren't just a neural psychotic—no, sir, you are far more than that!"

Braithwaite slapped the floor, untwisted his arms, and curled to his side with his eyes jittering at Holmes.

"I-I me-me," he stammered, then stopped, visibly trying to control his outburst and physical disability.

"R-Reggie and m-me g-grew up t-together," Braithwaite continued. "I-I invented the Eshocking machine. I-I wanted to c-cure myself. R-Reggie p-put m-me in Kan... Kandinsky." Braithwaite's body went limp, the fight drained out of him.

"You invented the Eshocker?" Holmes said.

"Y-yes..."

"You confronted your childhood friend, Reggie Sinclair?"

"Y-yes..."

"And when Dr. Sinclair laughed at you—"

"Y-yes!" Braithwaite wailed. "H-he laughed at m-me!"

"When he laughed at you," Holmes said, "and refused to acknowledge your technical contributions and your expertise... when he refused to acknowledge that you are not insane, and that indeed, you are an entirely rational and intelligent man—"

At this, Braithwaite clutched at his hair, ripping at it, clawed at his face, ripping at it, and shrieked a stream of incomprehensible syllables.

Holmes waited for the man to calm a bit, then continued:

"You suffer from a malady, in which you do not have complete control over your movements. You fall down. Your body twists. Even your mouth and vocal cords are not fully under your control. However, your mind is quite rational. You knew what you were doing, Mr. Braithwaite. Dr. Sinclair Eshocked you one too many times while refusing to admit—even to himself—how valuable your contribution was. So you turned your creation on him. You waited until he was weak—from what, Mr. Braithwaite?"

"S-s-s-s-s... old-old..."

"Old Ones Serum," I said softly. "You took advantage of Dr. Sinclair when he was seeing colors perhaps, unable to keep his eyes open... when he was out of his senses and drunk, as well."

"Y-yes," Braithwaite blubbered. "I-I strapped him into the Eshocker. No struggling. G-gagged him. Just as he did to us all, I did to him! And he deserved it, he did!" His voice gained strength, and Jacobs gasped.

"Y-you Eshocked the doctor," Jacobs groaned.

"I-I did! I-I did it, and for all of us, Willie!" Braithwaite cried.

"No, sir. You did it for yourself. For revenge," Holmes corrected. He lifted his hand from the calf, glanced at me, and turned his back. Bending, he leaned into the Eshocker box. "I've attached the blue wire, Mr. Braithwaite, just as you did when you murdered Dr. Sinclair."

"That won't do it," Jacobs rasped.

"No, it won't," Holmes said, "but you see, Mr. Jacobs, I've already removed the transformer from the other Eshocker that's always in this room. With Dr. Sinclair strapped into this Eshocker and gagged, Mr. Braithwaite could take his time. A simple twist of some screws, and he lifted the transformer from the other Eshocker. The transformer is not that heavy, and it's portable. Mr. Braithwaite placed this additional transformer behind the variable and fixed resistor units in this Eshocker. There's plenty of room in the box to place another transformer. The two AC wires were already there, waiting for him, attached to the first transformer. He unscrewed the other ends of those two AC wires, one from the variable resistor unit, the other from where it was attached to one of the two forehead electrodes. He simply screwed the wires into the second transformer and attached its two AC wires to the variable resistor unit and electrode."

"*What?*" I said.

But Willie Jacobs understood Holmes. He was an expert with modern machinery. He had built the tram machine with his father. He had helped Dr. Sinclair and Bligh Braithwaite wire these Eshockers.

"Mr. 'olmes is right," Jacobs rasped. "It ain't no effort to add a secon' transformer to the Eshocker. When 'e's not sufferin' from them twitchin's, Bligh can wire anythin' faster than anyone I ever known."

"And then after murdering Dr. Sinclair," Holmes said, "it would take no effort to return the second transformer to the other Eshocker from whence it came."

"Exactly," Jacobs said.

"But how did it kill?" I asked.

"The transformer increased the voltage applied to the

victim," Holmes explained. "Getting sixteen volts of AC using one transformer, Braithwaite pumped out far more voltage using that second transformer. A simple calculation indicates the voltage was sixteen volts multiplied by sixteen volts, for a total of 256 volts of alternating current, surely enough to kill any man."

"Y-yes." Braithwaite had ceased weeping. He was clearly proud of what he had done. Still stuttering, his eyes glowed as he explained. "I-I designed the Eshocker for easy building and service. P-plenty of room for the s-second transformer."

"Dr. Sinclair was overworked and under a lot of stress. I suspect he was not well—" Holmes suggested.

"A heart condition," I added.

"Y-yes," Braithwaite confirmed. "H-he had a weak heart, and in many ways. H-he went easily into the chair. After k-killing him, I-I returned the s-second transformer to the other Eshocker. An easy m-matter. Twist-off screws."

Would Dr. Sinclair have died from heart failure had Braithwaite not electrocuted him? Had the murder really been necessary?

I assumed it had been necessary for Bligh Braithwaite. Sinclair had stolen everything from Braithwaite, he had stolen his very life. Braithwaite must have wanted to take Sinclair's life, in return. I'd never forget the murder scene. Dr. Sinclair's chest ripped down the center, his burned brains, guts, and flesh, the pools of coagulating blood, the charred remnants of the white doctor's coat. The brains dripping from the ceiling and the medical supply cabinets.

I've had enough of murder, I thought.

"My old friend," I said, "surely we can do this without

killing that calf. Mr. Braithwaite has confirmed your deductions and admitted his crime and its method. There is no need to show him how he killed Dr. Sinclair using this animal."

Holmes straightened himself and turned to me. His hand reached to the calf's head again. The animal was so placid, innocent, unknowing...

"Of course, Dr. Watson. I never intended to kill this poor beast. The animal was present just in case Mr. Braithwaite needed extra motivation to tell all. Yet given what Dr. Sinclair took from Mr. Braithwaite, I suspected our man would break, weary of his silence, and tell us what we needed. He doesn't wish to be hanged—do you, Mr. Braithwaite? I will vouch for you if you cooperate with us, and my word is powerful with lawmakers. Don't worry, Dr. Watson, we will do without the animal."

"Holmes," I cried, "that's wonderful!"

"And now," he said, "without further ado, we must design and create a *Killer Eshocker*."

PART THREE

BATTLE ON THE THAMES

46
DR. JOHN WATSON

London

The four of us—Sherlock Holmes, Willie Jacobs, Bligh Braithwaite, and I—worked day and night, rarely leaving the back room of the asylum. I missed Samuel's first Christmas and wondered if Mary missed me as much as I missed her. Willie Jacobs, knowing his life would end soon, worked as hard as he could to help us build the machines. Braithwaite also worked hard, but in his case, because he wanted to avoid a death sentence. At the request of Dr. Sinclair's executors, Miss Klune had taken over the direction of the asylum until it could be sold. Once it was made known to her that our continued presence was vital to rid the city of the monsters in the Thames, she undertook to supply us with food, drink, and beds—for a fee.

My strength returned, and I was able to set aside my cane. Holmes had been correct about pulsing the doses of Eshocker treatment to clear my mind of the creature infestation. Others in London reported successful treatment, as well, and Timmy often stopped by to help us build the machines and supply news from the outside world.

"Miss Scarcliffe an' Maria are missin'," he told us as he wound the last of the coils around the huge transformer. "If Moriarty 'as 'em, I ain't 'eard."

Holmes lifted a harpoon over his head as if to throw it, then set it back down on a work bench. On the floor, loosely wound copper coiled around the cable that would send an alternating current through the harpoon. He stepped around the cable, leaned on a table holding the short copper pipe, and smoothed down his trousers. He'd neither shaved nor combed his hair in days.

"I'll send word about Miss Scarcliffe and Miss Fitzgerald. The authorities must find them and put them under heavy guard. Moriarty will want them back. They are his only hope of getting gold from the tram machine." He brushed hair off his face, speaking about the powerful Dagonites as if they were a minor point. His mind was on the Killer Eshocker and the creatures in the Thames.

On December 31, 1890, as we finished building the components of the Killer Eshocker, Lestrade marched into the Whitechapel Asylum and notified us that he had finally convinced his superiors that Mr. Willie Jacobs spoke the truth, that Miss Switzer had attempted to kill him with a lethal injection of drugs. Lestrade arrested her on the spot.

"I have to say, Holmes, that your written statement on behalf of Mr. Jacobs certainly helped matters. Miss Switzer will also stand trial for the murder of Caroline Brown," the Inspector added, much to Holmes's satisfaction.

"The attempted murder of Mr. Jacobs should keep her imprisoned until death," Holmes said. "His signed statement, as given to the Yard, should go a long way toward convicting her of Brown's murder. She will hang for what she has done. Mr. Braithwaite, London does not treat its murderers well."

With Holmes's recommendation that Braithwaite be committed for life to the Whitechapel Lunatic Asylum, Dr. Sinclair's killer would suffer a fate much better than that of Miss Switzer. Holmes argued that, by designing the Killer Eshocker with Willie Jacobs, Braithwaite would save many lives. Was this justice? It could be argued that Amy Switzer should also be committed to the asylum, for after all, aren't all murderers insane in some way? To take another life—whether out of greed or jealousy or the perverse desire to watch someone die—required that a murderer ignore his or her basic humanity. We are human because we have consciences, we know right from wrong.

"Now let's get this device onto the steamer," Holmes said. "Men are waiting for us already. They've hammered the metal plates to the sides of the steamer. The dynamo is onboard. It's time, gentlemen."

We left Bligh Braithwaite with Miss Klune and the inmates, and this time, the three of us—Sherlock Holmes, Willie Jacobs, and I—clambered onto a police carriage and headed to the Thames. Carts loaded with the Killer Eshocker components followed us.

Passers-by gaped at the components and at our carriage, but steered clear of us. Tomorrow would be a new year, and tonight, any sane inhabitant of London would have cause for celebration.

Mid-afternoon, and dark clouds drooped over the city, threatening a storm. The river thrashed beneath the wind.

Police guarded the dock where the steamer *Puritani* awaited us. At the riverside a strange crowd had assembled. Legless creatures, those with twelve arms waving Medusa-like above them; headless creatures with eyes bulging from naked purple flesh; froglike men with wings; wriggling wormlike things with suckers and with daggers for teeth; men who still looked like men yet had their faces beneath their necks—

"Holmes, these poor wretches look like the Dagonites at Swallowhead Spring in Avebury!" I exclaimed.

He nodded, but said nothing. His focus was on the Killer Eshocker components that the police were hoisting and loading onto the *Puritani*. The Dagonites themselves seemed to take little interest in our movements—their focus was on the turbid river and the monsters within, but they had amassed around the boat, too close for comfort, and had begun to chant.

"*Ufatu maehha faeatai tuatta iu iu rahi roa cthulhu rahi atu daghon da'agon f'hthul'rahi roa.*"

Jacobs shook. I put an arm around his waist and helped him, staggering, to the dock and past the Dagonites.

"Believers of the impure, of those from beyon' who come an' destroy us! Me father..." His voice hissed through his rotted jaw and now lipless mouth. He cringed and grew silent, but continued to shudder.

"Come," I said gently, "we must board the ship, and we need you, Mr. Jacobs. You are our only hope in this matter. You are a master mechanic and expert electrician. Please, we must kill these creatures who come from the beyond—" I could barely believe I was saying these things!—"and as you say, killed your father."

"*Aye...*" The word hissed through his broken mouth like wind through a tunnel. A hand quivered and rose to the infected scab around his nostrils. A finger poked, then a knuckle.

Marines lined the deck of the steamer. Holmes was already on the ship, outlining his plans to their captain.

"*Ebb'yuh dissoth'nknpflknghreet!*" a Dagonite shrieked above the general chant. A blob of green-scaled monstrosity, it kicked out with multiple legs, ramming a policeman with hammer toes and spike claws. The officer struck back with his truncheon, and the monstrosity shrieked more loudly.

The crowd screeched and moaned, chanting in a cacophonous drone that was like a razor to my ears. Several officers dropped their weapons and clamped their hands over their ears. Wondering how much more of the screeching I could handle, I pulled Jacobs more quickly through the crowd.

"*Yog'fuhrsothothothoth 'a'a'a'memerutupao'omii!*"

Gibberish oozed and trills soared, baritones rattled from the wormlike things.

"*Ch'thgalhn fhtagn urre'h nyogthluh'eeh ngh syh'kyuhyuh.* Cthulhu! Oh Deep Ones! Oh Great Old Ones! Dagon be all!"

They screamed in unison, in broken flurries that erupted randomly yet in a harmony that defied all logic. Interspersed with the gibberish and guttural rattling came human words: "Glory to Amelia and Maria, mothers of Dagon! Amelia, mother of the hordes that come from the sea! She gives birth at Half Moon Bay, where Cthulhu rose from the open sea!"

I shoved Jacobs onto the *Puritani* and jumped aboard after him.

A luminous fog rolled above the river, which heaved and raged against the shore. The *Puritani*, large and firm, held steady, and while part of me feared that the ship would suffer the same fate as the *Belle Crown*, I told myself that there was no choice but to ride the ship into the violent river and destroy the beasts.

As the fog gleamed an unearthly hue, it illuminated a tempest of creatures reeling along the water's surface and swinging upon the tips of the waves. Dirty clouds hung low and grasped the fog, then shifted with the wind.

Supporting Willie Jacobs with both hands, I stumbled across the lurching deck until a Marine clutching a rifle motioned me toward the engine room. Jacobs and I clambered down the companion-ladder, our bodies hitting the walls and rails on either side of us as the ship jolted. Finding the engine room, we also found Sherlock Holmes.

Along with a dozen other men, he stooped and lifted one of two main AC cables coming out of the transformer we had built in the asylum. The men shoved the end of the first AC cable through a hole in the ceiling, where others grabbed it and pulled it onto the deck. Another cable branched off this first one, and Holmes and his men now rammed this one through the same hole. The final step was to shove the second main AC cable through a separate hole in the ceiling.

Cables already ran between the steam engine and a huge dynamo, and thence to the transformer.

Jacobs broke free of my grasp, lurched, and extended one arm to the transformer, an enormous unit with one hundred coils of copper on its left side and three thousand coils on its right. With Braithwaite, he had designed this unit based on Dr. Sinclair's Eshocker. The killer version required no resistors to hold back the current that would blast out of the transformer. A slight grin flickered about the ruins of Jacobs's mouth, and his eyes moistened. He looked at me, and with tight lips, I returned his smile.

"When you signal," he rasped, "I'll tell the men to turn off the voltage, the dynamo."

"You can manage on your own down here?" I asked Jacobs.

When he nodded, I told him, "You see that red cord hanging from the hole where Holmes just pushed the cable? When you see the cord lift completely out of the hole, you'll know I'm signaling you to switch off the voltage. Got it?"

"Aye." Jacobs sank to the floor, head resting in cupped hands, shoulders hunched. While his mind was willing to do anything we needed, his body might not cooperate. Yet we could not trust anyone else with this task—only Willie Jacobs. He was the expert. The other men on this ship didn't have any notion about how the Killer Eshocker functioned. We dared not depend on them for anything but following orders and throwing harpoons.

As if he had divined my thoughts, Jacobs spoke up. "Don't worry, sir. I can manage. You're needed on deck."

I could not disagree. I turned and dashed up the stairs to the deck.

Wind blasted across the Thames and hit the *Puritani*, which slammed against the dock. The water wasn't high enough to slosh overboard—not yet, anyway. As soon as we hit deeper waters, anything could happen.

The first lieutenant stopped by me as I looked over the scene. "I hope your new harpoon works, Dr. Watson. We've tried cannons and dynamite. Nothing works." He appeared downtrodden, his eyes weary, his body slouched despite his military training.

"You've been out there, fighting those creatures all along?" I asked.

"Ever since the disaster with the *Belle Crown*."

It hadn't been that long ago that Holmes and I had taken a pleasure cruise on the Thames, only to nearly lose our lives to the... otherworldly beasts. Not sure if the harpoons would work either, I could say nothing to reassure the man. He took one look at my face and sagged even more. Then he wandered off, stumbling as waves hit the ship, to help his men throw one of the two large cables overboard.

Attached to the end of that cable was a copper pipe screwed to a large copper plate, which would ground the Killer Eshocker.

Ocean salt water would have conducted the electricity well, but even in these tidal reaches of the river, the Thames didn't contain sufficient salt—its waters alone would not conduct enough current to kill the creatures. The Eshocker required two harpoons to be fired: one into the head of a creature and the other into its tail or the rear of its body, depending on the physical attributes of the creature in question. How did one hit a tiny creature's head? How did one hit the rear of a blob that lacked a tail or hindquarters? How did one hit a creature with writhing tentacles? How did one hit anything that flitted in and out of reality?

The two harpoons lay on the deck. One connected directly to a cable attached to the transformer in the engine room. We'd wound the copper coil loosely around the cable and then tightly around the harpoon, which was crafted of brass and steel. Braithwaite had explained that copper was too soft, that the harpoon should be strong, of hard metal. Jacobs had agreed with him, and also told us to use steel clamps to hold the coil tightly to the harpoon. Holmes and I had done as he suggested, and ten clamps secured the coil to the weapon. We had constructed the second harpoon in the same way, except that this harpoon's cable was attached to the main cable leading to the copper tube and the copper plate.

Holmes scrambled up the stairs to join me on the deck as the *Puritani* got under way.

"Holmes," I shouted above the roar of the engine and the fury of the wind and water, "do you think she'll hold better than the *Belle Crown*?"

"There is no way of knowing," he yelled back. "If our method succeeds in killing the largest beasts before they turn on us, then we might survive. Otherwise, we could end up as before—in the water, freezing to death, dying as our former shipmates did."

Bobbing across the choppy waves into the middle of the Thames, the *Puritani* slowed, and two officers lifted the harpoons and aimed them at the water. Holmes and I swiveled, holding onto the rails behind us as we watched the men on the other side of the ship. Again, my mind flashed back to the *Belle Crown*, when a huge tentacle had risen over Holmes's head, ready to drill his brains into his body.

Beyond the ship, not close enough to smash a man's head

but within reach of the cabled harpoons, *a creature rose.*

Dozens of eyes glittered through the fog, and bat wings unfolded over a mouth drilled into the middle of a bulbous body. The mouth opened, and phosphorescent teeth jutted out like claws.

Over the roar of the engine and the machinery, the creature screeched up tuneless scales and back down them, its voice clacking at the highest notes.

"Throw the harpoons!" Holmes yelled.

Spurred into action, one man launched his harpoon at the thing's mouth, while the other harpoon snapped through the wind and skewered the lower part of the bulbous body.

The first harpoon snared the creature's mouth, dropped off, and fell into the waves. The bat wings descended and folded over the mouth, and they scraped the other harpoon into the water, as well.

"A disaster," Holmes muttered, pulling me from the rails and across the lurching deck, where I pulled the red rope from the hole leading to the engine room.

The cables on the deck ceased vibrating, and with a loud grunt, the Killer Eshocker switched off. *Thank you, Willie Jacobs*, I thought.

"Pull them in," Holmes commanded, and the men pulled the harpoons and cables out of the water.

Stooping by the red rope, I noticed that the harpoon that had pierced the beast's mouth was coated in a film of grease, or pus. I shoved the red rope back down the hole, and Jacobs switched the machine back on. When I rose, holding the harpoon, I saw that Holmes had hoisted up the second harpoon and aimed it at the beast's mouth.

"Launch it, Watson," he cried, "and aim low!"

The creature disappeared beneath the surface. Holmes backed up a few steps, and I did the same.

"Get ready," he hissed, his sharp eyes upon the water, scanning for a rupture in the waves.

Small glowing blobs with tendrils floated in clusters along the surface. Some broke free, rose up into the wind, and burst, spraying green splotches that spread like spilled paint over the water. I squinted, seeking the giant creature—a tentacle, a sucker, a glittering eye.

"There!" Holmes cried, pointing with his free hand.

The creature erupted from the water mere yards from the *Puritani*. The men behind me shouted.

"Kill it!"

"Kill the infernal beast!"

"Throw the harpoons!"

Holmes's harpoon streaked through the air and pierced the creature right beneath its bat wing. As the beast rose and shrieked, it unfurled its wings further to catch the wind, and before it could re-fold them, I shot my harpoon with all my strength and it punctured the bulbous hide nearest the water.

A screech shattered the wind—skittered up sharp scales, crashed like a tidal wave down multiple octaves.

"We have it!" Holmes clapped me on the back, and the men cheered.

Glittering eyes bored down at us, and the bat wings glowed over our heads. The creature spasmed, puffed its hide out, as if trying to expel the lances but failing, then puffed in and out while a greenish ooze poured from the two wounds. Yards from the boat, the mouth yawned open, wide enough to consume a man in one gulp, the claw-like teeth snapping—clicking shut, whipping open, clicking shut again. Everyone on the steamer cowered against the far rail of the boat, except for Holmes, who stood rooted, staring in fascination at the beating wings and snapping teeth.

The beast's eyes glittered, dozens of them, like a single sheet of ice, and then exploded. Green pus and gelatinous eye fluid spattered across Holmes's hair and coat. He wiped his face clean with a hand and grimaced. A smell of rot and mold saturated the air—a stench of fetid decay that seemed a thousand years old.

The Killer Eshocker cables hummed on the deck, sending huge amounts of voltage into the thing—the Old One, the Deep One, whatever the Dagonites called these creatures.

It sagged into the water, its wings drooped, its mouth closed. It whined, long and low, a keening that sent the tiny green blobs and their tendrils skittering across the waters as dandelion fluff flies on the breeze. Still the voltage sizzled into the beast, crackling now along the skin, shooting orange along its wings, burning the flesh and whatever beat inside this creature from beyond.

It faded—*briefly*, it faded and almost disappeared into the rift that led… elsewhere. But it flickered back into view, still attached to the harpoon and its deadly cable. The voltage pumped into the bulbous thing, and it bloated with red-hot fire, bulging and bulging until finally, it burst. An explosion of hide and organs and blood of all forms and colors rankled the air with a smell unlike anything I'd ever encountered. It was as if all the corpses in the world were rotting beneath my nose. I gasped, choked, clasped a hand over my nostrils, pinching them shut. Slime rained upon us and slicked the deck. Gore spewed up, and as the *Puritani* jerked, the wind caught the bloody muck and carried it off.

"Watson," Holmes choked, "the signal!" I yanked up the red rope, and down in the engine room, Jacobs switched off the machine.

We'd slammed the creature with a devastatingly high voltage, enough to kill it before it could retreat to its realm. But it was only one creature, and by killing it as it faded slightly into the otherworld, we'd sealed one large rift, or so I hoped.

The Marines and the seamen alike were in a sorry state. One vomited over the rail into the Thames, another hung his head, retching on the deck.

"Gentlemen," Holmes said, "prepare yourselves. We are still far from the end."

"But," I said, "the newspapers indicated that only a few large beasts have been seen in the river. If we dispatch a few more, can we not safely assume that the infestation has been cleared?"

"No, Watson. The *Puritani* will cruise these waters for as long as it takes to hunt these creatures down and kill them."

The boat spasmed. Several men slipped on the gore that had exploded from the beast. Holmes and I stared at each other.

"We'll work for a few hours," he told me, "and then another crew should come onboard and continue this task."

By the time we'd killed two more creatures, our current team of men could do no more. We were all coated in gore and stank to high heaven.

We dragged ourselves down to the engine room, where

we found Willie Jacobs, as close to death as a man can be. He was on the floor by the Killer Eshocker transformer unit. He would die beside the giant machine that he had built, just as his father had died by the giant tram machine they'd built together. Thankfully, Willie Jacobs's body was intact, whereas his father had suffered a much worse fate. Still...

"Not this, too," I whispered sadly.

Holmes crouched by Jacobs and grasped his hand.

"You're a good man, Willie," he said, "and an even better friend."

"Aye," the dying man said, "an' so are you, Mr. 'olmes, an' also Dr. Watson."

Did I see tears in Holmes's eyes?

I, too, crouched by Willie Jacobs, who had saved Mary and Samuel from an assault in my own home. His eyes were dead but for a pinprick of light. His breathing was shallow and slow. His fingers dabbed at his nostrils.

"Kill 'em that killed me father," he rasped. "Get 'em all, Mr. 'olmes."

Holmes opened his mouth to answer. No words came out for a long time. Finally: "Watson." The word was soft. "Watson." Yet softer.

"Yes." My voice trembled. "He's gone."

The wind had died, and so had the day.

Night sank, as did our hearts.

We would both miss Willie Jacobs. He had suffered a short and terrible life.

To this day, I can say with absolute certainty that Willie Jacobs was one of the finest men I've ever had the honor of knowing.

47
PROFESSOR MORIARTY

Whitechapel

"Cthulhu! Cthulhu! Lord Dagon!"

I raised a fist and joined the chant.

My nemesis, the arrogant Holmes, and his puppy, Watson, had dragged themselves off the *Puritani* and left for the warm comforts of home. Little did they know how people truly suffered. I employed men who would otherwise be rotting in prison. I employed boys who would otherwise starve on the streets. Holmes had taken Timmy from me, and where was the boy now? On the streets, whereas working for me, the boy had eaten well, slept on a soft sofa in the shelter of my den. They had snatched him as a wild animal snatches a suckling from its mother's den. Where was the civility in that?

With the crowd thinning, I had to be on my way. These onlookers were deformed and crippled in ways that shocked me. In front of me, a woman had lost both arms but had five legs, all jellylike and propped on huge, webbed feet. Beside her, a man inflated and deflated like an accordion. And the head... I shuddered to see it—spherical with ears in the back, mouth on the top, and dozens of eyes littering the front.

The top mouth opened and a chant rose, and the deformed around him joined in.

"*Yog'fuhrsothothothoth 'a'a'a'memerutupao'omii!*"

I edged away and scurried through the night streets, intent on one thing. I had to find Amelia Scarcliffe and Maria Fitzgerald. They'd escaped, and with them went my chance to produce and claim the tram machine gold as my own. With them went my chance to control these deformed lunatics, the Dagon gang, with their secret knowledge of opening the gates to gold and power.

My den profits were plummeting. Addicts were no longer addicted. All the fault of Sherlock Holmes, the arrogant meddler.

In the distance, I heard the faint chanting of the Dagonites.

"*Aauhaoaoa DEMONI aauhaoaoa DEMONI aauhaoaoa DEMONI!*

"*Ch'thgalhn fhtagn Innsmouth Innsmouth INNSMOUTH!*"

The last word was a long howl, and stayed in my head as I dipped into an alley, racing to my sanctuary.

Innsmouth.

I would have to discover what *Innsmouth* meant.

48

DR. JOHN WATSON

London

Holmes fidgeted with his beakers, his test tubes, and then the hypodermic needle in his desk drawer. He twisted it between his fingers, then set it back in its case. Plucking up his violin and bow, he straightened, shut his eyes, and began playing. It was an eerie, low tune, and spellbinding. The newspaper dropped to my lap, and I also shut my eyes, letting myself drift into the music.

A rap at the apartment door jolted us both, and Holmes's bow screeched to a halt. I jumped from my chair, but he waved me aside, and opened the door himself. His face brightened.

"Inspector Lestrade! Do come in." He waved the policeman into the room.

"Good afternoon, gentlemen," Lestrade said. "Are you busy at present?"

"Busy? No." I knew what Holmes would say next, and he didn't disappoint me. "Why? Do you have a case that requires my services?"

Sitting down in the chair next to mine, Lestrade set his hat on his lap. His fingers played with the hat rim, and his foot jittered. Holmes threw himself into his chair by the Gothic revival table and leaned forward, elbows on his knees. His eyes focused keenly on our visitor.

"No," he said, "I see it is not a new case, but unfinished business that brings you here. What, then," he asked, "may I do for you?"

"The creatures are mostly gone from the Thames now, Holmes."

"That is a relief, is it not?"

"Certainly," Lestrade agreed. "But I am concerned about a few things. For one, will these creatures return from wherever they come? How do we know that they are gone permanently?"

"They are gone, for now," Holmes declared, leaning back in his chair, "just as the tram machine is simmering, the otherworldly rifts of the Thames are simmering. All is under control. *For now*."

"How do you know this?" Lestrade persisted.

Holmes had explained all to me days earlier, for I, too, had been baffled by the disappearance of the monsters that had plagued not only the river but also my own mind.

"I'm surprised it's taken you this long to come here and ask me," Holmes said with a hint of a smile.

"I've been busy," Lestrade said, "with other matters, such as helping the military. We've been moving men on and off the *Puritani* twenty-four hours a day to kill the beasts. You know we had to fix the harpoons and cables several times, and without your Willie Jacobs, we had some difficulties with the transformer."

"Ah, yes," I piped up, happy at any time to praise Willie

Jacobs. "He was a true hero, Inspector. He risked his life and went to the limits to do what he promised and to do what's best."

"Well, yes, and so—" Lestrade returned his attention to Holmes—"explain this Killer Eshocker method to me. My men have been using it in the river for a week, yet we don't know how it's killing these things. Tell me."

"Gladly." Holmes's smile widened, as he educated the Inspector. "At first, I wanted to test the Eshocker treatment—and yes, it's interesting, is it not, that Dr. Sinclair's Eshocker actually *is* an electrotherapy tool?—on an animal infected with the microscopic creatures. Our test demonstrated sufficiently that, administered in pulses of voltage, the Eshocker did indeed eradicate the infestation from an animal's brain. We supplied an electrotherapy dose of a *duration* required to kill whatever was in the brain without killing its host, a lamb. Yet we had to *pulse* the dose to kill additional creatures that seeped into the lamb's brain from what I loosely term the otherworld. I believe the voltage seeped into this otherworld and somehow sealed the rifts that enabled the creatures to enter the brain."

"You have evidence of this?" Lestrade asked.

"My evidence is that the method cured Dr. Watson and has now cured many hundreds of Londoners who were similarly infested, or infected, by these creatures. It's not the proof I prefer, Inspector, but in this case it must suffice. I deduced that I could use a similar method on the creatures in the Thames. They were larger, and hence, the rifts into the otherworld must have been larger, as well. Much higher voltage was required."

"But why didn't our dynamite, bombs, bullets, and even cannonballs destroy these creatures? Why only the Killer Eshocker?"

"Because," Holmes answered, "the Killer Eshocker harpoon is attached to the source of enormous electricity—an electricity that flows into the creature and across the rift. Dynamite, bombs, bullets, and cannonballs just knocked the creatures back or maybe put holes in them, which apparently healed as they flitted in and out of our world and the otherworld. An explosion—from, say, dynamite—means that chemical energy converts quickly into high-temperature gas, which expands and creates pressure waves. These pressure waves can knock the creatures back, but they cannot close the rift between our world and the otherworld. The creatures can simply duck across the rift and avoid the explosions. The only way to seal the rift is by high voltage that travels across the rift with the creatures. In the otherworld, the voltage reacts in ways we cannot imagine here, and the rift closes. It's the same concept as with the tram machine, which only produces gold due to a mysterious catalyst in the otherworld. It is not magic, Inspector. It is *science*."

"This is why we didn't have to pulse the Killer Eshocker voltage," I added, and when Lestrade's eyebrows rose, I explained, "because once the harpoons and the high AC hit the creature, it crossed to the otherworld, taking the voltage with it, and the rift sealed. No other creatures could come into our world through that rift."

Unfortunately, Holmes had filled me in with more than he was willing to share with Lestrade. Particularly disturbing were Holmes's answers as they related to Mary and Samuel's return.

"They are safer in hiding, Watson," he'd said. "Earlier, when Professor Fitzgerald uttered those incantations from the *Dagonite Auctoritatem* and constructed mechanisms that opened the rifts, the creatures entered London. Eventually, the creatures swarmed into the Thames. The river holds no special attribute for opening rifts and bringing these creatures into London. The tram machine did possess such attributes. I am sorry, Watson, but much as I dislike concluding it, the fact remains that these gates might be opened again—anywhere, at any time, and for reasons we cannot fathom."

"Then how are Mary and Samuel safer in *hiding*?" I asked, then sadly answered my own question. "Because the danger is ever close to *me*."

In our sitting room, the curtains were closed for the night. The fireplace warmed the room, where minutes earlier, I'd read the newspaper and dozed a bit, listening to Holmes mutter and fidget and play his violin.

But outside, the unknown cosmic horrors remained. Somewhere, they seethed. The world was not safe, and my family was better off staying away from me—a thought that filled me with despair. The battle was not over against Dagon, the Old Ones, the Deep Ones, Cthulhu—whatever form these creatures took.

Our homes, the walls surrounding us, gave us a sense of security, but we were fooling ourselves.

With a pinched expression, Holmes returned to his chair and gazed at our visitor and then at me.

"It is over," he said, "but only *for now*."

I thought of Timmy Dorsey, Jr., huddled somewhere tonight. I thought of Professor Moriarty, secluded where we could not find him, most likely devising plans to kidnap Amelia Scarcliffe and Maria Fitzgerald again, hold them prisoner until they agreed to open these monstrous gates for him and unleash hell upon earth. My breathing quickened, as did my heart.

Holmes's eyes narrowed.

"Yes," he said, apparently guessing my fears, "there is more to come, Dr. Watson. The fight against evil has but begun, and we are far from finished."

At this, Inspector Lestrade rose, popped his hat back on his head and tapped the brim. When he spoke, his voice was more forceful and firm than I'd ever heard it.

"You have no idea, Mr. Holmes," he said. "A creature—the Dagonites call it, *Cthulhu*—has been seen off the coast of Innsmouth, Massachusetts. Multiple reports, including police bulletins and newspapers, claim this Cthulhu is the size of many whales and possesses giant tentacles, each of which can crush a ship with one blow. Classified documents report that Cthulhu looks like an immense mutated octopus with wings, and also that it possesses great intellect that rivals yours."

At this Holmes bristled and drew himself up. His eyes narrowed with concentration.

"Inspector," I muttered, "surely you exaggerate."

But Lestrade shook his head.

"I'm afraid not, my dear fellow," he said. "Imagine the gate that had to open to let Cthulhu through... although the people—if you can say that they *are* people—of Innsmouth claim that Cthulhu has been here all along. He rose from the depths of the sea, they say, and—" he added—"they worship him."

"Innsmouth. *Cthulhu*," Holmes said, as if half-believing the story. "A monster beneath the sea." No hint of mischief played in his eyes.

As for me, I was too stunned to comment.

Lestrade ambled to the door, then turned.

"I wanted the two of you to rest for a few days before I filled you in on the crisis of Innsmouth and this Cthulhu. But we can't wait much longer. Holmes, we will be in touch shortly with instructions for you and the Doctor about making the journey to Innsmouth—"

"And... what? Destroy this Cthulhu monster?" Holmes exclaimed. "That would require an army."

"Possibly, but as you said earlier, dynamite, bombs, cannonballs, guns—nothing kills these things nor closes the gates. Our government wants your intervention, Mr. Holmes."

Picturing a gigantic octopus with wings and the intellect of Professor Moriarty and Sherlock Holmes terrified me. Even my experience in the war hadn't prepared me for a battle against otherworldly creatures, let alone one such as Cthulhu.

"I should also tell you," Lestrade said as he opened the door to leave the flat, "that Innsmouth is the center of the world's Dagon cult and its depravity. The residents have devolved. They are bizarrely deformed."

"There were cultists on the shores of the Thames with such deformities," I said, "when we boarded the *Puritani*."

"No, Dr. Watson." He frowned. "The Innsmouthians are much further gone, and there's nothing the government or military can do for them, so say the American police. The people of Innsmouth are no longer *human*."

Cthulhu and Innsmouth...

Holmes and I were about to embark on an adventure unlike any we'd ever known.

ACKNOWLEDGEMENTS

Thank you to my husband, Arie Bodek. As a professor of physics, he helped me finetune and proof the actual wiring schematics for the den, hospital, and extreme treatment mode Eshockers. Yes, I possess the schematics from which these machines could have been built in 1890. While there were electrotherapies in Holmes's time, nothing came close to Dr. Sinclair's Eshockers.

A parting goodbye is in order to Willie Jacobs. I've written a lot of books and stories, and like most authors, I have some favorite characters. Willie Jacobs ranks right up there in the number one spot, which he shares with only a few others. Willie, you rocked me for months!

My thanks to Steve Saffel at Titan Books NYC, and also to Sam Matthews and Laura Coulman at Titan London.

ABOUT THE AUTHOR

LOIS H. GRESH is the six-time *New York Times*-bestselling author of twenty-eight books and more than sixty-five short stories, as well as the editor of the anthologies *Innsmouth Nightmares* and *Dark Fusions*. She is a well-known Lovecraftian writer whose works have appeared in *Black Wings of Cthulhu*, *The Madness of Cthulhu*, and many other anthologies. Her work has been published in twenty-two languages. *Sherlock Holmes vs. Cthulhu: The Adventure of the Neural Psychoses* is the second in her new trilogy of Holmes thrillers. Lois is a frequent guest of honor author at large fan conventions and has appeared on television series such as the History Channel's *Ancient Aliens* and *Batman Tech*. You can follow her adventures with Sherlock Holmes at www.facebook.com/lois.gresh and www.loisgresh.com.